TRUTHS

Visit us at www.boldstrokesbooks.com

TRUTHS

by

Rebecca S. Buck

A Division of Bold Strokes Books

2010

ISBN 10: 1-60282-146-1
ISBN 13: 978-1-60282-146-0

This Trade Paperback Original Is Published By
Bold Strokes Books, Inc.
P.O. Box 249
Valley Falls, NY 12185

First Edition: April 2010

CREDITS
Editor: Ruth Sternglantz
Production Design: Stacia Seaman
Cover Design By Sheri (graphicartist2020@hotmail.com)

Acknowledgments

The publication of *Truths* has taught me what a team effort publishing a novel is. Thank you so much to everyone at Bold Strokes Books for your efforts with my book and for making me so welcome. I can't wait to work more with you!

Gratitude especially to Radclyffe, both for liking this book in the first place, and for creating and guiding the amazing organization that is BSB, which truly feels like home.

There aren't sufficient words of thanks for my editor, Ruth Sternglantz. Your (mostly) gentle nudges have truly made this the best book it could be. You've also convinced me that maybe I am a writer after all. Thank you.

Huge thanks and love to all my family and friends who have supported me, in ways big and small. I can't mention everyone. To Mark Spray, Jacqui, Charlie and Sharon Serej, Amy Fitzsimmons, and Sonja Šterman, for everything you've done in your different ways. The title of Most Enthusiastic Supporters has to go to Jeff and Eileen Buck.

I have the deepest appreciation for those who made their way through my drafts or part-drafts and gave me their opinions: Mark Spray, Michelle Ward, Debbie Silberman, and especially Rachael Udell. Raych, as you already know, I don't think it would have been published without you.

I also give thanks for a song by Joan Jett, called "Watersign", which kept me sane through my worst moments of writer's block during the creation of this novel.

If I've missed anyone, I apologize. And thank you.

Dedication

For everyone who has ever had to search for an elusive personal truth and fought to hold on to it. Keep a tight grip.

2008

'I've had enough of you, I'm going!' he spat at me. I fought the surge of indignation that required me to respond. *This isn't my fault*, I wanted to scream back at him. Let it go. The conclusion was what I wanted to achieve, after all.

His eyes seared furiously into mine. Now I had to suppress laughter at his impotent rage. Frustration at his stupidity, hilarity at his lost temper. It was a moment of realisation; that was as deep as my feelings reached. It was as though my core, where the genuine emotions dwelt, was Kevlar protected. Sod it, fuck off.

He had his own moment of realisation. I wasn't going to cry or rise to his taunt and retort. Briefly, he seemed ready to explode, turning a comical tone of purplish red. Then, speechless still, but with the last word to his advantage, he was gone with a rather pathetic slamming of the door.

Alone, I looked around my sparsely furnished flat, righteously triumphant. I overrode the slight sickness in my stomach and the moist heat stinging my eyes. I flicked the stereo on and let the obscenely loud music compliment me on my victory.

1808

Hang. Dead.

The only words that filtered through the haze, ominous echoes, yet strangely meaningless. The disapproving frown of the black-capped judge was surely directed elsewhere. She heard a gasp of horror over her shoulder. Why?

The firm men's hands grasping at her arms were warm but too persistent, pulling her towards the steps.

Automatically, she descended with them. Step, step, step, stumble, step, step. A gloomy corridor, a breeze caressing her neck, guttering lanterns. Been here before, but going deeper this time. Long shadows looming.

The echo returned, pursuing her: hang, dead, hang, dead. A sudden stutter of her heartbeat, a hot pulse of fear. But numb thoughts. Nonsensical sounds, nothing more, not yet.

Turning a corner, the clanking of keys, the grinding of the iron lock. Stern bars giving way, allowing them through.

A shadow rising from a gloomy desk, tattered uniform, limpid eyes, thread veins, and thin grey hair. Too fat for his buttons.

And then the nausea of realisation.

CHAPTER ONE

2008

That alarm was beeping incessantly, but too early, I was sure. I rolled over and peered at the red digital numbers. 8.03. They faded into a blur. My head pounded with an ache that could only be the result of the half bottle of Southern Comfort I had downed as a nightcap. Thank fuck there hadn't been a whole bottle left. The alarm was still attempting to wake me; I reached over and whacked the *off* button.

My legs were unnaturally heavy as I lowered them to the floor, dubious as to whether they would do their job properly as I attempted to stand up. Upright, but unsteadily, I rubbed my eyes and tried to think as the room finally came to a standstill. Work. That meant clothes. Where had I dumped them? A crumpled pile in the chair at the foot of my bed told me I should look in my wardrobe for clean ones. What about breakfast? My stomach flip-flopped at the thought. I headed for the small blue-tiled bathroom, hoping a cool shower would wash my cotton-wool head away.

It was by some miracle I was on the bus by 8.35. I sat in the first of the front-facing seats, looking desperately through the windscreen, trying to avert the daily motion sickness, which today was so much the worse. The lukewarm shower (I was too much of a coward to turn it to cold) had helped, and I had achieved dressing in my fresh black jeans and skinny T-shirt without too much of a problem. Now I thought about getting through the day ahead. No lingering on other thoughts; fuck him.

1808

'Lizzie's back.' There was hilarity in the man's voice. 'Won't be leaving this time!' he said, snorting. My name is Elizabeth, she thought. It was all that was left to her now.

'So she is.' The limpid eyes were looking her up and down. Shiver. 'Welcome back, Miss Cooper. Lizzie. Knew we'd be seeing you again. You have the devil in you, missy, only one way to cure that.'

The first furious tears, not of fear but of rage, welled. Vision blurred, throat aching. 'I didn't do it.' Cracked lips, a retort which just had to come out.

'Judge and jury say otherwise, Lizzie. You know they're right.' He was looming over her, grinning. Her gaze fell lower; one of his brass buttons had fallen from his blue uniform jacket, leaving a mess of threads. More tears, but now she fought them. Do not give him the victory.

'Paperwork's done already, love, knew you'd be back y' see.' More grinning. Yellow teeth, one absent from the front. A shudder of revulsion and a rising of the bile inside her. 'Down to Mrs Beckinsale with you now, get you settled. Not that you'll be with us for long, naturally.' A vicious chuckle to accompany the wave of terror he saw in her.

'Come on, Lizzie.' The first man pulled her arm. Another black passageway. She had been kept in a cell near the court stairs, innocent until proven guilty. Now guilty, they were leading her into oblivion. A fitting preparation for what was to come. Dizziness, almost glad of the strong hand at her elbow.

'Lizzie,' the voice called from behind her. She stopped but did not turn, dread seizing her. She waited expectantly. 'I'll see you later, Lizzie.' Sick to her stomach, but denying him a reaction, she went towards the gloom.

2008

Nottingham, with its compact, modern city centre of bustling shops and thriving coffee bars, showed little evidence of its grimy industrial heritage, let alone its pedigree as an important medieval market town in the heart of England. It was a thoroughly up-to-date city and not at all picturesque, but it had always been my home and I was comfortable here. The centre was already full of its daytime inhabitants: mothers and children, pensioners, students. The good working population were already at their desks and counters. In my jeans, canvas rucksack slung on my back, I suppose I seemed more like one of the students than someone on her way to gainful employment. Just one of the reasons most people did not see what I did as a 'real job', whatever the hell that was. A job not starting until 9.30 a.m. didn't mean it wasn't really a job.

Soon I left the frantic commerciality of the main shopping streets behind, trying not to feel too superior. I was as prone to indulging in retail-worship as the next person; not having the money did not make me any better than those that did. I climbed the hill that led to the old section of the town, breathing steadily to convince myself I was actually in better condition than I was.

At the top of the hill, I crossed a busy road, which seemed to separate the present from the past. Ahead, everything seemed more subdued. Old red-brick, white-windowed Georgian industrial buildings kept their secrets, of this Midlands town's nineteenth-century heyday. People did not come here to look at them, and it always struck me that they had not quite resigned themselves to being relics, rather waited patiently, quiet with a secret pride, for a time when they might be useful again. A recollection of their history always moved me; I preferred these sturdy, gentle buildings to all the grandeur of a gothic cathedral.

A delivery van up ahead started its engine as I crossed an area of flagstones, now deserted, which had once been the town's marketplace. The information board was covered in blue graffiti. The Victorian church to my right was a fashionable pub these days. It was pleasingly impossible to be romantic about history, even here. Time went on, the past receded. I should have remembered it was important to move on with the days and months. The past was not a place to linger in, but that was just what I did every day.

The Museum of Law and Justice, my place of work, was located in the old Shire Hall and County Gaol. This stern building became visible rather suddenly as you rounded a curve in the road, though you barely noticed the bend as you walked. You saw it even before you noticed the huge medieval church opposite, which overshadowed it. Set back from the pavement by the width of five stone steps, the sandstone edifice was carved into columns and looked like it needed a thoroughly good wash. It was supposed to be imposing, commanding, terrifying. Instead, I smiled as I crossed the road and climbed the steps. I felt welcome here; this was my gateway to history, to forgetting the real world for a while.

I entered the four-digit code in the pad to the side of the employees' door, like a magic word to take me back in time. I turned the heavy brass handle and passed through into the shadows of a side hallway.

1808

Footsteps on stone; long echoes. Keys jangling and iron locks scraping. A pitiful squeal of hinges. A shorter passage; a wooden doorway; worn stone steps. An odour to turn the stomach.

A woman, older than herself and taller too. Broad shoulders and thick arms, red hands. A face that was tired rather than severe. Dull grey eyes. Equally grey dress covered in a stained white apron, straining a little at the waist. Stitched tears and patches in the skirt.

She was pushed forward. 'Elizabeth Cooper.' The information came from over her shoulder. 'Thief. For the rope.' Cold disbelief and again the assertion in her head. I didn't do it. I didn't do it. I didn't do it.

'In y'come then, missy, I'll not be expectin' any trouble from y' since there's not a lot of good can be had from it in your case.' Local accent, harsh and rough, but somehow more kindly and familiar than she expected.

More steps forward. Lime washed walls. Long wooden table, well scrubbed. Guttering lanterns. A window with bars and no glass sending a fierce breeze through the chamber, enough to chill her heart. The grey daylight of late on a rainy day did nothing to illuminate the place. Gates clanking and locking behind her. No way out. Not ever.

Two women alone in the gloom. A curious empathy, against the rules, unspoken and unexpected, yet she sensed it very clearly. How was empathy possible? She was empty, dead already. Dead. Hang. Dead. The echo in her head was loud, constant.

'Let's 'ave y' in 'ere then,' said the woman, and the transient empathy was shattered. Through a heavy wooden door into a large chamber. The stench grew stronger. Only one lantern here and a grate but no fire. No heat at all. A tiny barred window, too high in the wall. The light seemed not to be able to penetrate.

Benches along the walls, and now figures in the long shadows, which danced maddeningly as the candle guttered in the draught. Women with obscure faces turned her way.

'This is Elizabeth Cooper,' came the guttural tones from behind her. 'Make sure she knows the way of things.' The harsh jangling of keys sealed her into the chamber with the ephemeral women.

2008

Passing into the main reception hall of the Shire Hall, my footsteps echoed around the silently imposing room. High ceilings, stone columns, armorial shields, and oak panelling. It was surely no accident, the resemblance to a Victorian church. Doors to other passageways, stairs, led off mysteriously to the right. In this warren of a building, I still did not know where they all went, even after over a year of working here.

I meandered to the reception desk, where the museum visitors would buy their tickets as soon as the doors opened—providing there were any visitors of course, which was by no means certain. I slipped behind the desk to scrawl my name in the signing-in book.

'Mornin',' a voice said from the office containing the monitors for the CCTV and the supplies for the reception desk.

'Good morning,' I said, turning to see Jim, the usual receptionist, middle-aged, bland enough but not someone I counted as a friend. It was an incestuous sort of place to work, this, rife with rumours and bitching, and I had decided long ago to be careful who I made friendships with. There was nothing really wrong with Jim, but nothing made him stand out to me either.

'All right?' he enquired, cheerfully.

'Yeah, fine thanks,' I replied, there being no chance I was going to explain my hangover and its cause to him. Forgetting to ask after his well-being, I slid out from behind the desk and through the doors to the side, which took me into an oak-panelled corridor at the side of the courtroom.

A few turns later and through another coded door, and I was at the shabby staffroom, a small hole at the very end of the corridor, right next to the supervisor's office, with a kettle, stained and chipped mugs, some leatherette chairs that stuck to your skin in summer, and a walk-in closet that acted as a cloakroom.

I made my entrance reluctantly; as usual, the cleaning staff, whose shift had just ended, were gathered, cackling over their tea. A couple of other colleagues were sitting with mugs in their hands: Jade, a rather useless student, and Mike, a retired man who was here for the pleasure of the job, not the money. Neither of whom I counted as friends, either. Politenesses were exchanged again and my head started to pound. I dumped my bag on the small bench in the cloakroom and departed the staffroom once more, following a familiar route, back through the entrance hall, through one of the doors marked 'staff only', and then climbing a back staircase that was painted in a shade of blue that always reminded me of a hospital.

Five minutes later I returned to the staffroom, transformed. That was the idea at least. In reality, I was dressed in a not-so-well-cut black jacket, with pretend corseting at the waist, and a black floor-length skirt with a torn hem. The costume made me a Victorian prison wardress, and despite my disdain as I glanced in the smeared mirror, the visitors seemed convinced enough.

Pulling my hairbrush from my bag, I turned my back on the people in the room and brushed my long light-brown hair out in front of the mirror. Without the natural dexterity required, I plaited it into a long tail which I coiled round into a bun at the nape of my neck. It was as close to a period hairstyle as I was going to manage, and, let's be honest, I was the only one who worked in the place who cared about such things anyway. Jade had pink highlights in her hair. Very fucking Victorian.

I usually liked the way my reflection looked once I had done my hair; it brought out my big hazel eyes, which I vainly regarded as my best feature, and emphasised the heart shape of my face. Today, it merely drew attention to the slightly greyish tone of my usually pink skin and to the dark shadows underneath my eyes. I brushed some dust from the sleeve of my jacket and went to work.

1808

Motionless for a moment, and wondering what to do. Then one of the women was on her feet, a shadow no longer, but a pale face, flickering with the lantern. 'Maisie Burrows,' said a girl's voice. A gesture to the other shapes in the gloom. 'These are Jane Larkin, Mary Smith, and Gilly Stevens.'

Vague movements and mumbles in the darkness as her gaze began to penetrate its thickness. A rasping cough from a large woman, Mary Smith it seemed, who appeared far older than Elizabeth.

Was that a smile on the face of this Maisie Burrows? Inconceivably, it seemed so. 'You'll grow used to it before long,' she said, in tones too mature for the years of her voice. 'This is the day room. We sleep through there and Mrs Beckinsale lets us to the table for eating.'

Fighting the echoes, she could not do anything but stare silently. Still the smell turned her stomach. A curious look from Maisie. 'You can talk, can't you?'

'Yes.' The first time she had spoken here. Her voice unfamiliar and large in the murk. No more words. Had she ever known any more words?

A scuffling in the corner of the room drew her attention. 'Don't mind the rats,' said Maisie. 'They're as hungry as the rest of us.'

Was that humour? No, the tone was bitter. Empathy with rats? How could she be here? Sickness rose in her throat again and she swallowed hard. She drew in a deep breath and choked on the stench, the dankness of the chamber.

'So'—Maisie was still talking, she knew words aplenty—'what did you do?' No answer. Then the injustice pushed a reply to the surface.

'I didn't do it.' The melancholy in her own voice struck her dumb again.

'Course not,' Maisie said, 'none of us did.'

I'm not like you, Elizabeth thought.

'But they've found you guilty of something upstairs, ain't they? Look at we four ladies—two thieves, a bawd, and Mary, who struck her husband with her skillet, but only hard enough to bruise 'im.' She sniggered. Elizabeth looked at the women, tried to apportion the crimes to the indistinct figures.

'Stealing in a dwelling house,' she said blandly, as though it applied to someone else. 'They say I'm a thief.'

'Another one 'ere, Gilly,' Maisie called across to the most obscured of all the female shapes, farthest from the light. 'That makes three, you, Gilly, and me,' she said. 'What sentence did they give you?'

It was such a light question. The echoes hammered against the inside of her skull. Hang. Dead. Dead. Hang. The gloom was suffocating suddenly, the inconstant illumination dizzying. The air was rotten, like a tomb. Her tomb. There weren't the words to answer the question. Her stomach lurched and her bowels felt loose. The walls spun around her, mocking her. The floor was closer than it should have been, pushing up towards her. Then, there was nothing.

2008

'Come on, out 'ere, let's see you, scum, the lot of you, I'm sure,' I called, in my best local accent, to a small party of visitors, a speech I now reeled off with barely any hesitation. They were in fucking early this morning. Quite often I didn't have to move from my chair until after eleven o'clock. Typical that, today of all days, the tourists were keen. A family with two children; an elderly couple; a young man and woman, who seemed to be together, holding hands. Fools.

I had reached the point where the composition of an audience really did not affect what I had to say to them. Wanting to amuse and impress people had been a feature of my first month or so here. Now, after a year and a half, a longer time than many of those imprisoned in the gaol had lingered here, my words were pretty generic. I went on, the familiar words slipping out more or less before I thought them. 'What are you lot in for then? Any murderers?' They had been allocated crimes with the purchase of their tickets, and the elderly man and the boy, who looked to be about twelve, raised their hands tentatively. 'Oh good,' I said, regarding them with a sinister, and most likely queasy, smile. 'You look the sort. This is where it ends for you then. This is the exercise yard of the Victorian prison.' I brandished my black polished cane about me, a little wildly. 'It is also where we are going to hang you.' Mock horror and giggles from my spectators as they glanced up at the noose on the gallows, swinging gently in the breeze. A giant stage prop, the gallows in the yard, a huge framework of wood stained black, a platform reached by a steep run of steps. It was so high the noose was nicely silhouetted against the sky when the visitors first came into the yard. Most of them thought it was genuine and loved to gaze up and nudge their friends and family. People's fascination with brutal death never ceased to amaze me. I guess I felt it too, why else would I be working in this place?

'You're lucky really though, before 1868 you'd have been hanged in public on the steps out front.' A little more genuine revulsion, as they remembered the way they had entered the museum. 'But for some reason, in 1868 they stopped public executions and moved them in here. We still get a good view at least. Since you've been convicted after 1872, it'll be the long-drop for you. A quick death, providing you get a good executioner, your neck will break instantly. Of course if the rope is too short you'll strangle, and if it's too long your head might come off...' I trailed off, a certain triumph inside me that even the cocky young man looked a little disturbed at the notion. 'It's better than you would have got on the steps outside though. There it was the short-drop, where you'd just dangle and strangle slowly, for up to an hour, unless you could pay someone to pull on your legs and make it a bit quicker.'

Now on to my favourite part to deliver, the moment I would finally get a reaction, maybe a real connection with the history of this place if I was lucky. 'When you murderers are dead, remember we can't bury a murderer in consecrated ground, so you'll be going under here.' I tapped the flagstones at my feet with the cane. 'In fact,' I gestured to the wall on my right, where some square slabs, carved with simple lettering, were mounted, 'these are the grave markers of real murderers who are actually buried under your feet.' A pause for dramatic effect. Give me a fucking Oscar. 'We'll put quicklime in your coffin so your body dissolves faster.' A little squeal from the young woman, who clung to her boyfriend; down-turned eyes from the whole party, who suddenly, shifting on their feet, seemed a little less at ease. At least the reality of this place had hit them now. I had no damn idea where the bodies of the murderers really were. They could have been at the other end of the yard entirely. Or non-existent inventions to scare the visitors. I had been really worried about attention to historical detail when I had first taken this job. Then I realised sensationalism and getting the visitors through as quickly as you could were more to the point.

I smiled. 'So, the exercise yard. This is the only bit of open air you'll get in this place, and it will be where you spend any time when you're not in your cells. Before the prison system was reformed, you'd be allowed to do pretty much as you wanted here, but the Victorians decided that wasn't good enough and brought in a far more disciplined system. So since I'm an enlightened Victorian myself, I could make you march round in orderly circles, in silence, and you won't even be permitted to look at your fellow prisoners.' I waved my stick menacingly. 'You can see evidence of some of the people who were here before you on that wall there.' I pointed to the building side of the yard. 'Can you see the graffiti? The names are on record as those of men who were imprisoned here before the stricter system was brought in. Some of them were counting down the days.' I gestured at the tally marks inscribed in the bricks. 'Don't forget, in those days, they weren't counting down the days of their sentence. Up until the mid-nineteenth century, this prison was a holding prison, not the punishment in itself, just a place to hold the criminal until their sentence was carried out. These markings could be counting down to a whipping, transportation to Australia, or maybe death.'

Letting the word hang in the air for a moment, I moved a little to my left and pointed towards a dark doorway to the side of the yard. 'You'll have time to look around the yard in a moment. First, you are going down into the oldest part of the prison, the pits and the dark cells. The name is appropriate, I think you'll find. The pits are the oldest cells—or I should really say dungeons—in the prison, dating back to medieval times, carved into the rock below the building. The dark cells are for punishment and were used into Victorian times. Disobey me by talking or laughing,' I glared at them at this point, 'and you'll be locked in there, with no light and no human contact, your food will be thrown through the hole to you, and you will use the floor as your toilet. So try to catch your food before it hits the floor.' My comment got the sniggers it deserved. 'Prisoners coming out of there have been so ill they have to be helped up the steps to the gallows.

'Look out of the window, through the bars, when you're down there. You'll see some houses. They're built on what used to be Narrow Marsh, the city's worst slum. Bear in mind two things: firstly, those houses don't have proper sanitation and the smell coming up from down there is almost as bad as the one in your cell. Secondly, you probably know people down there. The residents of Narrow Marsh are well known for their bad ways. During a police chase they lower their washing lines into the streets to help the criminal escape. Your family and friends could be down there, just a wall away. You'll hear children playing in the streets and you'll hear drunken shouts and fights coming up from the pub that is still at the bottom of the cliff here, the Nag's Head. Go down, have a look around, and when you come back I'll answer any questions and tell you what it was like to be transported to Australia.'

Thank God, I thought, as I sent the group through the doorway to examine for themselves the horrors of what was, for most people, the most frightening part of the prison. On a busy weekend, I might have to deal with more visitors, delivering this first part of the speech again, before the previous group emerged. Thankfully, this was a weekday and I had a few moments to myself.

I struggled to organise my thoughts into anything but a craving for sleep. I gazed at the carvings in the prison brickwork, my mind inert and languorous in the warm early summer sunlight. Mercifully, I was too hung-over for any meaningful contemplation. I didn't want to think about why another relationship hadn't worked. I didn't want to think about drinking so fucking much and the way my head was now pounding as my just reward. In truth, these days, it was better not to think too much at all. Feeling as though I was seeing my surroundings through a haze, I turned my attention to the dark, gaping entrance of the pits and waited.

CHAPTER TWO

2008

The children were the first to emerge from the lower part of the prison. They looked around the yard, pretending not to be interested in what I or their parents told them, but unable to hide that interest entirely. I recognised that nonchalant, hands in the pockets stance, the faint hostility with which they looked at me as the one who was trying to educate them, while all the while they could not help their gaze travelling in fascination over the gallows, grave markers, and graffiti. Most days, I took some pleasure in the fact that, by sparking their curiosity with my performance, I might have encouraged a child's interest in history generally, maybe for the rest of their life. Most days. Today, I just wanted them to get out of my yard as soon as possible. I waited, leaning against one of the supports of the gallows, for the rest of their party. When they reassembled, and no one seemed to have any questions for me, I strolled, less formal and imposing now, to the set of doors further along the yard; they followed me.

'In here, those of you sentenced to be transported will find out what it's like. We used to transport people to America, but America's independence in 1776 stopped us doing that. So we chose Australia instead. If you survive the very long sea journey, which you will spend locked below decks, you will be expected to undertake hard labour when you get there, helping to build the prison and houses of the local settlements. When your sentence has been served, you will be free to return to England if you can afford your passage back. If not, you will be allocated your own piece of land to farm. Your story could still be a happy one—many transported men and women went on to lead prosperous lives and have families in Australia. We stopped transporting people in the 1860s, and there was a lot of whining about harsh conditions, but if you ask me it was an easy sentence. Many prisoners were released early and took part in making Australia the country it is today, one of Britain's most successful colonies. So have a look around. When you come out, go through that door there,' I pointed to the end of the exercise yard farthest from where they had entered, 'that leads to the section of the prison built in 1833, a more modern prison. That's when prison started to be the punishment in itself, along with hard labour and solitary confinement, so you could reflect on your sins. You'll see what Victorian prisons were like and you can decide for yourself which system you think is best. Now, all of you, get out of my sight.' This morning the half-snarl in my voice was more genuine than usual.

They smiled at me, and I returned the gesture weakly, before stalking off, stick in hand, back into the shadows near the entrance to the yard. I knew I had no more visitors for a while. Part of the first part of the tour, conducted by my eighteenth-century turnkey colleague, involved herding the tourists into a cell and slamming the heavy door on them. The squeak of the old hinges and the resounding thud of the door were audible throughout the gaol and especially from where I waited, just below the barred cell window. Shortly after being released from the cell, the 'prisoners' would be guided down the stairs into the part of the building set up to represent the women's gaol, where they could be expected to spend at least ten minutes observing how in the Victorian era the women washed laundry for the whole prison, before making their way through a tunnel to the exercise yard where I waited. If I hadn't heard the slamming of the cell door, like today, it was a pretty safe bet I was at ease for a while.

When the visitors had disappeared into the next building, I perched on the dusty wooden steps of the gallows, warm in the sunshine, rather than on the small modern chair provided for me in the dark corner of the passageway. It was odd really, how relaxed I felt here, surrounded by bars and locks and the remains of executed murderers. The regulations of my job meant I could no more wander freely around the building than any prisoner, and while there were no visitors in the gaol I was as isolated down here as anyone suffering solitary confinement. But somehow, that was how I liked it. The thick walls and heavy doors that had imprisoned so many men and women seemed rather to protect me from the outside world, gave me a sanctuary, a place to hide. I did my best not to dwell on the fact that the only place I was truly happy these days was in a building constructed as a place of judgment and imprisonment and just how socially challenged that suggested I was. It was quiet here, and if I wanted to think, I could. And if, like today, I wanted to pretend there was no life outside these high brick walls, nothing to think about or to get drunk over, the confines of this place allowed me that comfort too.

1808

Dizziness and a haze of darkness. Elizabeth tried to open her eyes. They wouldn't open. A shadow loomed over her, and she knew they were open already. Lantern light glimmered closer to her. Beneath her body it felt damp. Was she on the floor? She remembered the rats and gave a start.

'You're with us again are you?' said a voice, closer than she expected. A softer voice, less accented. Not Maisie, another woman. Older, but not aged. 'Don't try to get yourself up, darlin', stay lying down.'

A wave of nausea made her body heave. Cool fingers soothed her forehead, smoothed her hair. Her mother's touch. But not her mother. Who? 'Who are you?' It came out as a croak.

'I'm Gilly, darlin', the other thief.' Gentleness, a hint of laughter even, in the tone that seemed to overwhelm her own fear. Hot tears rising, but bitterness in her mouth. And hunger churning her insides. 'You fainted clean out, darlin', right on the floor.'

Elizabeth remembered the blackness, the oblivion. Death. The echo came from nowhere and she cried out softly.

'Oh, darlin', what is it?' A voice to draw the fear from her. The words were there now, but they came accompanied by sobs.

'Death,' she said, 'death. That's my sentence. I'm going to die. And I didn't do it, I mean it.' Aching throat and chest ready to burst. Hot tears on her cold skin.

The other woman, Gilly, seemed stunned. 'Death?' The word was small and cold. In it was a realisation of her own escape. 'But surely not? Maisie and I, we're to be transported, and we're thieves if you believe them upstairs.'

More heaving sobs and Gilly's hands strong on her shoulders. 'You're not me, are you?' The words she spat with some bitterness, with all the injustice she felt.

'And what's so special about you that they want to kill you, darlin'?' A slight edge of resentment but hidden by sympathy. An invitation to tell the tale, reveal the pain of the injustice. However, there weren't the words for that story, not now. There wasn't even room in her head to remember it.

'I don't know,' she murmured instead. She swallowed a sob, but still her shoulders shook.

'Someone can speak in front of the judge for you.' Gilly's words were hopeful rather than certain. 'He'll commute it and you'll be on the boat with us. You'll see.'

'It wouldn't work.' Numb hopelessness was all she felt.

'And why not?'

'I just know.' Not the time for explanations. Would there ever be a time for explanations? How long did she have?

Gilly's hands gripped hers. A glimmer of comfort in the dark, despite herself. Elizabeth gripped back and closed her eyes, so there might be nothing but her own darkness and the human contact. Soothed for a moment. Then the sickening stench again, of mould and urine and worse, and the damp at her back. What was she lying on?

'Where am I?' she whispered to Gilly, wishing she could make out the other woman's face more clearly.

'This is where we sleep,' came the reply.

Elizabeth put her hands to whatever it was she lay on. Straw mattress, damp and rotting. Now the sounds came, scuffles not far from her head, women's murmurs in the room outside. Metal against metal, somewhere distant. A faint cry that must have been from the streets outside, below the cliff. A world outside which carried on, would not even notice her absence from it. She began to sob again, and Gilly's hands could not soothe her.

❖

2008

Silence was all that reached me from the corridors of the gaol above. Thank fuck for that, since my headache was steadily getting worse. I was probably hungry; I didn't usually go without breakfast. The thought of food was still pretty repulsive, and pointless anyway, since I wasn't allowed back up to the staffroom until my designated break time. Fire safety regulations apparently. Like there were any visitors to guide to safety.

The museum was not the most popular with tourists, despite my morning flurry today. It was quite common to spend hours on end waiting. We were supposed to clean the exhibition, sweep the flagstones, check for damage, but it wasn't a duty any of us took especially seriously. It was an old, dusty prison, for God's sake, and we weren't paid enough.

On some days, I got on better with my colleagues than I did today. When Chloe, a history student who was usually on duty as the Victorian prisoner in the women's prison, and Mark, a guy just a year older than me with a real connection with this place and his role as the creepy turnkey, were at work, we would often gravitate together on one of the several levels of the building, generally to whinge about the management or share a joke or two. It was usually in a place from which we could all scatter quickly at the sound of approaching footsteps. It was easy enough to improvise a reason why two costumed inhabitants of the prison might be caught chatting if a visitor slipped through unexpectedly, but none of us appreciated the sharply patronising tone of the supervisor, Karen, if we were found to have left our posts when she conducted her random walkabout inspections.

If Mark and Chloe weren't working, like today, I had no real reason to go anywhere, so I tended to patrol my exercise yard and lurk on the gallows steps in the sunshine. It was quite a little suntrap, my domain. On one side, rising so high I could not stand far enough back to see the roof, was the wall of the gaol and the Shire Hall above it. A layer of red brick, carved with prisoners' graffiti, then the level where the cells were, where a row of arched, barred windows in sandstone looked sternly outwards. Above this the building rose again in aged red brick, with white Georgian windows. It hid its secrets well. Most of the upper floors were offices these days, and the building gave little real hint of its sinister past on those higher levels. I hated that so many people worked in the offices above, whinging about the monotony of their jobs while traipsing in and out of the building whenever they chose, with barely a thought to its history or their own relative freedom. I didn't consider the people who worked on those upper floors colleagues; they didn't live the history of this place as I did.

From where I sat on the steps of the gallows, I directly faced the entrance to the yard through which my captives would come, blinking, having emerged from the dark tunnel from the women's gaol. The sinister entrance to the pits was to my right, a shadowy, forbidding doorway that even made me a little nervous. The entrances to the transportation exhibition and the more modern part of the prison were across the sun-bathed yard to my left.

Surrounded on three sides by buildings, the other side of the yard was enclosed by a tall red-brick wall, which loomed in on you, giving the whole area a very enclosed feeling. Sometimes, I climbed to the platform of the gallows and onto the guard railings closest to the wall, in order to peer over it and look at the city beyond. The hustle and noise always took me by surprise, and I found the view ruined by the modern glass structure of the new court building in among the old textiles factories. I would gaze for a few minutes, contemplating the continuity of history, and retreat back into my own little piece of the past. I was safe here, in my prison. I often thought of the prisoners who had been trapped inside these walls, longing for the freedom to even peep over the wall, let alone be able to leave by the front entrance every evening as I could do, and reflected how screwed up it was that their gaol was my refuge. But then, I told myself, their perspective of the outside world they longed for was probably far different from mine. Life had surely been simpler so long ago. Freedom brought its own bloody problems and hiding behind these walls meant I didn't have to face them for a few hours at least.

I suppose I was almost territorial about my exercise yard. I wondered if the warders of days gone by had felt the same way. It was one of the ways I spent my idle time, imagining the people who had once inhabited this place. I had studied history—I had a bloody degree in it—I knew not to romanticise it. Academically, I had seen beyond the myth of the clean and idealised past created in countless films and television adaptations of classic novels; my research cut through the costumes and candlelight. I knew the facts and figures of population growth in cities during the industrial revolution, understood the resulting brutality of the squalor endured by so many of those who had turned to crime over the centuries. I knew the filthy conditions inside the gaol would not have been much worse for many of the prisoners than their lives on the outside. Many of them would have been illiterate and with a life expectancy not much beyond thirty. Facts and evidence: they were the historian's staples and I knew enough of them to have a good grasp on the reality of this place. I suppose somehow, though, I did not connect completely with it. How else could I lounge on the steps of a mock-gallows in an exercise yard where people were executed and buried in quicklime?

Today, any contemplation of history was about as far from my mind as it was possible to be. I leaned back on my elbows, covering my black costume with dust from the steps, and let the sun warm me through. My head was still pounding. I was never going to drink again.

How many times had I said that? But this was different. This was all down to that fucking bastard. I should've known two months ago it wasn't going to work. I didn't even fancy him, for God's sake. It was more a case of, at the age of twenty-five, I really thought I should have a boyfriend. People I'd known at school and university were all getting married and having children. I hated the thought of being pregnant, let alone the screaming brat it would produce, and I'd only had a handful of serious boyfriends. One had lasted almost a year, but I had known it wasn't love as soon as the initial excitement—or maybe relief—at having a boyfriend had died down. This latest one—Paul his name was—had been nothing more than a good idea at the time, which had soon turned out not to be. We'd spent a month holding hands and pulling each other's clothes off half-heartedly, and a month arguing about every conceivable subject. Something about him just made me uncomfortable. I was glad he had finally fucked off last night. I'd been drinking to celebrate being single again, of course I had. Or perhaps I was quietening that echo, the one that followed me from year to year. Maybe I'd been wrong.

A heavy thud followed by a squeal of delighted alarm reached me from above. Thinking that lounging on the steps of the gallows was not the best place to be discovered by my next party of prisoners, I got up and went to lurk in the shadows to wait for them.

1808

Drifting in and out of sleep on the damp straw. Always dark, even with her eyes open. Surely it wasn't night already? Eternal darkness. Dead. Hang. Hang. Dead. The echo taunted her, awake and asleep. Drifting into sleep again, falling, falling. Dying. Aged two-and-twenty and healthy, a strong girl they'd called her, and now dying. Impossible. Yet it was to be.

Alone now, Gilly's hands nowhere to be felt. No murmurs without, but a vague sound of scraping chairs, farther away. The women were still there. Elizabeth felt hot now, burning, but her fingers were icy when she held them to her face.

More shapes in the gloom. Low to the stone floor, on the straw mattress, a chair loomed nearby. There was a bucket near the arched entrance to this cell. That was what it was, a cell. A gaol cell, where she would spend her last days. Heart raging against the injustice. The bucket was the source of the bitter odour of stale urine.

Elizabeth sat up and waited while her balance restored itself. Why was she alone? She eased herself to her feet and moved unsteadily to the doorway. Now, she caught their voices in the first chamber.

The darkness of the sleeping cell seemed to pull her back towards it. She wanted to lie on the straw and wait for death, she felt its draw. But hunger stirred in her stomach. Still alive now.

She tore herself from the shadows that clutched at her skirts and moved towards the voices.

The women were seated around the long wooden table, pink-faced Mrs Beckinsale at the head. Her keen eyes saw Elizabeth first.

'Gracin' us with y' presence, Miss Cooper, or will y' be keepin' to y' bed for the rest of t' day?' A snigger from Maisie, the eyes of the four women on her now. Too much attention. It was lighter in this room now; candles burned on the table, the smell of their tallow adding to the acrid atmosphere. 'Gilly, give 'er some stew.'

Gilly stood and reached for the handle of the ladle which protruded from a dish in the centre of the table. Pungent over-boiled cabbage filled Elizabeth's nostrils. Gilly took up a small wooden bowl and spooned two ladlefuls of a liquid substance into it. Then she put it on the table at the side of her and gestured that Elizabeth should sit beside her.

What was in her bowl was not stew. More like cabbage, served with the water it was boiled in. Glancing along the table, no bread in sight.

Opposite her, pale face made yellow by the candles, Mary Smith gazed at her. A broad woman with heavy features, probably past her fortieth year. She had an odd scar on her left cheek. An unnerving gaze, strikingly even and constant. Elizabeth looked away.

Next to her, Jane Larkin, a smaller, younger woman with very dark hair from beneath her cap, spooned up her cabbage eagerly, her whole body rocking slightly. Not interested in Elizabeth at all.

'Go on then, eat up, or y'll be hungry later.' Mrs Beckinsale's voice reminded her of her mother's. She fought a sob rising in her throat and lifted her spoon.

The taste was foul, the texture, at once watery and viscous, almost made her sick, there at the table. But she returned her spoon to the bowl and took another mouthful. It was at least warm in her belly. Mary Smith stopped her gazing and returned to her own meal.

Mrs Beckinsale, she noticed, ate the same cabbage soup they did. A moment of curiosity about the older woman sparked in her. Did she live at the gaol too? What of her husband? Another spoonful of the cabbage. She was surprised at how little was left in the bowl already.

As she ate, she glanced sideways at Gilly. She knew her voice and her hands, but the other woman's appearance was unfamiliar. Gilly had pink skin, despite the candlelight and the shadows. She ate her food slowly and properly, drinking the water from the side of the spoon. Older than Elizabeth, but not above her thirtieth year. Auburn hair beneath her cap, a vaguely crooked nose in profile. Straight shoulders and a slender form. Nothing at all coarse; she seemed to be in the wrong place. This morass of odours and seething shadows did not seem to be a reasonable environment for her, any more than it felt like it was for Elizabeth.

Another spoonful of cabbage. Still alive, hunger soothed if not satisfied. Still alive. But with the assurance came the opposite echo, just beneath. Hang. Dead. She let her spoon fall to the table. Mary Smith glanced up at her again. She remained in her chair and fought the tears. The other women were looking. Let them. And the thought brought a curious comfort. Not alone, not dead, not yet.

2008

Small groups of two or three people insisted on plaguing me until the middle of the afternoon. I spent my half-hour lunch break alone in the staffroom, wondering if everyone else had maybe gone home and left me, but really quite grateful for the solitude.

By three o'clock, I was relaxing on my gallows steps once more, the shadows beginning to extend over the yard and putting me half in the shade. My headache had subsided, but I still felt tired, and despite my best efforts, my thoughts persisted in going back to a consideration of my latest failed relationship and a possible future of spinsterhood. Those distant days when I'd contemplated something very different threatened to intrude on my reflections. Six years and still the doubt. I stared blankly at the red brick ahead of me and worked on blocking the echoes from my mind. Much though I didn't feel like more work today, I was also deeply uncertain that I wanted the freedom of closing time to come. The prospect of returning to my flat and fighting the thoughts that always threatened to intrude on my peace of mind made my enclosed gaol yard seem even more comforting as the day drew towards its close.

It was always peaceful in the yard by this time in the afternoon, providing there were no parties of schoolchildren to deal with. Not many people chose to start a tour of the museum this late in the day, and the chances were, if there were no more visitors now there would be no more for the rest of the day. The museum officially closed at four thirty, but no one would be admitted after four, which was always a blessing.

By this time, I was virtually lying on the steps, my legs extended to the floor and my head back on a higher step. I was not especially concerned that I would be discovered in my relaxation, since I knew Karen the supervisor would be doing her end of the day paperwork and trying to get home as quickly as possible. The cell door would warn me of the threat of visitors. Besides, I had developed an odd kind of sixth sense by now; I generally knew when someone was lurking nearby. It happened sometimes: a visitor would sneak through without the customary ceremony of the cell door above, the supervisor would take a different route than usual and wait in the shadows just to observe, the curator would conduct a quiet tour of sponsors or researchers through the yard, or a colleague would creep up for a chat or for the fun of making me jump. All were possible, and without even really trying, I nearly always knew when someone was there. I guess I was so used to being alone in my yard that when my territory was invaded, I sensed it instantly. It was a sound out of place, a slight shift of the shadows, a feeling of being watched. So I was quite comfortable, in my odd repose, that I would be able to be at least respectably upright before I was discovered.

The sun was warm, and it felt good to stretch out and relax. There was a slight breeze disturbing the still air of the enclosed yard and moving my hair slightly. This was my place, I was at home here. Here I pretended to be something else, and my real life didn't matter. For all my complaining, I loved my job. It was a soothing thought. I looked up at the few white clouds in the blue sky, thinking how quiet the yard was, as though the city outside had disappeared. I breathed deeply and closed my eyes.

Suddenly I had the feeling someone was in the yard. I felt a fear in the pit of my stomach I had never felt in all my days working in this sinister place. I sat upright and looked around, yet somehow, I could not move any farther, I could not get to my feet. The fear seemed to melt into anger and pain inside me, powerful feelings with no foundation in reality, in the empty, peaceful yard. I wanted to call out, ask if someone was there, but found I could not make the words come out of my mouth. I was frightened by my own inability to do anything. Then I seemed to see a woman standing in the entrance to the yard that led to the women's gaol. I didn't recognise the girl, though she looked younger than me, with blond hair, and she was dressed in old-fashioned clothes. Not a costume, not the Victorian women's prison uniform one of my colleagues wore. A tired brown dress, a white cap; poor clothes, like I imagined the servants and factory girls to have worn in the first part of the nineteenth century, before Victoria was on the throne. She belonged to an earlier time, before the prison discovered strict regimes and uniforms, earlier than the Victorian picture I presented to visitors daily. I looked at her for a moment, and then she turned and went to walk away.

'Boo!' I jumped out of my skin and opened my eyes to see Bill, the grey-haired museum caretaker, looming over me. It took me a moment to realise why I was on my back on the gallows steps. I sat upright instantly and studied Bill with some suspicion.

'Was I asleep?' I asked, stupidly, my head still foggy.

'Fast on,' he retorted, smiling.

'How long were you there?' I demanded.

'Not so long.' He chuckled. 'Came down to lock up and there you are, sleeping beauty.'

'Lock up? What time is it?' I was pretty sure it had been just after three when I had settled myself on the steps. Surely I hadn't dozed off for longer than a couple of minutes?

'It's four. There's no one in, so we get to go home early,' he informed me, to my bewilderment. I'd been asleep for nearly an hour. And I'd not heard Bill coming into the yard. What if it had been Karen or a tourist? What if someone had thought to actually look at the CCTV monitors? Fuck. Maybe my sixth sense wasn't so hot after all.

Bill was still smiling his amusement at me. 'Good night last night was it?' he asked indulgently.

'No, the opposite,' I told him grimly.

'Drowning your sorrows?' he enquired, as I pulled myself to my feet and tried to restore some semblance of dignity.

'More or less,' I replied. 'Doesn't work though, does it?'

'It can help, love. But a good night's sleep is a better help most of the time,' he advised good-naturedly.

'I'll be trying that one tonight I reckon,' I told him. 'Home time then?' I confirmed.

'Yep, we're lucky today. Tell you what, you go straight up, I'll check through,' he offered.

'Thanks, you're a star,' I told him with a smile. Normally, as the last guide the visitors saw, it was my job when the museum closed to take the route they would through the museum and make sure there were no stragglers, sheep-dogging those that were there to the exit as quickly as possible. Bill usually just locked the doors and turned off the lights after me. I'd get out of here a good fifteen minutes quicker if he did the checking for me. 'See you tomorrow then,' I said.

'Yep, sleep well.'

'Thanks,' I said, heading into the building to climb my way back up the several flights of stairs to the staffroom.

As I left the sunshine and Bill's company, an uneasy feeling struck me again. The detail of my dream clarified itself in my head and I remembered the girl with her dark blond hair. I was pretty certain there was no one like that working here, but I supposed there was a chance there was someone new I hadn't met yet. Or it could have just been a dream. Did the girl have a name? Was her face familiar? I ransacked my memory of the dream as I climbed the stairs which took me to the next level of the prison, level with the entrance to the women's section.

A distant door slammed, the sound of Bill at his closing-time duties. Along a short, shadowy passageway and then right, into a longer one, to take me to the steps that would let me climb to the level of the building that the courts and staffroom were on. The lights here were all electric, since there were no windows open to the daylight. I passed the deserted lair of the turnkey, illuminated in gloriously theatrical slime green lighting. And a name seemed to filter into my head. Elizabeth.

Elizabeth? Most of the bloody women that had ever passed through this prison were called Elizabeth. That or Mary. I must have seen the name Elizabeth on the information boards around this place tens of times a day.

Suddenly the lights went out.

The atmospheric green was replaced by pitch darkness, in which I could barely make out the door I was heading for. I overreacted instantly, having never been very keen on the dark. My heart thudded and I dashed headlong for where the door had to be, only a few feet in front of me. The thick darkness behind me almost seemed to push me forwards, to eject me unceremoniously from its gloom, and I did not dare look over my shoulder. I sensed the gaol, large behind me, corridors and doorways and metal gates and cells, caves below it, most of which I didn't even know. I felt the cold air which seeped through it, felt the emptiness. When we left it, the electric lights turned off, it was a gaol once more, not a museum of curiosities, and the cold dark of its past echoed into the present. I didn't belong there. Let me out.

With some relief I opened the door and virtually fell through it into the small hallway on the other side, which led to a metal spiral staircase up to the staffroom corridor. I paused in the light, realising how hard I was breathing. How fucking ridiculous. So Bill had flicked the switch that turned all of the museum lights off, thinking I'd have made it out already. It had just been the unexpectedness of being plunged into darkness that had scared me, of course. I made a point of never being frightened by the history of this building. I certainly did not believe in the spirits of the past haunting the present. Even if they were, it wasn't likely to be their idea of fun to turn all the lights off, was it? I found the idea of ghosts uninteresting and overrated. Without that, what was there to be frightened of about history? Nothing.

Elizabeth Cooper.

The name seemed to have planted itself in my head from nowhere. Did I know someone of that name? It sounded familiar in some way. I couldn't think of anyone I knew. A celebrity maybe, someone in the news? I couldn't recollect anyone, but it was hardly an unusual name, I must have heard it at some point and now I was ascribing it to some dreamed-up girl at work. Why even make that connection? For fuck's sake. It really was time to go home and sleep.

1808

One day slid by and then another. For all their misery, Elizabeth would have seized them with both her hands and stopped time, if she could have done. The echoes were as regular as a clock ticking. Death. Hang. Death. Hang. Tick. Tock.

Sleep had felt pointless, as she had lain on the damp straw on the floor of the cell. All five women shared the straw, and she was conscious of their reduced space because of her presence. But there was Gilly, close behind her, and for that she was glad. Living, warming breath on the nape of her neck, the other woman's tired grey skirts pressing against her own poor brown ones. Too hungry for sleep, the echoes too loud and the shadows too deep. Gilly moving slightly, sighing, already unconscious. And then sleep had come, dreamlessly, to silence the echoes until the light crept between the bars again.

Days with nothing to do but wait and listen to the time dripping away. Elizabeth, used to the bustle of her housemaid's duties, felt pointless. She was waiting until they killed her. It was the only purpose of her life now, and it was no purpose at all. The pattern of her old routine haunted her memory, and the colours of her life flooding into her head only heightened the injustice. No one had listened, and in the end no one had cared.

Was she even a memory in their heads now? Or a ghost already?

Would they watch as she died? Would anyone watch, or would she hang, dying in the street, as passers-by just shrugged and went on their way? The image of herself, noose tight about her neck, body straining for life in a fight which was impossible, was not real. She had seen a man hanged once, on the very steps where she would meet her own death.

It had been a cold day in late autumn. She had been in town, a rare hour free of work, when she had been drawn by the movement of people in the street towards the front of the Shire Hall, knowing perfectly well what drew her, and that it should not, inescapably compelled nonetheless. She had simply climbed the hill, filled with a dark curiosity, and stared at the wooden platform that had been erected, the loop of rope swinging from it. She did not know for what crime the man had been condemned and did not like to ask those around her.

Knowing she should not stay, she was somehow fixed in her place, her heart throbbing violently, as the condemned man was brought out, arms tied behind his back. The image of his face, unexpectedly calm as the hood had been placed over his head, had haunted her in nightmares for weeks afterwards.

Elizabeth had closed her eyes, only opening them again when she heard the strangled sound the man made as the noose tightened around his neck. She had been mesmerised by the painful slowness of death to have mercy upon him. The cloth that had been hung around the bottom of the platform to hide the worst of his agonies had come loose and every moment of his body's fight for life was visible before her. He had made sounds as though he was trying to talk for nearly half an hour, as she had stared, transfixed, unheeding of the thinning crowd around her. His clothes had been stained dark where his bladder had released, and foul liquid had run down his leg to pool on the cobbles below. His body had still been twitching and jerking on the rope when she had walked away on weak legs an hour later, her stomach uneasy. Yet she'd felt a perverse elation at having witnessed such a death. Now, looking down at her living body, she moved her legs. It was inconceivable to imagine her muscles contorted in those death throes. Despite the echoes, it was too horrible to be possible. Imagining it numbed her thoughts.

Mary Smith attempted to read the Bible to pass her days, hissing with laughter periodically. Elizabeth watched her and wondered just what part of Scripture made such humour possible. Mary was sentenced to be whipped for striking her husband with her skillet. She was to be taken to her home village and led at the back of a cart, naked from the waist upwards, and given twenty lashes through the village. Elizabeth studied the broad woman's face and saw no sign of fear or dread. Her punishment seemed too awful to consider. It was long moments before Elizabeth realised she'd be glad to exchange sentences with the other woman.

Jane Larkin wrote letters in an ill-learned hand and passed them to Mrs Beckinsale to be sent to their recipients. In between letters, she paced between the cell and the day room and muttered to herself. Elizabeth remembered the description Maisie had given of the small, hard-faced woman. Bawd. Elizabeth wondered what Jane had known in her life, what manner of life it had been. It must take some suffering, she knew, to sacrifice your reputation, your own body, for the paltry money men would pay. Jane's clothes were of a finer cut and fabric than any of the other women's, but in the old fashion and filthy about the hems. She fidgeted with her dark hair beneath her cap constantly. She had known things of the world which Elizabeth could barely conceive of. And she was to be transported for seven years for it.

Maisie and Gilly, thieves together, passed their time quietly sewing. They mended for the whole gaol, and, it seemed, most of the turnkeys' families too. It was too dark, even when there was full daylight outside and a lantern alight within, for sewing not to be a chore, and both women looked up frequently, rubbing their fingers to their eyes.

Maisie Burrows, with her white blond hair, was young, just turned sixteen and oddly proud of her youth. She seemed to have no comprehension of the journey she was to be forced to undertake, nor the conditions in which she would be kept in the Antipodes. Transported for fourteen years. By the time she was free, halfway around the world, Maisie would be young no longer. Already her voice was older than her years, and the shadows below her eyes were dark against the rose she maintained in her cheeks by continually pinching at them.

Gilly was the only one of the women who Elizabeth felt any connection with. The others were criminals, sinful and coarse. Gilly was a convict too of course, but her voice was soft, her eyes contemplative. The other women were awkward with her once they knew the sentence which hung over her head. Gilly had been only kind.

On waking, the women took it in turns to squat over the slop bucket in the night cell. The last to use it took it to the door which led out of the day room, where it would wait, uncovered and fouling the air, until Mrs Beckinsale came to unlock the door and lead the woman to the place in the gaol where such things were disposed of.

Breakfast was shared with Mrs Beckinsale at the long table. A ladle of gruel, grey and gelatinous, and tepid water to drink. And then trickling hours until the middle of the day. There was bread then, and more water. More hours stretched until the cabbage soup of the evening. Gilly assured Elizabeth there would be a little meat on Sunday. It seemed an odd thing to look forward to.

Mrs Beckinsale was a benign presence. She drifted between motherly and stern, but there was never cruelty in her tired eyes. The women followed her rules, her routine: her way. To all intents and purposes, the women's gaol was her gaol. Gilly told Elizabeth she was married to a turnkey in the debtor's gaol and they lived somewhere in the upper reaches of the building. Elizabeth did not envy her keeper in her life. It seemed as inevitable a death sentence as her own was, only more lingering.

The first morning, Elizabeth had sat awkwardly on the bench, watching the other women. She had lain on the damp straw, before becoming restless and pacing, her path criss-crossing with Jane's. In the afternoon, she had talked to Gilly and silenced the din in her mind with details of the routine she could expect. While she was here. Before she died.

By the second day Elizabeth was sewing alongside Gilly and Maisie. Her hands were busy and the concentration on her stitches through the gloom dulled her thoughts slightly. Maisie irritated and troubled her all at once. Gilly's calm rippled through the dank atmosphere and soothed her.

It was growing dark on the evening of her third day. Pointless to keep count; better to count the remaining days. But the date of her death was not appointed yet. While there was no date, it was an ethereal thing, just echoes, nothing more. There was still life; there was hunger and there was food, scant though it was. There was cold and there was the warmth of five bodies on the damp straw to carry her through the night. It was an odd life, removed from the world, another existence entirely. But it was still life. Routine was bringing comfort, empathy beginning to soothe her into a forgetfulness of what was to come.

'Lizzie Cooper?' A voice from the gaol, outside of Mrs Beckinsale's domain. A man's voice, heard before. A start as she heard her name, and then a shudder. Too fat for his buttons, one of them missing, a mess of threads.

'Elizabeth.' Mrs Beckinsale bustled into the day room from the outer chamber where she had been marking something in a large book. There was an urgency in her expression. She is afraid of him too, Elizabeth thought. 'Look sharp, missy, it's Mr Charles that be wantin' you,' she said quickly. Elizabeth rose from the bench and glanced anxiously at Gilly who had been sitting by her. Concern and curiosity at once in Gilly's eyes.

'What for?' she asked of Mrs Beckinsale.

'Why should I know? Come on, girl!' Her keeper's firm hand gripped her arm and pulled her towards the gate. A rattle of keys at the woman's waist, and then the gate was open to let him in.

A moist smile, the yellow teeth exposed, the dark space where a tooth should be. The button still missing, and now another one loose. Food stains on his coat. Dread in the pit of her stomach.

'Lizzie has a visitor, Mrs Beckinsale,' he said, mocking in his voice. But there's no one to visit me, she thought.

'Lucky girl,' Mrs Beckinsale beamed. Anxiety in her eyes, unmistakeable.

'Who? I don't know anyone,' she said. It was true in its simplicity. No family, and those who had been kind to her had abandoned her, condemned her.

'It's a lady, thinks she can help you,' he said.

Mrs Beckinsale's face was too strained for the happy words. 'In't that wonderful?' she enquired with forced lightness. Neither the man nor Elizabeth answered her.

'Help me?' A glimmer of hope made her blink.

'Yes, come with me,' he was taking her arm to lead her. 'I'll have her back soon enough, Mrs Beckinsale.'

'Yes, Mr Charles,' was the meek response.

❖

The gate crashed closed, metal against stone, behind them. A sense that she would sooner be behind it than outside, here with him.

The shadows of the corridor ahead of them were dark, but all the time there was the faintest glimpse of a distant light. Someone to help. But who? Was it possible? A pounding of her heart; the hope strengthening it, despite herself.

Two sets of footsteps echoing and returning to her ears. Brightness and then shadow, as they passed one lantern and then another. Not ascending. The gaol was built on a cliff. No respectable visitor, no one who could help, would surely be asked to sink down into its depths. They would have to go up, somewhere. Someone to help. Mind racing, despite the pall of hopelessness and disbelief. One friend after all, when she had thought they had abandoned her.

Silence between them, though they walked side by side. Not quite silence. Heavy breaths rasped in his throat, the keys at his waist rattled with every step. When would they turn? When would they go higher? How deep was it possible to be in this building?

Slowing and stopping at a doorway, bathed in the halo of light from a lantern which hung next to it. The door to a staircase perhaps? Keys turning in the lock. Taking a step towards the door, unconsciously almost, a step towards the light, drawn like a moth.

The door creaked open. Darkness beyond, not even a glimmer of light. Sharp force against her back, as his rough hands shoved her into the obscure shadows beyond the door. A cry that must have been her own, and then falling. Cold stone bruising the heels of her hands, the fire of pain in her leg as her knee crashed into the floor. Tight fear and complete blackness. No light, no help, no friend. There was no staircase, no way to ascend. She was betrayed and the realisation turned into rage.

Light swung dizzyingly around the chamber as the lantern was brought within, placed on an iron hook near the door. Rage became terror as the door slammed closed.

Walls of sandstone, carved into the cliff. Smell of damp, underground, like a grave. Elizabeth turned to face him. Light behind him, face in shadow. Fear consumed her. She slid away from him, cowering against the wall of stone at the back of the chamber. It was cold, solid, immovable as she pressed herself to it. Damp through her clothes, but she was sweating.

'On your feet, Lizzie, let me see you.' The words were a snarl. Impossible to move, to obey, to escape. Quicker than she thought he could move, he was above her. Hair almost ripped from her, hand clamped to her head, pulling her to her feet. Pain throbbing through her leg. Hard to breathe.

'When I tell you to do something, you do it, Lizzie, didn't y' know?' Sudden movement and an explosion of pain along her cheekbone as the heavy fist struck her face. A cry of agony. Her cry. She caught herself against the wall, the grains of the sandstone sticking to her hands.

'You didn't really think anyone would help you, did you, Lizzie?' Sardonic words, spoken through a yellow smile. Missing tooth. Tears rising and an ache in her throat. No. She hadn't thought it, hadn't allowed the hope. Not so stupid. There was only darkness and desolation. Laughter now, as she fought not to cry. 'Ah, Lizzie, no one cares. You're a corpse already. Three weeks from now, you'll be cold underground.'

Three weeks? She raised her eyes to his cruel face, imploring despite herself. 'No one told you, Lizzie? Date's set. They're measuring the rope out as we speak.' More laughter. Sickness rising.

Looming closer to her now. Sour milk on his breath. 'So, Lizzie, it don't matter a bit what I do with you now, you see. No one will know and no one will care.' She stared at him. His belly pressed against her first as he stepped closer.

'Please, sir...' she began, pleading, despite the rage of injustice deep in her core. The fear and repulsion were greater.

'Oh, Lizzie, you don't have to beg me,' he crooned. She bit her lip until it bled into her mouth. 'You just be a good girl, and I'll give you what you deserve.'

Rising horror, rage at his smile. She fought him, clawed at him, scratched his face, but he was strong and his laughter echoed in the room. A hand clamped around her throat, choking her. She strained for air, motionless, gasping.

'Imagine what it'll be like to die,' he whispered. She wanted to scream, but the hand was too tight. Her eyes were stinging and her head was swimming. And she suddenly saw the reality of her own death. Three weeks. Panic rose and she struggled against him.

'You just be a quiet girl, Lizzie,' he said, hand gripping tighter, as his free thick fingers tore at her clothing. His touch on her bosom then, bruising her flesh. Tearing of fabric, and then damp, cold air on her exposed skin. His eyes crept over her.

'Bet I'm the first one to see 'em, Lizzie, aren't I? First and last!' Hands touching her nakedness, releasing her throat. Gasping and coughing, unable to draw enough air in. Shame at his touch, vomit in her throat. Her hands trembling.

'Please, sir, please don't,' she implored through the thick pain in her throat.

'In my gaol, Lizzie, I do as I please,' he snarled. Anger in his eyes, or something that appeared like it. Another lightning movement, his hands hurled her forwards, to the dirt of the floor again. Not able to catch herself, her chin scraping the stone. Trying to lift herself, but his weight suddenly behind her, on top of her, pressing down, hands at her skirts.

And then pain, sharp and deep, as her body was invaded. Shame burned her cheeks, rage tore through her insides, but his weight covered her, pressed her flat to the floor. She looked at the flagstones and tasted the blood in her mouth. She tried not to think she would be better off dead already.

2008

There was a message from Paul waiting for me on my answer-phone when I arrived at my flat. I lived on the outskirts of the city, in a not-so-bad area which was apparently up and coming, though I had seen scant evidence of any positive trend. It only took me a short while on the bus, since I was early enough to miss rush hour. The blinking green light on the phone was not a welcome sight as I passed through the hallway.

'Jen, it's me. Sorry about last night, let's get together and make it up. Tomorrow night, I can pick you up at about six? Let me know.'

'Oh, sod off,' I said out loud when the message finished. It hit me in that moment; I wasn't remotely tempted to meet him tomorrow, or ever. Never would be good enough. I just didn't care. Two months out of a lifetime wasn't a lot to have wasted on him. I felt my own bitchiness as I thought it. It wasn't really his fault. I knew I'd done nothing to make the relationship work, and, ultimately, I had achieved what I had deserved. Single again. Maybe I should simply content myself with being that way.

I deleted the message. Doubtless he would survive the disappointment. Full marks to him for trying though.

I went into the kitchen and flicked the kettle on. The empty Southern Comfort bottle jeered at me from near the bin. I scowled at it and left it where it was. A rummage in the cupboards told me I really needed to get myself out to the supermarket. It would have to wait. A crumpled packet of Pasta 'n' Sauce was a sufficient meal for one; it said so on the packet after all.

As I poured the powdery contents of the packet into a saucepan, measured out the correct amount of water to mix in with it, and turned on the gas, I thought how pathetically fixed the routine of my life had become. It didn't matter that my relationship with Paul was no more; his impact on my day to day life had been minimal anyway. I'd kept him at arm's length, not wanting the intrusion of having to make changes to my life for anyone but myself.

Instead, I was locked into the same pattern, days sliding by, each one indistinguishable from the last. My only refuge was my voluntary imprisonment behind those high prison walls, the only place where the truth I resisted so fiercely seemed not to be able to touch me as I immersed myself in the history and the enforced regime of my work. But I was losing my resolve, I sensed it already; the thoughts were even penetrating my quiet hours in the exercise yard. There was only so much longer this routine could go on. For all my pretending and hiding behind the bars of the gaol, I was free to do exactly what I wanted after all. I was just too damn frightened to face the truth of what that was.

CHAPTER THREE

2008

A plate of orangey-coloured, herb-scented, overcooked mush and cup of green tea (it'd be good for my system) in hand, I perched on the edge of the saggy peach sofa. I took a tentative nibble at a forkful of pasta. Not too bad—enough MSG to make it quite palatable in fact. I blew on the forkful to cool it down.

My eye was drawn to the newspaper, still open on the coffee table at the employment pages. I'd drawn a couple of red rings around potential jobs, but that had been three days ago, and I'd not taken any further action yet. The truth was, nothing seemed quite right.

I'd graduated three years ago with a good history degree and the world had supposedly been my oyster. Yet the delights of a career had yet to open to me. I'd tried admin, looked into teaching, considered academic research. I'd been told I could be an accountant with a history degree. Well, that was just great. I just could not find anything that offered me the life I wanted. Whatever the hell that was. I lived a life of perpetual indecision. Boyfriends came and went without much regret. If you'd asked me to define my type, I wouldn't have been able to. It was the same with jobs.

So I'd taken a job with pay more suited to a student summer job, which involved dressing-up in a costume and shouting sensationalised history at tourists in a building which horrified most people. Not the career choice most people had been expecting of me, it had to be said. I remembered the optimistic predictions my teachers had made for my future, based on my outstanding school exam results. My university tutors, impressed by my dedication to history and a studiousness that had come largely from using academia to block out any confrontation with real life, had told me I was suited to postgraduate research. Somehow I didn't see myself as a professor one of these days. I just didn't know what I did see myself as. My parents would be happy for me to have anything that could be called a career, and I knew my mother especially was just waiting for me to come to my senses. Perhaps I was a disappointment to her. But even in that I found a little of the joy of rebellion. My school and university friends were mothers, secretaries, teachers, nurses, marketing assistants…and I was a Victorian prison wardress. There was something perversely satisfying in that.

The pasta was beginning to congeal as it cooled and was suddenly less appealing. I took one more mouthful and laid the plate aside. Actually, I couldn't imagine a better job than mine. The pay was derisory, the management laughable at times, but still something about my daily immersion in such an important building appealed to me. I was a historian, after all. I was beginning to think a job in a museum, maybe as a curator, might appeal to me. Yet I was reluctant to relinquish the fun of my work, the dramatic licence I took in helping the past reach through and come alive. Besides, there was something to be said for spending the days in costume, pretending you were a character from a previous century. It was a good way of avoiding confrontation with reality. Which is exactly what my parents would have said to me too. Maybe they were right. Deep down I felt that same old uneasy sensation that told me I knew exactly what I wanted, only I did not want to recognise it. In the end, my prison was really an escape and there were not many jobs that offered that. What I needed was a life I didn't feel the urge to escape from. I just had no idea how the fuck I could go out and get it.

I reached for the remote control and turned on the stereo. The volume I'd been playing it last night made me jump, and I felt a twinge of guilt for my neighbours. I turned it down and lay back on the sofa to lose myself in rock. Every word of the lyrics, every nuance of the singers' voices; I listened to it and imagined the words were about me. It was my form of meditation. Soothed, I felt the tension dissolve for the first time today.

1808

Pain in her leg as she followed him back through the patches of light of the passageway. Concentration on her feet, not stumbling, one foot in front of the other. His broad back a shadow in front of her. Dry mouth, taste of barely swallowed acid. Three weeks. Hang. Dead. Did it matter now?

Pain deep in her body, unfamiliar. Her throat still tight and aching. The urge to sob, but her eyes dry. An odd calm, like the stillness of death already. Sound of his grating breath as they walked and the recollection of it, panting, close to her ear. Panting. Pushing. Hurting. Finally a moan of fulfilment and then laughter. Blood drying, crusting on her lip, her pulse strong in her cheek. No hope now. Dead.

Thunder of keys and gates, too loud. One hand clutching her torn dress against the prying air. Grains of the stone still on her hands, the smell of the underground in her nostrils. Buried. Three weeks.

A pulse of relief. Mrs Beckinsale. Empathy.

'Brought her back to you, Mrs Beckinsale,' he said.

'So I see, sir.' She did see, Elizabeth knew it, felt the inspection of the tired grey eyes. She saw everything.

'Turns out her visitor had made a mistake, couldn't help her after all.' The cruelty of the lie returned to her. But she hadn't believed it, had not allowed herself to hope.

'That's a pity, sir.' Bland meekness, but Elizabeth saw the shadow behind Mrs Beckinsale's eyes. She understood.

'A clever one this. She gives you any trouble, call for me.'

'Yes, sir. Thank you.'

'Well, good night then, Mrs Beckinsale. Lizzie.'

He left. Neither woman answered him.

Grey eyes looking her up and down. Mother. Mrs Beckinsale was a mother, or had been. Elizabeth felt it. The tears were there now. Fingers turning her face to see the blue bruise on her cheekbone, examining her torn clothing. Nothing but empathy. And Elizabeth saw it then, helplessness too. As helpless as any of her charges.

'Now, don't cry'—the words were brisk, but the eyes were soft— 'it won't help.'

The door opened. The rush of foul air, and at the same time, the comfort of the four gazes turned upon her. Someone would know. They would know. 'Gilly, you look after her, mind,' said Mrs Beckinsale, before turning away and locking the door behind her.

Gilly and Maisie were both on their feet. Even Jane appeared curious. Only Mary Smith's gaze was disinterested. Gilly came closer, peering through the gloom, as though she had not perhaps seen correctly.

'What did he want then?' demanded Maisie. Elizabeth turned staring eyes on the younger girl.

'Hush, Maisie, darlin', hush,' Gilly said gently. 'Elizabeth?' Fear and compassion combined. Warmth, a hand on her arm. Flood of relief, shame, and grief. Tears fell. Her legs buckled under her and she was on the floor, sobbing at Gilly's feet.

A moment of bewildered inaction, and then Gilly was crouched on the floor beside her. 'Oh, darlin', what is it?'

Elizabeth looked into Gilly's face. She knew her grief was infecting the other woman, as surely as if it was a disease in the enclosed cell. Maisie and Jane were both on their feet, near to her. Even Mary had moved to the edge of her bench. A threat to Elizabeth was a threat to them all, for they were as powerless as she was, as Mrs Beckinsale was. It was not just concern for her or inquisitiveness that made them come to her now. It was the need to understand the danger.

Gilly squeezed her arm. Three weeks and it wouldn't matter. Why tell them, why face the pain of it in the retelling? The sobs hurt her bruised throat. She coughed.

'What happened?' It was Jane's voice this time, the first words she had bothered to direct at Elizabeth in the whole day.

'Yes, darlin', can you tell us?' This was Gilly. They needed to know. Elizabeth could feel the tension in the room.

'He said I had a visitor,' she began, her voice broken.

'We know that much,' Maisie interrupted.

'Hold your bloody tongue and let her speak,' Jane snapped at the younger girl.

Hesitation. How to find the words? 'He said I had a visitor. Someone who could help me.' It was as though the glimmer of hope he had given her was still in her heart. She remembered it too clearly, the idea of a friend, of a way out. Not alone. Why wouldn't the light be extinguished? Her breath caught in her throat. 'And he took me to see her. But we didn't go up and see a visitor. We went to another place.'

The memory of the sandstone walls and the dirt of the floor arrested her thoughts and she fell silent.

'What happened, darlin'?' Gilly pushed gently.

'He told me I have three weeks,' she said, looking just at Gilly. She felt the desperation of the words as she said them.

'Do you mean?' No reply. 'Oh, Elizabeth.' Gilly's arm was around her shoulders now, but the warmth did not prevent her shivering convulsively.

'And he told me I might as well be dead already. And he choked me, and he tore my dress,' the words were pouring through the sobs now, 'and his hands were hard and too strong and the floor was dirty and he was heavy…and it hurt, it really hurt.' She turned and clung to Gilly's body.

'Bastard!' Jane growled. Maisie was staring at her. Gilly held her tightly. Empathy and concern surrounded her. But the thought came too, they were glad; glad it had been her, who was going to die anyway, and not them, who would have the rest of their years to remember. She would have experienced the same sentiments. With a cry of pain, she pushed Gilly from her, and staggering to her feet, fled into the night cell. She collapsed onto the damp straw, her sobs reverberating from the close walls.

❖

Her sobs had died away and she was lying prone, looking into the gloom. What did you see when you were dead, she wondered? Murmurs outside, in the day cell. Footsteps then, approaching. She turned to the doorway to see Gilly's figure outlined. Gladness flooded her heart. She did not want to be alone. She would be alone when she was dead, wouldn't she?

'Elizabeth?' Gilly's voice enquired across the darkness, checking to see if she was asleep.

'I'm awake,' she replied, sitting up. Gilly came to sit on the straw near her, taking her hand naturally.

'Oh, darlin', I wish I could say somethin' to help,' she said. It was such an expression of concern.

'There's no help, is there?' Elizabeth said weakly. 'There never will be, not for me.' Gilly drew her closer. 'Just three weeks. That's all forever is now.' Her words were cold. Her heart might as well have already stopped.

'No, darlin', forever's more than that. You'll just be in a different place, that's all,' Gilly said, pulling her into an embrace and smoothing her hair. 'And it's got to be better than here.'

'Do you think,' Elizabeth said, allowing the closeness, but her heart refusing to be warmed by it, 'that after everything, I believe in God or heaven? He abandoned me like everyone else. I used to dream of a better place, where my mother was waiting for me. Now I know it was all lies. This is all there is. Three weeks, and then nothing!' Her words were oddly high-pitched. Gilly still held her, motionless now.

'You have to believe in something,' she ventured.

'I did, once. This morning you might have convinced me. But not now...' Her body began to shake again, as Gilly held her tighter. Shadows circled them and somewhere a door slammed shut.

2008

The name Elizabeth Cooper stayed with me, even though I tried to ignore it. It was just odd I should have had such a vivid dream and been left with this name in my head. I still couldn't place where I'd heard it before.

As a result of an early night and large-scale consumption of green tea rather than Southern Comfort, I felt much better when my alarm started its beeping the next morning. It was another sunny day, and I was refreshed enough to be able to conjure something like enthusiasm for work.

It was a slow morning once again, but for some reason I found it harder to relax than I had the day before. I circled the exercise yard, climbed the gallows steps and descended them again almost immediately, uneasy in the confines of the high walls for once. I hoped no one was watching on the CCTV that scanned the yard. They generally weren't. Memories of my dream lingered. It was strange that after so long working here, the place had finally crept into my unconscious. Other people who worked here had occasional nightmares about it, and usually told us all about them in detail in the staffroom the next morning, but I never had. I suppose this hadn't really been a nightmare. Still, it was enough to keep coming back into my thoughts. I'd even checked the staff rota this morning. No new employees at all. There was no memo telling us a new prison inhabitant would be wandering around the place in the dress of a poor Georgian woman. There was certainly nothing pertaining to anyone called Elizabeth. I wondered where on earth I'd heard the name before, why it should be sticking in my head with such determination.

I'd read a fair few books about the history of this place, heard stories. Maybe I'd plucked the name from one of them? By lunchtime, my curiosity was getting the better of me, and, shunning the luxuries of the staffroom and still in my black costume, I made my way to the other end of the building and the museum library and archives.

The part of the building that gloried in the name of library was not as spectacular as it sounds—a smallish, plain room, at quite the opposite side of the building to the staffroom, and on the first floor. The walls were not lined with books as you might expect, quite reasonably, of a library; there simply weren't enough books on relevant topics to fill that many shelves. It seemed the history of the wretched people who lived and died in these walls was not a very worthy academic topic. That was one of the reasons academic history did not appeal to me. It seemed that, even in our enlightened times, histories of major figures went into minor details of their personalities, yet somehow studies of lesser people treated them as generic parts of population growth or widespread urban distress. I wanted to know the people. But the historical record just wasn't there.

Still, they had made an effort here, in the library. There was a reasonable collection of books on crime and punishment through the centuries, a few social and economic histories, and a small selection pertaining to the Shire Hall and County Gaol specifically. There wasn't a lot else to be done. It wasn't so much the library I was after, however, but the archives.

Despite my history graduate credentials, I had not spent a lot of time in the library since I worked here, and now I was there, I looked around, a little bewildered. I knew there would be a system of some sort, but like all library systems, it would be a mystery until its secrets were explained to me. Besides, the scale of my idle research struck me now; what were the chances of discovering if a name existed in the centuries of records I presumed were in the archives?

I stood in contemplation a moment longer, trying to ignore the flickering of the fluorescent light above my head that gave the room an uneasy yellow tinge. It felt a little like a school classroom, and I found it a strangely intimidating room. I stared for a moment at the empty librarian's desk with its piles of orderly papers. I'd considered being a librarian for a while, on one of my more perverse days.

At that moment, the man himself entered the room. In his early forties, hair already thinning and largely grey, with clichéd librarian's glasses and an impossibly ugly knitted jumper, he looked just like the sort of creature you would expect to find inhabiting a museum library. With him was a younger man, probably in his late twenties. My eye was drawn to him, for his difference to the librarian as much as anything. He was tall and slender, with blond hair tied back into a short ponytail. He wore jeans and a black shirt, a silver pendant in the place where his collar was open. A pointed face that wasn't wholly unpleasant to look at. Had to be a graduate researcher, no two ways about it.

The librarian looked at me in my conspicuous costume and, recognising me as a fellow inmate of this place, smiled warmly. 'Hang on a tick, I'll just sort this young man out, then I'll be with you,' he told me.

'Not a problem,' I assured him, my smile reaching both men.

'Just over here,' the librarian said, turning to the tall man and gesturing at one of the bookshelves. 'There's not a vast collection, but all our books on the eighteenth century are in this section. I'll let you have a browse, then I'll show you what archives we have.'

'Thanks,' the man replied. It was not enough of a speech to be able to catch whether he had an accent or not. As the librarian turned to me, I realised I had been watching and listening to them. It probably wasn't polite, natural though it seemed in such a small room. I smiled, trying to hide my slight awkwardness. Now it was my turn to explain what I wanted, while trying not to sound too crazy in front of my two-person audience.

'Hi,' I began, glancing at the librarian's name tag which told me he was called Kevin Donnelly, 'I work here,' I gestured at my costume, 'as you can tell,' I added, with an uncomfortable giggle in my voice, 'and I wanted to know about some of the prisoners here. Well, actually one in particular. I'm looking for a woman, I know her name, but I have no idea whether she'd be in the archives, or if I'd be able to find her, just by using a name?'

'You know her name?' he asked, with helpfulness suffusing his expression. It wasn't going to matter to him how I knew her name.

'Yes,' I told him.

'Then you're in luck,' he smiled, apparently excited, 'you see we've just put all the archives on a computer catalogue. It means you can search them by things like date and name of prisoner.'

I saw the researcher glance across from his perusal of the eighteenth-century shelf. Clearly his studies would benefit from such a tool too. I wondered what he was studying.

'That's fantastic!' I replied, feigning an enthusiasm to match Kevin Donnelly's, though the historian in me was genuinely rather impressed by this facility.

'I'll show you,' Kevin said, sliding behind his desk and bringing the computer out of hibernation. He turned the monitor so I might look at it too. The cursor flew to several icons, opening new windows, until a search page was in front of us.

'Surname?' he asked.

'Cooper,' I told him, feeling flushed with embarrassment that I'd dreamed the name. What if it didn't exist at all? For that matter, what if it did?

He typed the name. 'First name?'

'Elizabeth.'

His fingers tapped the keyboard again. 'Any other information?' he enquired.

'No. Sorry,' I said.

'Should be enough,' he assured me, hitting the enter key.

It took the computer seconds to flash up a new screen:

Elizabeth Cooper. Sentenced 27th February 1808. Stealing in a dwelling house: Theft of four rings, three necklaces, one silver mirror, and some fancy linen. Sentence: Death. Height: 5'4". Build: Slender. Hair: Dark Blond. Eyes: Hazel. Complexion: Fair. Distinguishing marks: None.

I looked at the information on the screen and I shivered involuntarily. Elizabeth Cooper did exist and somehow her name had made its way into my dream. How the hell was that possible? One word stood out to me in particular among the bright letters. Death. It seemed to be in bigger writing than all the other words. For a woman who had lived, and, I assume, died, in 1808, to be catalogued like this on a cold computer seemed suddenly obscene. Her name should have been inscribed in a faded manuscript that smelled of the must of the centuries. Still, it was fascinating.

'Is that all the information?' I asked. There was no date of execution, no more information about this woman's crime or who she was.

'That's it, I'm afraid. Records back then weren't always kept properly. Plus a lot have been lost or become so damaged that we can't read them,' he told me, unnecessarily. I knew the perils of original historical manuscripts and records. So many had been damaged by damp or fire, you sometimes got the impression that historical Britain was constantly either sodden or aflame.

'Well, thank you,' I said, unsure what to do next.

'Want me to print it for you?' Kevin asked.

'That'd be great, thanks,' I replied.

He clicked a few more times on the mouse, and I heard the printer whirr into life. And then stop. 'Sorry, out of ink. I'll go and get some, back in a tick,' he said.

'Okay.' I smiled as he walked past me and out of the door, presumably to some office storeroom.

I looked up at the ceiling and down at the floor. The room seemed suddenly too small for just me and the researcher. I could hear his breathing, the squeak of his shoe leather as he moved from one side of the bookcase to the other. I wished for a radio or a pneumatic drill, just some noise to block out the silence and the little noises of a stranger.

I glanced across at him. At the same moment, as though he felt my gaze fall upon him, he turned his head and looked at me. He smiled awkwardly. I returned the gesture, then looked back at the thin carpet.

'So, you work here?' he asked. There was an accent. Maybe a hint of Yorkshire? Certainly more northerly than here.

'What gives you that idea?' I returned, with more sarcasm than I had intended. I mellowed it with a slight laugh and a gesture at my costume.

'Thought you might just dress like that every day,' he replied, turning to face me properly now. Oh fuck, turn around again; I'm not doing conversation today.

'Nope,' I said shortly.

'It must be interesting,' he persisted. I wished he would shut up.

'Yes, it is,' I replied. No matter how many hours I spent sitting—or even sleeping—on my gallows steps, or sheltering in the murky shadows from the rain, just waiting for a passing tourist, I still defended my job as one of the most interesting possible to anyone who asked. That was why I was still working here, obviously.

'I'm researching, myself,' he went on.

'Oh really?' I answered. I had to admit I was a little interested in just what he was researching. 'What topic?'

'Changes in prison conditions in the eighteenth century. Though I've only just started, so don't ask too many questions.'

I wasn't going to ask any questions actually. 'I studied history at university,' I told him, not wanting him to think his academic credentials outweighed mine. 'I'm interested in people's stories. I studied the Chartists for my dissertation, but there was too much politics and not enough personality for me.' Sodding hell, why the beginnings of an academic conversation?

'Good place to work then,' he replied. 'I'm Owen,' he said. An introduction was a bad sign; it meant he planned our acquaintance to continue. I hadn't talked about history in a while though, it might be interesting.

'I'm Jen,' I told him.

'When do you finish work?' he asked.

'Why?' I retorted. Of course I knew why, I just wasn't sure I could be bothered.

'I just thought maybe you'd like a drink. Maybe we could talk about the history of this place. It'd be good for my research.' He shrugged and smiled. My body language was beginning to put him off the idea. I didn't really want to be rude though, and he seemed like a pleasant enough sort of a man really.

'I finish at four thirty, hopefully,' I revealed at last. 'If you want, we can meet in the pub across the road. It's pretty obvious.'

'Okay, you're on,' he said, and he smiled wider. Now the date was made, I was regretting it instantly.

I stood awkwardly for a moment. Now what? Thankfully it was at that point that Kevin bustled back in, jumper blaring, ink cartridge in his hand.

'Here we go,' he said briskly. 'Oh, and I remembered where I'd heard that name before,' he added.

My attention was immediately turned on him. 'Oh?' I asked.

'Yes, Elizabeth Cooper. It seemed familiar, but I see a lot of names,' he explained.

'Yes?' I said eagerly. Get on with it.

'Yep. Then I remembered. When we re-did the crime boards last year. She's on there.'

I suppose I should have been pleased with the logical explanation for how this name had got into my head. There was no mystery; the name wasn't part of my dream at all. The crime boards were the large boards around the museum that allowed the visitors to compare the number they received on their tickets with one on the board. This number allocated them a crime. Actually it did more than that; it ascribed the details of a real crime, the name of a real historical prisoner, to each of them. I was never much interested in the crime boards, but I had certainly read them, wondering if the cases described were actually real. It seemed they were.

'I never noticed,' I replied, trying to hide my disappointment. I had no idea why I should feel disappointed with the news. It should have been a relief.

'Yes, I think we chose her because it seemed so harsh, the death penalty for theft. But you know what the Bloody Code was like.'

I did, and understood that at the beginning of the nineteenth century the number of crimes for which a person could be executed had risen to levels that were hard to believe. 'Yep,' I replied. Kevin passed me my printout. Suddenly it didn't seem quite so interesting. 'Thanks,' I said. 'Well, back to work.' I left the library without another glance at the tall figure of Owen. I'd go to the pub across the road when I finished. If he was there, then we would see. If he wasn't, I wouldn't be devastated.

1808

Through the thick stench, the air smelled of morning. Her eyes were dry. Gilly was lying in front of her, turned away from her, on her side. Elizabeth gazed at her angular shoulders. Jane stirred and mumbled something sleepily behind her. Elizabeth blinked uncertainly. When had she fallen asleep? A memory of Gilly lying down beside her, arm wrapped around her, warming and protecting. A sharp stab of pain in her cheek. Different memories. Sudden sickness made her sit up, sweating. It was just at the moment the door opened and Mrs Beckinsale entered.

'Come on, wake up now!' she called. Her eyes fell on Elizabeth, and registered her concern.

'Mornin', Elizabeth,' she said. 'Find you well this mornin' do I?' Elizabeth understood the woman's anxiety that she should be well. Mrs Beckinsale did not want to confront the truth of her position, of her colleagues, of the brutality of her life. It was easier if Elizabeth was well again.

'Thank you, Mrs Beckinsale, I'm well,' she replied blandly, and saw the relief her reply engendered.

Maisie Burrows would not make eye contact with her as they sat for breakfast. Mary Smith sighed and coughed more than usual, but the cause of it was not definite. Rapidly cooling gruel, thin and insubstantial today, grey in her bowl. She stared at it and reached for her cup of brackish water. Body pulsing with pain, especially her leg and cheek. And elsewhere, as she sat on the wooden chair.

Jane Larkin kept gazing at her and shaking her head, swearing under her breath. Even Gilly, with her kind eyes, seemed to struggle for words. Mrs Beckinsale did not look at her either. Alone among them. She had not realised how much she needed their empathy already. And yet they were all changed by what had happened to her, the very air of the room seemed changed. Breeze blowing through the open bars, cooling her skin, ruffling Gilly's hair as it passed. However alone she felt, she was one with them at the same moment. Her life, however short its remainder, was also their life.

❖

Mrs Beckinsale opened a door in the end of the outer chamber that day, allowing them access to a small yard. The walls were high, though on the tips of her toes, Maisie demonstrated that it was possible to see over it and to the rooftops of the town beyond. Elizabeth was not inclined to look. Halfway up the cliff and with a sheer drop to the slums of Narrow Marsh below, it was unlikely any woman would risk an escape over the wall.

Fresh air filled her lungs, bringing the smell of the town. It was unchanged; the smoke of industrial production, the acrid squalor of the slum below, an edge of horse manure, but all the time a hint of the countryside beyond. She closed her eyes, forgetting the red bricks surrounding her and suddenly she was back in the town, on an errand for Cook. She was useful, she was safe, she was cared for.

The sounds were different from this height though. Elizabeth opened her eyes again. Down below a man shouted, his words indistinct snatches of sound on the breeze. A cart could be heard delivering ale to the public house at the foot of the cliff. There was a faint hum of machinery from a lace factory nearby. She was above it all, they all were. Horribly distinct from it, removed. Life was at the bottom of the cliff, and they were hidden from it by the red brick, separated by the cruel height. Maybe I'm dead already, she thought, and I'm up in Heaven, only it's all been a vicious lie and Heaven is really Hell.

She tilted her head back, feeling the bruises on her stretched throat, and looked at the sky. The heavy grey clouds had passed away and been replaced by a hazy blue. There was more light in the day room as a result. The sky was so constant. Ever changing, but only between shades of blue and grey and white. It would go on doing so when she was buried in her pauper's grave. For that was what it would be. Three weeks.

The cruelty with which she had been informed of her remaining time flooded back. Yellow teeth, too fat for his buttons, strong hands. Her tongue moved over the hardened blood on her lip and, stomach churning and despite the daylight, she remembered.

The memories made her tremble, from a recollection of the fear and from a sickening rage. She felt his breath near her ear again and tasted blood. She licked at where her teeth had reopened the wound in her lip. Her dress was still torn, but she had tied an apron over it, from Gilly's work basket. It was a servant's and no one would miss it. She would sew her dress later.

Noises from the town seemed to taunt her now. It was crueller to allow her to stand in this raised yard than to keep her locked in a cell. A last breath of the fresh air, and she retreated into the dim inside.

❖

In the afternoon, she removed her dress and, in her petticoat and slip, sat beside Gilly, sewing the tear. Maisie was still tiptoeing at the wall, fascinated by the glimpses she had of the city. Elizabeth thought of the girl being snatched from everything she knew and carried to a land of harsh heat and disease and further imprisonment. She wondered how Maisie would bear it. How would she herself have taken the sentence? Would she have felt she had escaped?

No. There could have been no justice, whatever the sentence. Innocent people were not sentenced. They were released, free to wander wherever they pleased. Her life was to be drained from her, but it had really already been taken, in the moment she was accused and the evidence presented. Innocent had become guilty, a criminal, and she had ceased to exist.

2008

After lunch, I went to look at the crime boards. Number A4-3000, Elizabeth Cooper, 1808. Crime: Theft of jewellery. Sentence: Death. There it was in large black writing. Scant information really, considering it was a real life, a real death I was looking at. There was something of a gimmick about it that made me feel uneasy. At least I knew now where I had got the name from. I thought about Elizabeth Cooper for a moment, imagined what sort of girl she might have been. Suddenly the reality of the history of this place struck me, and I shivered. I made an effort to put Elizabeth Cooper out of my mind.

Owen was in the pub across the road when I got there just after half past four. I wasn't sure if I was glad or otherwise to see him. At least I hadn't been stood up.

I loved this pub, the County Tavern it was called. Its façade was dark stone, almost green with age, which made it stand out in a street of red-brick and rendered Georgian façades. In fact, it had more in common with the grand exterior of the Shire Hall, which it directly faced, than the quiescent industrial buildings. I always sensed an odd relationship between the two buildings as they had stared at each other over the centuries. One grand, imposing, a place of judgment, punishment, death, and fear; the other small, unassuming, quaint almost, a place of indulgence, laughter, and who knew what. The steps where once thieves and murderers were hanged were only the distance of a narrow road from the door of the tavern. To sit in the pub and gaze at the sandstone columns, those notorious steps, the inscription above which telling which King George in particular the building was dedicated to, and to know all the time what was behind it all, I found a rather moving experience. It was one of those times when I valued my job most of all.

Today, however, such reflections were not uppermost in my mind. Owen saw me from the window as I descended the steps and crossed the road. I saw his pointed face white in the window as he smiled. I wanted to turn around and go home. It was a perfectly unreasonable response to have, but that part of me that knew this was all a charade thought it might really be better to give it up as a bad job now and spare myself the awkwardness, the wondering why I couldn't make myself like him. I made my way into the dark interior, which was all oak-panelled walls and grey slate floors, and fixed a smile as I made eye contact with him.

'What can I get you?' was the first thing he said, indicating his own pint of lager.

'I'll get it, you're okay, thanks,' I told him, turning and heading for the bar before he could even take a breath to protest.

I returned moments later with my orange juice. Truth was, I could have done with a drink, but I didn't want to be here long, and I knew the alcohol would be in danger of relaxing me just enough to enjoy Owen's conversation. I was happy at how quickly all thoughts of Paul had receded from my consciousness.

I took the chair opposite him and wondered, sipping my juice, what on earth we were supposed to talk about.

'Busy afternoon?' he enquired, breaking the ice.

'No, it was quiet really,' I responded. Thinking I should really make the effort, I added, 'It usually is on a weekday.' My turn to ask a question, I guess. 'So, did you find what you were looking for?'

'Some of it,' he replied. 'I'm still not exactly sure what I'm looking for. Ideas as much as anything.'

'Are you at uni here?' I asked.

'Yes, for my post-grad. My degree's from Durham.' He was pretty intelligent then; that was a good university.

'Where are you from originally?' was my next question, leaving me feeling like a student again. The set questions in any freshers' week: who are you, where are you from, what are you studying?

'From near Leeds,' he told me, 'so I'm closer to home now.'

'Oh, that's good.' I'd run out of steam on the conversation front. I took advantage of the pause, during which he glanced out of the window, to study him a little more closely. The skin of his cheeks was rough and uneven, I assumed from the impact of teenage acne. There was something unpleasant about the cratered skin that revolted me, however much I chided myself. A fine layer of stubble suggested he needed a shave. His blond hair was thinning into typical male-pattern baldness, leaving him with a rather high forehead. His eyes were a murky green, and intelligent. Still, something about his appearance left me feeling vaguely disturbed. Maybe it was more that I was perfectly aware that many women would find him handsome, while looking at him left me cold.

'It's an impressive place,' he said, gesturing with his head out of the window at the Shire Hall looming across the road.

'Yes, it is,' I agreed. 'So many people don't realise it's here. Tourist information's crap here.' It was a pet hate of mine, the way the important aspects of the town—particularly its fascinating industrial history—were passed over in favour of emphasising the shopping and drinking facilities. I sipped my orange juice again.

'People just aren't interested in the important things,' he said. That made me feel a little warmer towards him; we'd found something we agreed on at least. 'So, how long have you worked here?' he asked, turning the conversation to me in an instant.

'Over a year now,' I replied. 'The money's rotten, but I like it. There's not many history-based jobs around. I considered teaching, but y' know, there's children involved,' I joked.

'Yeah, you need danger money to teach these days.' He grinned, taking a long drink of his pint. His prominent Adam's apple moved up and down as he swallowed. Turkey-neck; yuck. I forced another smile. Stop judging the poor guy by his appearance; his conversation is decent at least. For fuck's sake.

We managed to chat, mainly about the study of history, our respective dissertations—his had been about the effects of population growth in the eighteenth century—and the opportunities to carry a passion for history through into a career, for about another half an hour. As I drained the last of my juice, he looked at his watch.

'Look, you know what, I've got to go. But it's been nice. Are you free tomorrow night?' He looked hopeful.

'Yes, I am,' I said before I could stop myself. Why the fuck couldn't I lie? Despite myself, I thought I might learn to like him. He came across as genuine enough, interesting. Besides, a night out didn't mean marriage. I'd look on it as proof of how little breaking up with Paul had bothered me.

'Good. You want to meet somewhere?'

'Er, yeah,' I tried to sound keen and casual at the same time. I really wasn't sure which one I genuinely felt. 'Somewhere in town?'

'Good for me. Do you know the Dragon, near the Market Square?'

'I do,' I confirmed. 'Shall we say sevenish?'

'Also good for me.' He fumbled in his pocket for his brown leather wallet and pulled out a small white card, a little dog-eared at the edges. 'Here, it's got my number on,' he told me. I took the card and nearly laughed.

'You have a business card?' I asked, raising my eyebrows.

'I know, it's pretentious,' he laughed at himself and consequently went up in my estimation, 'but it's handy sometimes.'

'If you say so,' I replied with mock-scepticism. He stood up, and for a horrible moment I thought he was going to bend down to kiss me. Clearly I imagined it, or he thought better of it, since he simply smiled again.

'See you tomorrow night then,' he said.

'Yep, about seven in the Dragon,' I confirmed. 'Bye.' Thus dismissed, he left. I watched him walk past the window, then waited long enough to be sure he'd be gone into the city before I left the pub and headed for the bus.

As the bus bumped and rattled its way towards my part of town, I stared straight ahead to avoid the onset of queasiness and contemplated how easily I'd managed to screw up my Thursday night. I wanted to hide away at home, watch some television maybe. Instead I'd got myself ensnared, going on a date I had no real desire to go on at all. Yes, Owen was friendly and intelligent, but I understood he wanted more than friendship from me and knew already he wasn't getting it. Quite why, as a free-thinking adult, I had found it impossible to say no to him I did not understand. It was less an indulgence of his feelings, more an attempt to run away from my own. Somehow though, in all this bloody running away, I only seemed to leave myself more trapped. It had happened with Paul and now it was happening with Owen. I was getting damn tired of trying to escape the whole time.

CHAPTER FOUR

2008

The evening dragged by. I picked at a cheese sandwich, not really hungry, and fought the urge to return to the booze. There was nothing on television worth watching so I picked up the novel I'd been trying to read for the last month, but there was no way I could make myself concentrate on the words contained within its sickeningly cheerful cover.

My mum had lent the book to me; it was a fun story about a successful, smart woman in her early thirties, who had moved to a new house in the countryside. She seemed, fortunately for her, to have unlimited finances and was busy getting to know the locals—or rather, one local in the shape of the dashingly attractive widower who ran the local wildlife shelter, demonstrating his suitability as a love interest with his tender ministrations to all manner of badgers, frogs, and wounded deer. Watching him heal a hedgehog with a broken leg had melted the heroine's heart and marriage seemed likely. Riveting stuff.

I was only about halfway through the novel, but whenever I picked it up I found myself generally inclined to throw it out of the window or submerge it in the bath, depending on where I happened to be reading it. Not only did I find the story entirely irrelevant to my own pitiful existence, it was also impossible not to see through my mother's intention in lending it to me: to present me with a picture of the sort of woman she wished I would finally grow into. I hated the inevitability of disappointing her.

Perhaps I judged my mum too harshly or I was being oversensitive; it was possible she'd just found it a good read and wanted to share it with me. But even in that I found a problem. I felt removed from everything she wanted to share with me, imprisoned in my own miserable world, distant from my family, from my friends who had all got themselves proper careers and adoring fiancés. I was sick to the back teeth of wedding invitations and the necessity for buying Christening and new home congratulations cards for various school acquaintances, former colleagues, and cousins. All it did was remind me how fucking alone I felt, not part of their world. No wonder I hid myself away in the shadows behind the gaol walls, my costume transforming me into someone else for those few hours a day. It was better than being me, with no idea what path I was on. I couldn't even make myself look forward to a bloody date with a perfectly friendly guy. It was hard to convince myself there wasn't something wrong with me.

I dumped the book onto the floor and headed for a hot shower. Shortly after that, I gave up on the day and retreated to bed. There was nothing for it but to wait until tomorrow night. There was an outside chance I might have a good time.

1808

The bruise on her cheek turned from blue to purple and then yellow, as the days went on. A whole week in this place. A whole week less to live. Sinking further into herself, into the echoes and the torment of her memories.

'Elizabeth,' Gilly said, sitting down beside her on the bench, 'have you done anything about asking the judge to commute your sentence?'

Elizabeth turned heavy eyes on her. 'It's pointless. I've told you already.' Even Gilly's kindnesses were lost on her today.

'It's never pointless,' Gilly replied, undaunted. 'I heard of a girl once—'

'I don't care what you heard once. Listen to me. It's pointless.' She had not meant to sound rude, and seeing Gilly's reaction she was sorry. Too few days left to spend them regretting a hasty speech. 'Sorry. You simply can't understand.'

'What is it, darlin'?' Gilly said, recovering herself. 'Why are you different to the rest of us?'

Is that what they thought? Unsure suddenly if she wanted to be different; they were, after all, everything she had left to her, the lingering humanity in her life. 'I'm not so different,' she said, 'only if you knew the whole story, you'd see why it's impossible.' Hang. Dead. Desperately inevitable.

Hand on her knee, pressing on the rough brown fabric, comforting through it. A living gesture of friendship. No friends left. Perhaps, for her final days, the beginning of a friendship? 'Why are you so kind to me, Gilly?' It was almost a protest. 'Why don't you just leave me to rot by myself like the others do? You've got your own burden to bear, just like them.'

'It's to ease it, darlin', that I'm kind to you.' Someone who's in a worse situation than you are. It makes you feel better, of course it does, Elizabeth thought. She would not say it though. 'It takes my mind away from the things I can't bear to think on.' An intimate revelation, quite unexpectedly. A kindling of warmth in Elizabeth's heart, where she had thought there would never be warmth again. 'And besides, Australia's not so bad. Eventually they'll let me out and I can start over. Without the thieving this time.' An admission of guilt?

'You mean you really did do it?' Elizabeth asked. Gilly did not seem like a criminal.

''Fraid so, darlin', I'm every bit as fairly convicted as young Maisie there. But you understand, needs must.' A sad shrug, a shadow of regret. What echoed inside her head, Elizabeth wondered? There should have been a distance between them now, the guilty and the wrongly guilty, but instead the admission drew Elizabeth to her. A moment's contemplation. 'Go on then,' said Gilly, her green eyes expectant.

'What?' Elizabeth asked.

'Tell me why it's all so impossible with you.'

'It's a very long story,' which she suddenly had the words to tell, she realised, looking into the green eyes.

'Does it look like I have anything better to do, darlin'?'

A sigh. Let the memories come and chase away the echoes. Go back before and then further again. When did it all begin?

'My mother died when I was twelve,' she began, hesitantly. Gilly only waited, her sympathy warming the air. 'I never knew my father. He died just after I was born. I had two older sisters, but I never knew them. Neither of them made it to five before the fever took them.'

Unfamiliar children, her siblings. Her mother had been hers and hers only. Her mother. Memories of unbending kindness pricked at her eyes. Don't dwell on the distant past, not now.

'Our family struggled for money after my father died. He was a watchmaker, and successful too, but he'd run up debts and most of what he left went to those he owed. We were really very poor but mother never accepted it, even when she had to take in needlework for money and it ruined her eyes. She was educated, you know, she even spoke some French, and she was determined I would be too. She had hopes I could become a governess, so she taught me to talk properly, read and write, and even to draw. We were happy just the two of us, hoping for the future.' Elizabeth paused, recalling for a moment what it had been to hope. She glanced up and met Gilly's soft gaze. Summon the strength to go on, she has to know the whole story. 'Then she died, just a week after my twelfth birthday, and there was only me left.' Her lip trembled, but she steadied herself with a deep breath.

'I went into service immediately, there was nothing else I could do. I was strong and I could read and write, so finding a position was easy. I had no one to visit and living-in was no obstacle. I had two positions as scullery maid before I was sixteen, and left them regretfully, with an excellent character, all written out.

'When I was sixteen, I went to be housemaid for a Mr Joshua Bourke and his new wife. It was a big house in town, on Greene Row, if you know it?' Gilly nodded slightly and waited for her to go on. 'Mr Bourke was very rich indeed, and it was a good position. He was often from home, about the country, shooting, taking his wife with him, and it made for light work, despite it being such a large house.'

Elizabeth paused. A flood of colourful memory, so distant now. She looked at Gilly. More words than she had spoken to anyone in friendship since…since when?

'What's the matter, darlin'?' Gilly asked.

'I'd not really tried to remember it before,' Elizabeth's reply was honest. 'I'm probably making no sense.'

'You're making perfect sense, darlin'. Go on.'

'I was happy there. Mr Simon, the head of the household servants, was stern, but the footmen were good humoured and kind to me, and I made a particular friend of the under-housemaid, Emily. Cook looked after us all like her children. I'd lost my mother four years by then, and I felt as though I'd found a new family, this time with sisters and brothers too.

'It was a beautiful house, you should have seen it. All pure white at the front, with rows of windows shining in the sun. There were fine carpets, swirling with red and gold in the bedrooms, so rich they made me dizzy to look at them. Every room had a huge great fireplace, all carved and moulded. There were always hothouse flowers delivered to put in crystal vases. The floor in the hallway was Italian marble, and I remember looking at it, polishing it, and seeing the sunshine and the blue sea and the olive groves. There was German porcelain that showed me deep forests and high castles, running streams, and even real china, which seemed to have come from another world.

'All of the fine furniture was from abroad, or else Mr Bourke had it commissioned especially. Mrs Bourke was very particular about what she sat on, or so the footmen said, who heard her arguing with the master about it.

'Mr Bourke was a kind man, and handsome too. He was unfortunate in his way though, since Mrs Bourke apparently thought him too handsome to have any control of himself. She was pretty enough herself, all fair skin and pale curls, but her figure was thicker than she wanted, you could tell from how little she ate and the way she sat.'

Recollections flooding back, details that should have been forgotten. And Gilly listening, remembering. Elizabeth's head, clouded by gloom and echoes for what felt like forever, was suddenly awash with colour and life. She could not have stopped the words if she had wanted to.

'She didn't like him talking to the female servants in too kindly a tone, and it made her rather on the sharp side with us too. Emily, my friend, heard her accusing the master once of illicit dealings with Mary, one of the scullery maids. Of course, there was nothing in it, Mary was quiet as a mouse, and the master was a good man. But Mrs Bourke was convinced, and poor Mary was forced to look for another place in the end. Mrs Bourke wasn't too popular with the servants after that, and that's not a good position for a mistress who is trying to run a house.'

'No, I imagine not,' Gilly agreed. Gilly had, Elizabeth knew, no experience of service. She was not completely certain what Gilly's life had been before, and resolved to ask.

'Mind you, I had some pity for Mrs Bourke, though you wouldn't think it after what happened with Mary. The master was kind enough, but he kept his money tight. And it was his money since the rumour was she was from a poor country family, her father a gentleman fair enough, but a gentleman with no money. It was a good marriage for her, but she never had any of his fortune for herself. Made her bitter against him, I think. I heard them myself, arguing about it, and he was saying she had everything she could ever want—which of course she really did—and she only had to ask and he would purchase her anything. She said she wanted to have the money herself, of course, but he couldn't understand why she would want to bother herself about it.'

Raised voices from the fine second drawing room, as she built up a fire in the next-door sitting room. A slight smile at the trials the gentry faced in their lives. And then down to the long scrubbed kitchen table, to eat beef and potatoes with Cook, the other maids and footmen. There was always wine mixed with water to drink and Cook made fresh bread for them every other day. Recollections of the laughter and smiles, despite the tired eyes and calloused hands, around the table. A pause in her story. Stone walls around her, the acrid stench, the gloom, and only Gilly. But Gilly was intent on her, her pink face showing interest and intrigue. How had this happy story led to this place? How had such bright light faded into thick darkness?

'So theirs was not the happiest of matches, as it turned out. She suspected him of dallying with the maids, and he wouldn't give her all of his money when she wanted it. Of course, they carried on from day to day well enough, and there were always house parties and balls and card games to keep them happy. We heard them arguing sometimes— servants always do you know—and once or twice there was broken pottery to clean up. I think she'd flung it at his head in one of her rages. But I was there seven years and everything stayed much the same way.

'I suppose it was about two years ago that things grew to be different somehow. I think the master had some money worries. Cook insisted he'd been losing it at cards, but I didn't like to think it of him myself. Whatever it was, they were forced to get rid of one of the scullery maids, one of the under-housemaids, and two footmen, which made life harder for us servants as well. Well, we heard them arguing more and more after that, and she was always short tempered with the servants. I think if she could have run the house without us, she'd have discharged us all there and then.

'It seemed strange at the time, since they had no money, but she started to leave the house more and more. They stopped going about the country so much and kept more to town, but she didn't seem able to keep indoors. Of course, because she was going out so often, she always hankered for new gowns and hats and more fashionable coats, and they cost money, so the master was even less happy with her, and their rows grew more and more fierce.

'One day, a man came calling for her at the house, a tall gentleman with a very fine coat. I saw him as I was going through the hallway, replacing candles, and she spirited him into the drawing room and closed the door, quick as anything.

'I didn't think on it again until about a week later, when I saw him, just leaving the house, when I looked out of an upstairs window I was polishing. At the same time, Mrs Bourke was less sharp all of a sudden, and her face was rosy again. The footmen had seen the gentleman coming too, always while the master was from home, and of course, we whispered amongst ourselves.'

Moments of merry gossip in the kitchen, or in the maids' sleeping quarters in the attics. Snippets of conversations overheard, glimpses through doors left ajar. She almost smiled with the recollection. It made the remembrance of the conclusion of the tale more excruciating.

'All the while, we knew there were worries over money, but Mrs Bourke was still buying new dresses, and bonnets with ostrich feathers, and strings of pearls. She always liked her fine jewellery, but she grew bored of it very quickly. Mr Bourke's mother had given her several fine pieces, but they were too dated for her. Emily was convinced the gentleman was giving her money. But I noticed items around the house were no longer in their proper places. The fine German porcelain jugs, an heirloom of Mr Bourke's, were gone one day, and brass candlesticks stood in their places. The second-best silver cutlery service was missing, and we had to make do with the third-best for when Mr Bourke's sister visited. Several of the fine linens for the table were gone, and one day I noticed, when I was dusting, a carriage clock that had been a wedding present to them was not where it should have been, only a dustless space on the table top where it had stood. It was odd I thought, that the master or mistress hadn't noticed their possessions moving, if there had been anything amiss, you know, and so I assumed they had grown tired of the things and packed them away or moved them.'

'Didn't you think one of the servants might have stolen them?' Gilly enquired, her mind trying to follow the path the story was going to take.

'At the back of my mind I did, but I didn't want to think it. Like I said, they were my family, and when do you expect a member of your family to be a thief?' Remembering Gilly's confession of her crime, she flushed, and went on quickly. 'I mean, we were well enough looked after, and I knew them all well, they'd all come with impeccable characters, the mistress insisted upon it. I mentioned it to Cook and to Mr Simon, but he told me not to worry, if the master and mistress had missed anything, he'd look into it, but it was not our place to interfere. It struck me that he knew more than he was saying to me, but it wasn't my own place to question him.

'Gradually, of course, it dawned on us all. It was Mrs Bourke herself taking their possessions to who-knows-where, and selling them, to get the money she wanted for her fancy coats and feathers and gowns with higher waists. Mr Bourke, preoccupied he was with his money, never seemed to have noticed, though he might have noticed she argued less with him and had more fine gowns than ever, had he given it a thought. She must have guessed we servants knew, of course, there's no way we could not have done, even in such a large house with so many fine things.

'Eventually, it was a different gentleman we saw coming to the house, when Mr Bourke was away from it, this one with not such a fine coat, but with a far handsomer face. Of course, we were discreet. Only one day, I didn't know he and the mistress had returned to the house, and I walked into the sitting room, without knocking, to build up the fire in the hearth. They were in there, sitting very close to each other on the French sofa. They both jumped to their feet, and went bright red when they saw me. I apologised and curtseyed and received her sharp words about knocking before I entered a room, and fled to the kitchens, quite frightened by what I had interrupted. Of course, Cook, who was like my mother, saw that something was out of sorts with me, and I told her what I had seen. She told me to watch out for the mistress and not to cross her path. I think she remembered what had happened to Mary, and thought Mrs Bourke might try the same trick with me, if I had seen something I hadn't ought to have done.

'I did as Cook said, of course, and when nothing was said, I thought it had passed.' Now the stream of words began to break down. Her voice cracked and she felt the burning injustice flooding back. 'If only I'd known,' she said softly, struggling against the rush of tears that threatened.

'What happened?' Gilly pressed, reaching for Elizabeth's hands.

A shaky breath. 'It was about a fortnight or so later, that Emily, who was prone to eavesdropping, heard the master and mistress arguing again, and she said it was bad this time. He'd finally noticed some of their missing possessions, when he had wanted to examine a fine necklace of his mother's, and she, having sold it, hadn't of course been able to produce it for him. Well, anyway, he accused her, but she'd flown into a rage, and wondered how he could think such a thing. She'd convinced him it must have been a servant who had stolen the things.'

She choked on the words, cutting the sentence off. She glanced up into Gilly's face and saw the understanding beginning to dawn. 'Oh, darlin',' Gilly breathed.

'The next day, the master searched the servants' quarters. He started with the footmen. Of course we all knew he'd find nothing, and wondered what would happen at the end of the search with some trepidation.

Then he searched the maids' rooms. We went with him, to show him which cot was whose. He pulled back the woollen blankets, one by one. When he got to mine, I saw there was something odd in the bed. A glint of metal caught my eye, and I stepped forward to see what it was. He was quicker, pulling the blanket from the bed entirely. I saw the jewels sparkling and I knew what she'd done. Hidden in my bed, when he examined the objects further, were four gold rings, one of them with an emerald and another with a diamond. There were two of her new necklaces and a fine pearl one of the master's mother's. There was a small silver-backed mirror the mistress kept on her dressing table. It was all resting on top of a piece of fancy linen, with Bruges lace at the edges.'

The details were not difficult to relate. The emotions—confusion, and then blood running cold with panic, rage at the betrayal, and then fear and helplessness, of there being no way out—were harder to tell.

'The master had me locked in the maids' attic, until I was arrested and brought to the gaol. I protested, I told them I was innocent, that I couldn't do such a thing. Why would I want to, I said, I had no other home, no other need for money, I had everything I needed, so why would I do it? But it was as though I had become dumb suddenly, because they didn't hear a word I said. They had their proof. And what could I do, say it was the mistress who had stolen all their possessions, so she could carry on in her fine clothes with her fancy man?'

She stopped and took a breath, feeling the recalled panic rising as though she were back there again. It had been just less than a month ago, but it seemed a lifetime. Now a month was more than a lifetime to her.

'But at the trial?' Gilly asked, wide-eyed with the horror of the tale now. 'Didn't you tell them then?'

'Yes. I'm not so loyal as to risk myself for a sly witch like she turned out to be,' she exclaimed, the anger pulsing through her now. 'After they had me in that cell, upstairs, asking me questions, I told them everything I could. I told them time after time until my throat was hoarse with it. But they wouldn't listen. A maid's word over a mistress's word, there was no hope of them accepting it.'

'But was there no one to speak for your character?' Gilly asked. 'Even I found someone, much good though it did me.'

'Emily visited me in the week I waited for the trial.' She remembered the clean white painted cell on the highest level of the gaol where she had waited, separate from the convicted criminals, still innocent by the letter of the law. The barred window let the daylight in and there was a hammock for sleeping in. Trapped, the walls closing in on her, she had felt desperation, had known it was hopeless. Only she had never thought it was as hopeless as it had become.

'Emily came into the cell with me, and she told me how they'd all spoken to the master for me, even Mr Simon. But they could do no more than I could. They couldn't accuse the mistress, and without that, the only conclusion, from the jewellery in my bed, was I had a good character, but I had gone bad and turned to thievery. I knew none of them would speak for me then. They had lives ahead of them, maybe marriages, children, or parents to support. They needed their wages, their board and lodgings. To declare under oath they'd seen the things they'd seen, just to save me, was impossible, and I couldn't even ask it of them. So they abandoned me. Emily never visited again.'

A tear ran over the yellow stain of the bruise on her cheek. Gilly was grasping her arm now, almost too hard, sharing her grief. Her green eyes were watery as she leaned in to rest her forehead against Elizabeth's. Elizabeth drew strength from her. She had to finish the tale, now it was nearly told. She went on in a whisper.

'I knew they would find me guilty. I stood in that court and I told them the whole truth, wondering if maybe someone would believe me, and at least knowing, before God, that I'd been honest. But it was hopeless. And what I accused her of only made me sound vicious and cast doubt on the goodness of my character after all. I thought they would transport me, and I prayed it would be for seven years and not fourteen.

'But, as I stood there, suddenly I knew I'd seen the judge before. He'd been a guest of the master once, to dinner. He was their friend. As if it all wasn't bad enough, the judge was their friend!' Tears fell more freely now. 'And I still hoped, even though I knew she'd been frightened by what I knew and that she would want me quiet. I'd be quiet in Australia. But she must have used her influence. Or maybe they just wanted to make an example of me, after all the things I'd said about a respectable gentlewoman. And then I saw the judge putting on his black cap, and I knew, but I thought it couldn't be real.' Gilly's arms were around her shoulders, and she pressed herself to the other woman, willing the echoes of the judge's words away. Yet they persisted, loud as they had sounded in the courtroom.

Hang. Dead.

2008

Owen Thomas BA (Durham). Phone number, e-mail address. I looked at the black italic print on the cheap white card. It was hardly a quality business card. Still, something about the fact that he had one impressed me against my will. I couldn't imagine myself handing over a professionally printed card with my details on. Not that a post-grad student had any reason to have a business card of course, it was bloody ridiculous.

It had been a long day at work. I had spent most of the morning dealing with a school party, enrolled for the special tour, entitled cleverly, 'Washing and Learning'. Now, supposedly, it was whoever was representing the female prisoner who was supposed to take care of most of this duty. However, when that female prisoner, who in this instance was Jade of the pink hair, chose not to arrive for work in the morning, with no hope of protest, I found myself dragged out of my comfortable exercise yard and into the unwelcome confines of the women's part of the prison. Donning a white pinafore over my wardress's costume, suddenly I was Matron of the women's gaol, there to oversee the children as they plunged the dolly and ponch into the tubs of sodden clothes and splashed carbolic scented water all over the small whitewashed room set up to represent the Victorian prison laundry. Then, since the last part of their trip was to see the exercise yard, I had to conduct them there, glad of the open air and daylight but forced to endure their idiotic giggles as I made them march around in circles, in an imitation of the strictly silent Victorian exercise routine. Hilarious. Somehow I never felt the history of the gaol ever made the deep impression it deserved to on the vast majority of the children who passed through in these big school groups. They were more interested that they could see part of my modern blue T-shirt peeping from underneath my jacket, and why I wouldn't let them climb all over the gallows. I loved children.

Contrarily, the long day had made me look forward to the evening out. I didn't fancy another evening on my own, the doubts beginning to creep in about Paul, and wondering if the emptiness in the pit of my stomach was as a result of missing him. Of course, when I was fully lucid, I knew I was glad to be free of him, without his thoughts and feelings to consider as I blundered my way through the day to day. There had been something reassuring about being able to say I had a boyfriend though, especially one my mother liked. Now, my liberty restored, I was busy making an even bigger mess of my life by giving Owen the impression that he had a chance with me. Paul had at least become familiar company, there was some comfort in that. I had no idea what to expect from Owen at all.

I had deliberated over what to wear for a short while. Following fashion was never really my thing, still, I liked to look halfway decent in what I wore. In the end, black velvet trousers took precedence over the skirt I contemplated, but teamed with my heeled boots and a sky blue top, I looked smart enough. I smeared on the lipstick and eye-shadow, all very natural and understated, and brushed out my hair and let it cascade over my shoulders. Light brown hair and sky blue sat well next to each other in my opinion. The effort I made with my appearance was most definitely not for Owen's benefit; it was for my own self-respect as much as anything else. However unenthusiastic I felt, I could at least try to look as good as it was possible for me to look. If it meant I could look in the mirror and feel some confidence in myself then it was a successful venture.

I suppose that was the whole reason I was going ahead with this stupid date anyway; it proved I had Paul out of my system already and, even if I had no clue what I wanted in my life, I could still be found attractive. That I really didn't want a man like Owen finding me attractive was a minor detail I tried to ignore. I could enjoy a pleasant evening, hopefully some lively conversation, and then let him down gently having reassured myself that breaking up with Paul did not mean I would be terminally alone. Besides, it was another evening in which I could escape from my claustrophobic flat and the cycle of self-torture, denial, and trying to forget.

CHAPTER FIVE

2008

I arrived at the pub in town slightly early, and was surprised to find Owen already waiting for me. The pub, close to the centre of town, was already busy. It was a long, narrow place, on two levels, with the bar up a flight of stairs towards the rear. Modern furniture and a recent makeover meant it had little character, but there was at least decent music playing.

Owen was seated about halfway between the door and the bar. He stood up and waved to attract my attention. I smiled as I approached him, using the distance to inspect him once more. It was no good; there was nothing attractive to me about the man. He was slender to the point of thinness. The way the shadow fell over his face made it seem more elongated and even a little sinister. Can a smiling face even be sinister? He was wearing black jeans and a white shirt with very thin black stripes. The white only served to draw attention to his bad complexion.

I arrived at the table, and he leaned forward to kiss me. I kissed him back, brushing his pitted cheek very slightly. He did at least have pleasant aftershave on. There was hope yet.

He moved out from behind the table, pulling his wallet out of his pocket. 'I'm getting this one,' he told me, before I could argue. 'Orange juice?'

'No, thank you. I'll have a vodka and Coke please.' Something a little stronger than juice was needed.

I sat down on one of low stools that surrounded the table and watched Owen's progress to the bar. To my surprise, I saw at least two women take a second look at him as he passed. One even glanced in my direction, obviously to see if he had company. Beauty is in the eye of the beholder, I philosophised to myself. I resolved to look at him again and try to be objective when he returned.

It wasn't long before he made his reappearance with my drink. As soon as I took a sip, I realised it was a double measure.

'Thanks,' I murmured, on my guard instantly.

'No problem,' he replied, not apparently noticing my wary expression. 'So, good day?'

'It was okay,' I told him. 'We had a lot of children to deal with, which is always chaos of course.'

'I can imagine,' he replied.

'How about you?' I asked.

'Not so bad. A lot of reading and a lengthy discussion with my tutor.'

'Sounds like fun.' I hoped the conversation was going to become easier. Maybe a double vodka wasn't such a bad thing after all.

I thought for a moment. 'It's been hot today hasn't it?' The fucking weather? For God's sake. There was clearly no end to my inspiring conversational skills.

'Yeah, it has. More sticky than hot really,' he replied. 'Bet that's fun in your costume?'

'Yeah. Though really sunny days are worse, with it being all black. I spend the whole time hiding in the shade.'

'It's a good costume,' he said.

'You think?' I scoffed. 'I suppose it's dramatic, but it's hardly authentic is it?'

'I don't know, it makes you look pretty stern.' He smiled at me with a sparkle in his eye that made me uncomfortable. Discussing my costume was one thing, but my appearance in it was quite another.

'It's okay for scaring the tourists,' I said. 'Sometimes I like to stand in the shadows very still and then move suddenly, just when they think I'm a statue.' I grinned sheepishly. 'It's all a gimmick really, more about frightening and shocking people than teaching them anything.'

My change of subject did the trick. I had aroused the historian in him, and we managed a reasonable conversation about the merits of sensationalising history. All very intellectual and interesting. I managed not to notice his scarred skin or that protruding Adam's apple for at least half an hour. We were discussing how people seem to find the macabre fascinating, and I had downed all but a sip of my drink, when I noticed his gaze had fallen below my face, to rest somewhere between my throat and my cleavage. It made me wish I was wearing a higher collar. I had a sudden and rather bizarre idea of him as a vampire, watching the blood pulsing in my jugular.

'Another drink?' I asked, getting to my feet rather quickly. 'My turn this time.'

'Yes, please.' He smiled up at me. His lips were horribly moist.

'Pint of lager is it?'

'Yep,' he confirmed.

As I walked to the bar, I was pretty sure his eyes were fixed on my backside. Maybe I was wrong, but it was not a concept I relished. Owen was capable of a decent enough conversation, but I already knew there was no chance of anything else happening between us. I hoped I'd not given him any signals to the contrary. A pulse of anger shot through me. It was tempting to retreat into the toilets and look for the fire exit. But that would be childish. I pushed my way through to the bar to order the drinks.

When I sat back on my stool and put his pint in front of him, Owen's muddy green gaze was back on my face, and his expression seemed earnest and not at all sleazy. Was I just being too defensive? Maybe it was too soon after Paul to be one on one with a guy again.

'All right?' he enquired, as if he had sensed something was wrong.

'Yep,' I smiled.

'So, where do you live?' he asked. Back to me; just where I didn't want the conversation to go.

'Not far. I have my own flat,' I told him, as unspecific as I could manage.

'I share with two other post-grads,' he informed me. 'Both scientists though, so we don't have a lot in common.'

'No,' I said. 'Science was never really my thing. Too precise. Not that history isn't precise, but you must know what I mean.' I hoped the conversation would return to the safe ground of history. This time it didn't work.

'No, I had that sort of debate with them last night actually. You're lucky to live alone.'

I suppose I'd virtually told him I lived alone, but something about the way he said it gave me a nervous tension in my stomach. 'Yes, I am,' I returned. 'I'm fairly happy alone.' It wasn't really true, but it was about as clear a signal that I could give him that I wasn't interested.

'You must spend a fair few hours at work on your own too. Don't you get lonely?' He looked rather intensely into my eyes as he asked the question. I looked down at my drink, which this time was just a Coke, to counteract the double he'd bought me.

'No, not really.' There was no way I was getting into conversations of that nature. 'And I'm not really alone at work. There's always someone around.' I don't really know why I wanted him to know that, it just felt like something that needed to be said.

'Do you ever wonder if it's haunted?' he asked, surprising me by changing the subject. Thank fuck for that. I breathed more deeply. He sat back in his chair and ran a hand through his hair. He seemed relaxed and interested, nothing more.

'I don't really believe in ghosts,' I told him.

'Me either,' he agreed.

'I do feel like you can sense people sometimes though. Almost like they've made their mark on history, and a little piece of them is still left behind, just lingering there,' I explained. I hoped this would expand into another interesting conversation.

'I know exactly what you mean,' he said eagerly, to my dismay. No discussion there then. And a rather odd smile had appeared on his face. He leaned forward on his elbows. 'Jen?' he asked, in a conspiratorial tone that set my alarm bells ringing once more.

'Yes,' I replied, in suspense over what he might say.

'Do you have a boyfriend?' There it was, just about the worst thing he could have said. I felt myself flush, a mixture of discomfort, embarrassment, and anger.

'Not right now,' I told him honestly, 'but I'm not—'

'Because I really like you,' he went on, cutting me off. 'I can't believe I only met you yesterday. I feel like I've known you for ages.' If his words weren't disquieting enough, his face had lost the easy smile and he looked deadly serious. It bordered on frightening.

'Er, look Owen, I like you,' I began awkwardly, 'but, you know—'
He interrupted me again.

'Don't say anything now. I'm sorry.' He relaxed perceptibly. 'Let's
just talk a bit more.'

I truthfully didn't want to talk a bit more. But I felt a little sorry
for him. Plus, I didn't like the idea of leaving him on uncomfortable or
angry terms. Perhaps another drink and another half an hour or so of
getting to know me would make him get over it. I'd just be less friendly.
He'd go off me, hopefully with the same startling speed he had decided
he liked me.

I took a sip of my Coke and waited for him to say something. When
he didn't, I broke the ice. 'So, what do you think of the university?'

What followed was really quite a boring conversation, exactly how
I intended it to be. I let my attention wander. I looked at the group of
middle-aged women, dressed up to the nines, gathered cackling around
the table to our right. I watched two men in business suits make their
way to the bar. A couple a few metres away held hands over the table.
Lucky them. Someone near the bar was rattling a charity bucket. One
of the hazards of an evening in town, the charity collectors, going from
bar to bar, trying to give the drinkers a guilty conscience, or hoping
they'll be drunk enough to drop tenners into their buckets.

I looked back to Owen, who was telling me about an interesting
journal article one of his professors had written. 'Mmm, really?' I said
at an appropriate moment. I wanted him to think I didn't care less about
what he was saying. From the way he was going on, however, I didn't
think he'd got the message.

It was then that one of the girls who had served me behind the
bar began a round of the tables, setting a small glass dish on each one
and then placing a stubby candle, which she proceeded to light with a
cigarette lighter, onto each dish. Fantastic. Just what I needed, a romantic
atmosphere. As she made it to our table, I used the opportunity of her
coming between Owen and me to look away from him again.

A harsh jangling to my right told me the charity collectors were
nearby. I glanced across at the bucket. Breast cancer research was
tonight's charity. More to my taste than animals or children, I thought,
maybe I would give them my change when they reached our table. I
looked up at the person holding the bucket.

I glanced away and then looked again.

The charity collector was a woman, probably in her thirties. She was relatively short and very slim. Her hair was shaved close to the nape of her neck, the rest cropped in an unmistakeably boyish way, except it was longer at the front, where it reached into jagged points to frame her face. It was black, artificially black, though her skin tone suggested she was naturally dark. She was half-turned away from me, so I couldn't make out her face properly, but her profile showed a small nose and a slightly protruding mouth with naturally pink lips. In her ear she wore one silver hoop and one silver stud.

I looked her up and down before I realised I was doing it. I was half-hypnotised by her already, drawn to the way in which it was impossible to label her as beautiful in the strict sense of the word, and yet she was the most striking woman I had seen in a long time, if not ever. Her appearance rejected labels, defied definition in a way that excited and intrigued me. Her clothes sat so naturally on her slightly angular figure that she gave the impression of having made no effort with her appearance at all. Stonewashed black jeans, tight to her narrow hips and strong-looking thighs, and a black vest-top which skimmed over small breasts and showed off toned arms, the movement of her biceps clearly defined beneath her skin as she rattled her bucket.

I looked at her hands where she held the handle of the bucket, noticing the short nails and impression of strength in her grip. The several silver bracelets at her wrist looked heavy, as my eyes ran over her straining forearm. She moved on to the next table, turning her back to me, giving me a better perspective of her broad shoulders, straight back. The way in which her jeans squeezed her tight, small buttocks below a broad black leather belt drew my attention lower.

She moved so casually; her body language suggested relaxed confidence, a woman at ease with herself. I watched for a moment longer, strangely compelled. An ache had begun in the pit of my stomach and it only grew as my eyes followed her as she moved to another table, drawing smiles from the couple she rattled her bucket at. Then, to my dismay, the lights dimmed, leaving the interior of the pub to be illuminated by the candles and, though my eyes lingered on her, her figure became less distinct.

'What do you think?' Owen was saying to me. He thought I'd been listening to him, clearly. Couldn't he take a hint? I wanted to get up and walk out, leave him open-mouthed behind me. Only I didn't have the confidence, either to leave him in that way, or risk him following me when I'd be alone in town.

'Oh, I agree with you of course,' I returned, hoping my improvised reply would fit with the question he was asking me.

'I knew you would,' he said. A dangerously soft note had come into his voice now. 'You think just like I do.'

Not there again. I felt a little nauseous. I smiled weakly and wondered how to extricate myself from this politely.

'You know, I knew the moment I saw you we'd be friends,' Owen was saying with some enthusiasm. I regarded him warily, my skin beginning to crawl. He made me seriously uncomfortable.

'And I know you're only being careful, but you have to admit it, Jen, we do have a lot in common.' I didn't have to admit it, nor was I going to. 'We agree on so much,' he added. How drunk could he possibly be on two pints of lager? His expression suggested more than was logical.

'Look, Owen—' I tried, hoping to put an end to this, maybe salvage a loose friendship.

'Jen, you look beautiful in candlelight,' he crooned at me. I stared at him blankly. It was hopeless. 'I want to know you more, I really like you.'

I was actually frightened by the intensity of his gaze, the hint of lasciviousness in his tone. Overreacting or not, this didn't feel right. 'Really, I'm not—' I began.

'You know it feels right, Jen. It must have been fate that we met in the library. And I don't believe in fate.' He paused, and I was torn between horror and laughter. He reached over and tried to take my hand. I pulled back from him before he could touch me. I saw a faint dawning of realisation in his expression, a moment of anger too, and a seeming struggle to control it. 'I'm going to the loo and to get us another drink,' he said, a strain in his voice. 'Don't go anywhere.' He smiled. From the way he wavered as he stood up, I gathered that the two pints he had consumed with me were not the only intoxicating drinks he'd had that evening. That explained some of it, I suppose. But he was still creepy.

Alone, I pondered my situation. I could get up and flee now. To tell the truth though, I was genuinely frightened he would catch up with me before I'd made it onto the bus or into a taxi. Besides, he was drunk and I should take pity. Could I be that rude?

I was contemplating this when a pink plastic bucket appeared in my vision, being shaken rather vehemently. 'Donate to breast cancer research?'

I looked up at the woman holding the bucket again. Her eyes were dark with long lashes and, with a smudge of black make-up applied almost carelessly, were the most outstanding feature of her face. She was looking expectantly at me, a little impatiently. Unaccountably, I wanted to blush. 'Oh, yes, hang on,' I said, reaching for my handbag and fishing about in it for my purse. I felt her eyes on me as I did so and my hands grew hot and clumsy. I looked up at her again and smiled awkwardly. 'Sorry,' I muttered, as I opened my purse and looked for some change.

'No probs,' she said with an easy grin. Her pink lips parted slightly to reveal a glimpse of white teeth. Suddenly, I couldn't bear the idea that I would give her my change and she would move on, barely having spoken to me. I remembered this compulsion, this urge to talk to a complete stranger, that almost made me want to grab hold of her arm and prevent her walking away. I'd felt it once, maybe twice before. I ignored the echo of doubt the memory stirred, growing nervous in the pit of my stomach. Those fucking doubts had constrained me for so long, but they had kept me safe at the same time. And though I remembered feeling this way before, it had never seemed to consume me as it did now. Maybe tonight was the time to throw caution to the wind for once? What did I have to lose, at the end of the day? I only wanted to talk to her, after all. Just to talk. I swallowed the lump of tension in my throat.

'Are you doing well?' I asked, for lack of anything better to say. I felt giddy with how badly I wanted to engage her in conversation, with the sensations that swept in waves through my body that I could not ignore but refused to acknowledge. The candlelight flickered shadows over her face and she appeared vaguely puzzled by my abrupt question.

'All right, for a weeknight,' she told me shortly, clearly waiting for my contribution.

'Are you on your own?' I went on, risking her impatience.

'Yeah,' she said with a slight frown. 'My mate was supposed to be helping but she cried off with a sprained ankle. No stamina!' she said, and flashed a grin, before looking expectant once more. Suddenly an idea struck me. It was ridiculous, and if I'd have thought about it I'd never have done it. But I didn't think about it.

'You want some help?' I asked, trying not to look too hopeful.

'What do you mean?' she replied, looking slightly confused. All she wanted was my money after all.

I tried not to blush any redder than I already had and to keep the light-hearted tone in my voice. 'I mean, it's for a good cause, and I've got nothing better to do. I can come and help you collect,' I explained further. I was impressed by my own plan; I could escape Owen's company and not risk him finding me alone in town. It was more about escaping Owen than spending time with her, of course it was.

I saw her glance at my table, taking in Owen's empty pint glass. I followed her thought process. She hesitated for a moment, then she shrugged. 'Why not?' she said casually. Her words struck me sharply and infused me with greater confidence; why not indeed? I didn't owe Owen a thing, there was no reason for me to stay in the suffocating candlelight of the pub and endure his company a moment longer. I could get to my feet and leave with this woman, who knew nothing of me and expected nothing of me, but who accepted my suggestion with no more than a slight shrug. It was that easy.

'Great!' I said, with disproportionate excitement. I got quickly to my feet, shouldered my still open handbag, and made for the door, and freedom, before I had a chance to regret it, or to wonder what Owen would think when he returned.

1808

Gilly did not suggest that Elizabeth appeal against her sentence again. The older woman's kindness grew deeper with her knowledge and Elizabeth found some peace in the idea of Gilly, at least, knowing her truth. No matter that the servants at the house knew her truth too, that her mistress knew it better than anyone. The lie had obscured the truth, and in doing so had become the reality of her former life. A thief, sent to die on the gallows. If she was remembered, that was how it would be. Gilly knew now though, and believed her, and felt her rage and despair in her own stomach. Gilly would always know. A curious calm.

The slight freshness of the morning, the dread of another day arrived, soon to pass.

Odd taste in her mouth, as though the metal of the very iron bars that imprisoned her had begun to seep into her body. A wave of nausea, even though she had only just awakened, worsening as she sat up. Scrambling off the straw, waking Gilly and Jane, heaving over the foul bucket, but not enough food in her stomach, bitter acid in her mouth.

All of the women awake now, looking sleepily at her. Gilly's concern was evident. 'Elizabeth, darlin'? What's wrong?' No answer, looking into the stained bucket, more heaving, until her throat stung and her chest ached. Her eyes were watering, her face hot.

No breakfast, the gruel sent her back over the bucket. A sharp look from Mrs Beckinsale. By the bread at the middle of the day, she was recovered from the sickness, but there was still an uneasiness in her abdomen, a sense of something not quite right.

The same sickness the next morning, as a vicious wind whistled around the building. Gilly's hand rubbing her back, alarmed at the violence of her body's heaving. And Jane, rising from the straw, looking contemplatively at her. Mrs Beckinsale regarding her with a similar expression, as she failed once more to manage a spoonful of gruel.

Acid in her mouth again the following morning. Frightening now, mornings wasted in sickness, and not many mornings left. Looking at Gilly who knelt by her. 'What's wrong with me?' she demanded, close to tears.

'I know what's bloody wrong with you.' Jane's voice from just behind them. 'Seen it enough times before.'

Elizabeth and Gilly turned their eyes to her. 'Three mornings in a row you can't get out of the cell without bloody heaving, can't eat your breakfast?' There was an air of self-satisfaction, that she understood and they didn't, but also an edge of pity in her dark eyes. 'Have you stopped to think about whether you're due yet?'

Gilly's eyes registered her horror first. Elizabeth was a little slower. Then she realised how many days had passed. It was over a month now since she had been put in a cell. There'd been no flow. Over a month. She thought she would be sick again. Blood running cold in disgust and panic. She looked desperately at Jane.

'You don't mean it?' she demanded.

'I do, most certainly. As I said, I've seen it enough before. You're with child.'

'It's impossible,' Elizabeth cried. It was impossible.

Sickeningly though, it was not impossible. Too fat for his buttons, one tooth missing. His child.

'It's all too possible, my love, I should know all right,' Jane said, her sympathy grown a little in the face of Elizabeth's panic.

'But I can't be,' Elizabeth protested, not to Jane, but to the air, to the gaol, to God if He was listening. A memory of the shame of it, inescapable now. 'I really can't.'

A life inside her? She was dead already; she could not nurture a life with her cold blood. A life, where there had only been death. That glimmer of light, that wouldn't be extinguished? She put her hand to her belly, where she had felt unsettled. Life. But the echoes still there. Dead. Hang. Dead. Eyes turned desperately to Gilly, who was still silent, trying to comprehend.

'But I can't have a baby. I'm going to die. They're going to kill me!' Her cry woke Mary and Maisie, who were sitting up and looking at the small group, trying to understand. Gilly's eyes were full of tears, but she had no words of consolation. 'They'll kill the baby too,' Elizabeth said, and curiously, she knew she did not want it to die, even though it was his. Life inside her still. 'They'll kill us both!'

'Not necessarily, love,' Jane said.

2008

It had grown dark in the time I had been inside the pub, and I charged through the door into the orange glow of a street lamp. It was a mild night, and the streets were busy.

I was followed out of the pub by my new friend, looking at me with a mixture of confusion and slight annoyance. 'Oi! You know I had more tables to do in there?' she demanded, coming to stand beside me, bucket jangling.

'Oh sorry,' I ventured, disproportionately worried by her apparent displeasure. Was now the time for an explanation? But what was the explanation? I wasn't even sure of it myself. I was relieved to see her smile. She had a wide smile, which dimpled her cheeks and made me smile in return. Her annoyance seemed to transform into amusement.

'Look, where are you going next? Can we move on?' I asked, with some urgency. I wanted to be invisible by the time Owen grasped that I had abandoned him. I wanted to be alone with her. Oh fuck, no I didn't. No, I didn't. The truth was inescapable, however much I wanted to fight it. I squashed the thought and smiled at her again and waited to see if she minded taking me with her.

In reply she began walking up the road, away from the city square. She was an inch or two shorter than me, but she walked with a long stride and sure, quick steps. 'I don't have permission to go into them all,' she told me, 'so the next one's just up here.'

'Can I carry your bucket?' I asked helpfully, going with her.

'Yes, you can, you might as well be useful for something,' she said good naturedly, passing me the bucket, which was heavier than expected and rattled slightly with every step I took.

'So, what are you trying to escape from?' she asked. I looked across at her, and saw her grinning back at me. Our eyes met conspiratorially for a moment, and then, blushing, I looked back in the direction we were going.

'It's a guy I met yesterday. We were having a perfectly good conversation, then he came on all heavy. And creepy, bloody creepy,' I confided. I didn't mind telling her my business, she was no part of my life and it didn't matter. Besides, she really had a right to know why she had a new friend for the night. One of the reasons. I wasn't about to tell her I couldn't keep my eyes off her. That was something I didn't want to think too deeply about, let alone admit to.

'There won't be a second date then?' she joked.

'Er, let me think... No,' I replied wryly. 'I only hope I don't see him again now!' In truth I was a little nervous at the prospect.

We paused at the entrance to a busy bar. 'This is the next one. Since there's only the one bucket, we'll have to stay together. Just smile and ignore anyone that's rude.'

'Right, okay,' I said.

'And by the way, I'm Aly,' she told me, holding out her hand.

'Jen,' I returned. 'Pleased to meet you.' I took her hand in mine and shook it. Her grip was firm, her fingers warm, and I felt the heat shoot up the entire length of my arm. I released her hand quickly and giggled like an idiot to hide the strangeness of the situation. I followed her through into the hum of voices in the bar.

We visited several establishments in quick succession, and I barely had another chance to talk to her. I watched her though, and rather envied her easy confidence in her dealings with the people in the bars and pubs. Perhaps that was the fascination she held for me? I envied her self-assurance and casual manner. She flashed a pink-lipped smile here, a stern big-eyed glare there, and generally induced people not only not to hassle her, but also to part with their cash. There was a lot to envy and yet she was someone very different from me and I couldn't genuinely say I aspired to be like her. I just wanted to look at her and not stop. I found myself smiling as I watched her, delighted that I had encountered her and had nerve enough to tag along with her. I felt oddly excited. I guessed it was the drama of my escape from Owen the creep, something I would never usually have done. I told myself that was what it was. It was nothing to do with the woman who had facilitated my escape, she was just an interesting addition to the events of the evening. Still more people donated money to us, and I was surprised how heavy the bucket was growing, and also amazed when I looked into it and saw a thick layer of notes.

When we reached the end of the row of illuminated bars and hollow looking shops, closed for the night, we turned and made our way back towards the square. We had to meet the charity representative who would take the money. The bucket was beginning to become a security risk. I was carrying a small fortune.

'Are you all right with that?' she asked as we walked, the heavy bucket slowing me down slightly. She was grinning slightly at my attempt to look as though the weight was not bothering me at all. I wasn't fooling her, clearly. She didn't strike me as someone who would be easily fooled. I wondered just how perceptive she was and felt a little worried by the idea of her seeing through my defences. Not worried enough to be glad our time together seemed to be coming to an end, however.

'Yeah, it's fine,' I assured her. 'Not far is it?' I added, smiling and hefting the bucket so more of its weight was in my right hand.

'No, see that car? That's Pauline, who works for the charity.' I saw a car ahead of us, and a stout woman waiting just by it. When we reached the car, the woman smiled at Aly and took the bucket from me.

'Who's this?' she asked, smiling at my new friend and then me.

'This is Jen,' Aly told her. 'She suddenly decided charity work was her calling.' I giggled and Pauline's smile spread across her wide face. I wondered what she thought was the real reason for my carrying Aly's bucket. Clearly she thought *something* to cause her to smile in that way. I felt my face flushing, but my lips curled into a smile to match hers.

'Well, thanks for the help,' she said to me. 'I'm Pauline. Call us up if you're ever feeling charitable again, we can get you your own bucket.'

'Thanks,' I laughed.

'Feels pretty heavy,' she said, shaking the bucket. Then she put a lid over it and sealed it with strong tape. 'We both need to sign, Aly love, to prove I've sealed it here and not nicked any on the way back to the office,' she said. Aly took the pen and scrawled an illegible signature on the sheet of paper Pauline held out to her. Pauline inscribed her name next to it and tacked it to the top of the bucket with tape. It didn't seem a foolproof way of preventing theft from the bucket, but maybe I was too cynical.

'Want a lift anywhere?' Pauline said next.

Aly looked at me and raised her eyebrows in a question. Tension rose in my chest; I didn't want her to accept the lift and leave me stranded in town. I wanted to go somewhere and chat with her. But what if she didn't want the same thing? Why should she, after all? I dared suggest nothing so I simply shrugged my shoulders as though I had no real feelings regarding what Aly did next.

'Er, no thanks,' she replied, to my relief. 'I think we'll stop and have a drink somewhere. That's if you want to?' she enquired of me.

'That'd be great,' I agreed, trying to moderate my enthusiasm.

'Well, okay girls, have fun,' Pauline said, with a little wink at Aly. 'I'll call you and let you know the total,' she added.

'Thanks. See you soon,' Aly told her.

'Yeah, bye,' I added.

We stood and watched the car drive away. Then we faced each other. Suddenly, we were together for the sake of one another's company, and I felt awkward. Awkward but curiously satisfied with the way the evening was progressing. 'Where d'you want to go then?' she asked me, eyes settling on my face in a way that unnerved me slightly.

'I don't know,' I replied. I could have led us to any number of bars I tended to frequent when I did venture into the city on an evening out. But I wanted to see where she would suggest.

'I know a place, if you like,' she suggested.

'Lead the way!' I told her, fascinated to see where she would take us. And where this night would take me.

CHAPTER SIX

2008

I tried not to look at Aly at my side as we walked quickly through the city centre. If I didn't look at her I could convince myself there was nothing at all extraordinary happening, that a new acquaintance and I were simply going for a drink. That was all that was happening, after all. It was only when I looked at her that I felt hot and as though my legs might not make it to her destination of choice. My physical reaction to her appearance was not something I was prepared to dwell on, it was bloody ridiculous. Besides, it reminded me of the time I had felt this way before. That had been nothing short of a fucking disaster. Going there again was not a good idea. Going where? I kept my eyes on the pavement in front of me and refused the temptation to look at her.

The place she took us to was in a small side street. It was a café bar, which had adopted a style reminiscent of the sort of place I imagined you might have found in Paris, rather than the industrial Midlands. It was quiet inside, with hushed conversations rather than a general hubbub of noise. The red painted walls were intentionally shabby and stained, and candles burned in the necks of empty wine bottles on every table. It didn't feel in keeping with the place to order a vodka and Coke, so I settled for half a French lager, which, in truth, I preferred. To my surprise, Aly ordered a glass of white wine. I bought the drinks, saying it was the least I could do.

We sat at a table in the corner made by the front window and the wall furthest from the bar, Aly on a bench seat against the wall, me in a hard-backed wooden chair with a red cushion opposite her. When we were settled, I smiled at her, feeling suddenly shy. She was almost glamorous to me, though she wore less make-up and certainly dressed more casually than I did. It was still impossible to pin down just what quality of hers it was that made my face flush, but there was something undefined that held me almost in her thrall. I felt like I had pulled off some kind of coup, securing this confident, intriguing woman as my friend. At least, I hoped I had. I was terribly afraid she would find me boring and a quick drink would be the end of our acquaintance.

She was looking back at me across the table, something contemplative in her expression. 'I hope you didn't mind my hijacking you like that,' I said, wanting to break the ice myself, before she had the chance to form any false impressions of me from my silence.

'No, happens all the time,' she replied with a smirk.

'Of course, I expect it does,' I agreed, laughing at myself as some of the tension dissolved. Being with her seemed to make me relaxed and uptight all in the same moment. I took a sip of my lager, and she mirrored my action with her wine. I noticed she held the glass by its stem only, as is correct with chilled white wine. It was an oddly delicate action. Refined was not one of the first words I thought of to describe Aly, in her jeans and black vest, the bundle of cheap silver bracelets and bangles weighing down her wrist. I watched her hand as it returned to the table and released the glass. Though her fingers were quite thick, she had small hands, and her short fingernails were impeccably neat. She wore one very small silver ring around her little finger on her left hand. I noticed there was no wedding ring, and I was glad. Married women intimidated me. Not that I had expected her to be married and I almost laughed at myself for looking in the first place. I was conscious that I expected something very different from her, based on her appearance, and hated myself for stereotyping. I also frightened myself with the clarity of the realisation. What was I doing? I'd retreated from that danger years ago. But there was something so compelling about her, something that almost hurt me, somewhere deep inside. I tore my gaze away from her fingers and made myself think rationally. I was lacking in friends. It was her friendship I craved. I couldn't allow it to be anything else.

'So, how did you meet him?' she asked, breaking into my thoughts. For a moment, I wondered who she meant.

'Oh, er, it was at work,' I told her, as it dawned on me that she was referring to Owen. 'Which is why I'm worried I'll have to see him again.' It was almost inevitable actually. I tried to ignore the nagging in my stomach which suggested that abandoning him in the pub was probably not the wisest move. Fucking stupid really. The whole thing was turning out to be surreal. Now here I was with a woman I'd never laid eyes on before. A woman I found dangerously compelling in a way I recognised, despite my best efforts to suppress it. I wanted to laugh at the bizarre turn events had taken, but could not, quite.

'Where do you work?' she asked then. Her eyes were steady on my face and I felt as though she was weighing me up. I took her question as a good sign; if she wanted to get to know me she couldn't be judging me too harshly.

'At the Museum of Law and Justice. It's in the old Shire Hall and prison, up on High Pavement,' I answered her. I could see she'd never heard of it, and I wasn't surprised. 'I'm a Victorian prison warder,' I added, to make it sound more interesting.

She grinned, her eyes registering real curiosity. 'You mean you dress up?'

'Yep, all in black, and I get to wave a stick around and shout at people, and tell them I'm going to execute them.' It was this part of my work people were always interested in, not the history. I didn't mind, I suppose I would have been the same. I wanted her to think I did something fascinating for a living, not that I spent most of my time waiting around for visitors, preferring the company of buried murderers to the living world outside the walls.

'Sounds like fun,' she said.

'It is, at times,' I told her. 'So, what do you do?' I ventured tentatively.

'I'm a photographer,' she said. I was pleased she'd not said nurse or teacher or admin assistant. 'Or at least, I'm on my way to being,' she added. 'I'm saving up for my own studio. Right now I suppose you could say it's part-time. The rest of the time I work in my friend's music shop and help him do his books.'

'I've always found photography interesting,' I said, with some truth, though I'd probably have claimed an interest if she had told me she was a cleaner or a cashier in a bank. 'What sort of things do you photograph?'

'Well, the money's in weddings and all that. It's what I'm trying to get into. I do portraits too, of course. Anything really, as long as it pays.' She laughed wryly. 'Never thought I'd hear myself saying that when I was taking my art degree!'

I laughed gently with her. 'I know. I've got a history degree. I'm supposed to have a career by now, but I'm too busy playing let's pretend and shouting at people.' There was an empathy between us suddenly, some common ground.

'When did you graduate?' she asked. I knew she was trying to find out my age without asking bluntly. I used the same trick myself.

'Four years ago,' I informed her. 'You?'

'A little longer,' she grimaced comically, then looked up at the ceiling while she calculated. 'God, it's eleven years ago now,' she said finally. That meant she was somewhere around thirty-two. 'I'm getting fucking ancient!' she declared and I was glad to hear her swear. It relaxed the atmosphere between us.

'That's hardly ancient!' I returned, deciding that while she probably looked her age, she certainly looked good for it at the same time. Those few extra years she had on me only served to increase my fascination with her, though I disliked feeling so young and inexperienced in comparison to her. The revelation of my age didn't seem to have bothered her in the slightest. I wondered if anything I could say to her would faze her at all. It was apparent she took everything pretty much in her stride and that drew out my ability to talk to her. 'Where did you go to uni?' I asked.

'In London,' she told me. Well, that was another setback to my confidence; London always sounded vastly exotic to me, an exciting and sophisticated place, and she'd lived there, studied there. But while my confidence wavered, at the same time my interest in her deepened. There was no point telling myself I was envious of her now, despite her time in the capital. This sure as hell wasn't envy I was feeling. But what the fuck was it? 'How about you?' she enquired.

'Right here,' I said reluctantly. 'It was the best place for the course I wanted to do,' I added, to defend the fact that I had stayed in my hometown to study.

'Have you always lived here?' she asked, with no apparent condemnation in her tone, though I flinched at the question.

'Yep,' I told her, feeling the lack of adventure in my own life.

'Though I left home as soon as I could afford my own flat,' I explained, anxious that she wouldn't conjure up the picture of me as some little girl living at home.

'Yeah, I could never have gone back after I went to uni,' she said, agreeing. I wondered if she was judging me and hiding it well, or genuinely as accepting as she appeared to be. 'Me and my mum argue if we're left alone for two minutes!' she added. Her tone was unconcerned. She was so relaxed in her manner of speech, so casual in her bearing, I found it hard to imagine her arguing with anyone.

Her last words hung in the air, as we both took another drink. I watched as a rivulet of crimson wax dribbled from the pool around the wick of the candle, streaked its way to the neck of the bottle and ran over it, slower and slower until it finally solidified. I knew her eyes were on me, I could feel her gaze from the other side of the bright halo around the flame of the candle. I shifted slightly in my chair and kept my own eyes on the waxy trails on the body of the wine bottle holding the candle. I found I wanted her to look at me. Yet, even as I allowed it, it frightened me. I experienced my increasing temperature with alarm, as the silence between us grew heavier. I could not make myself look up and see her gaze levelled at me, and, with my eyes fixed to the bottle, it felt impossible to think about anything else. I needed to say something, shatter this tension. Was it all in my head, I wondered, or did she feel it too?

'I like this place,' I said finally, my voice a little rough, glancing around me as if I was really interested in our surroundings.

'Yeah, I don't get out that much, but when I do, I can't stand noisy places and bright lights,' she replied. 'See, I'm old before my time.' If she had experienced the mounting tension I had, her demeanour showed no signs of it. For some reason, that disappointed me slightly.

I smiled. 'If you're old, I must be too,' I rejoined. 'I hate most of the bars in town actually. I like the pubs better. And I'm not really into clubbing.'

'Me either. They only play crap anyway.'

'Hear! hear!' I said, pleased to have found yet more common ground. I thought for a moment, determined to allow no more lulls in the conversation. 'So, is Aly short for something?' I asked.

'It might be,' she said with a secretive look, 'but it's classified information.'

'Oh, I see,' I laughed lightly, though her amused grin made my pulse race unaccountably.

'Jen's short for Jennifer, I assume,' she added.

'Yes. Not much else it could be,' I said wryly.

A draught made the candlelight flicker. I looked out of the window at the night and saw myself reflected in the glass, bathed in the soft light. I turned my gaze back to Aly, who was looking across towards the bar. My eyes slipped down the side of her smooth neck to her collarbones. I lowered my eyes to the table as she faced me again, and I took a drink to ease my dry mouth, still watching her, as quite unconsciously, she traced a finger through the condensation on the bowl of her wine glass and put the moist finger between her pink lips.

An emotion stirred in me, an old feeling I thought I'd run far enough from years ago. I knew now it was inescapable, however hard I tried to hide. I knew what I wanted, even as I still told myself I didn't.

We managed to make light conversation until the bar began to empty. When we parted, we exchanged telephone numbers. During the taxi ride home, I tried not to think of her.

1808

'With child?' Mrs Beckinsale looked at Jane. Anxious, but not surprised. Elizabeth knew for sure then that their keeper understood exactly what had befallen her. 'Y' certain, Jane? 'Cause Lord knows it, I don't want to be causin' bother for nowt.'

'All the signs are there,' Jane told her. 'Don't this mean they won't put her to the rope?'

Mrs Beckinsale turned her eyes to Elizabeth now, inspecting her pale face. 'No, if it's certain, not 'til the baby's 'ere.' What Jane had said was true. Confusion and a beating heart. A baby, inside her. She'd never imagined it possible, even before. Now there was another life at stake. But nine long months, and then dead just the same? No, not just the same. Dead, but leaving life behind her, to go on into the world. Not the same at all.

'Y' sure y' late?' Mrs Beckinsale asked her brusquely.

'Yes,' Elizabeth confirmed.

'Well, the doctor will 'ave to be got then won't he? I'll go to Mr Charles.' The name hung heavy in the air. Elizabeth felt her pulse in the place where her cheek had bruised. Mrs Beckinsale caught her expression. 'All 'as to go through him, where doctor's concerned,' she said by way of explanation. A jolt of fear, and not only for herself now. An exchanged glance of worry with Jane, unexpected empathy. Gilly behind them.

'But Mrs Beckinsale—' Gilly said.

'Hold y' tongue, Gilly Stevens. I'll see all's well,' Mrs Beckinsale said. Surprising reassurance, a suggestion that it was safe to hope.

❖

Sitting, waiting. Bewildered. Elizabeth held her hands to her belly and wondered at the miracle inside her. For that was what it was. She had believed him; she might as well be a corpse already. Yet it wasn't true. Her body had rallied its life force to create a vital spark in her womb. It was not because of him; it was despite him. The baby would save her, not from death in the end perhaps, but from oblivion.

'Lizzie Cooper?' His voice outside. Blood freezing as she remembered the call once before. He had come for her. Frightened eyes met Gilly's anxiety. Mrs Beckinsale with them, her face grim, determined it seemed.

'Now come on, missy, doctor's been got for y'.' She took Elizabeth's arm. Impossible that she would not feel her trembling, walking towards him as he entered the outer chamber. The missing button was repaired. His face a scowl, dangerous eyes. Urge to back away, sickness returning.

'I've come to take her to the doctor, Mrs Beckinsale. He'll soon see to this.' A secret, a lie in his tone. She would not follow him again. A sudden knowledge: her life depended on it, she would not be alone with him again. His eyes were on her, and she knew he thought she was already dead. It struck her: that was why he had chosen her, not Maisie, who was prettier, or Jane or Gilly. It was her impending death, the idea that he would be the only man she would know, and that death would silence her. But she was not already dead and there was life inside her. Not dead, not yet. Go with him, and she would be! Mrs Beckinsale pulled her forward as she tried to hesitate.

Mrs Beckinsale's face was blank as she replied, 'Very good, sir. I'll be coming with y', see for meself what the doc has t' say.'

'That won't be necessary, Mrs Beckinsale.' A warning in his tone. Defiance in her face, an expression he could not but cower before.

'I reckon it will be, sir. Else she might fall down 'ere and now an' we'll 'ave to get the doc down 'ere anyway.'

Defeat on his face, and resentment of the tired-eyed woman whose mind was sharper than he'd given her credit for. 'Very well. He's waiting.'

Out into the corridors once more, but a third set of footsteps on the stone this time. Safe. His back ahead of her, as once before, but an odd feeling of triumph, where before there had been despair. Turning a corner sooner this time, and finally the stairs, rising up a level. Larger windows, with glass beyond the bars here. Gloom mixing with daylight, to create a calming grey. Rapping knuckles on a wooden door, and the call to enter. Sudden trepidation, but Mrs Beckinsale's solid presence behind her.

The doctor was a younger man than she expected, with thin brown hair and cuts from the razor on his face. His skin was yellowing, and he was very thin. He wore a black coat and reminded her of a preacher. He was nervous as they entered the small chamber, which had a large high window to provide light, a desk, and an examination table. Elizabeth eyed the table with a lump in her throat, and turned her gaze back to the doctor.

He was bewildered to see Mrs Beckinsale, and kept glancing between her and Mr Charles. His eyebrows were raised in query, as his eyes finally settled on Mr Charles. A slight shake of the turnkey's head and an awkward cough of acknowledgment. Elizabeth knew then that Mrs Beckinsale had saved her and her baby. Cold dread at the thought of what they could have done to her, in this light chamber, made her withdraw a step backwards. Or would the doctor simply have lied, and sent her to the gallows? Her hands were sweating as Mrs Beckinsale urged her forwards,

'Come on, up on the table, missy, let the doctor do his job,' she said. 'I think, Mr Charles, y' can wait outside for us.' The doctor looked nervously at the other man. What had he been promised, Elizabeth wondered? Their sheer power over her terrified her. But Mrs Beckinsale, with her determination, had defeated them. Mr Charles turned helplessly and left the chamber. Elizabeth looked to the hard table, and then the doctor. He looked as frightened as she felt. Mrs Beckinsale helped her to climb onto it and lie down.

Elizabeth endured the doctor's clammy fingers pressing her, the indignity of his examination, staring at the daylight that flooded into the room. The words she had told Gilly, the memories of her life before, seemed to filter through the bars with it. The housemaid she had been could never have imagined this. The shine of the Italian marble in the hallway drifted into her memory, and suddenly the false splendour she had so admired disgusted her. Her own home had been small and dull. Could the young girl she had been then have ever imagined she would be here now? It was just as impossible. She thought of her mother, who had seemed old to her as she lay dying, the consumption racking her with coughs. She felt a new connection to her. Elizabeth had the same eyes and nose as her mother. Would the child in her belly have them too?

The doctor completed his examination, and, as Elizabeth gathered herself and slid down from his table, he went to sit at the desk and set a piece of paper in front of him. He sniffed and rubbed his eyes. Then he dipped a pen in his ink and was about to write, when Mrs Beckinsale startled him into dripping the ink onto the wood of the desk, by going to stand just behind him and placing her hand on his shoulder. Elizabeth watched her, bewildered.

'Is it sure, Doctor?' she asked him.

'Yes,' he said, clearly intimidated by her. He seemed very young, suddenly. Elizabeth, hearing his words, breathed for the first time since she had entered the room.

'An' you're goin' to write y' confirmation now?'

'Yes, of course.'

'Well, Doctor…what's y' name?'

'Doctor Webb.' He sniffed again and scratched his nose.

'Well, Doctor Webb, you're goin' to say she's about a month along already aren't y'?'

Elizabeth and the doctor protested at the same moment. 'I couldn't, madam, it'd be a falsehood.'

'Mrs Beckinsale! Why?'

Elizabeth was quick enough to decipher that Mrs Beckinsale wanted it to look as though she had already been with child when she had entered the gaol. It was not only a lie; it was falsehood to ruin her reputation. Then she remembered her reputation was as a thief and a liar. She looked to the other woman for an explanation.

Mrs Beckinsale turned to her. 'Listen, missy, I don't know what that man out there had planned for you and y' child, with the fine doctor 'ere. Maybe it was nowt, but lookin' at 'im here,' she jerked her head in the direction of the doctor, who was hearing her words open-mouthed, 'I'm damn right sure somethin' was in the offing. Now Mr Charles 'as a wife he's right scared of and he wants y' dead next week, so he's won, don't he? If Doctor Webb 'ere writes his confirmation, an' we takes it to the judge, he's goin' to wonder, ain't he, how you, being in gaol over a month, as y' have, could be with child for less than that. Now, we can be hush, hush about it, but it's still more trouble than Mr Charles out there'll be wantin'. He won't want the talk, y' see, in case 'is wife gets to 'ear of it. So what I reckons is the best bet, is to 'elp 'im out a bit with this. Say y' were already with the child before you got 'ere. Then it's not 'is problem is it, and 'e won't be comin' botherin y' or the good doctor 'ere about it, will he?'

Elizabeth was silent for a moment. Dr Webb shifted uncomfortably in his chair, his fingers twitching around his pen. Looking at him, Elizabeth knew Mrs Beckinsale was right. She would not be safe, or free from the threat of the man who waited outside, unless she released herself from him. The truth was irrelevant to her life now. It had not saved her. Now a lie would allow her to nurture the life in her belly, to live for a little longer. She was astonished at Mrs Beckinsale's quick wits and her candour, the sheer force of her determination to protect her. To protect herself too. Elizabeth looked at her and nodded.

'Go on then, Doctor Webb,' Mrs Beckinsale commanded, her big hand clapping him on the shoulder. 'And, sir, y' breathe a word o' this that I get to hear of, and I'll make sure y' ain't the gaol surgeon no more. Y' reckon any other patients'd 'ave y'? Y' hoping t' go to Australia aren't y', sir, ship's surgeon for free passage on the convict ship? A new start, that's right, ain't it? Won't be happenin', sir, unless y' still the gaol surgeon, will it now?' He looked at her stunned for a moment, and then turned to his paperwork.

Mrs Beckinsale took the paper from him with a triumphant flourish. 'Good day t' y', Doctor Webb,' she said. The doctor managed to get to his feet and nod his head. He would not look at Elizabeth.

Outside the door, in what seemed a very dark passageway after the light of the doctor's chamber, the shape of Mr Charles lurked.

'There y' go, sir,' Mrs Beckinsale said to him, 'I'll let you get that into the judge's hands.' He looked at her warily. She walked a step towards him, leaving Elizabeth standing watching, astonished by her confidence. Mrs Beckinsale had seemed as frightened of him as she had been herself. Now she whispered venomously, 'And if y're thinkin' on not takin' it an' leavin' it 'til it's too late to save her from the rope, then y' might want t' look at the dates the good doctor's predicted.'

He looked confused and then, holding the paper up to the light, studied the doctor's scrawled handwriting. Bewilderment and then relief crept over his face. He looked first to Mrs Beckinsale, and then in disbelief at Elizabeth. She gazed at the flagstones below his feet. She wanted to tell the whole world what he had done. The injustice of the lie she was forced into, the idea that he would not suffer for what he had done, left her with a bitter taste in her mouth. But the truth would not help her now. It had not helped her before, anyway. The women in the gaol knew the truth. The baby inside her was the truth.

'I'll take 'er back. Y' get that upstairs now, sir,' Mrs Beckinsale said. She turned and took Elizabeth's elbow and pulled her away, down the corridor. They were silent, as they walked together, but the shadows did not try to tear at Elizabeth now. She had not been abandoned it seemed, after all.

2008

The next day, the Friday, was my day off. Since we were required to work weekends, one of my free days was always a weekday. I turned off my alarm clock and slept in late. When I awoke, I blinked at the crack in the ceiling, recalled that there was no reason at all to get out of bed, and determined to luxuriate in the warmth for a little longer.

However, my body was used to getting up at least two hours earlier, and there was no way I was going to drift back to sleep now. I let my thoughts wander randomly. I wondered what Owen had done when he discovered I had left him. I was glad I hadn't given him my phone number. Fucking creepy bastard. I tried to not to think about seeing him again.

Now I smiled to myself as I thought of the nature of my escape from him. I remembered Aly, opposite me in the quiet, candlelit bar, laughing gently. She'd given me her telephone number. Would I be brave enough to call her? In the morning light the intensity of the emotions she had engendered in me last night seemed surreal, possibly a result of drinking or the heightened adrenaline of fleeing from Owen. Still, I wanted to call Aly. My face felt warm but I chose to disregard it.

The telephone in the living room shrilled. I sat up in bed. I wanted to ignore it. Instead, I dragged myself to an upright position and padded in my bare feet to where the phone stood on top of a bookcase near the window. I picked it up and threw myself down onto the nearby beanbag. A passing butterfly of excitement flew through me. There was just a chance it might be her.

'Hello?'

'Hello, Jenny, I thought it was your day off today.' My mother. Only my family and remaining school friends called me Jenny these days.

'Hi, Mum,' I didn't mind really. We weren't close, but I loved her all the same. She had no idea about anything I thought or felt, but what did that matter when I didn't have to share a house with her anymore? 'How are you?'

'Oh, not so bad. Glad the sun's been out. You?'

'Fine. A bit tired. We had a school group yesterday.'

'If you're going to be a teacher, you'll be getting used to that.' With my mum I continued the fiction that I was considering teacher training. It seemed a worthy, well-paid career, besides they gave you a grant just to train.

'I know. But they're worse armed with wet prison laundry and carbolic soap flakes than they would be with history books and pens.'

'Have you got that prospectus?'

'No, I expect it'll be here in the next couple of days though.' It wouldn't, I'd not sent for it.

'Oh good. I'd like to see you finally getting somewhere.' She made it sound like an uphill struggle. For all my cynicism, I never saw life as an ordeal in the way she did.

'I'm not doing so badly anyway.'

'No, I mean it's been interesting for you working there. I suppose it'll look good on a CV too, but it's not a long term sort of thing is it really?'

'No, not really.' Agreement was always the best tactic.

'How's Paul?'

'I have no idea.'

'What do you mean? Is he busy?'

'I really don't care.'

'Oh, Jenny, do you mean? You do don't you? Are you all right? What happened this time?'

'I don't know really. Something did, and then he left. It just wasn't working.'

'But you seemed so happy, and I thought he was nice.'

'We were, briefly, and he was nice enough. Didn't last though, obviously wasn't meant to be. Don't worry, Mum, I'm happy about it.'

'That's what worries me, I mean, you're on your way to thirty...'

'I'm not even twenty-six yet!'

'You know what I mean.'

'Yes, I do. Did you get your plane tickets yet?'

'Oh, I tell you, that's been a bloody saga!'

'Why?'

Thankfully, I managed to steer the next part of the conversation in the direction of the failings of the holiday company who were supposed to be sending tickets for her trip with her best friend to Barcelona, and the evils of the registered mail system. I wasn't going to tell her about the debacle with Owen. She'd have been glad to know I'd made a new friend, but I didn't want to tell her about Aly.

It was at the end of the conversation, just as I was preparing to tell her I had to go and do something important, that she finally said something of interest to me.

'Oh, I meant to tell you, by the way, I thought you'd be interested more than anyone else. I was talking to your grandad the other day. He's been talking to your Great Uncle John, who has apparently been doing some family tree research.'

'Oh right?' I was dubious about the quality of the information I was about to receive, but something about genealogy had always fascinated me. It was about having a place in history, a connection with it. It was the idea that a series of chance meetings, marriages, and maybe romantic liaisons in the past had produced me, a unique product, just like everyone else. If I'd had more time and patience, I'd have been doing family tree research myself.

'Yes, well anyway, it seems like we might have Australian roots.'

'Australian? Are you sure? I thought Australian people had British roots, not the other way round?'

'I'm only telling you what your grandad told me. Apparently, your—what would it be?—great-, great-, great-, great—I think—grandad just appears in English records in about 1860, or around then anyway. Uncle John remembers something from when he was little, apparently his father had a carved kangaroo that he liked to play with, and he was told to be careful, because it was old. Your Great Aunty Kate, you know, Grandad's sister, says she remembers the kangaroo too, and she was a bit older, you know, and she was told it belonged to their great-grandfather, who was Australian. Apparently neither of them had ever really thought about it again, since their great-grandad had already been dead for quite a while, until the question came up of where he might have appeared from. Uncle John's doing some more research.'

'That's interesting,' I said, trying not to sound sceptical. Wooden kangaroos and hazy childhood memories? I suppose it was a start but hardly sound historical evidence. 'You'll have to let me know what he finds out.'

'I will. We could all be Ozzies!'

'Yeah, funny isn't it…'

'Oh, sorry darling, I'm going to have to go, I've got the gasman coming, it's why I'm not at work. He should be here about now. Speak to you soon.'

'Will do. Love you.'

'Love you too, Jenny, bye for now.'

'Bye, Mum.'

I hung up the receiver and contemplated going to back to bed. Instead I put two slices of bread in the toaster and ate my breakfast in my pyjamas. I thought about Aly again, unable and unwilling to prevent the thoughts. Part of me dreaded the sensation in my core that I could not quite define. Not again. And part of me hoped the phone would ring and it would be her.

CHAPTER SEVEN

2008

The phone did not ring again, but my mobile bleeped at me in the evening, telling me I had a text message. I'd given Aly both numbers, but I had thought she'd phone. It was a surprise to me then, when I read the text: *Hi Jen, hope u got home OK? Kno it a bit soon, but do u fancy a quik coffee 2moro? I'll b in town in the p.m. thort we cud meet wen u finish wrk? Let me kno. Aly x*

A wave of heat seemed to sweep through me. Don't be so fucking ridiculous. My mobile felt heavy in my hand. I read the message again. I was glad she'd not phoned, I'd have made an idiot of myself. Too soon for what? Coffee with a friend? Was I reading something into her words that wasn't there? I liked to look at the letters, clear on the phone display, not imagined. I thought of Aly holding her mobile, thumb working to input the message. I wanted to giggle stupidly. What was it about her? It was her confidence, her easy manner. She was so different to the people who usually wanted to be my friend. That was what it was. That was all it was. But even telling myself that, I felt an ache I remembered, one I thought I could stop myself from feeling ever again. I'd said no to it six years ago and lived with the doubts for all of this time, secure only in the knowledge that I had made my decision, correct or otherwise. But what if I didn't want to live the rest of my life constrained by those doubts, by a decision I'd made when I was a naïve student?

I sent a message back: *Hi Aly, yep, got home fine, hope u did 2? Not 2 soon at all, I finish at 4.30ish, so shall we say 5 in the place u took me 2 last nite? Let me kno if that OK, hope 2 c u then. Jen xx*

I was relieved to receive her reply moments later: *Suits me! Look 4ward 2 it, c u then xx*

Maybe my gaze lingered on those two digital kisses longer than it should have done. But I didn't let it into my consciousness. I didn't delete the messages as I usually did. I saved them in my mobile's memory.

1808

Another week crept by. Mary Smith was taken from the gaol for her sentence to be carried out, and then she would be free. Elizabeth watched her go, wondering what it would be like, to have been in the gaol, in this other world, and then return to the ordinary everyday one. Mary glanced over her shoulder once as they led her through the gate, and said goodbye to no one.

'Sour one, that,' Jane Larkin commented. Her conversations with Elizabeth had become more common as the time they spent together drew on.

'She didn't seem too unhappy,' Elizabeth replied.

'If I were her husband, I'd have hit her with the bloody skillet,' Jane said with a wicked grin. 'Good job there's nothing heavy in here, that's what I say.' She mimed hitting Elizabeth over the head with a large object and Elizabeth smiled weakly. There was never a light atmosphere in the gaol, but Elizabeth had related to them how Mrs Beckinsale had rescued her and stood up to Mr Charles, and her tale had brought the colour of triumph and satisfaction to the cells, for the moment.

'She certainly never cared about any of us,' Gilly added.

'Why should she? She was getting out of it today. Tries to murder her husband and gets twenty lashes, I steal some hankies and a gentleman's watch and I'm off to the other side of the world.' This was Maisie, who, contrary to the other women, seemed to have grown increasingly bitter as the days passed.

'You know you thieved more than that, Maisie Burrows!' Jane taunted her. 'How many years was it, picking pockets and cutting purses before they caught you? I'd swear you had my bloody coins from me once when I was crossing town after a good night's work.'

'Like you ever did a good night's work,' Maisie replied, her sarcasm sharp.

Gilly and Elizabeth left them to their banter and took up their sewing. It was later that day that Mrs Beckinsale, satisfaction on her face, brought her the information that her stay of execution had been officially granted until the baby was weaned.

Those words hung in the air. Until the baby was weaned. And then death. But suddenly the finality of it was gone. There was a future to think about, even through death. And even death had receded into the distance. There would be life before then. Even a life of shadows and gates and gruel was a life. She had to endure it now.

❖

Elizabeth was still sick every morning, but now Mrs Beckinsale saved her gruel, cold and congealed though it grew, for her to eat when she began to recover, a few hours after waking. Elizabeth found she had an appetite, even for the gruel and the hard bread and the cabbage soup. She felt the pull of the baby inside her, drawing goodness from her.

Mrs Beckinsale was kind to her. Without trying to hide it from the other women, she brought Elizabeth extra slices of bread, even a little cheese. When she could, she slipped her a leg of chicken or a slice of beef. It was not every day, and Elizabeth guessed the meat came from her own husband's table. She wondered if Mrs Beckinsale had told her husband about what had happened in the women's gaol. Somehow, she thought not.

Gilly and Jane were a source of support for Elizabeth, Gilly with her kindness and even Jane, with her no-nonsense conversation. Maisie, however, grew quieter. Elizabeth knew she resented the extra attention, the morsels of food, that her condition had brought her and felt sorry for the younger girl.

❖

The days merged together, all of them passed in obscurity and shadow. It seemed inconceivable that spring had become summer outside, and yet inside the walls it was still dank, the nights cold. Weeks and then months had slipped by, and the miserable gaol routine made it almost possible to forget they were all waiting for something, be it transportation or death. The world might have forgotten about them here, there might be no end to this existence. As the days passed, Elizabeth began to ponder the future. Not her own death. That had become unreal again, a distant happening. It was life that preoccupied her, the life in her womb, that already had such an influence over her own existence. What would become of the baby? No mother or sister. No kindly friend. The full horror of it struck her for the first time.

Her baby would be an orphan, child of a criminal, a pauper, friendless in the world. She imagined an orphanage no better than the gaol she sat in. Memory of herself, alone at just twelve years old, not even fully understanding what death was, only that it had left her deserted. And what had been the conclusion of her story, in the end?

That could not happen to her baby. She knew it then; the child in her belly was all there was. She looked up at Gilly, still sewing patiently in the dim light, constant as always.

'Gilly?' she said, the notion barely formed before she spoke.

'Yes, darlin'?' Gilly rested her work in her lap and blinked her eyes.

'When will you be transported?' It seemed a dreadful thing to ask.

'We don't know,' Gilly replied. 'Mrs Beckinsale says they usually know about a week or so before. We just wait for that. Depends on how many people they've got to take from all over the place, she says.'

Elizabeth regretted the sadness she had seen emerge in Gilly's expression. She knew the older woman was frightened of the journey, of what her future held.

'Gilly, I want you to take the baby,' she said suddenly, vehemently. Maisie, who was sitting by them, sewing, looked up, startled, but said nothing.

'You what, darlin'?' Gilly asked, just as astonished.

'There's no one else,' Elizabeth said, her desperation straining her voice. 'Really. You know I don't have any family or friends. They'll take it and they'll put it in an orphanage. I'd rather them kill us both now than that, Gilly. Take the baby with you.'

'I can't, darlin'. Think of it on that hulk, going all that way. And they'll be putting me in gaol and making me work for seven years when I get there. How could I?'

'But if you could, would you? Would you be its mother?'

Gilly's face softened. 'Of course I would, darlin', you know I would,' she said. Elizabeth closed her eyes and let the swirl of thoughts settle. There would be a way. She would find it.

2008

It was just as well it was a busy day at work that next day, being a Saturday. Weekends could be relied upon to bring a steady stream of small groups through the museum, and they were usually the days that passed most quickly. And I wanted the day to pass quickly.

I was also rather afraid Owen would make an appearance at some point, demanding an explanation. He had a right to it really, and it wasn't like he didn't know where to find me. I wondered if they'd let him into the museum, which you entered separately from the library, without him buying a ticket. At more than five pounds it seemed unlikely he'd go to those lengths. He could wait outside for me later, that was a very real possibility. But surely I wasn't that important, especially after the way I'd treated him?

I was only alone for a short time that day, during the lull which quite often followed my own lunchtime; after all, tourists weren't going to give up a leisurely lunch for a tour of a prison. My half-an-hour break ended at just about the time most people contemplate seeking out somewhere with reasonable lunch prices.

It was a dull day and spotting with rain, so I abandoned my usual seat on the gallows steps and instead went into the passageway through which visitors entered the yard. I leaned back against the cool brickwork and looked outside at the daylight. It was good to have a moment's break. I'd be able to hear from here when the next party were on their way down to me.

I thought of Aly again, I couldn't help it. I knew it was dangerous, the way she had crept into my mind. I didn't question why it was dangerous; I knew perfectly well what my subconscious was suggesting to me. I had grown used to distracting myself, ignoring that particular nagging. Maybe I was sick of guarding myself against danger, hiding from it constantly? I felt oddly pleased with myself. The hot excitement fluttered in my belly once more.

It was as I contemplated this that I heard a strange sound, out of place with the usual creaks and groans, rattling of chains, and slamming of doors. I listened harder. It sounded for all the world like sobbing, a girl sobbing, somewhere a little distant from where I stood. I took a pace or two towards the yard and lost the sound, so I retreated back into the building. It was still there. My first thought was that a child was lost somewhere in the frightening building. I walked some distance into the passageway and found, though I could still hear the sound, it did not grow any louder.

Worried for whoever was the source of what really were heart-rending sobs, I turned back towards the yard, since I was not supposed to stray from my place, and I did not want the responsibility of a lost child. I listened closely at the entrance to the dark cells, but the sounds were not coming from in there. In fact, they had faded again.

I went back slowly to my place in the passageway, listening. Nothing. Then I turned cold as a cry of pain reached my ears. The fine hairs on the back of my neck stood on end. It was a faint sound, distant even, but still full of horror. I felt suddenly nauseous and had to fight the compulsion to put my hands to my ears. From nowhere came a sensation of fear, terrible fear.

There was silence again. Yet still my stomach was in a knot of horror and I was rooted to the spot. I felt cold, very cold, as a draught crept in from the yard and ruffled my hair. Then, barely caught but seeming closer, whispered voices, female but indistinct. I turned my head in the direction they came from, but there was only the empty passageway, the damp stone and the iron gate. I felt the fear deep in my belly, and could not think clearly enough to look for an explanation. As the whispers died away, a pressure seemed to envelop me, only I wasn't frightened of it. Warmth spread through me, and I felt comfort. I felt empathy so deeply, I thought I could cry. Then, in a moment, it was gone. There was silence, the light drizzle, and I felt quite ordinary again.

'Fuck,' I said to myself. I shook my head and stamped my feet, sure I hadn't nodded off this time. I left my shelter and walked through the rain, which clung to my hair and made the black of my costume sparkle, and into the transportation exhibition. In there, hidden in a cleverly disguised cupboard, was a telephone. I dialled the extension of reception, and Jim answered,

'Hi, Jim,' I said, surprised at how calm I actually sounded.

'Hi down there,' he said.

'Could you get someone to check CCTV for me please?' I asked. 'It's probably nothing, but I thought I heard, well, a little girl crying, and I just want to make sure there are no lost kids about.'

'Will do,'

'Thanks.' I hung up the receiver. I chewed my lip and waited by the phone until it rang again. 'Hello?' I said, picking it up rather quickly.

'Can't see anything,' said Jim's voice. 'I've asked Bill to do a quick tour and check though.'

'Okay, thanks,' I replied, hanging up again. I wasn't surprised. After all, it wasn't just a little girl crying that I had heard. Just what the hell had I heard? I reflected for a moment as I left the transportation exhibition and walked back towards the gallows and entry passage. I'd heard people talk about voices before, chill feelings, hands touching them—ghosts. I didn't believe in bloody ghosts though. I mean, yes, if anywhere was likely to be haunted, it was this place. But ghosts didn't exist. I'd been here over a year, and I'd never had cause to consider it before. Still, the memory of the fear I had felt made me feel cold. The sky had grown more oppressive and grey, the rain heavier. I shivered. Then footsteps approached and a party of ten tourists, two families, emerged into my yard.

'Stay back there, you scum, or you'll be getting your clothes all wet. Don't you realise we want to sell 'em on once we've taken 'em off you?' My voice only wavered a little.

I managed, through some pretty serious pressure on the last lingering tour party, to get out of work by quarter to five. It was the first time I was genuinely glad to leave the building. Perhaps after a year it started to play tricks on your imagination? The safety of its confines had not been so reassuring today, at the same time as the freedom of the outside world seemed to hold greater promise. I walked quickly over the street, its cobbled surface gleaming with wet, though the rain was not falling now, a light wind having replaced it. Already I was finding my earlier experience difficult to recall exactly, and I turned my attention now to the direction I was walking in. Or, rather, my mind became irrationally preoccupied with *who* I was walking to.

I felt a glimmer of pleasure as I arrived at the little Parisian café. By day it looked more like the sort of place you would visit for coffee and cakes. I smiled at its friendly exterior.

Despite the large window, the inside of the café was largely in shadow, since it was positioned in a narrow street, with buildings looming opposite. The candles had not been lit today; instead, wall lights provided cosy but more commonplace illumination. I looked eagerly around at the few people inside. I couldn't see Aly.

Moments later, the door behind me opened, and I recognised her rather deep, mellow tones. 'Hello! Beat me to it!'

I twisted to look at her, feeling my temperature already beginning to soar. 'Hi,' I said, wondering awkwardly what else I should say in greeting. As my eyes made contact with the deep brown of hers, I fought the urge to blush again. What was it about her? I thought I'd remembered her pretty accurately, but the reality of her again, now that we were face to face and the full impact of her dark gaze was directed towards me, threatened to take my breath away.

We both ordered coffee, mine a cappuccino, hers a double espresso, and made our way to our table. Our table? The table we'd sat at the night before last, in the corner by the window. I couldn't help looking her up and down as I followed her. Plain black jeans this time and not quite so tight, but still snug around her firm thighs. Her black leather belt was loose about those slender hips, and she wore a blue shirt with the sleeves rolled up. I could see the hand with which she held her cup, my eyes running over the tension of the muscles in her forearm, and noticed she still wore the heavy silver bracelets. My gaze travelled over angular shoulders to the shaved hair at the back of her neck, a dark downy covering over the skin beneath. It looked so soft, I wanted to reach up and run my fingers through it. Shit, that was a strong urge. I tried to make it go away, looking away from her and down at the white foam of the cappuccino in my hand. But my eyes were drawn back to her irrevocably. The ends of her longer cropped hair had been tousled by the wind, and it stood up more than it should have done in places. As she sat down opposite me, I saw her eyes scan my appearance up and down, and I wished I wasn't in my usual work clothes of jeans and faded black T-shirt. At least I'd taken my hair out of its bun, and it hung loose and wavy around my face. I reached up a hand to ruffle my locks slightly and saw the way her eyes followed my every move. Tension gripped my abdomen, while I tried to maintain my outward composure, something she seemed to have no difficulty with at all.

'So, how are you?' I asked her, watching as she ripped open three paper packets of brown sugar and stirred them, one after another, slowly into her espresso. I looked at her face as she concentrated on her coffee, long lashes lowered, and saw she had smudged smoky eye-shadow above her eyes and that a few traces of a natural pink lipstick clung to her lips. Her skin was very clear and smooth, her cheeks slightly coloured by the wind. With her hair awry, her make-up faded, and her skin touched by pink, she seemed more natural and earthy than she had the night before last, and yet at the same time my irresistible, uncalled for response to her was even stronger than if she had appeared before me perfectly turned-out.

'Good, thanks,' she told me, pausing to taste her coffee and seeming satisfied. 'Though I've been working today, like you,' she added.

'Oh?' I said, glad of the opening for normal conversation, 'What have you been doing?'

'Not in the music shop. I've actually been discussing ideas with a shop who are thinking of getting me to take photographs for their next window display.'

'That's brilliant,' I said. Despite her characteristic laid-back air, I could tell she was excited from the way her eyes sparkled. It was difficult not to be transfixed by her eyes.

'Well, they said they'd let me know, so touch wood,' she said, rapping the table with her knuckles and making her bracelets clink together. 'How's your day been?'

'Not so bad,' I said. Then I hesitated. Would she think I was crazy? She appeared so open, so relaxed, I wanted to tell her about what I had experienced. I didn't think she would laugh at me. 'But one odd thing did happen,' I began tentatively.

'Oh yeah? Do tell,' she urged, more interested than I think I expected her to be. I described, as accurately as possible, the strange sounds and sensations I had experienced earlier in the passageway. I found them very difficult to relate to her, for they were sensations, ideas of sounds, more than they were clear or definable. Then, since she still gave me the impression she was interested and I found her easier to talk to than I expected, I said it was the second time that week that something strange had happened, and I explained, laughing at myself, how I had fallen asleep and dreamed of a girl, and been stuck with the name Elizabeth Cooper in my head. Then I told her the results of my research in the library.

'So the name at least I can explain,' I concluded. 'And that's where I met the idiot you saved me from too, in the library.'

'I'm not sure I saved you from him,' she laughed her deep, throaty laugh. 'And maybe you're being haunted.'

'Yeah, I might think so too, if I believed in ghosts,' I told her.

'I don't believe in them either,' she agreed. 'At least, not like in stories and that. I believe something though.'

'What?' I asked eagerly, genuinely curious to know more of how her mind worked.

'Well, I don't know exactly. It's more of an idea than something I absolutely believe. But you know, when you go somewhere old and you just get the feeling you can, well, sense the generations of people that have been there before?'

'Yes, I do, exactly,' I encouraged her.

'I think there's got to be something in that. I'm undecided I suppose. Part of me thinks it's because we have such good imaginations that we tell ourselves we can sense things, when actually it's all coming from inside our own heads. But someone once said to me that he believed that history wasn't really in the past. I didn't totally get what he was saying, but, roughly, he suggested that all of time is still existing in some sort of parallel to our own time, and when you sense people and see so-called ghosts, it's just those people living their own lives in their own time, only the lines that divide times have become slightly blurred. He went on about energy and stuff too. I've not explained it very well,' she concluded, looking at me to see if I understood.

I can't say I followed her explanation to the letter, but I found the gist of what she was saying an interesting idea. Okay, so most likely I would have found anything she said disproportionately fascinating, but there really was something in the idea she related that I found thought provoking. 'So, in other words, ghosts aren't dead people's spirits, they're living people, in their own place in history, which sometimes crosses over somehow with our place in history, and then we can sense them, or their energy at least?'

'Yes, you've explained it better than I did,' she said with a shrug. 'It sounds ridiculous I suppose, but just something about it rang true with me when I first thought about it.'

'I know what you mean,' I assured her, since something about the theory appealed to me too. It meant history was more like layers of time, stacked on top of each other. People talked about the weight of history, after all. Perhaps the history of a place was a building up of these layers, growing heavier and heavier with every passing moment. I voiced that to her. 'So, where I work, in the exercise yard, I'm there at the same time as the Victorian prisoners trudging in their circle, the earlier ones just milling around, and even as someone being executed? Like layers piled on top of each other?'

'Yeah, something like that,' she said. 'Maybe your girl crying was in another time.' She looked thoughtful for a moment. 'I guess it's like the saying when you shiver about someone walking over your grave— in another time, you're in your grave and someone can walk over it, but in this time, where you're alive, you feel it and shiver.'

'You're right,' I said, 'I'd never really thought about that saying before.'

We sat quietly for a moment, looking at each other. I was contemplating our words and their bearing on what had happened to me today. The notion that, just briefly, I had been connected with a different time, even if it was to feel pain and hear that dreadful cry, tempted me to believe it. Still, I was an unromantic historian, and I maintained a healthy portion of scepticism. I was inclined to blame my imagination. What I was not imagining, I was sure, was the way Aly was looking at me, her lips in a half smile, her eyes curious, expectant. I wanted to say something but found that words failed me.

'Well, that was deep!' she said at last. I laughed with her, glad to arrest the build-up of tension between us before it actually became an atmosphere.

'I know, and we've only just started our coffees!'

By what seemed to be mutual consent, our conversation was a little less meaningful for a while. I tried not to look into her eyes too much, and consequently found I could converse with her with relative ease. It was only when her gaze met mine that I felt my heart miss a beat and lost track of my words for a moment. She asked me more about history; I probed her taste in art. I told her my parents were divorced, not very amicably, and she told me hers were still married, also not very amicably. She had an older brother and a younger sister, where I was an only child. She collected for the breast cancer charity because her aunt had suffered from the disease and nearly died. We were both born and bred in the local area, only she had spent those crucial four years in London, whereas I had been nowhere of very great interest. I liked the experience of getting to know her, of understanding some of the depth behind that compelling exterior she presented to the world. I felt privileged, somehow.

I went to the bar and ordered more coffee, and, at Aly's insistence, a large slice of chocolate cake and two spoons. I hesitated myself, before the intimacy of sharing the cake, but it was a suggestion that came easily to her and I didn't see a way of refusing. I knew I didn't want to refuse, tremulous though the notion made me. For God's sake, it was only chocolate cake; I needed to get a grip. When I returned to the table, bearing a small tray, I noticed she was watching me contemplatively.

'Penny for them?' I laughed nervously, trying not to feel self-conscious.

'They're not worth that much,' she returned with a faint colouring of her cheeks, her eyes dropping to look at the cake as I placed it on the table between us. 'Now, grab a spoon and dig in. You've not tasted chocolate cake until you've tried it here.'

I obeyed her and spooned myself a good chunk of the tempting cake, from the side closest to me, sticky with icing. The chocolate was so powerful I could smell the delicious aroma before I raised the spoon to my mouth. The cake was moist and light, the glistening icing which coated it dark and rich, clinging thickly to my tongue, bittersweet as I swallowed it. It was grown-up chocolate cake: sharp cocoa and smooth cream, the slightest hidden suggestion of vanilla.

'Good?' she enquired, her pink tongue emerging to lick her lips, eyes watching as I spooned up another mouthful. I nodded and smiled my appreciation of the cake, blushing as her gaze followed the spoon between my lips, and I realised too late I'd taken too much and felt the icing clinging at the corners of my mouth. I licked at it as discreetly as

I could but could not help but notice the small smile that played on her own moistened mouth.

One more spoonful and the cake was beginning to taste far too rich. I put my spoon down and drank some of my coffee, its bitter edge the perfect combination with the rich, creamy cocoa of the icing which lingered on my taste buds. Aly had stopped eating for a moment too and put her spoon next to mine, the cake a semi-devoured mess of moist stickiness between us. I stared at it, wondering if I could manage any more, yet still so tempted by the way the thick, silky icing coated the remaining sponge. I turned my attention to her face and found she was looking directly at me. Ignoring the hammering of my heart, I grinned and tried to make conversation, 'So, if you eat chocolate cake all the time, and take three sugars in an espresso, how thc hell do you stay so slim?' I asked, only becoming aware after I said the words that they acknowledged that I had paid attention to her figure. She only smiled.

'You're not so fat yourself,' she pointed out.

The notion of her eyes on my body, assessing my figure, made me feel hot and more than a little exposed, 'No, but I have to watch it,' I told her as evenly as I could manage. 'Every calorie sticks to my stomach or my thighs.'

'I go to the gym quite often,' she said, 'sweat those calories away.' A picture of her—muscles working, skin glistening with sweat—came unasked for into my head. I willed it away and ignored the flush of heat low in my body. Dangerous? This went beyond that. Only I kept on walking towards it. I could think of nothing to talk about that did not lead me back to an acute awareness of my proximity to her, of the effect her appearance had deep inside me, of the way I wanted to look into her eyes and tell her my secrets and hide from her all at the same time. My stomach was a knot of nerves.

'Not a big fan of exercise myself,' I returned quietly, picking up my spoon again, as she did the same. The steel felt cold in my fingers and when I lifted it to my burning lips. We were consuming our way towards the centre of the cake now, our spoons crossing as we helped ourselves to the surprising sweetness of apricot jam and heavier saturated sponge in the middle of the sandwich. I felt the warmth of her hand as our fingers nearly brushed. I experienced the effect of that brief touch in my whole body and I drew a deep breath. I told myself this was a natural gesture of a new friendship, this sharing of the cake, but fire that raged inside me told me there was nowhere I could hide from the truth, as our spoons clashed against each other. What was it about the chocolate cake, the act of sharing it? It had broken the wall I had maintained so well in my heart for six years. I was losing control of the flood of emotion that came from behind it. The longing had been locked away too long, and somehow by sharing chocolate cake with me she had freed it. I knew I could not, would not, force it away again. I felt my skin prickling with sweat. I had to hide this dizzying arousal, she couldn't see it. It was too much, too soon. Besides, I didn't really know anything about her. I could still be wrong. How was I supposed to know how this worked?

'Oh sorry,' I mumbled, apologising for bashing my spoon against hers.

'I'll fight you for it,' she said, brandishing her spoon like a sword. I tried to laugh, but it stuck in my tight throat. The metal of her spoon was coated in thick chocolate, smoothed into streaks by the pressure of her lips and tongue as she had pulled it from her mouth. I stared at it and looked away, frantically trying to find something else to hold my attention. I ended up staring at the table as I put my own spoon down once more and took another sip of warm coffee. My eyes were inevitably drawn back to her face. She glanced at me as she put her spoon between her lips again and lingered, licking it clean. If she knew how much it tormented me to watch that smooth metal slide between her moist, slightly chocolatey lips, it did not show in her expression. Then she pushed the plate to me. 'Go on, last mouthful. Sure you can manage it.'

'No, you have it,' I said, wondering if my face was as pink as it felt. She couldn't know the feelings she had awakened in me. I'd be mortified.

'I insist.' She smiled easily, but I was acutely aware of the deeper contemplation in her eyes now. She had seen a change in me, I knew it. I tried to restore my temperature to a reasonable level by taking a steady breath. I spooned the last soft, gooey morsel of the cake into my mouth and swallowed it quickly. The richness was beginning to turn my stomach.

'Told you it was good,' she said, as I placed my spoon back on the plate.

'So you did,' I said. I managed to look at her again. As I did, her hand moved towards me across the table.

'How did you get chocolate there?' She smiled, brushing at a place on my face a good distance from my mouth. Her fingers were soft, and they were very warm. I pulled away from her touch as though they were white hot and likely to brand me. I drew another shaky deep breath and knew my face was red. Again, I looked away from her, only to find my attention drawn quickly, inescapably back to her.

Aly sat back a little now, regarding me evenly, considering something about me. I squirmed internally under her scrutiny, my pulse throbbing in my ears, and wondered what conclusions she was drawing. If she was right, how would I deny them? Could this be the most humiliating situation of my life? Helpless to say anything to avert it, I simply looked back at her.

Finally she said, 'What are you doing, Jen?' Her voice was soft, but there was a searching question there.

'What do you mean?' I asked, torn between humiliation that my feelings were so apparent, fear of what I felt and what her reaction to those feelings might be, and the temptation to fling myself headlong into the danger, open myself to her. And all the time, I wondered if I'd read the situation correctly. I could still be wrong. The uncertainty was unbearable. She appeared to deliberate for a moment longer, while I waited, at her mercy, for what her response would be. I couldn't bear her searching eyes on my face, so I looked down at the table once more.

'Look, Jen, let's get one thing straight, so to speak,' she said at last, sounding as though she chose her words carefully.

'Yes?' Could she tell how nervous I was?

'I know we've only just met, and I really want to us be friends, I like you,' she began. I smiled weakly and waited for the rest. 'But you do know don't you? I'm gay.'

It felt odd to me, once she had said it, that she had needed to at all. It seemed so natural, as though she'd told me something I was already perfectly aware of. Why should I have known, really? A reaction to her appearance, because I had stereotyped her maybe? No, it was more than that, it was a deeper sense. She'd not said as much, not even alluded to it. But I'd thought it, almost assumed it. I'd been so wrapped up in my own reawakened feelings that I'd not even questioned the assumption. I'd just known. It wasn't so important suddenly. In the place of that confusion was a new question, so much more significant. Why was she telling me? If she just wanted to be friends, it was irrelevant. By its very nature, her statement suggested she was interested in more than friendship between us. But was I?

Six years ago I'd asked myself that question. It was like deciding to jump off a cliff, however much you wanted to swim in the cool sea below. Six years ago, I'd remained safe on the cliff, dry and still longing for the cooling water, but safe from the danger of tumbling onto the sharp rocks. Could I take the leap now? Her final word hung between us. She appeared a little uneasy herself, waiting for my reaction. My heart thudded and I looked into her eyes, made myself keep looking, and knew from my physical response there was no way I could deny anything. I didn't want to anymore.

'I know,' I said at last, my eyes still on hers. Something passed between us then, an acknowledgment of sorts, though I don't know of what exactly. Of mutual attraction? Possibly. I hoped so. A surge of confidence gripped me, and I took a running jump from the cliff. 'And I know what I'm doing,' I told her. I had no fucking idea of course.

CHAPTER EIGHT

2008

It was difficult to go on with the conversation after that moment, though, to begin with, we tried. I was as aware of her watching me and considering my reaction to her statement of her sexuality, as I was of my own dizzying whirl of thoughts and sensations. Nothing had really changed at all, and yet everything was different. Somehow, even in our awkwardness, we were companionable, but the openness brought a flood of other tensions. I imagined sitting with a man and hearing him say, 'By the way, you know I'm straight, don't you?' It would be extraordinary in the ordinary nature of the admission. Yet it would make the potential between us exactly what it now was between Aly and me as we looked at each other across the plate covered in chocolate cake crumbs. Only I found sitting across from Aly far more exciting than any moment I'd ever shared with a man. My awareness of it frightened me a little.

In so many ways she had only told me what I'd already assumed, already reacted to. But somehow giving it a label heightened the strain I felt, the thrill that went with it. Though she was thoughtful now, she did not appear to view what she had told me as some major revelation. To her it was just a statement of fact, of course. To me it was so much more. It was the label I had avoided, never been able to imagine attaching to myself. It was why I lived in confusion, why everything was a maybe and nothing a definite in my life. When I looked at Aly I wanted it to be definite, for the first time, but even now I felt that shadow of doubt hanging over me. How could I be sure? For that matter, how could she? There was no trace of hesitancy about her, she radiated supreme self-confidence. I wanted that for myself, but somehow could not imagine making such a definite statement about myself as she had just done.

She was looking at me again as I reflected on this. She abandoned all pretence at continuing with a light conversation at that point and looked at me earnestly. 'You haven't run a mile,' she said gently.

'No,' I replied, the honesty swelling inside me in response to her gaze, 'I don't want to run.' To my alarm and embarrassment, I felt the stinging of hot tears at the corners of my eyes. I blinked them back, hoping she hadn't noticed.

'I'm glad,' Aly said. Her face was pinker in tone now, a new tenderness was in her eyes as she spoke. 'I like you, Jen,' she said carefully.

I knew she didn't mean just as a friend.

'I like you too,' I returned shyly. My quiet words were in marked contrast to the elation that filled me until I was light-headed. It felt like the first time in my life I had ever spoken the whole truth. The first time that mattered, at least.

'I know,' she told me and it almost felt like a relief, as I understood that she had already seen past the locked doors of my doubts, the mistruths I presented to the world. Clearly those doors weren't as strong as I had thought. Or maybe I had just been waiting for someone with a key to fit the locks.

'How did you know?' I demanded.

'Let's just say you didn't hide it as well as you thought,' she said with a gentle smile. I looked at the table in embarrassment, my face hot.

'It's okay, Jen,' she said, 'I'm very happy about it.' Her smile was wider now, as I stared at her in disbelief. Then her face became more serious and I felt a pang of fear, that having come so far everything could still be lost. 'But the only thing is,' she said softly, 'the night before last, you were on a date with a guy.'

'That meant nothing,' I said quickly, feeling almost defensive. 'I mean, look what happened.' Surely she did not doubt the validity of the feelings that were now laid so bare in front of her? I implored her with my eyes to believe me, to forget about Owen, to look deeper into me and see how much I wanted her. Because I did want her, I couldn't deny it.

'I know,' she said, 'you didn't like him. But don't rush into anything we'll both regret.'

I didn't know whether I was grateful for or frustrated by her candour, her patience. She smiled and reached to touch my hand just slightly. The knot of pain in my chest was loosened a little. The notion that there was anything for us to rush into had, in fact, made me giddy.

'Look, we'll go home now shall we? Tuesday, after you've finished at work, we can get together again, talk maybe?'

'That'd be good,' I agreed. I didn't want to part from her. I wanted those questioning eyes to draw out my honesty as she had already begun to do. I didn't want to go home and be alone with my thoughts; for once I was frightened of being on my own. This felt real, here with her, and alone I knew I risked retreating into my old mental hiding places. I didn't want to go back to my miserable flat, to find it much the same as ever, while I knew everything had changed. But what else was there to do?

1808

Thoughts of the future preoccupied Elizabeth, until she could think of barely anything else. The old echoes had been replaced by new ones, of a baby's cry of hunger, her own despairing sobs when she found herself alone and motherless. It was unthinkable that she had been saved to carry this child, only for it to be born to that. There would be a way. Impossible to keep herself from talking about it.

The door to the small yard had been thrown open again, and Elizabeth and Gilly were seated next to each other on the flagstones, backs against the wall. The sky was pale grey but bright. The women were silent, immersed in their own thoughts. It was becoming more and more common for the two of them to leave Jane and Maisie to their own company and bickering, and seek a quiet place. Often they did not talk.

The sickness was no longer plaguing Elizabeth in the mornings, and sustained by Mrs Beckinsale's kindnesses, she felt remarkably healthy. A swelling of her stomach, which she could feel more than see, had made the presence of the baby inside her so real nothing else filled her thoughts.

Today, she looked across at Gilly, who had leaned her head back against the wall and closed her eyes. Her throat was long and pale, her face whiter than usual. Elizabeth felt a burning concern for her. Gilly was such an important part of her hopes for the future. Still her mind raced, searching for a way to make it possible.

'Would you really be the mother to my child?' she asked softly, making Gilly open her eyes. She looked tired. Elizabeth felt responsible, as though every bit of kindness she received from the other woman was draining her somehow.

'I've told you I would, darlin', if I could.' Gilly smiled weakly. Elizabeth knew her questions only brought home to Gilly the sentence she faced.

'If I found a way?' she pressed.

'Darlin', you won't. Can't you think of anyone else?'

'No. There's really no one.'

'I'm not so sure I'd be a good mother anyway, in the end,' Gilly said.

'I'm sure you would,' Elizabeth said, convinced. 'You're so kind and gentle.'

'I'm a thief, darlin', don't forget that.'

'But you're not like Maisie,' Elizabeth protested. 'You might have stolen something, but you're not like a real thief.'

'I am, darlin', according to the law.'

'No. You didn't go around just stealing in the street did you?'

'No, I didn't.' A touch of indignation, remembered pride.

'What did you steal exactly? You never told me.'

'Two loaves of bread, half a pound of ham, and two shillings.'

Elizabeth looked at her. It was something so small, so simple, to have thrown this soft-natured woman into this other life. 'Why did you take them?' she enquired.

'Like you, it's a long story,' Gilly said.

'Tell me,' Elizabeth said. For a time at least, her thoughts would not be of herself and she welcomed the notion.

'Very well, darlin'.' Gilly's eyes glazed and she seemed to look into the distance, although the brick wall of the yard was only feet away. 'I was raised by my aunt and uncle, in a village, Arneby, if you know it?' Elizabeth shook her head. 'It's only a small place, surrounded by fields, with a big oak tree in the middle. Just a cluster of houses and a church, really. A lot of the people that live there are farmers. But my uncle, he was a stockinger, with his own frame. I was raised by him and my aunt, who was my mother's sister, because they didn't have any children of their own. I had two older brothers and three older sisters when I was born, and my mother and father couldn't cope with another mouth to feed. So my aunt took me in. They were so kind to me. They kept chickens and a cow, and there were always fresh eggs and cream, and vegetables from the garden.' Here Elizabeth saw the tears in Gilly's eyes as she remembered. 'My uncle even taught me to read, since he said there was no point in girls growing up to be of no use to anybody. Aunt Louisa couldn't read, and she always laughed at him when he said it. They were happy I think, even though there wasn't much money.'

Gilly paused and sighed. Elizabeth wondered how this idyllic picture had been so horribly shattered. She waited for Gilly to go on.

'Aunt Louisa sewed the seams for my uncle and she taught me to do the same. We knew how to look after the stocking frame, putting oil on it, setting the threads up ready, collecting the loose ends. There was a row of wide windows that the frame stood in front of, so there was always enough light, and we kept the panes so clean you'd have thought there was no glass.'

Elizabeth saw that Gilly was actually smiling. The bittersweet flood of memories affected her too, and she felt the hot stinging in the corners of her own eyes.

'His work paid well enough to support us all, at least until I could be married. I never met anyone I wanted to marry, mind. But it would have come in the end. I was six and twenty when it all went to ruins. The bigger manufacturers, they started to set up workshops with more than one frame in, and they made cut-ups, which aren't as good quality as the stockings my uncle made, but they sell for cheaper, so people buy them. Some of the stockingers survived all right, if their middlemen were good to them, but the man my uncle dealt with saw his chance to make money. Prices fell for my uncle's work and they put pressure on him to go into one of the workshops and start making cut-ups. He said they were an insult to his trade and he wouldn't. And then Aunt Louisa was taken ill. It was so sudden. One minute she was in the kitchen cooking and bustling in to bring my uncle and me our supper, and the next minute she was cold in her bed, dead. I remember looking at her, when my mother came to see her laid out, thinking she just looked like she was sleeping, and willing her to wake up. I missed her terribly, of course I did, but my uncle was destroyed. She'd been all he lived for and now she was gone.'

Pain in Gilly's eyes, as Elizabeth had not yet seen it. A clue to the echoes that haunted the other woman.

'Of course, I couldn't have married if I'd wanted to then, I had to keep house for my uncle. But he wouldn't work. He just sat in his chair, all bathed in the light from the windows, and he wouldn't move. It was awful, the way he just stared into nothing and hardly seemed to hear me when I spoke to him. And the money stopped coming in. I even tried the frame myself, I'd watched him at it for so long, but I didn't have the strength to work it fast enough. Then we didn't have the feed for the cow or the hens, so I had to sell them. Even then, when all I could give him for his supper was a morsel of mutton and a piece of dry bread, he couldn't bring himself to work. He barely spoke to me. I took in sewing, to try to scrape some money together. More often than not I gave him the food and there wasn't enough left for me.'

There was no hint of martyrdom in her tone, simply fact. Her pupils flickered, as though she was seeing the memories.

'I couldn't bring myself to go to my mother. I wanted to show I could look after him, and I couldn't bear her busying herself in our house, trying to make him sit at the frame again, reminding him of Aunt Louisa, because they both looked alike.

'Eventually, I couldn't always afford even bread. My uncle was growing thinner, and suddenly he seemed so old and fragile. I was taking some sewing back across the village one night, when I passed the open door of some people we didn't know very well on the opposite side of the village. On the table was a whole loaf of good bread and some ham, already sliced on a platter ready for serving. I couldn't help myself. It didn't even seem like stealing. I was just going to take the bread and ham. I crept into the house, ever so quietly, and I knew the people were in the back parlour, because I heard their voices. I took the loaf and gathered up the ham. I folded my apron over so I could carry them. Then I saw on a shelf—there was another loaf of bread. I thought of my uncle well fed for the next week, and even enough left for me, and I folded that into my apron too. I was leaving the house when I saw the money shining on the corner of the table. I thought how many stockings my uncle would have had to have woven to have earned it, and how many meals it would buy us, and I took it. That was when their servant came through into the kitchen and cried out.'

Gilly paused to draw breath. When she began again, her voice was shaky. 'If I'd only taken the food, they might have understood. My father spoke for me at my trial, told them how things had been, and it earned me some sympathy. But it was the shillings that did it. They said if I was starving, then food was what I needed, but clearly I had the makings of a hardened thief if I had seen the money and thought to take it.'

Elizabeth imagined Gilly standing in the same dock as she herself had stood in, filled with the same desperation to defend herself and the same incapability to do so. Gilly was guilty of her crime, but Elizabeth marvelled at the cruelty of a world that could convict her. She almost heard the judge pronounce his sentence, that Gilly would be transported for seven years. She saw Gilly's face as she heard her fate, the tears flowing down her cheeks.

As if Gilly was following her thoughts, she went on. 'I was luckier than you. Australia for seven years. I knew it was the slightest sentence I could expect, and I was relieved for that. But it seemed so terrible. Even now, I don't know what I'm to expect. My mother and father were in the courtroom and I heard her cry out. She came to visit me soon after, and my sisters did too, and they write to me. My father can't bear to come here. My sisters would, but they can't get into the town, they don't have the money, and they're in service in the country, and daren't tell anyone about me, in case it brings their characters into question too. So I told them not to come.

'As far as I know, my uncle's still mourning Aunt Louisa. Of course, he couldn't live on his own, so the house and the stocking frame were sold and he lives with my mother and father now.'

Gilly concluded in a calm voice. She looked at Elizabeth for a long moment, and then her face crumpled slowly, and she began to weep, in a way Elizabeth had never expected she could. Her whole body trembled, and the strangled sound she made drew Jane to the door to see what the matter was. Elizabeth reached for Gilly and thrust an arm around her shoulders. Gilly had given her so much, and now she returned some of the kindness to where it was needed most at that moment.

❖

Gilly and Elizabeth returned inside together, to find Mrs Beckinsale looking for Elizabeth. She handed her an old tattered shawl and a mug full of milk. 'Take this, and be quick about it,' she said sharply. 'I've got to get the mug back. The shawl's for if y're cold.' Elizabeth swallowed the milk down in several gulps, glad of it in her empty stomach.

'Thank you,' she said, feeling as she did with every kindness that there were not sufficient words to express her gratitude to Mrs Beckinsale.

'Can't 'ave the baby starvin',' the older woman replied, before taking the empty mug and striding purposefully away.

'She never had favourites before you got here,' said a voice behind Elizabeth and Gilly. Maisie was watching them, scowling. 'A bit of milk for us would be nice, now and then,' she went on. 'I'm still growin' but doesn't think of me, does she?'

'You just shut your mouth and save your breath,' Gilly snapped at her.

'Should've thought about that before you started thieving, shouldn't you, love?' Jane weighed in to the conversation.

'So should've she!' Maisie said, gesturing at Elizabeth. 'And before she got herself in trouble.'

'I never stole a thing!' Elizabeth exclaimed.

'Got herself in trouble?' Gilly's voice joined hers. 'That's what you think is it, Maisie Burrows? Well, that just shows what a child you still are!'

'Well, how do we know she didn't? Get Mr Charles out there and smile at him, wink, lift her skirts a little, and then look at her, they've not hanged her yet and she's getting milk and shawls and meat. I've a good mind to call him over and smile at him myself!'

Indignation and resentment rose in Elizabeth's heart. How could Maisie's thoughts, the girl's bitterness, be directed at her who had only ever tried to be kind? It was impossible. Suddenly, sickeningly, she saw how being locked in this place had made her into another person: a convicted thief and a liar, who had acted only on selfish and scheming impulses. Maisie spoke as though she knew the reality of Elizabeth's character based only on what she had seen in this gaol, and it made her feel ill to think of another mind turned against her, accusing of her actions she was innocent of.

The determination rose fiercely inside her; she would fight not to lose her truth, not allow it to be overwhelmed by these long shadows or imprisoned by the locks and bars and walls. Maisie could think what she wanted to, Elizabeth knew her own truth, and Gilly shared it with her, ensured it was not obliterated by the darkness. Now she knew a little of Gilly's truth too. She felt her connection to Gilly more strongly than ever. Gilly was the key to her future, she knew it with a firm certainty that soothed her.

Jane was looking at Maisie with an expression suffused by disgust. 'You go and smile at him then, Maisie, and when he's got you on the floor and he's drooling all over you, you think about that cup of milk you're doing it for.' Her words were venomous, infused with bitter experience.

'You should know!' Maisie retorted.

'Yes, I should,' Jane replied, full of dignity and restraint.

'You just keep quiet, Maisie, if you've got nothing good to say,' Gilly told her.

'Nothing to say to all of you anyway,' Maisie spat back. Elizabeth looked at her and saw a petulant child. What had been her story? Maisie seemed very alone suddenly, and she was sorry for that.

❖

It was evening. They sat in the day room, the darkness swallowing them gradually, the tension between Maisie and the rest of them still raw, when the door banged open and Mrs Beckinsale entered. Behind her was a very tall, thin woman, with hair that appeared red where it could be seen at the edges of her cap. Her hem was too high from the ground, as though she'd grown since the dress had been made. 'This is Catherine Dyer,' Mrs Beckinsale told them. 'Jane, you look after her, make sure she knows the way of things.' Elizabeth looked at the tall, frightened woman, trying to make out the features of her face through the gloom. Catherine Dyer blinked. A memory of herself in the same place, peering at the shadows, and Elizabeth understood why Gilly had been so compelled to kindness. Catherine Dyer was terrified and bewildered, and Elizabeth wanted to comfort her.

Mrs Beckinsale still hadn't left the room. 'And I might as well tell y' now. Catherine's to be transported too. They've set a date, y'll be leavin' us in ten days' time.' She closed the door quietly as she left.

There was silence in the shadows. Maisie did not rise to exercise her curiosity in the newcomer, and no one thought of the comfort of Catherine Dyer. Ten days.

2008

Outside the café, Aly and I faced each other to say goodbye. It had been almost easy to take the first steps towards intimacy with her in the enclosed atmosphere of the café, but here, in the open air, everything felt different. The reality of what I had embarked on hit me and it struck me that my whole life could be about to take a new path. I looked into her eyes and wondered how it was this woman could have effected such a change in me.

'I'll text you,' she said, leaning in to give me a brief hug, which I returned hesitantly, growing hot as I felt the press of her breasts on mine.

'That'll be great,' I said. There seemed to be nothing more to say, so I smiled awkwardly. 'See you on Tuesday then.'

'Yep,' she said with a grin, fully aware of the awkwardness between us but apparently not the slightest bit bothered by it, 'looking forward to it.'

'Me too. Bye then.'

'See you.'

I turned and headed for the bus stop quickly. I didn't glance back to see if she had walked away, or if she still watched me. Yeah, like I was so hot she couldn't take her eyes off me. I laughed out loud at myself and a group of teenagers looked at me as if they suspected I was insane. Maybe I was, but, hey, I was happy.

It felt like no time at all before I was sitting at home, on the sofa, the flickering television lighting the room now that night had fallen. I drew my knees up to my chest and wrapped my arms around them. I wasn't remotely tempted to get drunk tonight.

Staring blindly at the television screen, I replayed the time I had spent with Aly, my face flushing and an absurd level of excitement tightening my insides. I recalled how easy I had found it, in the end, to admit I liked her. It hadn't felt at all strange to me, and to tell her was, as a result, only natural. She drew the honesty from me as if by magic, demolishing six years of barriers and lies as if they had never existed.

It hadn't been like that with Clare, at university. I let my mind drift back over those six long years, to remember the only other woman who had compelled me from the first moment in the way Aly did. She had made me want to hide away, feel ashamed of my cowardice and youthful naïveté in the face of her own openness. It had been so simple for her and she had never understood why it wasn't so straightforward for me. When she had finally challenged me, I had run away, told myself it was natural to wonder about these things, that it meant nothing. I remembered her words. *You don't even know yourself, Jen. I've tried, I really have, but you have to decide.* I'd avoided Clare after that. After a few months, I'd no longer ached when I saw her. I'd made my decision, as she had told me to, made it the only way that had seemed open to me. I had tried to force myself into thinking there had really been no option, that I had been correct in turning away from those emotions. And now I knew, as I really had all along, that I'd been wrong.

I thought about Aly again. I couldn't stop thinking about Aly. She was my proof I had been wrong all these years; my reaction to her, both physically and emotionally, was not something I could lie to myself about. Everything would change now. Surely, that change would be for the better? I thought about it too much, over and over, round and round, until it frightened me. What would this mean for my life? My own idea of myself? One thing was for sure, my easy, comfortable denial could last no longer. The self I had always presented to the world's days were numbered, inevitably. But I was already twenty-five, for God's sake, could I make such changes now? How did I even begin? How would I tell anyone?

My attraction to Aly was one thing, sectioned off neatly from the rest of my life. But it wouldn't work like that. I wouldn't want it to work like that. It was the fundamental way in which she would change my entire future that had frightened me away from all such possibilities before. I had grown used to my routines, my well-tried system of avoiding the truth, and if it constrained and imprisoned me,

I was at least safe. The freedom Aly offered was attractive but seemed likely to overwhelm me.

As I grew more tired and the night drew on, putting the distance of hours between Aly and me, I felt the terrible uncertainties threatening to intrude. What if it was just Aly? Okay, there had been Clare too, and I had been briefly distracted by an entirely straight woman named Gwen in my last job, but being attracted to three women in my whole life felt like a tenuous thing to base my entire future on. Yet I could not imagine being able to let go of what was developing with Aly. At around midnight, with sleep still a distant prospect, the 'maybe' came back into my thoughts. Fuck. Fuck. And fuck again.

CHAPTER NINE

2008

I didn't sleep at all during that night. I tried going to bed, but that only made me feel wider awake than before. I listened to music, took a warm bath, drank hot milk. Still wide-eyed, I watched the first signs of dawn with some relief. Work would definitely be a welcome distraction today.

Thankfully, it was another busy day. But the weight of uncertainty, of longing, of being in danger of losing my own self, hung heavily about my shoulders, and I don't believe I was a very entertaining tour guide that day. It was easy to go through the motions of my performance, complete with stick brandishing and generic insults, but it was difficult to convey any sense of connection with the past, or even to have a sense of humour, when my thoughts were firmly elsewhere. A woman with short dark hair made me think of Aly. A couple holding hands as I threatened to hang them made me think of Aly. A family party of grandparents, parents, and children frightened me with their happiness and reminded me how much of a disappointment I already was to my mother. What effect would this latest development in my life have on her and everyone else I cared about? A man with a camera in the next tour group made me think of Aly again. Every damn thing made me think of her, or of what impact she would have on my life.

I wandered around the yard, not able to settle on my gallows steps or modern chair. When I did pause for reflection between tour parties, I chose to lean against the wall in the darkest corner of the yard. I looked at my surroundings, the place I almost felt part of. The date with Aly had not changed me, I was still the same person who had lingered for a year and half within the shadows of these high walls. Except the hiding here, immersed in the history and my character, had always been my means of escape from the world and today, for the first time, they didn't have the power to distract me. I knew why; it was because I didn't want to escape the world this time. I wanted to climb onto the platform of the gallows, poke my head over the walls and shout at the world, tell it I finally knew what I wanted. So why the fuck was it so hard to get a grip of myself and feel happy about it?

The staff schedule for that week came out on Sunday. I discovered, peering at the sheet of paper that decided all of our lives for the next seven days, that I had been allocated Tuesday as my day off. My heart sank at once. Tuesday was when I would see Aly again. If I wasn't going to be at work, and therefore in town, she might not be able to meet me. I wasn't at all relieved, as I suspected I might be. I was actually dismayed. I realised at that moment how keen my anticipation of seeing her again was. Whatever the complications, the simple fact was I needed to see her again. I was nervous that having to rearrange our plans would make the whole thing too inconvenient for her and cause her to reschedule. My insecurities told me she must have better things to do than meet me, and I was lucky she had any time for me at all, without me messing her around. Plus, I didn't want to postpone being face to face with her again because I wasn't sure I could wait longer than Tuesday tormented by this unending confusion. I strongly suspected seeing her again would give me the clarity I needed.

I sent her a text message when I got home, my heart pounding as I pressed the keys: *Hi Aly, how r u? I not at work Tues, do u stil want 2 meet? Can b anotha day if better? Let me kno. Jen xx*

I was thankful for the impersonal nature of text messages, glad she couldn't see the way I blushed crimson at the idea of sending her those two little 'x's at the end of the message. She was quick to reply: *Hi Jen, I'm gud, ta, hope u r 2? Tues stil gud 4 me, if that OK? How bout we meet 4 lunch sumwhere? Wat do u reckon? Aly xx*

Delighted and anxious all at once, pleased by her matter-of-fact manner (could she have been any other in a text?), I replied instantly: *I gud 2 thanx. Lunch sounds gr8! Anywhere in particular? xx*

It really would have been quicker to conduct this conversation over the phone, but I didn't think I could manage to speak to her right now. I wondered if she suffered the same tensions, or if she simply preferred to text. Maybe she was taking pity on me. The reply came quickly once more: *There's a place I like on my side of town. If u stay on ur number 28 bus thru town, 2 the stop called Westgate Street, I'll meet u there. Sound OK? I thought at 1 o clock ish? xx*

I think I'd have gone wherever she suggested: *Sounds fine 2 me. C u then. xx*

I contemplated my message before I sent it. It didn't sound very friendly. I pressed the key to send it anyway. The date was made. It had been very easy to do it that way. Seeing her again, I fully expected to be a different matter.

1808

Ten days. The atmosphere in the gaol had changed instantly. A nervous tension gripped all of them. During the dark of the night, Jane paced the night cell and Maisie turned in her sleep so much that she disturbed both Gilly and Elizabeth.

Catherine Dyer, who was aged about twenty, was also a thief, and she was to be transported for fourteen years. She'd stolen cloth from her employer to make clothes for her small twin brother and sister. That was all they had managed to glean, before she had begun to sob. Her continual weeping only added to the heaviness in the air of the cell.

Daylight brought no relief. Elizabeth's own mind was in a state of panic. Ten days, and then alone. Ten days, and Gilly snatched from her. Ten days, and her only hope for her child's future taken away on a hulk to the other side of the world.

Gilly herself was calm. But she did not go out of her way to be kind to Catherine, even when the girl was still crying in the morning. By the time it had been light for an hour or so, Elizabeth was disturbed by the mood that had settled over the other woman. Gilly's story had stolen into her heart, and the boiling injustice that was ever below the surface in her emotions threatened to overflow. Gilly was as much a victim of the cruel world as she was. To have known Gilly, she thought, she was almost glad she had been found guilty and imprisoned here. The world that had treated them so harshly had faded, there were only these cells, they only had each other. In some ways it was a better world than the one they had known outside, she thought sadly. If only they could stay locked together until death took her; that would be something. But now the peace she had found in Gilly's company was to be savagely wrenched away from her.

Ten days. It was such a small amount of time. Hopelessness as she stared at her gruel, the desperation of trying to plan when there is nothing to work with. Gilly in the heat of the Antipodes; her child abandoned; her own body cold beneath the ground. It was all she could see.

Mrs Beckinsale waylaid her after breakfast. 'What do y' mean by not eatin' y' breakfast, missy?' she demanded, drawing Elizabeth away from the other women, who were wandering back into the day room.

'I couldn't,' Elizabeth replied. Mrs Beckinsale's concern was a relief to her. A glimmer of an idea. Mrs Beckinsale had known what to do before. Tell her. 'It's with the news that the others are being taken away, Mrs Beckinsale. I don't know what I'll do without them.' She would not confess all of her hopes at once, only to have them dashed.

'There'll be others like 'em soon enough,' Mrs Beckinsale said. It seemed an insult to say it.

'No, Mrs Beckinsale, there won't,' she protested, and then took a breath to quieten the strain in her voice.

'There won't be another Gilly Stevens, if that's what y' mean,' Mrs Beckinsale said, understanding in her tones. 'Don't think I don't see who y' friends are.'

Tears rising again, the struggle against them. Choosing her words carefully, the hope, the chance still there. But what if there was no way? Desperation in her eyes as they met those tired grey ones. 'I know, Mrs Beckinsale, but Gilly's more than a friend to me.' She swallowed through the lump in her throat. 'There's no one to take my baby, you see, and I had hoped she would. She said she would, if she could.' It was honest, Gilly had said that, exactly.

'Y' silly girls! How in this world is she goin' t' manage that then?' It was not contempt, it was almost pity.

'I don't know, Mrs Beckinsale. We'd not thought of it all. Only I know she's the only one I want to be my baby's mother.'

Concern and sympathy deep in the older woman's eyes. The thought came again: Mrs Beckinsale was a mother. Or had been. Contemplation then.

'We could ask the judge about y' sentence. He might commute it, since you'll have a child to care for,' Mrs Beckinsale said. Looking for a solution that was easy, within the rules. Memory of the judge at the master's dinner table. Influence she could not fight. Words twisted to make her sound vindictive and insubordinate. The mistress determined on her death. She had thought it, long nights ago, and ruled it out already. She would not put herself through the false hope. Besides, by the time it was concluded, Gilly would be gone and there would be no one when she was returned here, alone, to wait for death.

'No, we can't, Mrs Beckinsale. It won't work, you know it won't.' Hard to say the words, truth though they were. Cling on to the other hope, the slight chance.

'Well, I don't know what you're expectin' me t' do about it!' Mrs Beckinsale said briskly. But Elizabeth saw something different in her eyes.

'No, sorry to trouble you with it, Mrs Beckinsale. I'll eat my bread later.'

'See that you do,' Mrs Beckinsale said, before striding away, her boots loud on the stones. Looking at her retreating back, the glimmer of hope grew brighter.

❖

Gilly was quiet that day and eventually went to lie on the straw of the night cell. Elizabeth allowed her her solitude. Maisie, Jane, and Catherine were in the yard, speculating what Australia would be like. Elizabeth hated to hear them and sat with her pile of sewing instead, the needle motionless in her hand.

The swelling of her belly seemed to increase every day now. She put her hand to it and thought of the baby within, closing her eyes. Her life was pulsing into the child's veins, leaving her and nourishing the new existence. Her body would be hanged, but the part of her that was transforming itself into a separate human being would not be. The baby was her innocence; it could not be accused of the crimes she had been, and it would not be punished for them. And in the child, her innocent self would continue to live.

An abrupt memory of the carved sandstone walls, pain in her cheek and in her body, dirt on the floor, and his weight, his whispers. He had been wrong. She was not dead already, and now part of her was not going to die. It seemed bitterly fitting that it was he, who had told her she would be dead in three weeks, who had given her the spark of life inside her. The memory of the pain, the horror of the child's conception made her shiver with disgust and recollected fear. Yet she would not unmake the child in her womb.

The child would have a good life. She would fight for that with every breath, before they took that breath from her. The next ten days would decide it. The child would have a good life. Was it a boy or a girl? Whichever, it would be hers. Through her, it would be her mother's. The lines of connection would always be there, long after she was dead. There would, she imagined, be children, her grandchildren, and their children. Their hanged ancestor they would forget, if they'd ever known of her, but she saw the connection to the years to come, as if the cord that tied her to her child also tied her to her future grandchildren. She would never know them, but ultimately, she would triumph, living on into the future, when he had told her she might as well already be dead. Maybe one day, some descendent of hers would pass through the town again and gaze at its factories, its fine houses, its gaol, and know the connection was there. A feeling, a memory not their own, an unexplained thought perhaps.

And what she passed on to the future was pure. Her life was a lie now, her death would be a lie. Not only would the baby be her innocence, it would be her truth. Grown from a union of horror which she was forced to pretend had not happened, but known to the women in the gaol, the child would know one day its mother had loved it through her pain. She stroked her belly over the baby and smiled to herself.

Then the panic returned. Ten days. There had to be a way.

❖

Towards late afternoon, three days later, Mrs Beckinsale came looking for Gilly. She passed Elizabeth a morsel of what turned out to be fried liver, and then went to wake Gilly from the doze into which she had slipped on the damp straw. Moments later, Gilly, with heavy eyes, was following her out of the day room. Elizabeth watched them curiously. She heard Maisie's snide remark to Catherine, about Mrs Beckinsale's favourites, and chose to ignore it.

Gilly returned after a short time, her face transformed. Her green eyes were bright and her cheeks flushed. Elizabeth looked at her keenly. Was it distress or happiness that had so transformed her features? Every time she looked at Gilly, her heart fluttered. She thought of Gilly with her child, and longed for nothing more. But it was beginning to seem an impossibility. Her mind was numb from the effort of trying to think of a way it could be achieved. Now she hoped Gilly would look her way. To Elizabeth's alarm, Gilly seemed to look anywhere but at her.

For the next four days, Elizabeth tried to draw Gilly into conversation. She wanted to see if there was still any conceivable way of achieving her hopes. She also wanted to cherish the time that remained of her friend's company. Yet Gilly was strangely silent, and often wandered to a place where she could be alone. The pain in Elizabeth's heart grew. It was as though she had already lost her.

There were three days left when Gilly fell ill. In the morning, she awoke when Mrs Beckinsale entered the cell, but complained that she could not move, and that the scant light from the doorway hurt her eyes. Elizabeth looked at Gilly, lying prone and pale on the straw, with real fear. The memory of her mother's last illness swept into her thoughts and she felt a terrible dread settle on her heart.

The strain was telling on her anyway. Three days and Gilly, and all her hopes, would be gone. There had been no way after all. And now Gilly was stricken on the straw. If she recovered, it would be to be transported almost instantly. If she did not… Elizabeth could not bear to think of it.

Gilly took little food and did not move from the straw for that whole day. The next day, she tried to stand and then fell in a faint and had to be carried to their sleeping place. Her face was unnaturally flushed. Elizabeth soothed her, stroked her head, but Gilly seemed not to notice it, apart from to stir and mutter something incoherent. Eventually, in the afternoon, the doctor was called.

Doctor Webb was ill at ease as Mrs Beckinsale let him into the women's gaol. He looked about him continually, glancing at Elizabeth for a little longer than the rest of the women. He went through into the night cell and demanded more light. An extra lantern was brought, and he conducted his examination.

Afterwards, he made his report to Mrs Beckinsale. Elizabeth and the other women were silent, his words carrying easily to their ears. 'She is gravely ill, I'm afraid. More alarming though, madam, I fear it may be an illness that is easily passed from person to person. I recommend that the prisoner is moved to a cell on her own, until she recovers or otherwise.'

'But doctor, it's impossible. She's to be transported tomorrow,' came Mrs Beckinsale's protest.

'No, madam, she is not.' Doctor Webb's tone was firm. Elizabeth's heart skipped a beat. 'Even the journey to the docks would almost certainly bring about her end, not to mention the risk to the other prisoners. She must be kept quite separate.'

'I don't know, sir, if she's due to be transported, transported she must be.' Mrs Beckinsale's concern was palpable.

'In good time. If she lives, she can go on the next ship,' Doctor Webb said then.

'You can report it to Mr Charles and the governor, Doctor.'

'I will, Mrs Beckinsale, immediately. See that she is moved.'

'Yes, Doctor, thank you.'

Two turnkeys came then, to move Gilly to a cell where she would be kept alone. Elizabeth sat watching them carrying her limp body, stunned. Gilly would not be transported tomorrow! But where there should have been hope, there was only desperation. She had seen such a grave illness before. The idea that Gilly had been saved for her, only to succumb and die, even before she did, made her tremble. It was then, for the first time, she felt the baby stir within her.

2008

Monday was an alarmingly quiet day at work. There were no visitors at all until gone half-past eleven in the morning. For lack of anything else to do, I took the duster and polish into the Victorian part of the prison, and polished the display cases that were smeared with childish fingerprints. This part of the museum was much more of a conventional museum, with no lurking tour guides, just a mock-up of a Victorian cell, glass cases with various artefacts in them, and an example of a crank, which children delighted to turn, pretending to do their hard labour.

That done, I risked the displeasure of the management and went the way the visitors would, out of the upper floor of this part of the prison, past a row of stark white-painted cells, and back into the older part of the gaol. I then had to make my way through two iron gates, past where every so often there was an awful creak and thud as a tape-recording mimicked an execution in the condemned cell. I was now not far from the entrance to the women's prison again.

To my left was the door to the little room where we kept the cleaning supplies. I wondered what the visitors would think if they were able to open the ancient-looking studded door, and behind find a kind of cave, carved into the sandstone of the cliff on which the prison was constructed, now filled with polish and dusters, two vacuum cleaners, window spray, brooms, and other accoutrements needed to keep the place clean. The ordinary and the extraordinary juxtaposed, and with an oddly jarring effect.

I opened the door now and went into this room to put my polish back. As it usually did, the door slammed shut behind me, which was not so much of a problem, since the room was illuminated by a single bulb. It was a strange, shadowy place but had never frightened me. Even the damp sandstone walls curving around me had never seemed especially disturbing. It was fascinating, really, the way the building and the cliff mingled together and became one.

Having placed my polish away neatly—for Karen would even check in here to make sure we left it tidy—I thought I would venture up and see Mark, my turnkey friend. I went to the door and pulled on the handle. It didn't shift. I pulled again, with the same result.

Oh for fuck's sake. I put both hands on the handle and tugged harder. Still nothing. I felt an edge of panic set in; how would I let anyone know I was trapped here? I could hammer on the door, but it was thick and I knew, unless a new party of visitors arrived, there would be no one passing this way. Great. I tried knocking on the door, but its thick wood absorbed most of the sound.

I turned from the door and looked about the room for something to help me either make more of a sound, or maybe force the door. I wondered, could I ram it with the industrial vacuum cleaner?

Then the light went out. The darkness into which the room fell was complete, with not a hint of light. My heart began to pound. For a long moment, I was so disoriented I was afraid to move at all. I held my hand up in front of my face, tried to see it out of the corner of my eye with my night vision. Nothing. I might as well have become invisible. 'For fuck's sake!' I said it out loud this time, and my voice almost startled me as it sliced through the darkness. What was it with the lights in this building lately? Very slowly, I turned, estimating 180 degrees, so that I was facing the door again. I put my hands out, and felt it to my side, finding I'd turned farther than I thought I had. My total lack of vision was beginning to make me feel dizzy. A surge of panic seemed to make my other senses keener.

Suddenly there was a pain in my face as though I had struck it against something. I cried out and held my hand to the place. Fear set in, and I went back to hammering on the door, for what good it would do. In truth, the hammering was better than the oppressive silence. Only it wasn't silence now, I could hear that sobbing again. My skin felt cold with terror, but I was sweating. Then there was a pain in my body, a cramp in my lower abdomen. 'Oh, come on,' I shouted, to make a sound of my own and convince myself I wasn't going mad. I banged my fist against the wood of the door again.

The door opened. The gloomy light that flooded in from the corridor outside was like bright sunshine. 'What're you doing in there?' said Mark's friendly voice.

'Oh, thank God,' I panted, leaving the room and going to lean on the wall on the opposite side of the corridor.

'I was coming to find you and I heard a strange thudding. I thought you were a ghost!' he told me.

I smiled at him faintly. 'It wasn't funny,' I said, beginning to recover myself. In the familiar corridor, looking at his friendly face, his curly dark hair, his tatty, grey turnkey's tunic, the way he wore it with modern trousers and boots, I began to feel stupid. Still, I wished he'd close the door to the room and we could go elsewhere.

'What happened?' he asked, looking at my pale face.

'I was putting the cleaning stuff away,' I told him, 'then the bloody door stuck, I couldn't open it. Then, just to add insult to injury, the light went off. It is seriously dark in there with no light.' I was still breathing hard. I didn't tell Mark about the sudden pain I had felt, or what I had heard. Outside, with him, I began to wonder if I had imagined them after all.

He leaned into the room and flicked the light switch. 'Bulb's gone,' he said needlessly. 'I'll report it to Bill.'

'Get him to look at the door too, see why it's sticking,' I suggested.

'I will,' he assured me, 'though it must be a problem from the inside, because it was easy as ever to open from the outside. Strange that.'

Too damn strange for me. I didn't want to think about it. There were too many damn strange things happening lately. 'Well, thanks for letting me out,' I said, forcing a smile.

'Couldn't leave you in there, could I? Were you scared?' His smile was teasing. I often professed that this building and its history didn't frighten me.

'Not really,' I lied. 'I was just worried I'd be in there all bloody day.'

'The dangers of venturing to clean the place,' Mark said, rolling his eyes. Clearly I looked as though I'd recovered myself enough that all concern he might have felt for me had evaporated. 'Anyway, I was coming to tell you about four people have just come in, expect they're in court now.' The tour of the museum began with a mock trial in the grandeur of the Victorian courtroom, before the descent from the dock into the corridors of the gaol below.

'Oh thanks. I was wondering if anyone was coming today,' I replied, actually quite glad that I would have company in the yard before long. I didn't quite feel like being alone just yet. 'I'll wait with you,' I told him.

We went together to the turnkey's lodge with its eerie green glow. The stage lighting made it one of the least frightening places in the whole gaol. When we saw the first glimpse of a visitor approaching the gate along the corridor, I whispered to Mark that I'd see him later. I followed the visitor's route to the women's prison and laundry, where Chloe was waiting, in her brown and white Victorian prison uniform. I helped her hang some authentically dripping laundry on the washing lines, and told her, as she grated pink carbolic soap for the sensory delights of the visitors, how I'd been shut in the storeroom. She laughed at me and I tried to join in with her mirth. When we heard the cell door slam in the corridor above, the certain sign that it would only be moments before Chloe had work to do, I retreated to my yard through the dark passageway, more a tunnel than a corridor, that the visitors would take.

I managed to conduct myself as a strict wardress with little difficulty for the entertainment of the small group. They were a family, and clearly interested in what I had to say. Their questions helped me restore my nerves to what they should be. When they finally cleared the yard, it was time for my lunch break.

❖

When I returned to my station alone after lunch, the effects of the storeroom experience were still with me. The shadows that began to loom across the yard made me shiver. The doorway to the pits and dark cells lurked in my peripheral vision and I did not like to look at it. I didn't walk around the yard, uncomfortable with the idea of passing over the graves of murderers. It was a wholly unusual set of feelings for me, but it didn't matter how often I told myself I was being ridiculous, all my senses were on edge, and I felt some sort of threat from everything I looked at.

I suppose that was how I was sure there was someone in the entrance to the Victorian prison. I had perched on the bottom step of the gallows and was willing the day to pass quickly, when something—a sound, maybe a movement—told me I wasn't alone. My heart thudded, as I looked to the end of the yard. For a person to be in the entrance of the Victorian prison without passing me they would have to have been going the wrong way around the tour. I stood up and waited to see who would materialise. It would be someone who worked here, no doubt.

A long minute passed, and there was no one. Still, I was sure there was someone there, that I was being watched. Maybe the fear I had felt in the storeroom still lingered in my blood, and maybe I was being stupid. However, the feeling was genuine. My skin crawled as if I was in danger and my stomach felt tight. I remembered the pain I had experienced in the storeroom, deep in my abdomen. For a moment I was scared it was returning, but, breathing deeply, I knew this to be different. I was merely working myself up. What was happening to me lately?

From nowhere came the thought of Aly; I'd tell her about this tomorrow. Despite myself, I smiled at the prospect and felt the tension in my chest relax slightly. I'd spent far too long on my own staring at these walls, wandering about over the remains of murders; I was starting to go crazy here, hearing sounds that weren't there, feeling mysterious pains. It was really quite pathetic. The thought of Aly reminded me that outside of here there was something to look forward to. There was Aly, and whatever the confusion of emotions that came with thinking about her, I could not deny the excitement that, for a moment, obliterated all other feelings. I imagined her smiling in her relaxed way, the interest in her eyes, as I told her what had happened to me, how the place I worked in was finally getting to me. I knew at once I wouldn't mind confessing my newfound anxieties to her, however bizarre the reasons for them, and that, in telling her, nothing could feel as bad as it did trapped in my head while I was alone here.

To have someone I knew would be a sympathetic listener was an unexpected comfort. Thinking about the potential conversation with Aly reminded me how few hours there were until I would see her again and made me appreciate just how much I was looking forward to meeting her again. Getting spooked by bizarre happenings at work was insignificant compared to that. Feeling braver as a result, I began to walk down the yard towards the Victorian wing.

To enter what we called the Victorian part of the gaol, which had been built in 1833 and so wasn't actually Victorian at all, you had to pass through an archway in the walls of the exercise yard, then walk a few more feet to reach the doorway to the building itself. It was a tall building, of more modern red brick than the rest of the gaol, and it cast a shadow that made this whole end of the yard damp and green with moss.

I reached the archway, my heart still hammering, but maybe inclined to laugh at myself. Aly would laugh at me too, in that deep, throaty laugh of hers. There'd be no one there; if there had been, they'd have showed themselves by now. Or maybe Bill had come down to carry out some small duty and then gone back the way he'd come. There were endless possibilities. This tense feeling as I went through the archway was pointless.

A figure moved to my right. I almost jumped out of my skin, unable to prevent a strangled sound of frightened surprise. Then I recognised him.

'What the hell do you think you are fucking doing?' I demanded, in a raised voice.

Owen looked back at me, apologetic. 'I'm sorry; I didn't mean to scare you,' he said, trying a small smile. I did not smile back. Now I was over my initial shock, questions were circulating in my mind. How long had he been here? What did he want? Why was he creeping around in the shadows? What was I going to say about the other night?

'How long have you been here?' I went for first.

'I was just coming through to talk to you,' he said. He was lying. I didn't know it from his face, but I was certain he'd been there longer. I'd sensed it. Besides, if he'd been walking through, he wouldn't have been behind the wall to my right when I came looking.

'Have you been watching me?' I said, shuddering to even think he might have been.

'No,' he replied evenly. 'I wanted to come and talk to you.' I would talk to him. Just not yet, there were more questions before I would even feel comfortable standing near him.

'Why did you come this way? Why not wait upstairs for me?' I demanded, my manner not softening.

'I wanted to catch you where no one was listening,' he said, and I ignored the sinister connotations of his words. He was creepy, yes, but not that creepy. I was overreacting. I took a deep breath.

'But how did you get in?' I asked, wondering if he really had paid the admission fee. 'And how did you know the way?'

'I was upstairs, wondering just that, when that family came out. I asked them if they'd seen you, and they said yes. So I went through the door they came out of, and followed the signs backwards until I got here.' He shrugged as though it was perfectly acceptable.

'It would have been better if you'd waited upstairs,' was all I said. It wasn't in me to be cruel. 'What did you want to talk about?'

'What do you think?' he replied with some bitterness. I suppose that was fair.

'Well, I can guess,' I said. 'Look, I'm sorry, but it just wasn't going to work, was it?'

'I thought it was working better than you, obviously.' He looked hurt.

'I know. And to be honest, you came on a bit heavy for a first date.' I had to be brutal; this was no time for tact. I wanted him to get the message this time.

'Heavy?' he asked. He seemed to have no understanding of the concept.

'Yeah, heavy,' I confirmed. 'You know what I mean.'

'Not really. Look, Jen, I like you. Is that a crime?'

'Yes! Or no, but it is when you seem so sure so soon...' I felt like a hypocrite. I'd probably spent less time in Aly's company. But then, I was still floundering in some confusion about my feelings. I certainly wasn't inflicting unwelcome declarations of them on her.

'But what if I am sure?' he protested.

'You can't be!' I exclaimed, exasperated. His Adam's apple bobbed as he swallowed.

'I've seen you before, Jen,' he said.

What the hell was that supposed to mean? If he wanted to put me at my ease, that was not the thing to say. Unconsciously, I took a step back from him. 'What do you mean?' I asked, not sure I wanted to know.

'I've been to the museum once before. I took the tour. About a fortnight ago. You told me you were going to hang me.'

I was speechless. He hadn't looked remotely familiar to me. But then I must see hundreds of people every week, why should I remember one of them in particular? What I was more concerned with now was why the fuck he hadn't mentioned this before.

'Why didn't you tell me?' I demanded.

'I suppose I was shy about it,' he replied.

'About what?' I asked.

'Well, when I saw you here, in your yard, in your costume, I mean, I really liked you. I thought you were really sexy.'

It would have been hard to be more disturbed by his words than I was then. 'You liked my character you mean?' I enquired, trying to understand him and not wanting to at the same time.

'No. Well, yes, but it was you really. I could see how interested you were in history. Not many people are that interested. And I liked the way you looked.' His eyes flickered down over my costume even as he said it. I shifted uncomfortably on my feet.

'You should have told me,' I said. Too fucking right. If he'd mentioned this before, there'd have been no chance I'd have gone for a drink with him.

'I didn't want you to leap to the wrong conclusions about me.' He shrugged.

'Well, now I'm leaping to different ones,' I said. This was just too much. 'Will you just leave please? I'm sorry I walked out on you, it was rude of me. I just didn't know what else to do. I'm flattered that you like me, and maybe we can be friends. But right now, I want you to leave.' I said it with some vehemence, almost taking myself by surprise.

'Maybe we could try again? I could show you I'm different to how you think?' he suggested, looking hopeful. 'We have so much in common.'

'We may do. But I'm not interested,' I said. Could I be more frank about it? Still he stood there looking at me. Time to strike the final blow. I'd not considered it before, but as he gazed at me, I realised it had to be done. 'And anyway, I've met someone else I *am* interested in.'

His face turned red. I wondered if he was going to shout. He looked more angry than wounded, and instantly I wished I could retract my last statement.

'I see,' he said quietly. His eyes seemed to look right through me. 'Who is he?'

I wasn't going to put him straight about that. Nor was I likely to even hint at who I might be interested in. 'It isn't any of your business,' I told him, hostile to the idea that he had even asked.

'I see,' he said again. Still, his face spoke of repressed anger more than any other emotion. He made me nervous, as though he might explode at any moment. 'Then I'll leave you alone.' His eyes lingered on mine for a moment, then he turned and went back into the Victorian prison. I retreated across the yard, in the opposite direction to him. He'd left me unsettled. I hoped I'd seen the last of him. Maybe it was the experience of the storeroom earlier, perhaps it was that last look he'd given me, maybe it was misplaced instinct, but somehow I knew I'd see him again. And that notion worried me in a way I couldn't justify even to myself.

I ate take-away pizza for my dinner that evening and immersed myself in music until I fell asleep on the sofa. I finally crawled into bed at about two in the morning, thoroughly glad the next day was my day off. I was looking forward to seeing Aly too. I made the admission to myself with no reservations, a warm glow suffusing me as I drifted back to sleep.

I tried not to think during the time I spent getting ready and travelling on the bus to meet her, the next morning. When I tried to consider my feelings, they swirled around and around in my head and twisted themselves into contorted notions. Yes, the maybe was there again, the haunting question, floating with all the other ideas. But I knew I needed to see her. That was simple enough. Let everything else wait until then.

She was waiting at the bus stop when my bus pulled in with a dramatic hissing of brakes. She waved as it approached, to make sure, I assume, that I saw her and actually got off the bus. I noticed some of the other passengers looking at her, and it gave me an odd thrill to think she was waiting for me.

I felt shy again, walking towards her as she waited. She wore blue jeans today, a studded black leather belt, and a black shirt open over a white T-shirt. Even the loose shirt did not disguise her figure entirely, and the fierceness with which my body responded to the sight of her caught me by surprise. A touch of make-up at her eyes again. For me? I wondered, a smile of excitement twitching at my lips. I went over my appearance again in my mind: black jeans, sleeveless jersey top with an embroidered slash neckline. It had an ethnic feel about it that I liked but I'd not wanted to seem like I'd made an effort. Yes, I'd done my make-up too. So I'd made an effort. I just didn't want her to know it.

'Hi,' I said, smiling at her.

'Hello.' She grinned back. There was a new tension between us, but I had expected it to be there and it didn't frighten me. I only hoped to keep my composure and not reveal the turbulent emotions I had no chance of suppressing.

'I made it,' I said, meeting her gaze for the first time, catching my breath as her eyes looked directly into mine.

'Not too hard, was it?' She seemed to mean far more than simply following the directions to the correct bus stop and I was sure both of us were aware of the implication in her question.

'No, not since it was the same bus,' I said simply. 'So, where are we going for lunch?'

'Hungry?'

'Yes, actually.' I was also keen for us to move on from the greeting, the standing facing each other on the pavement, wondering what to say next.

We walked silently awhile, down what was a largely residential street, with leafy beech trees at intervals along the pavement. Both of us were thinking, but the silence was companionable enough, despite the knots my guts were tying themselves into.

'Good few days?' she asked eventually.

'Eventful, actually,' I told her, 'especially yesterday. *He* came back for a start.' I saw her glance across at me for a moment.

'The one from the pub?' she asked. Did she sound slightly anxious herself? I wondered what it was that could have made that slight strain intrude into her normally laid-back tone. Concern for me? Maybe more than concern for me? I was conscious that I liked the idea. It was easy, I found, not to be so confused when I was by her side.

'Yes, and I sent him on his way. I'll tell you the whole story later,' I said, hoping she was reassured. She was quiet for a few moments as we walked.

'You know, you're going to have to suggest where we go next time,' she said at last.

'Yeah, sorry,' I agreed, pleased to think there would be a next time. I'd not thought much beyond today. It seemed oddly decisive, as though everything depended on the next few hours.

'Oh, I don't mind,' she said, 'just I'm sure there're places you'd prefer.'

'I'm happy either way,' I assured her. I enjoyed seeing the places she liked, learning something about her through them.

'Well, it's just here,' she said, as we came to a shopfront. I saw it was a delicatessen sandwich bar, and I looked at the name above the door.

'A French café and an Italian sandwich place?' I asked her, raising my eyebrows. 'You're very Continental.'

'I just like places that are a bit different,' she explained. 'I guess I got used to the variety in London while I was there.'

Unintentionally reminding me of her worldliness compared with my own lack of it made her vaguely intimidating to me again. I smiled past it. 'Looks good,' I said.

Inside, there was a long counter, with a glass front, and all manner of sandwich fillings and salad, all very fresh and appetising, set out to choose from. There was a delicious scent of garlic and herbs. Aly greeted the small dark man behind the counter as though she came in here often.

'Usual?' he asked her.

'Of course,' she replied.

'What's the usual?' I whispered to her, bewildered myself by the range on offer.

'Are you ready?' she asked, eyes laughing. 'It's an olive and rosemary focaccia, with smoked soft cheese, sliced tomato, basil, garlic mayonnaise, and parmesan slivers.' She looked at my expression. 'It took me some time to perfect the combination,' she confided. 'To begin with, I just went for tomato and mozzarella on ciabatta, with a drizzle of mayo.'

I watched as the man gathered up the ingredients to make her sandwich. He made it remarkably quickly, and handed her a plate. I wondered how on earth she was going to eat such a mountain, then felt flustered as he asked me for my order. 'Er,' I hesitated, 'I think I'll try the herb focaccia, with mozzarella, tomato, basil, and garlic mayonnaise, please,' I managed.

'Nice choice,' Aly said by my shoulder. I smiled and relaxed, finally.

Aly insisted on paying for lunch, since she'd invited me, she said. We took our sandwiches to one of the four round red-and-white gingham-covered tables set up in the small space in front of the counter. I was glad the café owner disappeared into the back of the building somewhere as we ate, since it was quiet in the café and everything I said and every movement I made left me feeling conspicuous while he was present.

'How the hell are you going to eat that?' I asked her as we settled.

'Just watch and learn,' she retorted. I did watch, as she crushed the bread between her fingers. A small amount of mayonnaise oozed from the side, but she merely turned the sandwich to eat that section first. How she opened her mouth wide enough to take a bite was a mystery to me, but somehow she managed, and then put the sandwich down, her mouth full and mayonnaise at its corners. I laughed at her, more at ease than at any other time in her company, and turned my attention to my more delicate sandwich.

The necessity of chewing the focaccia bread and managing the dribbles of delicious garlic mayonnaise kept us pretty much silent as we ate. Though I was forced to concentrate on my food, I couldn't help glancing up at her continually, looking away just when there was any danger of her eyes meeting mine. She seemed to make the air vibrate with invisible waves, I was so acutely aware of her presence across the short distance of the small table. When we'd both finished, and wiped at our mouths with the paper napkins, Aly took our plates to the counter. She waited there a moment, as I watched, apparently considering something, and then she came back to the table.

'You know,' she began, her eyes unexpectedly animated and her manner less relaxed than previously, 'I was going to order coffee. But then I thought, well, my place is only ten minutes' walk from here. Do you want to get coffee there?'

'Oh, the old coffee cliché?' I joked, before realising what I was implying and turning red, a wave of embarrassed heat sweeping through me.

'I mean, if you don't want to, it's fine,' she added hastily, seeing my colour.

'No. I mean, it sounds good to me. I'd like to see your place,' I said. My heart beat a little faster at the thought, and my stomach flip-flopped once or twice. But I did want to. The protective wall of my confused emotions seemed to have disappeared. I rose on slightly shaky legs and followed her into the street.

CHAPTER TEN

2008

She had actually overestimated how far her home was from the café. It took barely five minutes of fairly rapid walking for us to arrive there. It was just as well, for as we walked, too quickly for much conversation, the sky turned heavy, promising a summer shower would soon fall. Her house was down a cul-de-sac of late-Victorian terraces. It was at the very far end, red brick and stern, though neat, with a pot of deep pink petunias in the small front yard. I hung back near the red-painted front gate as she took out her key and unlocked the front door. The click of the key in the lock sounded very loud. Everything met my senses more loudly or with a greater intensity than it should have done, as my legs weakened at the thought of actually being in her home. Alone with her.

'Come in then,' she said, leading the way, 'before it rains. Don't expect it to be very tidy though,' she added flippantly over her shoulder.

The front door opened directly into the living room of the house. I pushed it closed behind me and looked around with interest. I couldn't have imagined what her house would be like, but I wasn't sure this was it.

'It's rented, by the way,' she informed me as she saw my gaze travelling around the room, 'so please don't think magnolia walls and beige carpets are really my thing. I'm not allowed to decorate.'

'I wish someone would paint the walls of my flat,' I returned, glad she cared about the impression her home presented to me. 'Any colour would be good. Landlord couldn't care less though.' I paid less attention to the décor, and looked instead at the elements in the room which seemed more to reflect her personality. A large, comfortable sofa, in crimson, with a navy fleece throw over one side; a tall bookcase, stuffed with books and bending magazines, in no apparent order; a stereo with a haphazard scatter of CDs surrounding it. The coffee table was of dark wood, with a plain clear glass vase filled with red tulips, their fleshy pale green stems left long, allowing them to droop gracefully, alluringly. There was a photographic journal resting near it, and a book with a creased spine open, face down. On one of the walls was a framed Impressionist print—my artistic knowledge was not good enough to tell me by which artist. A lingering scent of sandalwood incense pervaded the room.

Above the pine fireplace, the top of which was loaded with candles of varying colours and heights and a statue of a graceful black cat arching its back, was a very large photograph, vivid against its black background and dark oak frame. My gaze was drawn irresistibly to it: a broken string of pearls in the foreground, becoming blurred towards the back of the perspective, much larger than life; one or two crimson rose petals, with drops of water glistening on them, resting on the same white surface as the pearls, casting dark shadows; and behind them all, slightly out of focus, a red apple, with a bite taken out of it, a trickle of juice running from the white wound in its skin. An old-fashioned metal key, brown and rusted with age, rested close to the apple. It was such a simple picture, and yet so sensual, vaguely disturbing.

'Did you take that?' I asked turning to her, the impression it had made on me evident in my voice.

'Yes,' she said, and I saw the pride in her smile.

'It's beautiful,' I breathed. It was a word I rarely used, but nothing else would do it justice.

'I'm glad you like it,' she said softly, her eyes shining.

'What does it mean?' I asked, tearing my gaze from her face and back to the photograph, wondering if it could give me some further insight into her personality.

'What do you think it means?' she asked, coming to stand a little closer to me and regarding the picture with me, her head tilted to one side, as if looking at it for the first time, as I was.

'I don't know,' I replied, worried that I wouldn't do the intrinsic meaning of her photograph any justice.

'Tell me what it makes you think about,' she prompted.

'Well, the apple makes me think of Eve and the forbidden fruit, you know…' I said tentatively. 'Or Snow White and the poisoned apple. But it's blurred, so maybe the meaning isn't certain.'

I looked nervously at her and found her smiling at me, an expression of pleasure on her face. 'Go on,' she said.

'I don't know…' I paused to consider. 'The rose petals and the pearls make me think of love and romance, and, well, femininity, but the pearls are broken and the petals look like they've got tears on them. They're blood red, which could be frightening or just romantic. And I'm not sure if the key is a bad thing, in that it could lock something away, or a good thing because it represents freedom…'

I turned to her again. She wasn't looking at her photograph at all now, only at me, her expression reflective. 'How did I do?' I asked with a nervous laugh.

'Perfectly,' she said softly before seeming to collect herself. 'I mean, you picked up on the whole point, things can always have more than one meaning. Something can be good and bad. Eve ate the apple and it gave her knowledge, an understanding of the truth even if she was expelled from Eden for it. Snow White found true love through being poisoned. A key can lock or unlock something.'

'So nothing is certain?'

'Something like that. Or more like things appear differently, depending on the perspective you're looking at them from. I keep this photo in here because I like to ask people what they see in it. Some people think it's entirely positive. Other people feel sort of threatened by it, like it's something sinister. One of my friends thinks it's about nothing but sex,' she laughed easily, 'which is exactly what I would expect of her.'

I smiled and found myself wondering just how many friends she had, and what they would think of me. I expected to meet them, at some point, I realised then.

'You're one of the only people who saw the double meaning in it,' she said. 'You saw what my intention was.'

'Oh sorry,' I said, 'I should have just gone with my first impressions, I guess.'

'Don't be sorry,' she replied. 'I like that you saw right through to what I was trying to achieve. You didn't just see the photo, you saw me too.'

Her expression became more serious and when our eyes locked the intensity was too much and I turned quickly back to the photograph, my throat tight, and unsure what to say anyway. I wouldn't have trusted any words at that moment.

'I can show you more of my photos later, if you want.' Her tone was dismissive, but I knew she was keener than that.

'That'd be fantastic,' I replied as casually as I could manage. I wasn't really seeing the photograph at all now, though I still stared at it. I was only aware of her, feeling her proximity as she stood close to me.

'But now, coffee?' she asked, more matter of fact than I felt, moving away from me slightly.

'Er, yes, please,' I said, pulling my gaze away from the photograph but not quite able to look at her.

'Milk and sugar?'

'Just milk, thanks.'

'You can come through, or take a seat here, up to you,' she told me. Not wanting to be apart from her, and not trusting my thoughts if I waited for her alone, I followed her through the doorway to her kitchen, where a window faced her small back garden, and there was a wooden door to access it. The house was really quite tiny, but the kitchen, with its pine units, seemed almost spacious.

I sat at the round table in the middle and watched as she filled the kettle and reached into a cupboard to find two mugs. As she stretched up, her shirt and tee rose with her arms, and I glimpsed the flesh of her back, smooth and quite pale. I looked away, uncomfortably aware that my hands were growing hot. I found a heady feeling of suspense pressing on me, as the silence between us grew. Even before I'd realised it, my eyes were back on her. I watched the movement of her fingers as she unscrewed the lid of the coffee jar and spooned coffee into the mugs. She paused and pulled at her loose shirt sleeves, revealing the skin of her forearms and that familiar cluster of bangles which jangled with every movement. I looked to her other unadorned wrist, noticing she wore no wristwatch, and was oddly fascinated for a moment by the structure of the bones where they were visible beneath the slightly tanned skin. My gaze slid over her hand to her fingers as she secured the lid of the coffee. The veins in the back of her hand were blue and close to the surface, as if she was warm and her body attempting to cool itself. Those hands looked so strong, so capable. I pulled my focus away from her to the surface of the table and drew a deep breath, trying to dispel feelings that were quite clearly out of all proportion. But they wouldn't be banished, and I couldn't help but look at her again as, with a rattle of bracelets, she reached up and pushed at a stray hair.

My eyes lingered on the back of her neck, watching the slight rise and fall of her square shoulders with her breathing, which struck me as a little laboured. She did not turn to face me even when she had finished with the coffee cups, and I could not help but think she was hiding her expression from me, conscious that I was watching her. I knew, for both our sakes, I should break the silence between us, which by now felt as though it had stretched eternally, but I could think of nothing to say. She leaned on the kitchen counter; her stance appeared awkward, different from her usual relaxed pose. She drummed her fingers as though impatient, as the kettle began to hiss and gurgle, the water approaching boiling point.

She turned abruptly and I felt myself blush, as though she had caught me in the act of doing something illicit. I was almost frightened of what she might say. She looked at me and smiled slightly. I noticed her cheeks were coloured too, and her gaze was less direct than I had become used to.

'You said just milk, right?' she said, as though it was an effort to say anything at all.

'Yes,' I replied. The tension between us was undeniable, and in our inability to say more than these simple phrases we both acknowledged it. She looked away from me and crossed the kitchen to fetch the milk from the fridge. She did not look at me again as she turned back to the empty mugs. Blue jeans looked damn good on her, I reflected. She adjusted her shirt sleeves again, as though she was uncomfortable, as the kettle boiled in a cloud of steam.

To ease the tension that threatened to suffocate me, I gripped my hot hands together and forced myself to look around me, away from her. Behind me was a door which clearly led to the stairway. Beside it hung another photograph, this time simply a close-up of an eye, the iris deep brown, with an indistinct reflection at the centre of it, which seemed to be something and yet nothing at all. It had a similar unnerving quality to the other photograph. I wondered if all of her photographs had that same indefinite edge to them. It was fitting, I decided, since Aly herself defied any attempts at precise definition.

I was contemplating this when suddenly she was beside me and I almost jumped to find her so close. She put a mug of steaming coffee on the table in front of me. I thanked her in a barely audible murmur, as she placed her own beside it, and flicked on the radio quietly.

'You don't mind do you?' she asked. 'I always have the radio on when I'm in the kitchen.' In her words I sensed a renewed effort to dispel the tension that had arisen between us, and, hearing that casual tone I had become accustomed to, I found I was able to turn my attention back to her without too much difficulty.

'No. I like to have music all the time too,' I assured her, forcing myself to speak more than one or two words and, in doing so, growing more relaxed myself. I was only sharing a cup of coffee with her in her kitchen after all. For God's sake, what was wrong with me?

She came to sit opposite me and wrapped her fingers loosely around her mug of black coffee. 'So, why was yesterday eventful then?' she asked.

'Long story,' I answered, rolling my eyes.

'The creepy guy came back?'

'Yes, he did.' I remembered the way she had tensed at that information earlier and studied her reaction for any sign of tightening, resolving to explain right away that I had no interest in Owen whatsoever, if she appeared dubious at all. However, she was merely looking back at me, waiting for an explanation, her expression casually interested. 'But that wasn't the first thing that happened,' I said, deciding to start the story from the beginning and thus make Owen a less significant part of it. I told her about the incident in the storeroom, even including how frightened I had been, and the mysterious pain I'd felt. 'You know,' I said, as I concluded the tale, 'if what we were saying before is right, and time is, well, layered on top of itself, then I'd say someone, in some time, is very unhappy.' I'd pondered this earlier, and dismissed it as illogical rubbish. Spurred on by her apparent interest, I wondered what Aly thought about it.

'That's not really surprising, since you're in a prison,' she reflected.

Then she grinned. 'Hey, maybe you're psychic or something, and you can sense these things, you know like the guy on telly.'

I laughed at the suggestion. 'I think it's all in my imagination, personally,' I returned, 'though, I must admit, I wasn't so sure then.'

'Perhaps someone's trying to tell you something from across the centuries,' she suggested lightly.

'Yeah, I'd consider it, but what? That they're in pain? To be frightened of something?'

'You'd think it'd be clearer, wouldn't you? If they were going to make all that effort,' she agreed. 'You'll have to see if anything else strange happens.'

'I'll keep you posted.' I laughed and, watching her reaction, went on. 'But I tell you what, I was on edge enough from that, really jumpy, I really didn't need a visit from Mr Creepy.' She looked more interested in what I said now. I wondered what she was thinking, what signs she was searching for. It struck me suddenly that she had insecurities of her own, and my uncertainty thus far had done little to soothe them. I wanted her to understand that, when I was with her, my doubts disappeared, but I had no idea how to voice it.

'Did you bump into him in the library again?' she asked.

'No. Believe it or not, I caught him sneaking around right down in my part of the museum.' I related the whole story to her, from how I'd sensed he was there, through the details of our conversation, to his disturbing parting gaze. I only left out the fact that I had told him I was interested in someone else, since that was far too frank an admission of my feelings towards her than I was ready to make in the middle of a conversation about something else entirely.

'He's more than creepy,' she concluded as I finished. 'Do you think he'll be back?'

'I really hope not,' I said emphatically. 'I mean, I'm sure I'm being too sensitive, but there was something not quite right about him, you know? And when he said he liked me in my costume, it made my skin crawl.'

'You think he got the message?' she asked.

'Seemed to. He looked pretty upset about it.' I shrugged. She was taking the whole thing rather seriously, when I just wanted to forget about him. 'Maybe he's a reasonable guy after all,' I added, hoping to ease the tone of the conversation slightly, 'just…misguided.'

She laughed gently, a mellow sound deep in her throat that my whole being responded to. Then she raised her coffee cup. 'Here's to escaping from misguided creeps!' I lifted my own mug and clanked it gently against hers. Our eyes met and stayed fixed for a moment longer than was comfortable.

'Jen?' she asked, placing her mug back onto the table, a level of emotion in her tone that was new to me.

'Yes?' I said in return, lowering my own mug, my eyes following it, wanting to look anywhere but at her. Slowly, she reached out a hand and touched it to mine, where it rested on the table. Again, her touch burned my skin but this time I did not move away. Her fingers moved against mine. I let them, heat pulsing from the place she touched and through my entire body. I felt sick and ecstatic in one moment. My breath quickening, I looked across at her, felt the draw of her dark eyes, saw the pink of her lips. There was a question she did not quite dare speak in her face, in her touch. The surge inside me was too powerful and something changed in an instant. I felt the release, an almost painful relief that made me dizzy for a moment.

'Oh God,' I said, pulling my hand away from hers and holding both of my palms to my burning cheeks. She was quiet, watching me. 'I don't know what to think anymore,' I said, voicing in one sentence the tension of six years, or longer. 'You make me feel like this,' I said, accusingly. Tears welled in my eyes. 'And I don't know what to do with it. I've always just ignored it, and now you're sitting there and I can't. I want it to go away, but I don't really.' My voice cracked and a tear fell, but I couldn't stop the flow of words, of emotions, I wanted to pour them into her, let her deal with them for me.

'I know I was wrong, but I'd got used to being wrong. Until I met you. It's only been a few days, not even a week, which is stupid, how can I know? I hardly know you! But I feel like something's changed in me. And I want you'—I paused, shocked by the frankness of my admission, before going on—'and I don't know how to deal with it. I've never felt quite like this before and I want it to be a secret again. But I can't make it go away. I've never felt so fucking uncertain about anything and so sure about it at the same time.'

She listened to me patiently through this. Now she reached for my hands and took them both in hers. This time, they did not burn me; their warmth was soothing. 'Jen,' she breathed, 'it's not easy. Believe me or not, I know what you're feeling.' She stroked my fingers with hers and my skin tingled, the sensation spreading along my arms. 'And, if you ask me, you're more certain than you think you are. But it can take time. You have to come to terms with it.' Her voice was soft, almost a whisper. I felt less like she was advising, more like she was confiding. She gripped my hands more tightly. 'But it doesn't have to be so complicated,' she said, 'if you don't want it to be.'

Her words were alluring in the gentlest sense. Her long lashes were black against her cheek as she closed her eyes for a moment, as if a thought had crossed her mind that she was uncertain whether to share with me or not. She raised her gaze to me and smiled. I tried to return the smile, though my lips trembled. Now she took one of my hands and enclosed it, warm in both of hers, and brought it up to her mouth. I was paralysed, my eyes fixed to her face, barely daring to breathe as she kissed the tips of my fingers with the slightest contact of her lips. I felt her breath against my skin and I shuddered. She must have felt it through my arm. Then she released my hand and I missed the warmth of her touch instantly. I ached for her in all of my body. But the ruins of the walls that had held me back so long were still there, cold and hard inside me, just enough to stumble over. I looked past her and out of the window.

'It's raining,' I said unevenly. The drops were large against the pane. She turned to look.

'So it is,' she replied. A moment's pause, then—to my surprise— she stood up and shrugged her way out of her shirt. My gaze followed the angles of her shoulders, the movements of the muscles in her arms. Her arms were more tanned than the skin that stretched smoothly over the hollows of her collarbones and the base of her throat. She wasn't wearing a bra and I saw the shadows of dark nipples beneath the white fabric of her top. It had risen a little way above the waistband of her jeans and that studded belt, revealing the slightest hint of the pale skin of her hips and toned stomach. I forced my eyes back to her face and saw her eyes shining. I watched, hypnotised and curious, as she opened the back door and looked out at the rain. She took two or three steps outside, face turned upwards to the sky. The heavy drops made darker blotches on her clothes, ruffled her hair, streaked silver over her bare skin. She stretched out her arms and I was transfixed by the movement of every muscle and tendon beneath her skin as she did so, by the contrast between the pale skin on the inside of her forearms and the more tanned skin outside. I watched her, sitting motionless in my chair, not questioning the eccentricity of her actions, simply captivated by her.

She turned her face to me. The streaks of make-up over her cheeks gave her a vulnerability I had not seen in her before. 'I love summer rain,' she said, by way of explanation, laughter in her voice. 'Come on, Jen.' She held her hand out to me, taking a step back towards the door. I laughed. It was impossible not to be drawn towards her. I stood up and I went to her. I took her damp hand and stepped outside. I felt the first few drops of rain, chill despite the heat of the day, as a shock on my hot skin. Her hand still gripped in mine, I turned my face upwards and closed my eyes. And the rain began to work a trick on me. Had she expected it? The heavy drops dissolved something in me, the traces of the walls that had constrained me simply melted away. Water trickled over my face, down my neck, soaked my clothes, and I wanted it to drench me, saturate me, transform me.

I opened my eyes and looked at Aly. She was watching me, the rain dripping from the short ends of her hair. She could have been crying, the water streaming down her face. Her skin was glistening all over now, her T-shirt clinging to her form. Her hand was still hot in mine. As we gazed, dripping, at each other, the radio in the kitchen switched to a rock ballad. A woman's voice, haunting and full, sang of a love to ease away all of the pain. Aly reached out her other hand to me and grinned with serious eyes. As I put my hand in hers, she drew me towards her, until our bodies were pressed close, and she moved with me to the rhythm of the song. Her arms surrounded me; I felt her hands, pressing the wet cloth to my back. Tentatively, I put my hands on her, one on the saturated tee, the other on her slippery skin. Her eyes were close now; too close almost, it made me dizzy to look at them. I could feel her breath on my wet skin, the movement of her ribcage beneath my hands. We moved slowly with the song, the rain drenching us steadily, but the warmth between us growing. Her hands stroked gently over my back, as she pulled me even closer.

'Are you afraid?' she whispered after what felt like an eternity of rain, and music, and her body against mine.

'No,' I murmured back. The word *maybe* no longer existed for me.

When her lips pressed against mine first, it was a shadow of a kiss. She pulled away, raised a hand to my cheek and caressed it. I leaned towards her, as she moved her mouth to me again, and I returned her kiss. Rainwater trickled around our joined lips, into our mouths, was cold mingling with the heat of her breath, her tongue. I ran my hand over the curve of her spine, into her wet hair, and pressed myself to her, thirsty for her, with a thirst that all the rain that fell around us would not quench.

The song had ended and the announcer's voice was droning in the background when she drew gently away from me. 'Let's go inside,' she said.

Aly's bedroom had the same magnolia walls as her living room, but with the red curtains drawn against the daylight, the room was bathed in a crimson glow. The door clicked closed behind us, and a sickening tension rose in my throat. It eased as she brought her lips to mine again, and now moved her kisses over my cheek and onto my throat and my whole body responded to her. A longing for her hands and her lips began in every cell, with no conscious trigger from my brain at all. I couldn't think; I was dazed with my need for her.

As we kissed, hands caressing skin which was now drying, sticky and growing hot again, my sodden clothes felt heavy and cold against me, hers a wet barrier stopping me from touching her. Driven to confidence by the urge to put my hands on that concealed, pale skin, it was me who first hooked my fingers under the hem of her T-shirt, attempting to remove it for her. She did it herself in the end, pulling it over her head in one easy action. Her small, achingly perfect breasts were pink from the contact with her wet clothes, her nipples dark and hard. Desperate to touch her, I raised my hands, then hesitated. She took my wrists, so gently, and pressed my hands to her chest and I caressed her, her flesh soft beneath my fingers. If my caresses were faltering, it was from the newness of it, for I felt not the slightest reluctance.

Following her lead, I removed my top next, feeling her eyes on my skin as I revealed it to the cool air of the room. Then I stood very still, eyes closed, as she wrapped her arms around me and unfastened my bra. I wriggled out of the straps and heard it drop to the floor. Oddly, it was not my breasts that felt exposed, even as she pressed herself to me and I felt them crushed against her own, but my back, where her hands now caressed the length of my spine. I opened my eyes again, and reached for her mouth with mine.

It was while she kissed me, with a growing passion, that her hands worked on the fastening of my jeans and loosened them, and she slid her hands over my hips as far as the band of my underwear. I put my hands onto hers, urging her to pull my jeans lower. She grasped the waistband and pulled them urgently down my legs, until I stepped out of them. She did not stand back and look at me; she pulled me close and explored my newly exposed skin with her fingertips, until finally her hands were easing my underwear lower.

Naked though I was, I had never been less self-conscious. My whole body was burning for her; even her slightest touch sent shivers over the entire surface of my skin. Now her gaze did drop, for a lingering moment, looking at me, at my body. I gazed into her eyes as they came back to mine, and I recognised her desire as my own reflected.

My hands were at her waist now, but she pushed me back and unfastened her belt herself. I watched, fascinated how such a simple action captivated me. The ends of the belt hung loose and she undid her jeans. Her glance up at my face had something mischievous in its lasciviousness, as she pulled her jeans, and her underwear with them, down her legs and stepped out of them.

I drew a deep breath and looked at her unashamedly. She seemed to invite it. Her legs were strong and slender, her hip bones prominent to the sides of her flat stomach. She had a small black tattoo near her left hip, a word in ornate lettering that I couldn't read quickly enough, and a star, surrounded by tendril swirls. I blushed as my gaze travelled from her breasts to the secret triangle of dark hair at the meeting of her thighs.

She was close to me again, all of her soft skin pressed to mine, and I felt I was melting into her. She urged me towards the bed with her hands on my shoulders and we dropped onto it together, her above me. Her mouth was on my throat again, and then her breath hot on my breasts, her tongue teasing. I gasped. She raised her head and smiled. 'There's more yet,' she whispered. I could only return the smile through a haze of arousal. Her hand touched the inside of my thigh, very high, as her mouth caressed my breast once more. I squirmed beneath her, but her hand was deliciously insistent as it rose higher, and finally I was helpless under her touch as her fingers slid into the place I most wanted to be touched by her.

I put my hands on her back, felt her becoming damp with sweat. Her hand worked against me as she kissed me on the mouth again, her tongue pushing between my lips as her fingers mirrored that action lower on my body. My moan of desire seemed to come from the deepest part of my being. I ran my fingers over the soft shaved hair at the nape of her neck and around to her face, stroking her smooth cheek, feeling the movement of her jaw as she kissed me.

She altered her position, her mouth leaving mine, as she took my wrist in a rather firm grip and pulled my hand lower, pressing it between her taut thighs. I felt the curls of hair, the moist heat very close to my fingers, as she released my wrist, encouraging but not forcing. I eased my fingers forward and felt her wetness. The pressure of her own hand on me became more rhythmical, as I, trembling with desire by now, finally allowed my fingers to explore her. I heard her catch her breath and, moving my hand again, saw her eyes grow a little wider. That slight widening of her pupils, caused by the movement of my hand against her satin wetness, was the most erotic thing I'd ever seen. Dizzily, I reached my head up to kiss her again.

I was lost in her deep kisses, my inexperienced hand doing the best it could, as she circled her hips to help my fingers and in so doing crushed her body to mine with every movement, her own hand moving in time with her hips and making me giddy with pleasure. With my free hand I caressed her back, her perfect buttocks, even her upper arms, wanting to touch every part of her. There was nothing but her warmth crushing me, her hand sending waves of pleasure throughout my body, her ever hardening kisses and her hot skin, her slippery flesh, beneath my fingers.

I was intoxicated by her, as I felt the pressure building between my thighs. I groaned deeply against her mouth, and she understood my need, pressing harder with her fingers just where I desired that touch most. My climax burst suddenly, surprising me with its intensity. I grasped at her back as my body gripped her hand, and I cried loudly with the release, not closing my eyes as I usually did, but keeping them locked to hers. I wanted her to see how powerfully she had affected me, as she broke off the kiss and looked back at me.

'Oh, Jen...you're beautiful...' she panted, her words ragged, eyes on my face. She bucked her hips towards me and I watched her expression, in sheer awe, as I felt her whole body shuddering against mine.

Afterwards, we lay under the covers of her bed, warm and relaxed. Her arm was around me, my head rested on the soft skin of her chest. I didn't experience a sudden sting of regret, as I had always thought I might do. I wasn't left unsatisfied. Far from it. My heart was ready to burst out of the confines of my chest with the excitement of being free at last. My whole body still glowed with the lingering pleasure. I smiled to myself.

'What?' she enquired softly. I hadn't been conscious she was watching me.

'Nothing,' I replied, since there was simply no way to voice what I was feeling.

'Are you happy?' she asked then.

I turned my face to her properly, so she could be sure of my honesty, 'Absolutely,' I replied.

'And does that surprise you?' I was amazed how well she had read me. Or maybe she hadn't read me at all, perhaps she simply remembered.

'Yes, I guess,' I told her honestly, sure of her understanding, 'but I'm glad.'

'Me too,' she smiled. There were remnant smudges of her eye make-up on her face, her cheeks were still flushed pink from her climax. The tips of the hair that framed her face were still damp and spiky. I leaned towards her and kissed her lightly on the lips. The erotic haze had faded, but still the softness of her mouth under my kiss caused a hot surge somewhere deep inside me.

I rolled onto my back, putting my head on the cool cotton of the pillow, and looked at the ceiling. She did the same, though we kept our hands entwined. The duvet was soft and warm against my skin, the bed comfortable beneath me. Her bed. It made me smile to myself again.

A thought came to me then. 'Aly?' I said, my smile in my tone.

'Yes, Jen?'

'Are you going to tell me your full name now?' She rolled over onto her stomach and grinned down at me.

'If I do, I might have to kill you,' she told me.

'I'm prepared to risk it,' I retorted.

'What do you think it is?'

'I've not really thought about it,' I replied. 'Though I'd expect Alexandra. Or Alison?'

'Nothing so plain,' she said, rolling her eyes. 'All right, brace yourself. It's Alethea.'

'Alethea?' I repeated. 'I've never heard that before. But I like it,' I added.

'You don't have to say that,' she grinned.

'Honestly. It's pretty.'

'Pretty? Suits me down to the ground then,' she said with mild sarcasm. 'But I do like its meaning.'

'Oh? What does it mean?'

'Truth,' she said simply, 'in Greek, that is. You know, like you can be called Faith or Hope or Charity or Patience?'

'Truth,' I said, unexpectedly moved. 'It suits you perfectly.'

'I don't know, but I like the idea. It's why I got the tat.' I remembered the small black word near her hip bone, the star next to it.

'That's what it says?' I said.

'Yep. And the star means truth too, y' know, like a light in the darkness.'

'I was too distracted to read it,' I said, flushing with the knowledge I had seen the black ink inscribed on her skin. It seemed so intimate. Truth. I knew, then, why the notion affected me so: she had helped me find my truth, liberated me of the doubts I had carried with me for so long. For the first time in what felt like my whole life, I felt free and honest to myself.

She was grinning at me now, a certain unmistakeable intent in her eyes.

'Shall I distract you again?'

1808

Gilly was alone somewhere in the gaol, maybe breathing her last, and Elizabeth could not go to her. It was as though she had already been snatched away to that distant world. She prayed to the God she'd given up on that Gilly would not die.

The turnkeys finally came to escort the other women from the gaol. They were to be taken to the docks at Hull. It would be months before they knew anything but the wooden compartments of the hulks, the rolling of the sea, and the interminable sickness of the journey. Elizabeth's heart beat in her mouth as she stood near the table at which they ate together and looked at the women for the last time. She saw the trepidation in their eyes and wondered what the future would hold for them. It seemed odd to think that after all these days of close confinement with them, breathing the same air, living their life as one, she would never know what became of them. At the same time, she envied the uncertainty of their future. Hers was decided. One day, they would be free in that distant land, able to hope again. Contemplating their sentence, the echo of her own returned to her. Hang. Dead.

What should she say to them? What was there to say? They were oddly silent. Maisie and Catherine, who had become friends, only looked at her and nodded their heads. Jane, however, took her hand.

'That baby's lucky,' she said.

'Not so,' Elizabeth replied, feeling the tears sting her eyes.

'Yes it is. You'll see,' Jane answered.

'I'll remember you,' Elizabeth said, wondering at Jane's words, so laden with kindness and certainty. 'Good luck.'

'And I'll remember you, love,' Jane assured her. She did not wish her luck; Elizabeth knew there was no point in that.

Tears in the dark eyes as Jane released her hand and was led away.

Complete solitude now. She sat on one of the benches and closed her eyes. It was as though the other women were still there, their energy surrounded her. Would they always be here in some vague way, she wondered? Was her own life somehow seeping into the stones of the gaol, always to linger here? It was oddly comforting.

Yet opening her eyes again, she felt only the emptiness. Jane and Maisie and Catherine's lives had moved on to another stage. It was a dreadful stage, no doubt, but it was a moving on nonetheless. Something she would never do.

The baby moved again inside her. She put her hand to the curve of her swelling belly. Yes, she would go on to another stage. She would be a mother and bring a new life to the world, even if she did not live to see it grow and blossom.

Doors slammed somewhere, and she thought she heard a cry, a

woman's cry. Reverberating footsteps, running. The loneliness brought a sense of foreboding. But the sounds were distant, almost of another world. Suddenly it seemed all there was in existence were the outer chamber, day room and night cell, the tiny elevated yard, and she and her child were the only occupants of that world. She wanted Gilly, her light in the darkness, and longed for her recovery until her heart ached.

❖

As soon as she saw Mrs Beckinsale, she demanded news of Gilly.

'She's doin' better today, so y' can rest easy about her tonight, I reckon,' Mrs Beckinsale told her. Elizabeth's heart leapt.

'Do you think she'll make it?' she asked, scarce daring to breathe the words.

'I'd 'ave said the chances are she will, like as not.' Mrs Beckinsale's words were matter-of-fact. The sparkle in her eyes was not. Before Elizabeth could press her further, she was gone, to attend to some duty. Elizabeth barely saw her that day, not even in the evening, when she brought her soup to her, but did not stay to share the meal.

The shadows were large with no one else to fill them. Elizabeth thought of Gilly, to banish the cold of the night away. Gilly would make it. She closed her eyes and prayed again. If God had made Gilly well, then maybe He was watching over her after all. Gilly and the baby, her light, her truth, the safe knowledge of her innocence, the life that would continue beyond her own miserable existence: they were all that mattered now.

It was on the dank straw, with the rustlings of the rats close-by, that she most missed the other women. The floor of the night cell seemed vast, with only her at rest in the centre of it. In the darkness, she imagined the rats, closer to her than usual. Where there had been gentle breathing, murmurings, there was only the wind and the distant echoes. She heard a shout from the town below, as keys jangled somewhere closer and hinges creaked. A gate was clanking regularly in a metallic rhythm. Elizabeth wrapped her arms around her own body, and sang songs of her childhood in her head, and to her child. Eventually, she was asleep.

❖

Sensation of being watched. Morning, but not time to wake up yet. Opening her eyes. Joy and confusion. Gilly.

Gilly leaned over Elizabeth, as she looked up, blinking. 'Gilly?' she said, dazed, wondering if she was dreaming. The recollection came to her. Gilly, gravely ill, but maybe going to live. She struggled to sit upright.

'Gilly? Are you well again?'

She saw Mrs Beckinsale in the doorway, watching them.

'Mrs Beckinsale? What is it?' Her heart pounded. It was so strange, it had to mean something was wrong. The light was very dim, but it looked like Gilly was smiling.

'I'll let y' tell 'er y'self,' Mrs Beckinsale said, backing out of the night cell. Gilly took Elizabeth's hand and Elizabeth felt the warmth of her excitement against her own cold skin.

'What's happening, Gilly?' Elizabeth asked, still anxious.

'It's such a wonderful thing, darlin', you won't believe it,' Gilly said in a loud whisper, as though someone other than Mrs Beckinsale might be listening.

Elizabeth felt a renewal of hope inside her. She shifted her position and tried to dampen the spark. Hope was always dashed.

Gilly went on, 'It was Mrs Beckinsale, darlin', she thought of it. Who'd have known she could?'

'But what?'

'I wasn't ill at all, I was just feigning it,' Gilly said.

'What?' Elizabeth's mind swirled with confusion. Gilly pale and stricken on the straw. Gilly with warm cheeks, unnatural. Gilly barely moving or talking for three days and taken to a cell on her own. Not real?

'It was so they didn't take me. So I could stay here with you—and the baby, darlin'. Mrs Beckinsale said it would work and it did.' Gilly's happiness infused her words.

'But the doctor said...' Elizabeth began. Then she remembered Doctor Webb writing the confirmation that she was with child with the wrong dates, at Mrs Beckinsale's insistence. She remembered that the doctor had been under the sway of Mr Charles before that. She recalled Mrs Beckinsale's threats to make sure he lost his position at the gaol, his chance of a free voyage to Australia.

'I don't know what she did,' Gilly was saying, 'she just told me the doctor would come and look at me, and that he'd say I was sick, too sick to go to the boats. And he did.'

Elizabeth remembered the conversation between the doctor and Mrs Beckinsale. He had said Gilly was likely to die if taken to the docks; that she had to be kept away from the other prisoners. And all the time, Mrs Beckinsale had been behind the lies she pretended to be so alarmed by. So why had he been telling her? Of course, it struck her then. Mrs Beckinsale had known they would hear the conversation, the women in the day room. For it to work, Catherine and Jane, and especially resentful Maisie, had to believe the lie too.

'Why did no one tell me?' she demanded. The lie had snared her too.

'I wanted to, so badly, darlin'. When you were nursing me, smoothing my hair, and I wasn't really sick at all. But Mrs Beckinsale said I musn't. It needed to be real to everyone, even you.'

Elizabeth felt the hurt of exclusion, of being tricked as they all were. But all the time, her heart was singing. It did not matter now. Gilly was alive and well, had not been snatched away to the sea.

Hope flickered. 'But what are we going to do now?' Elizabeth demanded. 'They're still going to take you eventually and, like you said, there's no way.'

Gilly's fingers pressed against Elizabeth's. 'Mrs Beckinsale says there's a way, darlin'. She's not told me yet, said I didn't need to know yet. But she says there's a way.'

The spark grew and hope, finally, flared brightly within her.

2008

I found myself unable to leave Aly. I couldn't think about going home, nor could I tear myself away from the warmth of her bed and her kisses, her hands. As afternoon became evening and she lit candles on the bedside table, my craving for her was still insatiable. She infused me with confidence to push away my reservations and in so doing to discover pleasures that reached deeper inside me than anything ever had. To lie folded in her embrace seemed the most natural thing in the world and it was difficult to imagine I'd ever doubted it.

She wrapped herself in a black silk dressing gown to bring us coffee and biscuits in the place of an evening meal. My appetite was only for her. When we eventually slept, it was with legs entwined, skin pressed to skin.

I woke up to find her sitting on the side of the bed, still undressed. There was enough light creeping around the edges of the curtains and penetrating the red material for me to see her quite distinctly. For a moment I just gazed at her naked back, her angular shoulders, her ruffled black hair. My thoughts cleared in an instant and brought with them warm memories of the night before and a surge of happiness that made me smile widely, as I propped myself up onto my elbows.

'Good morning,' I said at last. She turned, and I was unable to prevent my eyes sweeping over her breasts, remembering how they had felt beneath my hands, my tongue.

'Good morning,' she returned. 'I don't have to ask if you slept well.' She smiled and my heart swelled in my chest.

'What time is it?' I asked, suddenly remembering I had to go to work today.

'Don't worry. I have to work at the shop today, so I'm up early. It's only seven thirty—you've got plenty of time.' I relaxed, put my head back on the soft pillow and stretched my arms. I wanted to say something to reflect how momentous the day before had been for me, but nothing seemed appropriate. I hoped she understood, felt in my heart that she did.

She stood up and began to dress. I watched, fascinated. Her actions were so ordinary, as she pulled on first underwear, then those black stonewashed jeans I remembered, and a royal blue sleeveless top which clung to her breasts and the slight curve of her waist in a way that sent surges of heat through me. Even the simple fact that she wore no bra made my hands grow sticky as I gazed at her, my eyes shamelessly lingering on every detail of her body and the clothing she donned. However commonplace her actions, the fact that I was lying naked in her bed, watching her in the crimson light that streamed through the curtains, that my hands had intimate knowledge of that body she now dressed, made the whole thing seem extraordinary. I felt oddly pleased with myself.

When she was dressed, she pulled back the curtain just a little, to let a stream of daylight invade the room. I shook off my captivation with her, not wanting her to catch me staring so intently, and sat up on the side of the bed. She gathered my rumpled clothes from the floor and put them on the bed at my side. 'Can I lend you some clean underwear?' she offered.

While she bent to a drawer to find me a pair, I looked around a little more. Something shining in the corner of my eye drew my attention to the bedside cabinet at my side of the bed. I looked, flushed, and wondered whether to mention I had noticed.

'Er, Aly?' I began, compelled by something more than the joke I treated it as.

'Yes?' she said, not looking up as she pushed her drawer closed and straightened up.

'What are they for?' I giggled to hide my embarrassment, my curiosity. She looked at me and then followed my gaze to the silver handcuffs which dangled decoratively from the handle of the drawer in the bedside cabinet. She smiled knowingly at me and narrowed her eyes, as if she was trying to see through my joke.

'Decoration?' she suggested with some sarcasm. I felt my face flush. 'Or maybe more. Who knows, spend some more nights with me and you might find out.' A different lascivious expression crossed her face as she said this, though she hid it with a smile. I was silent, the heat that built inside me seeming to clog up my throat and make it impossible to speak. The thought of more nights with her was irresistible; the idea of pushing more boundaries enticing. I was already captivated by her, the cuffs were entirely unnecessary. But they could be fun. I tried to laugh and blushed as the sound was rather more strangled by my arousal than I expected.

Her knowing smile reached right into my core, as she passed me the clean underwear and bent to kiss me lightly on my lips. Mercifully, she went downstairs, leaving me to dress. Her underwear was a little too tight for me and pressed against my body in a way that was not entirely unpleasant. As I wriggled into creased jeans that were still damp in the seams, I could hear her moving around in the kitchen downstairs. I wanted to go down there and kiss her, draw her back upstairs and into bed. Fuck, I'd never been so voracious when it came to sex before. It made me chuckle happily to myself.

I heard the kettle boil in the kitchen as I pulled my T-shirt on, reliving as I did so the memory of undressing with her. It was as well that she had to work today, because, if the choice had been entirely mine, I'd have been tempted to call in sick and simply spend the day with her. I wanted to know everything I could know about her; I wanted to spend long, luxurious hours just talking with her. I didn't want to go into work and stare at the exercise yard walls, alone and with no way of contacting her. I didn't want to hide in my history today, locking myself away from the world. That world had Aly in it and I wanted nothing more than to be with her.

I glanced in the small mirror that hung on one of the bedroom walls, noting the tangle of my hair, remembering her fingers twined in it with a shiver of pleasure. I suppose work was unavoidable, but at least I had plenty to think about to get me through the day.

CHAPTER ELEVEN

2008

At work that day, I felt sure everyone would notice something different about me. I was different, after all. I felt so changed, I was almost disappointed when I found everything much the same. Jim at reception was blandly polite, my costume was still tatty at the hem, the shadow of the gallows stretched to the same point on the flagstones, and the moss still grew over the far end of the yard. Yet there was a puddle of water remaining from yesterday's downpour, and the old bricks were perceptibly a darker, damper red. It was all the same, yet slightly different.

I wanted to tell every visitor, every colleague what had happened to me, how full and happy I felt. Aly's underwear was a constant pressure beneath my skirt, and she stayed in my mind continually. I seemed to still taste her on my lips. Even telling tourists about executions and the horrors of the dark cells, I could barely keep the smile from my face. In my moments of reflection, perched on my usual step, I listened for the unhappiness I had felt here yesterday, and previously, for the sobbing, the cries, even for the pain. I didn't feel them once, nor did I hear anything out of the ordinary. I knew it had simply been my imagination, maybe a build up of tension that had now been released.

I had to wait until the next evening to see Aly again, since she had to help her friend with the stock-taking at his shop until late that night. It felt like a hell of a long time. In the afternoon, unable to hold back the desire to contact her any longer, I sent her a text message: *Hi. Just wantd to say that I was thinkin about u. R u havin a gud day? Lots of love xxxxx*

It took her about an hour to reply. I had smuggled my mobile down into the museum with me, and felt its secret vibrations just as I told an elderly couple they were about to be transported to Australia. I looked at it as soon as I had a chance: *Hi yourself! I've not thort about u all day ;) Shop work just rocks. Hope ur day just as gud. XXXXX*

I smiled at the message. The ironic tone conjured Aly up to me almost as clearly as if she'd walked into the museum.

It was as I was leaving for the day, for once quite happy to emerge from the confines of my yard, that I passed Jade, whose hair was now streaked with both pink and blond highlights. As we both slid behind the reception desk to sign out, to my surprise, she grinned knowingly at me.

'You're looking very happy,' she said accusingly.

'Am I?' I returned, startled by her interest.

'Yes, and I know that look. You've got yourself a new boyfriend haven't you?'

I wondered how on earth she knew I'd broken up with Paul in the first place. I'd not made a point of informing her. The fucking grapevine in this place was lethal. Now, I smiled broadly at her question.

'No, I haven't,' I said, with complete honesty that made me want to laugh out loud. I saw her about to argue with me, so I turned quickly and walked across the shadowy flagstones of the entrance hall to the exit. Outside, the sun was breaking through the clouds which had lingered all day, and I blinked at the bright light, still smiling as I turned to walk towards the city centre.

My own flat was strangely unfamiliar after my one night away. I found myself some food, took a shower, sat in front of the television, but everything felt out of place and different. I thought of nothing but Aly, and now that I was entirely alone, with no impending threat of a tour group, the detail of the memories rushed back into my head in full colour. I wondered, would it be too much to text her again? And tell her what? That I was thinking about her still? My fingers hovered over the phone for a moment, tingling, and then I thought better of it and tried to concentrate on the television. Five minutes later, the phone vibrated its way nearly off the edge of the coffee table as a text message arrived. I pounced on it, flushing with the idea that it would be her.

Hi darling, I'm out with John tonight, but I remembered that there's a program on that u might want to record. It's about teachers. Channel 4 I think, 10 o'clock. See u soon xx

It wasn't Aly. Whose bright idea was it to buy my mother a mobile phone and teach her to text in the first place? Of course, it was mine, and as I cast the phone disgustedly back on the table, I felt annoyed at having given her the means to intrude on me like that.

Once she had, however, the damage was done. I couldn't help but think about it. What would she say if she knew how I had spent last night? Now there was a question. My mum wasn't an especially prejudiced person. She seemed rather proud of herself for being friends with a gay guy at work, actually. But a friend and a daughter were rather different things.

The anxiety that had provided the foundation for my old doubts crept back horribly, and I couldn't stop it. My mouth felt dry at the prospect of trying to tell my mum, let alone the rest of my family. It had been one of the reasons, perhaps even the most significant one, that had driven me to fight the feelings so hard before. People had a fixed image of me in their minds. It was all very well to enjoy subverting that in theory, in secret; I'd grown so used to it that the fact that I was lying didn't seem to matter anymore. I'd train to be a teacher. I really liked being with Paul, but was just as happy single. I was satisfied with the direction my life was taking. The lies had become my truth and I fed them to the people who should have been closest to me without a qualm. But to tell them they were wrong about me? To tell them the truth? That seemed impossible.

Of course I've never hinted to anyone in my family that I might be anything other than straight. It just wasn't the sort of conversation I could ever have imagined having with either parent, especially when I had been so anxious to deny it to myself. Even as I thought about it, I realised it was the first time I had been able to think about myself in that way. I'd never really identified myself as anything; I'd forced myself to be just the same as everyone else. Now, everything had changed. It struck me as rather bizarre that I'd not contemplated it before this point. It had felt so natural to be with Aly in the end, and labels and identities hadn't mattered. They'd not mattered at all. Thinking of Aly made me wish she was with me tonight. I had no doubts at all when she was with me.

Now I became aware, with a growing sense of dread, that labels and lifestyles did matter to the rest of the general population, which included my mother. If I'd never thought about it, not even through the course of today, how could I expect them to understand? I couldn't imagine my mum talking about me, and the fact that I wasn't married, and saying, 'Oh, no, actually, Jenny's a lesbian.' Jenny's a lesbian. Jen's gay. Jen likes girls more than boys. Jen's queer. The phrases circulated through my mind, they felt awkward, as though they didn't belong to me.

Yet at the same time, and quite unexpectedly, the same phrases made a secretive sort of smile want to creep onto my face. Suddenly I had chosen an identity for myself, and any one of those simple phrases told the world. It was right for me and they needed to know. Did I have the nerve? I felt a constraining fear, of pinning myself down, of stereotyping myself. I was still me, unique and individual. I'd only just tasted what it was like to have the freedom to be myself. I didn't want to go from that to merely being a label in people's heads. Surely, that was as bad as hiding behind the walls I had built up over the years, behind the lies I presented to the world? Could I hold on to my newfound freedom and manage to tell the people I knew and cared about? Their image of me as an individual was incorrect, a lie that had been dismantled in less than a week by one striking and indefinable woman. How would they cope with the truth? It made me feel a little queasy to contemplate it. I thought about the new bottle of Southern Comfort in the cupboard…

My mobile vibrated against the table once more. I was more guarded with my emotions as I picked it up this time: *Hi gorgeous. Just wantd to say gudnite. Mayb I can say it in person 2moro nite? ;) 6.30 stil gud 4 u? C u then XXXXXXX*

The anxieties vanished in an instant. I replied quickly: *Hi again sexy, gudnite 2u 2. Hope u not been workin 2 hard? 6.30 gr8 stil. Here's a gudnite hug&kiss ;) xxxxxxxx* I wondered if it was too much, too affectionate. I had to restrain myself not to pour more of my emotion into it. I couldn't wait to see her tomorrow. Talking to her would again banish the doubts, the uncertainties, I was sure.

❖

We had arranged to meet late enough to make it an evening out, rather than a grabbed sandwich or coffee. I actually made the journey back to my flat after work, despite the fact that I could probably have killed the time shopping in the city. I wanted to change from my work clothes, take a shower, have a moment to collect my thoughts. I also made sure the flat was as tidy as it could be, thinking there was an outside chance Aly would come back here with me tonight. My heart fluttered at the prospect, though I couldn't quite imagine her sitting on my sofa, lying in my bed.

I changed into a dark denim skirt which actually gave me a waist, and a black sleeveless T-shirt with a scooped neckline. I smiled at myself in the mirror as I ruffled my freshly washed hair. I'd rarely felt this confident in my appearance when I was going out on a date.

When I saw Aly waiting outside the shop we'd designated, I realised it was the first time I'd seen her dressed for a night out. I had a very strong image of her in my head, but seeing her now, after only a day's separation, I was conscious that my picture of her had been bland and two-dimensional. My stomach actually lurched at the idea that she was waiting for me. Despite the warm day, she was wearing black leather jeans, low on her hips, revealing a glimpse of her toned stomach, and a tight scarlet T-shirt that demonstrated clearly that she looked after her body. Her usual silver bangles were in place and there was a silver pendant around her neck. Her hair looked intentionally unruly and her make-up was slightly heavier than I had come to expect, especially around her eyes.

'Hello, stranger,' she said, as I approached, feeling the warmth mounting in my body already. She reached out and wrapped me in an embrace. Even as my heart quickened, an acute awareness of our position in the middle of the street swept over me and I couldn't help but wonder if anyone had noticed us. She may have perceived my slight discomfort, because she released me quite abruptly, a faintly ironic smile playing on her lips.

'Hello,' I said, hoping my warm smile would make up for my stiff reaction to her display of affection. My heart was filled with excitement and happiness to be with her again, but here was something I hadn't yet considered; if she had been a man, I'd have easily taken her hand now, even kissed her in the street. Suddenly, I was horribly conscious of the people around us, their eyes, their thoughts, and a sense of our difference from them. I shook my head and concentrated instead on her eyes, watching me, and tried to cast my worries aside.

'Good day?' she asked nonchalantly. I knew she'd seen the shadow in my expression and made an effort to appear more relaxed than I felt.

'Pretty average, really,' I told her, as it had been. 'No strange feelings or sounds, no bad experiences with stuck doors.'

'Mine too,' she replied. 'Not that I have bad experiences with doors, of course, and the only strange sounds at the shop are wannabes trying to play their favourite riff on the guitars.' She laughed lightly and I couldn't help but join her. 'So, where are we going?'

It was my turn to choose the place we would go to. In truth, I'd rather not have had the responsibility, since it felt as though there was a lot to live up to. The places I'd been before seemed cheap and gimmicky compared to the ones she liked. However, there was one place in my mind. 'This way,' I said, setting off along the street.

I found it more disconcerting than I would have expected, walking beside her. Every time I looked at her, every word we spoke, reminded me of the last time I had seen her, of being in her arms, in her bed. My skin tingled with the urge to touch her again. But somehow, I knew I couldn't, not here and not now. She strolled along at my side, hands in her pockets, apparently unconcerned.

I was glad when we reached our destination. It was a small pub named the Queen's Head, in a crooked old building, in one of the streets which led up to the higher ground where the Shire Hall and gaol were situated. I'd only been in once or twice, but I liked the atmosphere and the beer. 'Well, this is it,' I told Aly, looking for her approval. I was glad to see her smiling up at the quaint, leaning building,

'I like it already,' she said.

Inside, it was quite dark, although a shaded lamp shone down on each table, and there was still daylight pushing through the darkness from the small casement windows. Our drinks in hand—Aly with her idiosyncratic white wine, me with my half of real ale—we chose a table, not far from the bar, but also with a good view out of the window. It was a raised table, at which we had to perch on stools, and I felt a little self-conscious. The pub was full of dark alcoves, where it was easy to make out figures, but not their faces, nor which direction they were looking, and I couldn't help but think that they were staring at us. I wondered at myself; when Aly and I had been sitting together before, I'd been pleased to think about people looking at us. Now, happy though I was every time I looked at her, I was bothered by their attention, by their thoughts and conclusions. I took a good drink of my ale and a deep breath. This was fucking ridiculous.

'Are you all right?' Aly said, clearly noticing my tense posture and looking concerned.

'Yeah, I'm good,' I said dismissively. Then, looking into her face properly, I felt guilty for my thoughts. 'I've missed you,' I told her with more feeling.

'It's only been a day!' she said with a gentle chuckle. Her laugh melted something inside me and I relaxed.

'And what's wrong with that?' I retorted. Her eyes were sparkling at me now, and it made me want to forget everything else in the world.

'Nothing. But I'm not that great, am I?' she joked.

'No, I guess not,' I returned, 'don't know what I was thinking.' We laughed together, as I forgot every other person in the pub. I didn't see a shadow of doubt behind her eyes, and I thought she couldn't possibly understand what I had been thinking and feeling. I might discuss it with her later, I wanted to be honest, but I needed to think a little longer about how she would take it. After all, in so many ways, I knew nothing about her.

Our conversation flowed easily after that. She talked about her job in the shop, how she had known her friend since she was seventeen, and how he played drums in a band which was actually very good, but only really toured local pubs. I felt a twinge of envy; not that there might have ever been anything but feelings of friendship between Aly and her drummer friend, I had no doubts on that score, just that he knew her so well, had been her friend for years.

I told her about my friends, all of whom were busy embarking on careers or marriages. She asked what my future plans were, and I told her I had no idea and rapidly turned the conversation to her photography. Apparently, she was getting a roaring trade in civil partnership ceremonies, though she wished she had more time to be more artistic in her photographs. 'When I've made a bit more, I'll be able to set up my own studio, instead of having my spare room as a dark room,' she said, determination in her tone. 'Mind you, digital's the way it's all going, and for that you just need a good computer.'

The pub began to fill with people, as night fell outside. We'd made it through three drinks apiece when, unable to keep my doubts a secret anymore, I suddenly blurted out, 'So, tell me, how the fuck am I supposed to tell my mum about all of this?'

She looked at me curiously. 'All of what?' she said, though I was pretty sure she understood instantly. I saw a slight strain come into her eyes, undermining that usual confidence for a moment before she recovered herself. Maybe she would have more empathy with my feelings than I suspected.

'You know what I mean,' I said, 'about you. Or more to the point, about me.'

'How do you think she'd react if you just told her?' she asked, more compassion for my emotions infusing her words now.

'That's just the thing. I don't know. I'm not even sure how I'm reacting to it myself, if you know what I'm saying. It's not even been a week!' Once again I found it frighteningly easy to be honest with her.

'It's been a lot longer than a week, if you ask me,' she rejoined gently.

'Well, yes, but you know...' I admitted.

'I'd say don't tell her just yet,' she advised. 'Yes, you need to eventually, but you need to feel really sure in it, before you try to explain it.'

'I am sure,' I told her. And I knew in that moment that it wasn't a mistruth, I genuinely meant it. God, it felt good to be sure about something for once.

'I know you are,' she assured me, 'but what I mean is, if she asks you questions about it, will you feel confident enough to give her the answers she needs?'

'I don't know,' I said, my mind racing through the sort of questions my mum might conjure up.

'You see, that's it,' she said, 'you don't just have to know it's right for you, you have to be able to convince everyone else that it's right too. If you care about their opinion that is. Which you shouldn't do, too much. Really it's bloody unfair, having to justify ourselves all the time.' Her tone modulated from advisory to resentful and I began to see that beneath her confident and nonchalant exterior there were issues that angered her, perhaps insecurities too. It only drew me to her more powerfully. 'We should just be able to do what we want, really, without having to explain it at all,' she added with less bitterness, when I didn't reply instantly.

'But it's my mum,' I protested.

'I'm not saying don't care about her,' she said, 'just that you can't live your life according to someone else's ideas about what you should be doing.'

'What was it like when you told your parents?' I asked, curious. I thought I saw a shadow creep over her face slightly and wondered if maybe it would have been better not to have asked.

'Oh, not so bad, y' know.' She paused and shrugged, and I could see the memories in her eyes. 'They were surprised, I have to say, which shows how little attention they really paid to me I guess. They asked me why, which I always found a bit odd. Dad wasn't sure what to do with himself, and Mum had this kind of fixed grin. She said she supposed it explained why I never wore dresses and I almost laughed at her. But they got over it in the end. I think it helped that I didn't actually have a girlfriend at the time, so they didn't have to see me with another woman and think about it.'

I wondered how many girlfriends she'd had, what they'd looked like, how long they had been with her. I was curious to know more about her rather than jealous. I wanted to ask but didn't have the courage. Besides, I was finding her revelations about herself and the opinions she clearly couldn't help but express fascinating, and I didn't want to interrupt her.

'You see,' she went on, 'the trouble I think some parents have is they still see their kids as kids. Even if their kids are straight, they don't like to think of them touching and kissing and fucking and all that. They don't have to though, their kids just do the same as everyone else and they don't need to think about it at all. It's not like a straight girl's going to go home and say, 'By the way Mum, I like to do it doggy-style.' Parents don't like to think of their kids having sex any more than kids like to think of their parents doing it.' She paused and smiled a wry smile that was very close to a sneer. 'But then you walk in there and say you're gay, and suddenly they're confronted with the idea of your sex life. I mean, it should be the same as a girl saying to her mum that she likes tall, dark men more than blond, short ones or whatever. But it's not like that in their heads. It's not just about being gay, as I see it, it's also about not being innocent in their minds anymore.'

I was captivated by her eloquence, the depth of her thoughts. I wondered how many hours she'd spent contemplating these things. She spoke about them with an undertone of bitterness in every word. I wondered if it was inspired by that fixed smile of her mum's when she'd told her. I suspected that she had not told me the full story of her parents' response, or at least moderated it in an effort not to frighten me. But I could well imagine the same fixed smile on my own mother's face. It was a daunting thought.

She must have seen my discouraged expression, because she smiled a more reassuring smile and added, 'But you don't have to worry about it right away. I was twenty when I came out, and I'd known for sure since I was sixteen, so I didn't tell them as soon as I knew.'

'You've known for that long?' I asked, slightly disbelieving.

'Yep,' she replied. 'Oh, don't get me wrong, I sometimes wondered if I knew myself as well as I thought I did. I even wished that it would go away and that I could be normal. But it didn't and I got a grip in the end and accepted that I am normal. Just gay.'

'That easy?' I said, still astonished.

'No, not that easy at all.' Her face was serious now. 'It was hard to come to terms with being different at first. But I couldn't do anything about it. By the time I was twenty, I knew it wasn't going to change, not ever, and I didn't want to lie about it. That's why I came out then.'

Watching her, I knew: her strength had grown from this internal conflict, the final self-realisation. 'You see,' she concluded 'the thing is, it doesn't really change. In the end, you realise that's a good thing.' Her easy confidence had returned to her now, and I was relieved, 'I mean, when did you first start to think about it?' she asked. Her question startled me a little.

'You won't believe me if I say when I saw you in the pub last week?' I said lightly.

'Not in the slightest,' she confirmed.

'Okay,' I said, taking a deep breath. 'I'd thought about it when I was at school, I mean, you do when you're a teenager don't you? I thought it was just something everyone did. And I suppose I had a bit of a thing for one of my teachers. I liked her more than I should have, I mean, but I didn't look at it in a sexual way.' I laughed awkwardly at myself. The words felt as though they were hurting my throat; they'd been sealed inside me for so long, growing large and heavy, and it was an effort to speak them. But Aly was listening, with eyes that were soft and interested, and I knew that not only was I able to tell her, I had to tell her.

'But I forgot about it. I never had a boyfriend at school, I just wasn't interested. But it's not like I fancied the girls, so I told myself there was nothing in it.' I paused again, and looked up at her to see her still listening to me intently. 'I suppose it was in my first year at uni. I met a girl there called Clare. There was just something about her...' My voice cracked as I remembered the way I had felt when I had looked at her, how I had engineered the situation just to be able to talk to her. 'I suppose I knew then. She knew too. But I was scared and eventually I convinced myself I was wrong and I stopped seeing her.' Even now, I didn't want to relate the details of our final conversation, the way I had felt for the following weeks. Besides, I thought, looking into Aly's face, it didn't matter anymore.

Aly reached her hand across the table to mine and took it in her warm grasp. My body responded to her touch with an easing of tension, a flicker of arousal. I let her hold my hand; if anyone was looking, what would they see? I wanted the contact with her far more than I cared about the people around us. My eyes lingered on our joined hands and I was flooded with happiness.

'And I suppose I've just been pretending it wasn't there since then,' I went on, wanting to bring the story to its conclusion. 'I've had a boyfriend or two, and, don't get me wrong, I did like them in one way or another, but there was always something wrong. And whenever we broke up, I always had the thought that I might have been wrong at uni. Deep down, I knew what I wanted, but I tried not to think about it. I lied to everyone, including myself, until I believed the lies.' I looked up into her eyes and moved my fingers against hers. 'And then I saw you,' I said. In the end, it had been that simple.

She nodded a slight acknowledgment and smiled at my last words. 'See, you've known for a while. It's just taken some serious coming to terms with,' she said soothingly. I squeezed her hand in return. Now that she knew about the lies I had told, I felt absolved of the dishonesty and my heart was lighter. It had brought me no closer to how or when I would be able to tell anyone else the truth, but I knew then, with her warm hand wrapped around mine, that I would do it.

We talked our way, about lighter matters again, through another drink. It was getting late, and I could feel the effect of the alcohol significantly by now. I could tell from Aly's flushed cheeks and slightly glazed eyes that the wine was working on her too. I began to wonder where the night would end. Should I suggest we go back to my place?

Aly drained her wine glass. 'Another one for the road?' she asked, grinning at me.

'Why not?' I replied, 'I like getting drunk with you.' I would ask her to come home with me, I decided. Another drink gave me a little longer to frame the question. She eased herself off the stool and made her way to the crowded bar. I watched her go with a glimmer of warm pleasure, my eyes dropping in a brazen appreciation of her figure in those tight leather jeans, which turned into an excitement that tightened my throat, as I thought of taking her home with me. She pushed around the corner of the bar, where the queue was less significant, and I lost sight of her. I looked down at the grain of the wooden table.

'Hello, love, all right?' A slightly slurred man's voice made me look up suddenly. He was talking to me. For fuck's sake, this was not what I needed.

'Yeah, great thanks,' I replied as coldly as I could.

'Want some company?' he persisted.

'No, thanks, I already have company,' I told him firmly.

'Where is he then?' he returned. He was clearly drunk, or he would have buggered off already.

'Toilet,' I said simply.

'But is he good to you?' he went on, moving about on his feet as though he was incapable of standing still.

'Look, mate, I'm just not interested, all right?' I said finally, in a tone that should have allowed no arguments. He was beginning to make me feel uncomfortable now.

'Aw, darlin', you don't need to be like that,' he said, drooling and struggling to focus on my face. 'I'm interested in you.'

'Well, you shouldn't be, so just leave me alone, would you?' I said, frustration mounting.

'What's your name?' he said, apparently undeterred.

'None of your business. Look, I've told you I already have company.'

'Yeah, but where is he? Not here.' He laughed as though he'd told a hilarious joke.

'Right here.' Aly's voice jerked my attention away from the drunk. She put our two drinks down on the table and glared at the man. 'She's told you, she has company. So just fuck off back to your friends. If you have any.' I was blown away by her confidence. She was shorter than me; he was over six feet tall, but she was the one with fierce anger in her face. I watched her, stunned and oddly fascinated.

The man, in his drunken state, was more confused than he would have been if he were sober. There was a strange pause, as he tried to make sense of the situation. In the gap, I was uncomfortably aware that Aly had spoken rather loudly, and that several pairs of eyes were looking in our direction. I watched as comprehension dawned on the man's face.

'You're fucking dykes aren't you? Fucking freaks. Shouldn't be allowed in a normal pub to lead decent blokes on.' He spat the insults at us, and I thought for a horrible moment he was going to grab hold of Aly as he lurched unsteadily towards her. She remained calm, took a step away from him and one towards me. I was compelled and horrified by her all at once. I felt as though every eye in the pub was gazing at us now, and my blood ran cold. They all knew; they'd all heard what he said. His apparent disgust shocked me to my core. But Aly wasn't retreating.

'Too right, mate, we're dykes,' she said, her words full of hostility and anger. Before I could do anything about it, she had pulled me to her and kissed me full on the mouth.

For a fleeting moment, I wanted to sink into her kiss; I even felt the pull of her aggression. In the next instant, I was aware of the attention of the crowded pub as though there was a spotlight turned on us. We were like intruders into their world, and Aly was using me to revel in it. The man meanwhile let out a kind of defeated cheer, only drawing more attention. But thankfully he was lost for words.

Suddenly her kiss felt like a betrayal of me, of my insecurity. I know my mouth tightened against hers, making her withdraw. She barely looked at me but gripped my hand and practically pulled me from my stool. We left our new drinks on the table.

I let her pride lead me out of the bar and into the street. As soon as we were outside, I snatched my hand away from hers, and looked at her with eyes brimming with tears.

'What the fuck was that?' I demanded of her.

'I was showing that bastard where to get off,' she retorted, beginning to see my anger but not softening in the face of it.

'No you weren't!' I replied, my rage no doubt fuelled by the beer I had drunk. 'You were showing off. You were showing off to everyone in there, that you didn't fucking care what they thought. But you didn't give a fuck about whether I cared, did you? Did you even think about who it was you were kissing?' I looked at her, saw the realisation in her eyes, and watched it turn to resentment. I was going to cry, because I had wanted her so badly, she'd drawn my deepest truth from where I kept it safely locked, brought it out into the open and now she'd betrayed me, and everything I'd always feared had happened to me in that pub. To hide my tears, I began to walk away from her, down the hill.

'Don't just walk off!' she snapped, and I paused, waited for her, but did not turn to face her. It must have angered her further, as she caught me up, because her eyes were blazing. 'And what's your problem anyway, that some people you've never met know that he was right, you are a fucking dyke? Because you know something? That's what you are!'

I turned to her now. It felt as though she had taken a hammer to my fragile emotions, my newly emerging confidence. 'Do you think I don't know that?' I snarled at her. 'I just didn't fancy showing the whole bloody pub quite so explicitly. You just used me to show them that you didn't care.'

'You say you know it, Jen, but do you?' I heard insecurity in her tone now, beneath the anger. 'I mean, you decided so fucking quickly didn't you? On a date with a bloke one minute, falling for me the next. Are you sure?'

Her words not only hurt me with the implication that I had been dishonest with her, they also shook me, since they tapped into the root of all of my insecurities. What if I was wrong? That eternal echo. But I'd banished it; she'd chased it out of my head. 'I am sure...' I began, only to be interrupted by her.

'Because you know, when a guy tries to chat me up, I don't have a conversation with him, I tell him to get the hell away from me,' she said bitterly.

'What, you think I wanted to talk to him? I was trying to get him to leave me alone! I just wanted to do it without attracting the attention of a whole pub. You might like them all knowing all about you, but there are some things I'd like to keep more private. You had no right...'

'So you've been hiding from the truth for six years and you're going to keep hiding are you?' she shot back at me. I had no idea how she could have said it, bearing in mind our earlier conversation. It seemed to be calculated to tear my heart to pieces.

'It's not for you to say whether I hide or not,' I told her quietly, and I walked away from her quickly down the street. This time, she didn't follow me.

❖

I managed to get into a taxi and make it back to my flat, all the time wishing I'd not walked away from her, but having no concept of how I could possibly have stayed. Once I was safely inside, I broke down, collapsing onto the sofa and crying into the cushions. It was so different to how I'd expected to return here, with her. Now, I was questioning everything. The fact of the matter was, in a cruel way, she was right. If I couldn't cope with a pub full of strangers knowing the truth, then how could I tell anyone I actually cared about? That's not why I was angry with her. It was her insensitivity, her disregard of all the insecurities I had confided in her. I'd expected more of her and my heart ached with disappointment and hurt.

Time passed, and, lying prone on the sofa now, I began to wonder what she was doing, what she was thinking. Maybe she'd go into another pub and get drunk, find another girl who didn't mind kissing her in public. My heart throbbed with jealousy. Why the fuck had I expected so much of her? I'd not known her long enough to expect anything. The alcohol was wearing off and I was beginning to feel sick. I went to the kitchen and blindly poured myself a drink of water. Suddenly, I felt horribly alone, caught between two worlds and not really belonging to either, tormented by lies that had been so solid and a truth that now felt so fragile.

In my pocket, my mobile vibrated. I caught my breath. It couldn't be anyone else at this time of night. I pulled it out, my hand actually shaking with apprehension. I couldn't imagine what she would say to me now. I looked at the screen through blurred eyes.

Where do u live? Tell me the address. We need to talk.

That was all. No love or kisses, no affection. But she'd stood there in the night somewhere and sent me the message. She wasn't drunk or in bed with another girl. Despite myself, my hopes rallied. I replied, mirroring her cold tone,

OK. Flat 2, at 320 Winchester Street. Kno where I mean?

I wondered: was she going to come over now, or wait until tomorrow? The reply was very quick.

I do. I'll be there soon.

Tonight it was then. I didn't bother to reply this time. The thought of her coming here, to my flat, invading my territory, unnerved me. What would I say to her? I wanted to be angry with her still, but worried my resentment would fade when I saw her. Was she coming here to say she thought it wouldn't work between us, that she needed to be with someone more sure of herself? Clearly she had some insecurities; what if they meant she couldn't deal with mine too? The prospect horrified me. I sat on the edge of the sofa and stared at the threadbare patches of the green carpet, waiting, feeling sick.

Eventually, my doorbell rang, and expected though it was, I jumped.

She smiled weakly when I opened the door. 'Hi,' she said quietly.

'Hi,' I returned, not smiling. 'You found me then?' As I had known I would, despite myself, just seeing her I softened. 'Come in.'

She followed me through the small hallway and into the living room. I felt oddly conscious of how small and shabby it appeared in comparison to her house, but she only glanced about her slightly. Neither of us sat down, instead we faced each other standing on either side of the coffee table. 'You've been crying,' she said softly, examining my face. I wondered just how puffy my eyes were.

'Yes,' I admitted. There was a silence between us, not in the least comfortable. I wondered what I was supposed to say next. It was actually Aly who spoke, preceding her words with a deep sigh.

'Okay,' she began, 'I'm sorry. I shouldn't have done that.' She looked into my eyes and down at the ground. I didn't doubt her sincerity for a moment.

'No,' I responded, and wondered at my own will-power in sounding so unforgiving. I was pretty sure I'd already begun to forgive her. When she raised those deep, dark eyes to my face again, I felt all anger melting. She was here in my flat, I was alone with her, and I wanted her. So now I knew she wasn't perfect. Of course she wasn't. I didn't need her to be perfect.

'I just get so angry with losers like that,' she said by way of explanation, when I said nothing further. 'And I was drunk too.' Now she looked sheepish and I wanted her all the more. 'And, if I'm honest, I think I got all possessive. I didn't want him coming on to you.'

'Possessive?' I enquired, my tone losing its cold detachment. I hadn't considered it like that. I'd assumed she'd grown angry because of his insults, had wanted to show they didn't bother her. I hadn't guessed that it was his interest in me that had infuriated her.

'Yeah.' She shrugged awkwardly. 'Maybe a bit protective too. I could see he was bothering you.'

'Am I supposed to be grateful?' I think she sensed that my tone was lighter now.

'No,' she said. 'You're not supposed to be anything. I just want you to know that I was thinking about you, not just myself.' She looked more intently at me. 'I suppose I was thinking about you too much.'

I took this information in and felt the remaining hurt evaporating. Where I had been disappointed, I found I was now ludicrously pleased that she felt protective of me. I could forgive her words spoken in anger. We had both been drunk after all. 'Okay,' I said, 'I'm sorry too.'

'You don't need to be,' she said.

'Yes, I do,' I said fairly. 'I don't know you well enough to judge you like I did.'

'And I shouldn't have said what I did.'

'No.' Just something about her meekness made me want to laugh. It was so unlike what I had seen of her so far. 'You insensitive bitch,' I added.

For a moment she took me seriously. Then she caught my expression and I saw her shoulders relax. Our eyes met, then our smiles, and then our lips as she caught me to her and we kissed. I clung onto her with relief.

'Don't tell me part of you didn't like it though?' she asked, leaning back to look at me with a knowing smile on her face. 'I felt you kiss me back to start with.'

'You've got me there. You're sexy when you're angry,' I confessed, pushing my mouth back towards hers. I wanted to kiss her forever. Her hands crept onto my body and I responded to her, began my own caresses. I slid my hands over the tight fabric that covered her back, and lower, to the soft leather stretched taut over her backside. Her fingers were more urgent then, grasping the hem of my skirt and raising it to my hips as she pushed me back against the wall, sliding her thigh between mine and kissing me harder. I moaned at the heat that swept through my whole body as she pressed with her thigh. Our fingers locked together and our kiss deepened. Unbelievably, my desire for her seemed to have intensified since our night together. She stopped kissing me for a moment.

'So, I think I need a tour of your flat,' she said in a thick voice, heavy with arousal.

'Maybe later,' I breathed, eager for her mouth again.

'No, now, I insist,' she grinned darkly. 'We'll start in the bedroom.'

1808

Gilly, alive and well. Her own heart full of hope, despite the lack of knowledge of what the future held. Gratitude for the woman who locked the door on them every night. And the baby moving in her belly, her breasts swelling so that she would be able to nurture it.

For three days, there were only Gilly and Elizabeth in the women's gaol. Despite the shadows and the stench, they were happy and life seemed eternal suddenly. They spent the time sewing, with long companionable silences, or sitting in the small yard, their backs resting against the red brick. Recollections of their former lives were passing; contemplation of the future constant but unspoken.

In the night cell, they lay on the damp straw together, Gilly's arms around Elizabeth. The dark of the night, the rats, the echoes could not touch them. There was warmth, and there was life, there was the light of hope at last. They were still wrapped in their embrace when Mrs Beckinsale opened the cell door in the morning.

Mr Charles visited the women's gaol on the third day, having only just learned that the sick prisoner had been moved. Mrs Beckinsale formed a broad wall between Elizabeth and Gilly and the man who stood gazing bewildered at them, as though he knew a trick had been played, only could not quite establish what it had been, or what the point of it was.

Elizabeth was not frightened of him now, though she resented his eyes on her, knowing the swelling of her belly was now discernable through her dress. And she shuddered. She felt the connection between the life in her body and him, as he looked, and found the triumph in it. He had wanted to kill her, and instead he'd given her further vitality. She reached for Gilly's hand and they stood strong together beneath his scrutiny.

It was after he had left them that Gilly turned to their keeper. 'Mrs Beckinsale, can you tell us yet? What are we going to do?'

Mrs Beckinsale sighed. Her tired eyes glanced first at Gilly and then at Elizabeth. They saw the anxiety in her face, but the spark of cunning too.

'It's taken me some long thinkin' on, I can tell y' that,' she replied.

'We're very grateful, Mrs Beckinsale,' Elizabeth assured her.

'I don't want y' gratitude,' Mrs Beckinsale said to them. 'I just want t' know that child has a good chance.'

Gathering them to her, she told them her plan.

Later, Elizabeth and Gilly sat in the gloom of the day room in the evening, holding hands and looking at each other with frightened eyes. This was going to require more of them than they could have suspected. Yet underneath the anxiety was excitement, joy, and a grim determination.

Both of them jumped when Mrs Beckinsale opened the door, followed into the room by two women, both of similar height and plumpness. Gilly dropped Elizabeth's hand and rose to her feet, as if they had been caught conspiring. 'These are Mary and Constance

Dunne,' Mrs Beckinsale announced, her eyes keen on Gilly. 'Make sure they get settled.' She left them then.

The two sisters looked around them nervously. They seemed vaguely intimidated, rather than frightened. Gilly and Elizabeth, their seclusion shattered, were silent. Then Elizabeth recalled her own first moments in the gaol and spoke out,

'Hello. I'm Elizabeth Cooper and this is Gilly Stevens. It's not so bad once you get to know it.' She heard the lie in her own words. It was so bad; it was only that she had Gilly now.

Mary Dunne, who was the slightly stouter of the two dark-haired women, looked back at her, and then at Gilly. 'Are you all there is then?' she asked, with remarkable composure.

'Yes,' Elizabeth told her.

'Cosy, ain't it?' Mary scoffed. Her harsh accent and apparent lack of concern for her new situation grated with Elizabeth. She saw the tightening of Gilly's shoulders and knew her friend felt the same. Why had they had to come? And tonight of all nights, when there were plans to be discussed in fearful whispers.

'Before y' ask, I'll tell y',' Mary said.

I wasn't going to ask, Elizabeth thought.

'We're here 'cause we tricked the old dear we worked for into payin' us double every week. Poor thing didn't know one day from the next, had no idea 'til her son came back from India or wherever the hell it was.' Dreadful pride in her voice. Elizabeth looked away from her, to her sister, clearly younger, who had begun to tremble.

'I've been in gaol before meself, but up in Leeds. They was goin' to transport me then, but they let me out, when it was proved it wasn't me that did it.' Mocking laughter. 'Of course, it's fair enough this time, I s'pose we're off to Australia. Was touch and go, Conny 'ere was sure we were bound for the rope, but I told her we was lucky, always were.'

Injustice made her mouth bitter. Gilly's silence told her how the other woman felt. She wanted to scream at them, tell them to leave her and Gilly to themselves. But the doors and gates were locked and the two women were part of their lives now inescapably.

Constance, the younger girl, was staring at Elizabeth, as she struggled for a response. Elizabeth looked back at her, wondering what

part in her sister's crime she had taken, and pitied her. Then Constance, still staring, took a breath and spoke in amazement,
'Say, are you with child?' Elizabeth clutched her hands to her belly, oddly defensive. 'How'd they cope with that in 'ere?'
Elizabeth looked at her blankly. She saw herself in Constance Dunne's eyes and shuddered. A fellow convict, with no regret of the crime other than that she had been caught, no doubt the child inside her before she'd even entered the gaol, probably as she'd committed the crime. But the truth was long and twisted, and it was Gilly's to keep.
'They manage well enough,' she said shortly. 'I'll show you where we sleep, shall I?'

2008

The tour didn't get any farther than the bedroom, not that there was anything of the flat worth seeing. Looking at Aly sitting on my sofa, drinking the morning coffee I had made her, I wondered how I had ever felt angry with her. The sun streamed in through the dusty window, and she was casually slumped, one foot on the coffee table, squinting a little in the brightness. I remembered snapshots of the night in my dark bedroom and I closed my eyes, growing warm. I opened them and she was still there. I'd take on the world, and I'd do it holding her hand. I could almost have picked up the phone and told my mum there and then. Almost.
I saw her glance up at the clock on the wall above the television. She turned to me. 'I've gotta go,' she said, and I was pleased that her words sounded partially reluctant. 'I've got to get home, get changed, and get my portfolio and stuff, then get back into town before nine.'
I knew she had a meeting with an independent book publisher, who were thinking of asking her to take photographs for the covers of their books. She was excited at the prospect, and her mind was already half on the interview she would have with them. I didn't mind, I was simply happy to share her anticipation with her.
She stood up and brought me her empty coffee cup. 'Thanks for the coffee,' she said, though her eyes said far more.
'You're welcome,' I replied, leaning in to her lingering kiss.
'Until later?' she said, finally pulling away.

'Yes,' I said. 'Hey, you know you're in town later?'

'Yes?'

'How about a museum visit?' I don't know what had given me the idea. I think I wanted to prove that, after last night, I wanted to see her in public. Perhaps I just wanted to share more of the everyday of my life with her? Maybe I wanted to let my real life reach inside the confines of the gaol for once.

'You mean come and let you hang me?' She smiled.

'Something like that. You can get in free—if you say you're coming, I'll tell them to expect you. I get so many free tickets a year.'

'Well, since it's free,' she said, smiling. 'If I come in the afternoon, at about two, that okay?'

'Yep, should be,' I affirmed.

'We can make more plans then,' she said.

'Sounds good to me.' I put the cup down and drew her towards me for one last kiss, before, slotting her mobile phone into her pocket, she left.

Five minutes later, I was dressed and smiling to myself in the mirror as I brushed my hair, when I heard an almighty crash from the direction of the living room. With no idea what could have possibly made such a destructive sound, I rushed through to see my window with a gaping hole in it, cracks radiating into the glass that remained in the frame. The curtain was flapping softly in the breeze and there were shards of splintered glass shining in the sunlight all over the carpet. What the fuck?

For a moment I couldn't work it out at all. Windows didn't just break. I looked at the sparkling glass in bewilderment, my heart thudding. Then I noticed a large stone, smooth, round and grey, just beneath the corner of the coffee table. Amazed, I tiptoed between the pieces of glass and picked it up. It was heavy, but certainly could have been hurled through my window. I looked at it contemplatively, about to curse the stupid louts that thought this sort of thing was funny, when I turned it over in my hand. On the other side of the stone was a word written in red marker pen, in block capitals: *dyke*.

I stared at it, and the fear rose in me. This was no random, because-I-was-bored act of vandalism. The stone had been aimed at my window, and with a message for me. But so few people knew. Yes, I admitted to myself, a whole pub full of strangers knew now, but it wasn't like they had any idea where I lived. My mind raced, searching for answers. I thought of the drunken man we'd confronted. He'd still been in the pub when I'd left, I was sure I'd have known if he'd followed me. Besides, he was probably too drunk to remember the scene he'd caused last night. It was a puzzle, but it was a disturbing one. I felt sick.

My first impulse was to call Aly. However, my hand paused as I reached for the phone. After last night, I didn't want to pose any more problems. She had an interview to deal with later too; I couldn't put this upon her now. I realised I was still clutching the stone. I placed it on the coffee table, turning it so that I could not see the writing, and thought for a moment. I had to call the agency I rented through, inform them. I dug out the number, trying to ignore those red, accusing letters and the way my hands were shaking.

In the end, I had to call work and tell them I'd not be able to get there until lunchtime. I had to wait in for the agency representative, who also dealt with the insurance on behalf of the landlord, and then the man who came to board over the window until it could be replaced later in the week. The wooden board cast an odd shadow over my living room. The stone still sat where I had left it on my coffee table. The representative had simply glanced at it, as if to check what I said was true, but to my relief he'd not wanted to study it. 'Must've been kids,' he'd muttered, frowning over his notes. I'd been terrified he'd see the word on the other side, and not only judge me, but tell me this whole thing was my fault and I'd have to pay for the damage myself.

❖

I stuck to the story that it had been kids when I got to work and met with concerned enquiries. The truth was impossible to tell. Besides, I couldn't work out what the hell the truth was. Mystified, I almost began to believe my own lie. It could've been kids, entirely at random. It could just be coincidence. Of course, I couldn't completely convince myself.

I was glad to be at work, not sitting at home in the shade of the boarded-up window. But the shadows of the yard seemed longer today, the dank corners deeper and darker. The gallows structure had taken to creaking in a disturbing fashion more suited to a horror movie, as the wood was heated by the sun. Somewhere, a gate kept clanking against its fastenings, as though a prisoner was rattling the bars, and, in the transportation exhibition, the tape which played a voice-over of the stories of some of those transported stopped working. It was as if the whole building and its props were as unsettled as I was. I wondered if the layers of history were trying to tell me something again, or if maybe I was simply adding my own nervous energy to all the other energies the bricks must have absorbed over the centuries. I heard no unexplained noises, experienced no pain, but somehow a sense of foreboding crept into my heart, and I felt as though it came not just from me and my broken window, but that the building around me infused me with it.

When the concealed phone in the transportation exhibition rang at nearly two o'clock, I leapt out of my skin. I had been leaning against the wall in the shade, considering the rows of windows on the back of the building, trying to work out which of the rooms I had been in, for the sake of occupying my mind. I crossed the yard quickly, curious as to why it was ringing.

'Hello, Jen,' Jim's voice said on the other end, when I put the receiver to my ear. 'There's a woman here says she's come to see you?' Aly. I'd not forgotten she was coming, in fact I was looking forward to her appearance with some pleasure, even through my anxiety, only I had not kept track of the time, since I wasn't used to starting work at lunchtime. I remembered now that I'd said nothing to Jim about her visit, being too busy explaining the calamity of the kids and the window. I felt better instantly, at the thought of having her with me in a few minutes.

'Oh, sorry, Jim. I forgot, with the window and everything,' I said into the receiver. 'Yes, she's my—er—friend, Aly.'

'Okay then, I'll send her for the tour first shall I?' Much as I wanted her here now, I quite liked the idea of Aly taking the whole tour.

'Might as well,' I said. 'Thanks, Jim. Anyone else in?'

'Yes, there's a family of four about to go into court, I'll send your friend through with them.'

'Okay, thanks, bye,' I said, replacing the receiver and closing the little cupboard that concealed it. I went to wait in the shadows, for when she would arrive. The incessant clanging of the distant gate had stopped, and the shadows were back in proportion again. The gallows still creaked unnervingly, but I was able to block it out of my hearing. I pondered on how powerful imagination was. With my change of mood, the whole character of the yard had been transformed.

I laughed to myself as I heard the cell door above slam, imagining Aly in the cell. Would she be interested or nonplussed? I thought about her in the laundry, looking at the dolly tubs, imagined what she would make of the women's communal bed. Then there were the footsteps in the tunnel that led to the yard. First, blinking in the sunlight, doubting a little whether they really had seen me, all in black and in the shadows as I was, came two young boys, both around the age of ten, maybe twins. Their mother and father followed, cautioning them quietly not to run, and drawing their attention to the lady, as I moved from the shadows and startled them.

Aly followed them out of the tunnel. I looked past them quickly, letting my eyes linger on her welcome face for a brief moment. I wished as soon as I saw her that I'd just asked Jim to send her down alone. There was so much I wanted to say to her. But I had a performance to conduct.

Self-conscious as I felt Aly's eyes on me, I went through the motions of stick waving and execution threatening. The boys were delighted with the concept of the bodies buried under the flagstones, and I thought even Aly seemed interested in what I had to say. Looking at her standing there, I couldn't help but wonder what the family thought of their companion on the tour. She was dressed in what I assumed was her interview outfit; black smart trousers and a black velvet jacket worn over a sleeveless top, carrying a black leather briefcase, which looked so professional and formal that it made me want to laugh. All on her own, she wasn't at all like a typical museum visitor. I wondered what Jim had made of her at reception.

When I sent the family down to examine the pits and dark cells, Aly lingered behind. I guess they thought she wanted to ask me a question. As soon as they had disappeared into the shadows, I went to her and took her hand in both of mine. I kissed her quickly, not wanting to risk more.

'Well, look at you,' she said, before I could speak, gesturing to my costume. 'You can imprison me any time, ma'am.' I smiled at her and blushed. I loved the fact that she was here, in my exercise yard. It was almost like having her in my flat. I spent as many God damn hours here after all.

'What do you think of it?' I said, holding off on what I really wanted to tell her, since she seemed so happy.

'It's interesting,' she said, 'and it's a bloody kinky sort of a place too, I can see the appeal.' I rolled my eyes at her irreverence towards the history, but laughed all the same.

'Can I take it the interview went well?' I asked, guessing as much from her playful mood.

'We're doing a shoot next week,' she said, and I could hear the pride in her voice, 'for two books. If they like them, then they'll think about some sort of contract.'

'They'll love them, I'm sure,' I assured her.

'Fingers crossed,' she said. 'How's your day going?' She must have seen the anxiety return to my face as she asked, because before I could say anything she demanded, 'What's wrong?' and her smile was replaced by concern.

I was silent for a moment, deliberating how best to put it. It was not the best chosen way when I began, 'Should it be this hard, Aly?'

I saw the worry in her expression then. I think she wondered if my fears of the previous night had returned in the short hours since she had left me. 'What do you mean?' she demanded, an edge of hostility in her tone.

'I mean, I thought we lived in enlightened times. I thought I'd have problems telling my family, but not that perfect strangers would throw rocks through my window.' I drew a shaky breath and clenched my fists to repress the surge of disquiet that swept through me.

'What?' she asked. 'Someone actually did that? How do you know it wasn't kids?' I told her about the word on the rock, and shared my bewilderment with her.

'Who knows about us?' I said fretfully.

'I haven't told anyone,' she said, slightly defensive, 'and besides, it has to be someone who knows where you live.'

'But there isn't anyone!' I said.

I heard a scuffle as the boys emerged from the entrance to the pits, followed by their parents. Aly was silent and I composed myself, in order to send the family to Australia. Aly walked with us along the yard, as though she was still interested in the tour. The moment they had gone however, she turned to me, taking my hand again.

'Look, I'll think about it, but I really don't know who it could be.

Maybe someone that knows me and saw me coming out of your door? It could be meant for me, not you. That's more likely.' Her words were not reassuring,

'But who the hell would want to throw a brick through your window?' I demanded.

'Actually, I don't know,' she replied, thinking. 'But there's people just take offence to the way I look, y' know.'

'The way you look?' I was surprised.

'Yeah,' she was remarkably casual about it. 'You wouldn't believe the comments sometimes. Though calling me a dyke's not a huge insult.' She laughed, but I could see the resentment in her eyes. 'You know, cut your hair and wear trousers and you must want to actually be a man, which makes you a freak and means people can say what they like about you.' She shrugged, though I heard the bitterness behind the words.

'I can't be as relaxed about it as you,' I told her.

'You get used to it,' she replied, then seeing my alarmed expression, added quickly, 'not that things like this happen a lot. I don't mean you get used to bricks though your window. But the names are water off a duck's back in the end. Besides, you look regular enough, you won't get it. Unless you're with me, of course.' She smiled at this. I couldn't quite return the gesture.

'If you're worried about going home on your own, come and stay with me tonight if you want,' she offered.

'That'd be great, if you're sure,' I accepted eagerly. I could be with her and feel safe. I didn't want to be behind my boarded-up window, remembering the glass shattered all over the floor.

'Course I am. It's not like you're just a random damsel in distress,' she said. 'Shall I meet you outside at half-past four? I've got some shopping to do before then, and we can get the bus together.'

'Sounds good,' I said. Quickly I leaned in and kissed her. She put her hand on the back of my neck and held the kiss longer than I would have done, knowing the family would soon be done in the exhibition. My knees felt weak. She released me moments before one of the boys came shuffling out of the doors.

I sent them all into the Victorian prison, Aly included. She winked obviously as she disappeared through the archway and left me smiling, despite the undercurrent of apprehension I couldn't quite escape.

CHAPTER TWELVE

2008

I wished, after she'd gone, that I'd found some way of making her stay with me all afternoon. Alone again, I felt the anxiety building up in me once more. I sang songs in my head to drown out the creaking gallows and the gate, which had begun to clank again. A cloud passed over the sun and removed all the long shadows, leaving instead a sheet of dull gloom over everything compared to the earlier brightness. A scruffy crow perched on the top of the wall and cocked its head to one side to look at me, cawing. I watched it as it flew away, and had a sudden feeling of being trapped, just like the prisoners here must once have been. It was so strong that I even went to check the doors to the yard, to make sure no one had locked them, as some sort of practical joke. They hadn't. For fuck's sake, I was going mad. Maybe it was finally time for a new job.

To distract myself, I went to read the crime boards again. My eyes were drawn back to Elizabeth Cooper. I wondered if she'd stood exactly where I stood now; if maybe in some layer of history she was standing here, dreading the death penalty that hung over her head. I wondered if she'd had any family to mourn her, any friends. I wondered what had compelled her to risk her life to steal the things she had done. They were small items to have cost her life. I thought of what I knew of the gaol in 1808. It was harsher in those days than the Victorian picture we presented to the visitors. Not so strict maybe, with less rules and routines, but the conditions were far worse. She'd have been executed in public too, on the steps outside. 1808. It was still the short drop then: her neck wouldn't have broken instantly, she'd have hung and strangled—a slow and horrific way to die. I shivered at the notion, almost feeling the rope around my own neck. How had she gone to her death? What sort of girl had she been?

I felt the hollowness of the history I spouted at the tourists every day. Did they ever really feel it? Did any of these names or crimes linger with them? I felt myself as negligent as the rest of them; I'd had no idea where I'd heard the name before, and I stood near this board every day. Elizabeth Cooper. I paused and tried to picture her. The girl from my gallows steps dream drifted back into my head: blond, small and terrified, younger than me. I tried to imagine what it would be like to face the gallows, and found I couldn't. Could anyone? And if we couldn't really connect with it, what was the point in what I did every day? It was a show, it was theatre, and I enjoyed it.

The notion made me feel ashamed, and my problems seemed small in comparison with Elizabeth Cooper's, whoever she had been. For a moment, I felt like our times really were layered with each other and I could feel her near me, her heart full of pain and injustice. Injustice? I wondered why I should have felt that particular sentiment.

❖

Holding on to the thought that I was far better off than Elizabeth Cooper had been, I was much calmer by the time I met Aly on the top step outside the main entrance at four thirty exactly. I know Jim, who was cashing up the day's money, had seen her waiting and no doubt recognised her from earlier. As I met up with her, Jade breezed past us, glanced at us, and actually looked back over her shoulder. 'See you tomorrow, Jade,' I said pointedly.

'Yeah, see you,' she replied, still staring.

'You know it's me they're staring at, don't you?' Aly said, unperturbed.

'No, they're staring at me too. I'm with you after all,' I said to her, and watched the faint surprise and then the satisfaction that spread over her face as she took in my words.

'You're happier than before,' she said with an enquiring look.

'Yeah,' I replied, 'actually, I don't know that *happier*'s the right word. But I feel better than I did. I've been thinking that there're people far less fortunate than me.'

'You mean like starving orphans in Africa?' she asked, raising her eyebrows.

'Well, yes, since you say it. But I really meant condemned prisoners in the early nineteenth century actually.'

'Oh of course,' she said, 'naturally. Well, whatever makes you feel better. Come on, let's get the bus.'

1808

The warmer breeze and longer hours of pale daylight had gone, replaced by the chill of early autumn. Friendship had proved impossible with Mary and Constance Dunne, the younger sister entirely dominated by the elder, whose company was insufferable. No remorse, no worry for the future. No justice.

The previous day had brought a new arrival, straw-haired, pock-marked Alice Whitworth, who, she claimed, had known Jane Larkin. They had shared a profession, and were about the same age. Alice had that same tired look about her eyes that Jane had worn. The reminder of Jane turned Elizabeth's mind to a contemplation of Australia, the horrors of the journey, but beyond that, the hope of freedom. Alice, with a coarse voice but quick blue eyes, was no more friendly with Mary Dunne than Elizabeth or Gilly. Her conduct suggested she would prefer to be left alone to contemplate her future across the seas. Elizabeth was happy to oblige her. Tension in the cells, the only relief was Gilly.

Her belly was large and heavy now. She'd been forced to adjust her dress. It did not matter that the air that crept through the bars was colder now, she was too hot all of the time, and hungry, no matter how generous Mrs Beckinsale was. Difficult to rest easily on the straw, but she welcomed every discomfort as a reminder of the new life that was drawing the goodness from her.

Tired, Gilly her only comfort. Together they shared their secret hope, the suffocating fear that they would not succeed. The other women were separate from them, insignificant. They drew away from them. Sleeping with hands entwined, days spent sewing, often in silence, but more shared between them than any words could ever convey. They were waiting for their moment, but they were also living the days of the only life they would know together. Dreadful and wonderful all at once.

It was a dull day, with rain falling outside. Elizabeth and Gilly were seated next to each other in the day room, the other women lurking in the night cell. They had tried to sew, but the failing light had made it impossible. Instead they sat, shoulders touching, lost in mutual contemplation. Elizabeth started suddenly, feeling the sharp kicks of the baby. Wordlessly, she took Gilly's hand and held it to her swollen belly, watching her face. Gilly's eyes were full of wonder as she felt the movement. 'Oh, darlin', I can feel it,' she breathed.

'He or she's going to be strong,' Elizabeth told her.

'Like their mother,' Gilly said.

'Like the mother they'll know,' Elizabeth replied, feeling the hope above the sadness. There was a way after all and it was to that she clung in the darkest hours of the night.

She saw the sadness in Gilly's own face, but also the determination. 'They'll know their real mother too, darlin',' she whispered. She dropped to her knees in front of where Elizabeth sat on the bench, and pressed her cheek to where the baby still moved.

'What if I'm a terrible mother?' Gilly asked, a cloud in her expression.

'You won't be, I know it,' Elizabeth said. 'I hope this child grows up to have your kindness.'

'Just be glad he or she will have your look about them, not mine,' Gilly said, more lightly.

'But you're beautiful, Gilly,' Elizabeth said, without a thought. She put her hand on Gilly's head, then pushed her cap back to stroke her auburn hair. Suddenly she felt like the older woman of the two. Gilly's hand came up to press her belly, to feel the baby as it stirred. Elizabeth noticed she was crying, softly.

'Gilly, please don't,' she murmured, fingers caressing first auburn hair and then pale skin at Gilly's temple, as Gilly laid her head in Elizabeth's lap. Gilly would carry her child into the future, she would find freedom, but Elizabeth understood the weight of that responsibility. Her future was decided, Gilly's was not.

'But how will I do it without you?' Gilly demanded, her voice weak and racked with pain.

'I don't know,' Elizabeth told her. There were no ready words of comfort. 'But I know that you will. And I will be with you. If this child has my look about him or her then you'll see me when you look at them.' It wasn't just for Gilly. She had to believe she would be there too, not in the ground, not forgotten.

'I wish there was another way,' Gilly said, for even the hope they clung to was only a last glimmer in the darkness.

'But there isn't,' Elizabeth said, resting her hand on Gilly's shoulder, as the baby moved once more. 'You know it's the truth.' Tears stung her own eyes now as Gilly raised her head to look into her eyes.

'You know you'll always be in my heart, darlin'. No one will ever take your place.'

Elizabeth looked back into the green eyes. Her tears fell. No point in promising the same, but a thought of a future she would still have a part in. She cradled Gilly's face in her hands, wiped Gilly's wet cheeks with her thumbs, and smiled through her own tears.

2008

I had never enjoyed sitting on a bus as much as I did at Aly's side. Even my usual motion sickness had vanished. The seats were narrow and I felt the pressure of her hips and the length of her thigh warm against mine as the bus bumped and rocked. Aly laid her hand on my knee, but her display of affection was subtle and hidden from the other passengers. Part of me wanted her to slide her arm around my shoulders, as the man in front of us did to the blonde who sat beside him, but I still felt constrained by the gaze of the other people on the bus. Though I was grateful for Aly's sensitivity after what had happened in the night, I was irritated by my own insecurities. I looked forward to reaching her house, having her to myself again. The closer we got to the end of our journey, the more excited I felt, and the easier I found it to forget my smashed window.

My improved mood lasted until we reached Aly's front door. Then we both stopped suddenly and stared in a kind of curious horror. Smeared all over the door was a brown substance we both hoped was soil from the garden, and, in white paint, stark against the red door, in huge untidy lettering, was written *filthy dyke whore*.

'Well, my insult's better than yours,' Aly said, but her voice was empty of laughter. The terracotta pot of petunias had been smashed on her doorstep. The strewn compost and shards of terracotta looked so disorderly, so violently destroyed; it seemed such a vindictive thing to want to do to a pot of pink flowers. I think it frightened me more than the words on the door.

'What the fuck's going on?' I demanded, not really of Aly, the panic rising in me. We'd both made the connection now; someone knew where we both lived. The chance of the rock through my window being some dreadful coincidence had disappeared completely. The whole thing seemed suddenly more sinister.

'The guy in the pub?' I ventured, since he was the only person I could think of who would have any sort of grievance against us both.

'I'd agree, but he was just a drunken bastard,' she said, 'and he was still in the pub. I don't know—it just doesn't seem right to think that it's him.'

'But who else is there?' I said, my anxiety evident in my tone. I really was frightened by the turn events had taken. Aly caught the edge in my voice. I saw the grave concern in her own expression, but she put her hand out to me.

'I don't know,' she said, pressing my fingers reassuringly. 'Come on, let's go inside.' I hated going closer to the door, stepping through the smashed terracotta and strewn flowers, but I kept my grip on her hand and drew some strength from the fact that she didn't seem to be as scared as I was.

When we were sitting in the kitchen, both cradling mugs of hot coffee, I asked her if she was frightened. Her demeanour was certainly agitated; I noticed the way she chewed the tip of her left thumb and fiddled with the bracelets at her wrist, before drumming her fingertips on the table.

'Not frightened,' she said, eyes hardening as though she slightly resented the suggestion that she should be. 'But I'm angry.'

'Has this ever happened before?'

'Yeah, all the time,' she replied, heavy with bitter sarcasm. She looked at my expression. 'Sorry,' she said, reaching for my hand once more. 'No, it's never happened before. I get crap a lot, from stupid ignorant idiots who can't cope with the way I choose to dress and cut my hair. But not this sort of hate.'

I had a terrible thought: this wouldn't have been happening to me a week ago if I'd chosen a boyfriend over this woman, if I'd not made this choice. In the moment I'd thought it, I wished I hadn't.

Aly must have seen the shadow pass over my face as I fought the idea. 'Please don't say this is going to change the way you feel,' she said warily. I knew then that she still harboured some uncertainties about my state of mind. I hated the idea that she might doubt me in any way and searched for a way to reassure both of us.

'It doesn't,' I replied, hearing how unconvincing I sounded. I squeezed her hand and tried to sound more certain of myself. 'Really, I still feel the same. It just makes you think about the consequences of the choices you make,' I tried to explain.

'But it's not a choice, is it?' she said, with some passion in her tone. 'You tried to fight it all these years and you still couldn't. I willed it go away when I was still a teenager and it didn't. You don't choose this, Jen, it's in you. And when shit like this happens, you have to face it, stand up to it.' Her expression had become almost fierce and I resisted the urge to retort that it was all right for her, who wasn't afraid and was used to the way the world perceived her, but entirely different for me, to whom all of this was new. I'd never really had to stand up for anything before, certainly not something that seemed to matter this much. Aly was looking at me as if she knew what I was thinking. 'If you let it scare you,' she said, with less ferocity, 'it can make you regret who you are. And you can't regret the way you were born, or you'll go mad in the end.'

'I feel like I'm going mad now,' I told her, not meaning to sound as though I was arguing.

She absorbed the sharp edge of my tone and simply nodded, reaching out to cover my hand with her free one. 'I know,' she said. 'But it'll be all right. We'll sort it out,' she assured me. I wanted to believe her, but I couldn't see how she meant to achieve what she planned.

'How can you be so sure?' I asked her.

'I'm not, I'm just choosing to be optimistic,' she replied with a small smile. 'What else is there to do, really?'

'It's hard, Aly,' I admitted honestly.

'I know, Jen,' she acknowledged. 'But this isn't about whether you're into men or women.'

'But you know…' I started to protest.

'No, Jen, it's not.' Her tone allowed no arguments and I looked back at her quietly. 'It's about some bastard out there who gets off on insults and breaking stuff, that's all. There's always a reason, if someone's going to do stuff like that.'

'No one would have ever done this to me before,' I protested tentatively.

'No, they wouldn't have called you a dyke, you're right. They might have just mugged you in the street, or broken into your house and nicked your stuff. There's always something that could happen. You don't stay home all the time, just in case someone wants to break in.'

'No...'

'And you can't hide who you are and the things you want, whatever people think of them. Come on, Jen, you know what I'm saying.' Her tone as she concluded was almost imploring. She didn't want to sit here giving me unnecessary advice; she just wanted me to understand. And I did. I knew then I didn't want to hide anymore, even if the risks of being in the open were greater than I'd anticipated. Aly's words only confirmed what I already knew: there was no going back, no re-building of the walls or re-locking of the doors. Despite my anxiety, I felt a sense of fulfilled pride as I recognised the truth of it.

'Yes, I do know what you're saying,' I said, as reassuring as I could be, 'and I didn't need you to say it either. I don't want to hide and I know it's not a choice. I'm sorry, I'm just shaken up by all of this.'

'You don't need to be sorry,' she said, squeezing my hand tighter.

Neither of us was very hungry, but she made us slices of toast, which we picked at half-heartedly. 'Tomorrow, I'll ask the neighbours, see if anyone saw anything,' she said.

'Good idea,' I replied, though wondering what good it would do, even if they had.

Later we sat together in the living room, her arm around me and my hand on her thigh as we slouched on the sofa. I should have revelled in being so close to her, but our contact came more from a craving for physical reassurance than any other reason. We tried to block out the idea of what was on the other side of the door by watching a DVD, but it was useless and we turned it off before the movie was even halfway through. To prevent the silence becoming oppressive we turned on the radio, but it was still impossible to relax.

It was completely dark, and had been for an hour or two. I was resting my head on Aly's shoulder, beginning to feel a little drowsy as she stroked my arm, when I jumped violently, hearing a sound at the back of the house.

'What was that?' I demanded at once, sitting up bolt upright on the edge of the sofa.

'What?' Aly asked, startled.

'The noise, out the back.' I said, my mouth turning dry. 'I swear I heard something. A crash or something.'

'It was probably a cat,' she said, but she got to her feet anyway and made for the kitchen.

'Where are you going?' I asked anxiously, still rooted to the sofa.

'To have a look, see if it's worth worrying about,' she said. I stood up to follow her, my heart in my mouth.

At that moment, we both very clearly heard a sound, like a blunt object striking a wooden board. We gave a start, exchanged glances, and rushed to the kitchen window. It was impossible to see anything in the blackness outside. It struck me that someone could be looking in at us from just feet away, and we wouldn't be able to see them. I shuddered.

Aly switched on the outside light and opened the back door. As soon as she did, I heard her exclamation.

'Oh shit!'

I pressed close to her in the doorway to peer over her shoulder. 'Shit,' I echoed, holding on to her shoulders to steady myself.

On the sill outside of her kitchen window, Aly had kept three painted pots, of basil, thyme, and parsley. All three lay smashed on the concrete floor of the yard. We looked down the garden. About halfway down, one of the planks which made up the six-foot fence was dislodged. I remembered the sound of something striking wood. It was the sound it would make if someone tried to climb over the fence and kicked it or had fallen against it. The electric bulb above us made only a small halo of bright light near the back door, half of the garden was in semi-shadow. Beyond was blackness. I imagined someone lurking in the dark, watching us. 'Aly,' I said hoarsely, 'let's go back inside.' I practically pulled her back into the kitchen and locked the door for her.

'It could have been a cat,' she suggested, as we pulled down the kitchen blind. 'They've knocked one of my pots off before, bloody things. We're probably over-reacting.' I was glad she had included herself in the statement too. I sensed that fear was beginning to creep into Aly's emotions, where previously she had only been angry. Knowing that it was not only me that was so affected by what had happened was some small comfort. At least we were facing this together.

❖

It was one of the most horrible nights of my life, only made bearable by the fact that I spent it with Aly. Uncomfortable with the idea of retiring upstairs and leaving the downstairs unprotected, we attempted to sleep on the sofa, having made sure the door was double locked and the curtains completely closed. We both dozed, and I maybe even got a couple of hours' sleep, but it was broken and uncomfortable.

'We could call the police?' I suggested, sometime in the early hours.

'Yeah, right. They'll ask a few details and give us a crime number,' she said. She looked tired, dark circles deepening under her eyes. 'For a start, they're too busy to care. And they're only just getting a grip on the fact that there's a law against homophobic hate crime now. They won't give a shit really. They'll just treat it as vandalism.'

I looked at her and blinked, too tired to think of a reply.

'What is it with people?' she demanded of the room in general, after a moment of silent reflection. The strain of the sleepless night was evident in her face. Her eyes were slightly red, with dark shadows beneath them, her cheeks paler than usual. I watched as her features contorted in anger. 'Why should there even need to be a fucking law?' Her words were bitter and fierce.

I was taken aback by her sudden fury. 'I suppose they struggle to cope with anything different,' I ventured at last, since she seemed to require an answer. I wasn't sure I was best qualified to give her one, and I felt useless, wanting to comfort her, but not knowing how to.

'I know that,' she replied vehemently, 'but what is it that gets in people's heads and makes them hate things so much? I can live with them not understanding, but why hating?'

'I don't know,' I said, aware that I'd not spent a lot of time considering it before. It hadn't been as important as it seemed now. I'd never really done anything likely to make anyone hate me. Suddenly a keen understanding of her resentment filtered into my consciousness. I was still intrinsically the same person I had been a few days before. If I'd not been subject to hate and prejudice then, why should I be now? The injustice of it struck me forcefully and I struggled to keep my own calm, to search for words to soothe her and myself. 'But you said you've not had anything like this before, so it's not everyone,' I said in the end, knowing it was small comfort really.

'No,' she acknowledged. 'But even reasonable people say the stupidest things.' Bitterness still dominated her tone. I knew she wanted to get it off her chest, and I watched her patiently, doing my best to keep hold of my own emotions for her sake, as she struggled to control the anger through her tiredness. 'Do you know, the other day, I heard a guy on the radio talking about it not being natural to be gay? He thought he was being quite reasonable, and obviously they thought it was acceptable to let him say it on air. He claimed he wasn't homophobic, but that people had to admit that it wasn't natural.'

I felt a flare of anger in me too, but had no words to express it. Aly did, though.

'It's people like that who should think about what they say. Nothing people do these days is natural! Is it natural for a man and woman to use a condom when they fuck, to stop her getting pregnant? No, not really, but no one except the Catholics has a problem with that. That's sensible. Is factory farming natural? How about wearing clothes, talking on the phone, eating processed food? None of it's natural, but that's all fine. Yet somehow who I want to share my bed with is some sort of issue for debate? It's more bloody natural than most things people do every day! When are people just going to get over it?'

I felt her rage, and knew now that the issues that enraged her were things I would have to confront as well. Though it was hardly an encouraging realisation, at the same time the way it united me with Aly gave me a stronger resolve than I would have anticipated. I wanted to be positive for both of us. 'Some people understand,' I said, hoping for myself that I was right, 'and most people that don't, still accept it, don't they? I think the world is changing.' I hoped I didn't sound too blithe or dismissive about something I was only now beginning to understand.

'But is it fast enough?' she demanded. As though my words had slightly surprised her, she was calmer now. 'There're still people that sound taken aback when they call for a photographer called Aly and find that I'm a woman, and not a bloke named Alistair or Alexander. Can you believe that? Because obviously pointing a camera is something only a man can do. People have such narrow minds, and I don't know what the chances are of them changing anytime soon.'

'Neither do I,' I replied, knowing there was no real way to reassure her. She had lived through the reality of the things she spoke of, while I'd shied away from them. I looked at her tired face and I saw that through her anger there was also vulnerability. She had chosen to dress how she pleased and desire who she pleased, and everything about her attitude said *screw what everyone else thinks*. Yet there was a part of her that still struggled with the lack of acceptance, did not understand why everything she did had to be so much of a statement. This sudden vision of her, underneath the surface, drew me to her further and made me want to be strong for her. I didn't want her to have to fight. I didn't want to have to fight either; it was something I'd never contemplated before. But if there was a struggle to be taken on, then I was glad she was by my side. I wanted to reassure her in the same way as her mere presence, the press of her hand in mine, made me feel better. I thought for a moment, searching for words to make her happier and to convey to her how I was feeling,

'You know, I don't care who hates me for it, I'm so glad you rattled your bucket in my face the other night,' I said, with a certainty that came from my very core. She had been staring straight ahead but now her eyes turned to examine my face. I managed a slight smile. 'I mean it. I can't say I'm going to be any good at all of this, and you know I'm scared, but I'm not going to let it stop me being who I am. I've done that for so fucking long, Aly, I'm tired of it.'

She reached out her hand and stroked my face. 'I'm so glad,' she said softly.

'You know you set me free, don't you?' I said, tiredness and anxiety making me emotional and more forthright than I would have been in a more rational moment.

'No I didn't, babe. You were already free, you just didn't know it.' She pulled me closer, into her arms, and held me tight. It was hard to believe there was any danger in the world while my body was pressed to hers and her arms surrounded me.

'Okay, you made me understand it,' I said, 'and I'll be damned if I'm going back on it because of some idiot that feels the need to break bloody flowerpots and windows to make his point!'

It was as though the hatred I had seen today, added to the need to reassure her, had consolidated my certainty. For a while it was enough to make me feel more optimistic, and I sensed that Aly, leaning her head against mine, began to relax and abandon her anger finally.

Whatever we said, though, the paint was still on the door, and the flowerpots were smashed on the ground. Someone knew where we lived. It was enough to banish any chance of sleep.

CHAPTER THIRTEEN

2008

It was a huge relief when the daylight began to filter around the edges of the curtains. I accepted another cup of strong coffee and the bowl of muesli Aly offered, and contemplated the day ahead.

'Will you be all right on your own?' I asked her.

'Yeah, I'll be fine,' she assured me. 'I'm going to do a round of the neighbours, ask if they saw anything, then I'll be off to work at lunchtime anyway.'

'Yeah,' I replied. I would be working all day too. I didn't relish the idea of the time alone with my thoughts, separated from Aly and trapped in my yard. I was actually hoping it would be a busy day.

'I'll meet you at the end of the day,' Aly said, and I felt grateful to her. I also knew she was really worried; it was visible in her heavy eyes, audible in the slight strain in her voice. The night had been frightening, but the day was unpredictable. Would the neighbours be able to shed any light? Would anything else sinister happen to us?

'Thanks. I already can't wait to see you again,' I said. 'And text me if anything weird happens,' I told her. 'I'll keep my mobile with me. I'll text you if I think of anything.'

'Okay,' she said. 'And we'll try not to worry, agreed?'

'Yeah, we'll try,' I replied, doubtfully.

'I'm sorry about this, Jen,' she said then, to my surprise.

'It's not your fault is it?' I said firmly.

'No, but...' she ventured.

'Really. I don't blame you at all. It's like you said, it's not like either of us has made a choice. It's just who we are. If some loser doesn't like that, they can go screw themselves.' The vehemence of my words and the clarity of my sentiments took me by surprise, but I was glad of them, even if just to see Aly's smile return, briefly.

❖

My day at work began with a large and interested group of visitors, spreading out over half the yard and laughing readily at my jokes. It lightened the atmosphere and I thought it boded well for distracting me for the rest of the day. However, to my dismay, all of the day's tourists had apparently come through in that group, since there was no sign of anyone else, even out in the street, as Mark informed me when he nipped down briefly for a chat.

After my previous day's reflections, I didn't feel like perching on the steps to the gallows, stage prop though they were. So I took to my modern chair, just beyond the last part of the daylight before the passageway. I checked my phone for messages. Nothing. Telling myself that no news was good news, but feeling a twinge at how much I was missing Aly, I folded my arms and tried not to think. Still, there was a knot of anxiety in my chest, which no amount of deep breathing and trying to think happy thoughts was going to unravel.

I had a headache, probably a result of the lack of sleep—plus the infusion of caffeine this morning—more than from actual anxiety. I put my cool fingers to my forehead and closed my eyes. As if from nowhere, the image of the prisoner, which yesterday I had given to the mysterious Elizabeth Cooper, flashed vividly into my head. I opened my eyes and blinked, disoriented for a moment, wondering if perhaps I'd fallen asleep. I didn't think I had.

I heard a door slam, but it wasn't the usual cell door that warned me visitors were coming. A gate somewhere swung on squeaking hinges. My headache was making me more sensitive to sounds. I closed my eyes and leaned my head back against the cool of the stone wall behind me.

That was when I heard the cries again. Not the heartbreaking sobs, but the horrific cries of pain or terror. My blood ran cold and my skin prickled. A pain stabbed low in my abdomen again, and I clutched my hand to the place. I heard a rattle of keys and another door slamming, and still the cries, more irregular now. My heart was ready to beat its way out of my chest. I went to stand up, move out into the daylight, but a pain stabbed down my leg and all of my strength deserted me. My panic was complete when I felt as though I was being pushed backwards against the wall. My throat grew tight as though there was a hand—or a rope—around it and I had the distinct sensation of not being able to breathe. I gasped and gurgled, but I was choking. Despite the chill that swept through me, my hands were hot and sticky. The woman's cries had stopped now, and I heard something else, a weaker, higher-pitched cry, like that of a child. In a moment it was gone. I still couldn't draw a breath, and now my chest ached for air. My eyes prickled and my heart fought the attack, but I expected it to give up any minute. I gathered my strength, my panic, and made one almighty effort to escape, pushing myself out of the chair.

I heard my own cry as I stood upright, and the sensation of choking disappeared instantly. I gasped for air and put my hands to my throat. Desperate to get out of the shadows and into the sunlight, I staggered into the open air and leaned on the gallows for support, trying to calm my mind. What the hell had just happened? I was terrified now, all of my senses on edge. Into my thoughts came Aly's suggestion of the layers of history. But that was a ridiculous concept. This hadn't just been an ephemeral feeling; it had been a real physical sensation.

My heart rate began to slow gradually, but I still felt light-headed. I bent over, sure I would faint if I didn't. I stared at the flagstones and tried to gather myself together, make sense of what had just happened to me. An idea came to me: panic attacks. I'd heard a friend whose mother had suffered from them describing them. Tight chest, irregular heartbeat, difficulty breathing, triggered by stress. Surely they were my symptoms? I was just adding colour to my panic with my overactive imagination. I felt oddly pathetic.

And yet, even as I stood, trying to convince myself, that same foreboding swept though me and I felt afraid. Suddenly I felt worried for Aly. I got out my mobile and sent her a message: *Hi, is everything OK? Just felt a bit worried. I just had horrible sensation of panic, thort somethin bad goin 2 happen, but gone now. Just let me kno u OK. XXX*

I was hugely relieved when in less than a minute I received her reply: *Hi, yep, I'm OK, plse don't worry. I'm just doing neighbours, dun about half, no one knos anything, typical. Keep in touch if u worried. XXXX*

I relaxed a little then, hearing her matter-of-fact tone in the words. But my senses stayed keen and, still tense, I remained standing in the middle of the yard, leaning against the gallows. It was the reason I heard the slightest of movements in the archway to the Victorian prison again.

1808

Pain in her abdomen that was worse than anything she had ever felt before. Breath taken from her. Fear now. The waiting was over. Almost willing it not to be, desperate to hold on to the connection, frightened of the emptiness beyond. And then the pain again, so that she thought of nothing else.

The straw beneath her back. Head in Gilly's lap, hand gripped tightly around hers. Let the pain stop. Constance and Mary lurking near the doorway, Alice just behind them. Their gaze was an invasion.

'C'mon now, girls, let me through then.' Mrs Beckinsale, her voice a comfort. 'An' y' can mek y'selves scarce too. Go on!' The prying eyes were gone.

'Now, Elizabeth, I'm goin' to look, see if it's comin'. I reckons it is though.' Mrs Beckinsale's big hands lifting her skirts, which were wet with the water that had flowed from her, pushing at her thighs.

Crying out with the agony and hot, so hot, despite the cold of winter that cut through the air in the room. Gilly's fingers cool on her forehead. Looking up into Gilly's face. 'It's all right, darlin', it's all right,' Gilly repeated.

'I can see its 'ead,' Mrs Beckinsale said. Its head. Her baby. She would be able to see it, to hold it, after all these long months. Joy despite the excruciating cramps, the fear. The murk of the night cell, the reek of the bucket, the dank straw. No place for a baby to be born, but the only place it could be. Conceived in pain, born in squalor, but grown of her life and her hope. Then the pain again, but worse and no thoughts of anything else. She screamed and heard the sound echoing from the walls. Gilly clutched her hand.

'Y've got t' bear down on it now,' Mrs Beckinsale said. Elizabeth took a breath and pushed with all of her strength, crying out as she did so.

'Again,' Mrs Beckinsale ordered. Elizabeth panted for air, her head swimming. Then she gritted her teeth and pushed again. Her body would surely split in two. The pain was impossible to bear. She had no strength. At Mrs Beckinsale's word, she pushed again. Then she closed her eyes. No more strength at all.

'Y' 'ave t' do it one more time,' Mrs Beckinsale said.

'I can't,' Elizabeth cried.

'Oh, yes you can, darlin', you're strong,' Gilly told her. She gripped Gilly's hand harder, and drew her strength from the other woman. She pushed again.

'It's got to be 'arder than that,' Mrs Beckinsale virtually shouted. Weakness, terrible weakness. But the baby needed her. She felt sick and tired and wanted to rest. Her skin was sticky with sweat. The pains had drained her. The baby needed her. With one last summoning of strength, she pushed down, sure the effort would kill her.

She felt the release of pressure, the movement of the baby slipping from her, into Mrs Beckinsale's hands.

'It's a girl. Y' 'ave a daughter,' Mrs Beckinsale said, her hands busy. Elizabeth tried to move, tried to see. Gilly was straining her neck. Then they heard the cry, a high-pitched protest at the cold world she had been born into. Mrs Beckinsale held up the child, wrapped already in the cloth she had brought, and Elizabeth looked at her daughter for the first time. Gilly pushed some of the wet hair from her sticky forehead and smiled down on her, as she took the baby in her arms. When Elizabeth glanced up, she saw the other woman had tears in her eyes. She kissed the baby's head, held her warm to her own body, and felt her own tears wet the sticky, fine hair.

Overwhelming love flowed from her into the child. Her daughter. The baby wriggled. Her life, her innocent life, there in her arms. Her connection to the future, the reason she was not already a corpse like he had said. So small, and so innocent. She smiled down into the wrinkled pink face and her throat swelled. Her truth.

❖

Gilly did not leave her side for hours. Elizabeth half-sat, half-lay on the straw, her back against the cold wall, still weak. Her child was cradled in her arms, and now she put her breast to the baby's mouth. She felt the strong pull as the girl began to suck. She willed the child to draw the life from her and take it into herself.

Gilly was fascinated by the child, her gaze barely moving from her small face and pink hands. Elizabeth watched her wonder and was glad.

It was then that the grief crept into her heart. The child was separate from her now, a new life feeding from hers, but not a part of it. She felt empty inside. Her daughter would go on, but she would not. For a terrible moment she fought a fierce resentment of Gilly, who would see the child grow when she could not. The child was hers, her own flesh and blood, it seemed inconceivable that she would be forced to relinquish that. How limited would her time be? How would she ever be able to let the girl out of her arms? She felt the child drawing on her milk and thought how impossible it was, that she would die and leave her baby alive in the world without her.

A sob caught in her throat. Gilly heard it and looked keenly at her. 'Oh, darlin',' she breathed, reaching up to wipe the tears that had begun to trickle down Elizabeth's cheek. Impossible to resent Gilly, who would never forget her, would make sure her child knew her mother had cradled her in tender arms and not wanted to ever let go. Elizabeth looked at the other woman and love poured from her. Take my strength, take my truth, take my life, she wanted to say to her. My child will need it.

❖

A day passed, and then another. Elizabeth was absorbed in the baby and thought of nothing else, spending hours looking into the pink face, willing the eyes that could not yet focus to see her, to remember her. Gilly was constant at her side and between them, by unspoken mutual consent, they pretended that the future, the time for action, was not approaching as rapidly and irrevocably as it was.

Then Mr Charles entered the women's gaol. He was nervous; he fidgeted with his buttons and did not meet Mrs Beckinsale's gaze. The baby cried and drew his attention to the day room. Elizabeth glared at him as he appeared in the doorway. He stared at the child, as if bewildered by its existence. Elizabeth rocked the baby to quieten her cries, and looked away from him. Let him gaze at her, let him see that she had won. There was a life in her arms despite him, not because of him, and he would not be able to hurt it. Close at her side, Gilly's hand stroked her back. Elizabeth heard anxiety in Gilly's quickened breathing and glanced at her to see the anger in those usually gentle green eyes as she looked at him. Gilly would fight with everything she had if it was needed, Elizabeth knew and trusted. For it might be needed yet.

The other women watched Mr Charles with greater curiosity. They knew little of him, certainly not the truth Elizabeth and Gilly kept to themselves.

He had turned away again, but his words to Mrs Beckinsale were deafening in the quiet gaol. 'I've come to tell you, Mrs Beckinsale. The next shipping to Australia leaves in nine days' time. And Lizzie Cooper will be executed in a fortnight exactly.'

His footsteps disappeared out of the women's gaol and away into the building. Elizabeth gazed into her baby's eyes and imagined she had not heard the words. The old echo returned to her. Hang. Dead. She looked across to Gilly, who had risen to her feet, her anxiety flushing her face. Their eyes met in fear and dread. For so long they had held each other and talked in whispers. Now it was upon them. Elizabeth banished the echoes from her mind. Before she could succumb, she had a life to save. Her child needed its mother, and its mother-to-be, to be strong now.

The baby grew remarkably in the next week. Elizabeth wanted with all her heart to think of nothing else. Her daughter had blond hair, just like her own, and her hazel eyes did resemble her mother's, she was sure of it. Rocking the child, feeling her pull at her breast, she wanted to forget the dreadful hours passing, the horror of what was to come, and what must be done before then. For while the trickling of time brought her own death closer, it also hastened on her last struggle for life.

The penultimate night before Gilly and the others would be taken away, bound for Australia, Elizabeth and Gilly sat, gripping each other, the baby in Elizabeth's arms, in the dark at the edge of the night cell while the other women slept.

'You haven't given her a name, darlin',' Gilly said to her in a whisper.

'I know. I wanted to ask you,' Elizabeth replied, just as softly. 'But I just couldn't…' Simply could not accept that she did not have weeks and months in which to think of a name. It seemed so final, when it was done. Yet she knew she could not stand to die not knowing her own daughter's name.

'She's yours,' Gilly told her. 'It's for you to name her.'

Elizabeth felt the warmth of the baby close to her heart. 'Verity,' she said. 'It was my mother's name.'

'So pretty,' Gilly breathed.

Elizabeth's eyes filled with tears. 'You'll tell her I named her, won't you?' she said, desperately. 'One day?'

Gilly held her tighter, 'Of course I will, darlin'. She'll know everything about you. She'll know how much you loved her, even here in the dark.' Elizabeth wept with the idea of the life her child would have, the picture of a little girl, growing, free. But freedom brought its own dangers, as she knew all too well, and the dreadful knowledge that she would not be there to protect the child haunted her.

'Oh, Gilly, you will love her, won't you?' she said, through the thickness in her throat.

'I love her anyway,' Gilly said, 'But even if I didn't, it'd be enough that she's part of you, darlin', and Lord knows, I love you.' Gilly leaned her head to rest against Elizabeth's. They were silent for a drawn-out moment.

'Are you frightened?' Elizabeth asked.

'No,' Gilly replied. 'Not of what we have to do, or of the journey. But I am frightened of not having you there with me.'

Elizabeth could not stop the tears as she pressed her face to Gilly's. Gilly's cheek was as wet as her own and their tears mingled. Tears dripped onto the baby between them and she stirred in Elizabeth's arms. 'But I will be with you, Gilly. Every time you look at her, I'll be there too.' She had to think it, to cling to it. It would be the only way she existed, in the child. Gilly had to understand it too.

'I know,' Gilly said thickly. 'And you'll be with me always, in my head, darlin'. And my heart.'

Elizabeth felt empty, unable to return the assurances. Always was less than a week, and then her heart would beat no more. Yet Gilly and her child would be in the world still. She would go with them and her soul would be free. 'I won't be frightened,' she told Gilly, desperate for the comfort. 'Not if I know you have her in your arms, as you're holding us both now.'

'I'll never let go, darlin',' Gilly said. Elizabeth crushed herself to the other woman, the baby, Verity, between them. She cried harder then, all of the tears she had falling onto Gilly's skin and dress, her baby's face and hands. It was dreadful, too awful that the moment was finally here. But it was as inescapable as the bars that kept them imprisoned. She wanted to hold her daughter, wrapped in Gilly's arms, and pass at that moment into eternity. With her tears, her life flooded from her.

As the beginnings of morning began to creep into the cold gaol, she held her baby to her breast for the final time. She felt the child pull the last traces of her vitality from her. She smoothed the thin hair, the colour of her own, and kissed the pink cheeks. 'Remember me, my precious truth, my own child,' she whispered to the face which looked back at her so calmly. 'Farewell, my Verity.'

She looked up at Gilly through her tears. 'She's yours,' she told the other woman. Gilly came to her and took the child in her arms. The baby squirmed at the unfamiliar hold, but did not cry. Elizabeth encircled them both in her arms.

'She will always be yours, darlin', we both will,' Gilly whispered. 'Don't be frightened. In my heart I'll be here with you, and in her, you'll be with me. One day, we'll see each other again.' Gilly's voice broke, and there was no more to be said. Elizabeth pressed her cheek to Gilly's, then her lips to the other woman's moist mouth. She bent to kiss her child, as the door creaked open quietly.

Mrs Beckinsale, compassion in her eyes, beckoned hastily to Gilly. Gilly looked into Elizabeth's eyes and they said their farewell silently. Elizabeth watched as everything she loved, the last part of her that was alive, left the cell. Mrs Beckinsale closed the door after them. Elizabeth sank to the floor, no vitality in her limbs to support her, and held her arms to her body, as though the baby was still there to cradle.

❖

'So the baby died?' Mr Charles demanded of Mrs Beckinsale. Elizabeth, curled on the straw of the night cell, listened, her heart numb, but terrified all the same.

'Yes, sir, in the night. An' Doctor Webb's been 'ere this mornin', sir, to fill out the papers and take the body. It'll be a pauper's grave of course, an' there's no family.'

'Why was I not called?'

'I didn't want t' bother y' so I didn't, sir. Seemed a waste for a dead baby.' His baby, Elizabeth could not help the thought.

'I'll have to speak to the doctor, of course.'

'Suit y'self, sir.' Mrs Beckinsale's tone became quieter. 'But y' know, sir, it was prob'ly for the best in the end. I mean, who wanted to deal with findin' the poor mite a place t' go, and with the questions they'd ask? Awful, the tales that people will tell, an' the ears they oftentimes get back to.'

Mr Charles could not have missed the veiled threat. Even Elizabeth could hear it in Mrs Beckinsale's tone. His answer sounded strained. 'Yes. Quite right of course, Mrs Beckinsale.' He stopped and cleared his throat. 'Ready for shipping the others out tomorrow, are we?'

'Yes, sir, more than ready,' Mrs Beckinsale said cheerfully.

Elizabeth heard his retreating footsteps with relief. He had not come into the cell, just as he never did. She thought of Gilly and her daughter. Still within these walls, inside this vast building of echoes and darkness, but beyond her reach now. She hoped the cow's milk suited the child, and her breasts ached, heavy with the milk she could not give to her daughter. She closed her eyes and imagined she was with them.

The other women were taken the next morning. Elizabeth watched them go from a seat in the day room, with little regret. Their questions, to which she had replied with blank stares, had become alarming. They wondered where the baby had gone, and Gilly too, vanished in the night. Mrs Beckinsale told them the baby had died and that Gilly had been taken ill and was being kept separate until they left for the journey to the docks. The other women had not been in the gaol for Gilly's previous apparent illness, and with no better answers, accepted what they were told without much concern. Elizabeth's tear-stained face, her silence, seemed to confirm it.

As they left, only Constance Dunne took Elizabeth's hand, and whispered quickly, 'I'll think of you.' The gesture warmed Elizabeth's heart for a moment, and then she was empty again, her mind with Gilly and her burden.

As Mrs Beckinsale prepared to close the door behind the women who went meekly with the turnkeys who had come to escort them, Mr Charles appeared in the doorway.

'Where is Gillian Stevens?' he demanded. Elizabeth's blood froze in her veins. She heard Mary Dunne murmur something to her sister. Silently, she begged the girl not to say anything. She watched through anxious eyes, as Mrs Beckinsale put her hands on her hips and faced him.

'Gillian Stevens is a thief, sir, and of no importance to anyone,' she told him.

'She is due on a boat to Australia, in order to pay for her thieving,' he returned. His tone made Elizabeth quake.

'So she is, sir.' Mrs Beckinsale paused. 'Only I've not seen 'er this mornin', sir.' Her tone was nonchalant.

His face registered her words, and he peered closely at her, looking for their deeper meaning. 'Do you mean to say, Mrs Beckinsale, that she has escaped somehow?' he asked through gritted teeth.

'Well, I don't know 'ow that could be, sir. I've 'ad the door locked all the time, so I 'ave.' She hesitated. 'Though there was a moment, now I recall, when I was called away, an' didn't 'ave time to turn the key.' In her expression was a challenge. 'But she was a good girl that one, can't see 'er takin' advantage like that.'

'Just where do you suggest she is then, Mrs Beckinsale?' His face was purple with repressed fury, though his expression was bewildered.

'Couldn't say, sir. Maybe she 'as run off, after all. Can't 'ave got far though, can she?' She turned to Mary, Constance, and Alice, who were watching and listening with interest. Elizabeth bit her lip with terror, as she asked them, 'Any of you girls seen Gilly t'day?' A hesitation in Mary Dunne's face, a blank expression from Constance, a slight smirk from Alice as if she began to understand what had happened.

Mary parted her lips, but then she said nothing. Mr Charles looked suspiciously at Alice, but she too maintained her silence.

Elizabeth tasted the blood she had drawn from her lip, as a rush of dizzy relief filled her.

Mrs Beckinsale looked back to Mr Charles. 'We'll call a search, shall we, sir?'

'Yes, Mrs Beckinsale, we will. With any luck, we'll find her before the ship sails. The woman's been here long enough.'

'Quite right, sir,' said Mrs Beckinsale.

Mr Charles strode away purposefully, and Elizabeth breathed deeply of the stale air. It was nearly done.

❖

A plain carriage, pulled by a pair of bay horses, drew up to the side of the river barge which would carry the convicts to the coastal docks. At the back of the barge, a line of men, chains about their ankles, were being guided onto the boat. Two turnkeys waited with three women, also in chains, who would board last. The river was busy with coal barges. Its gently flowing waters reflected the red bricks of the town high above, the factories on the top of the cliff, the gaol with its several chimneys. One or two of the men looked back in disbelief, as if surprised to see the gaol from the outside. The shortest of the women was looking about her, as if she wanted to remember every detail of her last moments on land in England.

From the carriage, a man dismounted. He was young and slender, dressed in a black coat, and looking about him nervously. One of the barge's crew came to address him, and began to unload several travelling chests from the carriage and onto the barge.

The man reached into the carriage and offered his hand to the woman inside. She climbed from the carriage gracefully, her well-cut black gown showing her to be of the respectable middle-classes. Her bonnet was broad brimmed and masked her face, but a coil of black hair could just be made out at the back of her head. She turned back to the carriage and bent to lift a large basket.

Side by side, the man and woman approached the barge. A man with a register checked them as they reached the gangplank. 'Doctor Webb, prison surgeon, bound for Australia,' the man told the clerk with false jollity, sniffing as he finished the words. 'Travelling with my sister, Mrs Butler,' he added.

'There's no sister on the list,' the clerk returned.

'Oh, no, I know. You see, my sister wasn't going to travel with me, but she was recently widowed, and I cannot possibly leave her alone. She has a child.' The clerk looked at the woman, taking in the mourning dress, the basket with its wriggling bundle. 'I've applied to the ship's captain,' Doctor Webb added, 'he gave me permission. He must have forgotten to write it down.'

This information seemed to decide the clerk's mind. 'Very well, Doctor, you may board.' He wrote a note in his register of the doctor's sister. The man and the woman climbed the wobbling plank together.

From the barge, they stood to look back at the gaol, rising stark and red up the cliff face. Both of them reflected on what they knew of its corridors and cells.

Gilly had protested the plan with all her heart. 'But why me, Mrs Beckinsale? Elizabeth could do just the same things as I can.'

For a moment, Elizabeth agreed with Gilly, and she saw the future bright before her. The moment passed so quickly. She glanced at Mrs Beckinsale, and explained for herself, firmly. 'No, Gilly, she's right,' she had said, summoning all of her courage. 'Don't you see? Almost every time he comes into here, he looks for me. They'll be used to hearing the baby crying. They notice me, Gilly. And they'll be making the preparations by then, you know they will.' She swallowed hard. The preparations for her death.

'And there's people that will want to see my life to its end too,' she added. 'I want to try it, really I do, but I can't. I won't risk it for the baby. You're my only hope. They don't see you like they see me. You can slip away, and they won't know. I could never do that, not now. They'll look for me and if they find me with the baby, they'll take it from me and they'll kill me anyway, and the baby won't have a mother at all, because you'll be gone.'

'They won't look as 'ard for you,' Mrs Beckinsale said, looking earnestly at Gilly.

Elizabeth's passion was convincing, and Gilly closed her eyes, consenting silently.

Yet she had not wanted to risk the journey to Australia. 'Why can't I just disappear into the town?' she had demanded of Mrs Beckinsale. 'I could find a way to travel, to London maybe. Or go north.'

'They'll look for y', missy, and then where will y' be, when they find y' and bring y' back 'ere? Y' might get away with it, well y' might. But if y' go on t' boat, I can tell 'em y've gone and escaped, and even if they look everywhere in the town, they won't find y' under their noses. I tell y' it's the only way to make sure of it. Y' can 'ave a new start there, an' if we manage it right enough, no one will be lookin' for y' at all.'

'But how will I get on the ship?' Gilly had demanded.

'Our good Doctor Webb is also makin' the passage, for no cost to 'is good self, since 'is services are required in the gaol there. The doctor has quite a name for 'imself 'ere, an' gaol work is all he can get. Mr Beckinsale reckons he wants t' go to Australia, since no one'll know 'im there, an' set up as a regular doctor. He's ever so worried that someone might take the chance away, Elizabeth 'ere knows that. I reckon he'll 'elp, with the right pressure put on 'im.'

Now Gilly stood on the barge and looked back at the gaol. The borrowed clothes were heavy about her, and the black hair the doctor had purchased from a wig maker was irritating at her neck. She looked down at the baby, no longer in a threadbare cloth, but wrapped in soft blankets in the basket, and smiled at her. Then her gaze returned to the gaol on the cliff. Her eyes followed the windows, until she saw the section where a wall seemed to enclose a yard, about halfway up the cliff. Her lips trembled, as the tears flowed down her cheeks, hidden from view by the large brim of her bonnet. 'Elizabeth,' she breathed. Her eyes remained fixed to that part of the building, until the barge drifted slowly away, and she could see it no longer.

❖

Elizabeth stood in the small yard and pressed her face to the cold bricks of the wall. Even on tiptoe, she could not see the river, and the barge that was being loaded on it. But she knew, standing outside, she was breathing the same air as Gilly and her child. They were beneath the same sky, and so close she could have run to them in minutes.

'Verity,' she said to them in a whisper, 'Gilly, keep me with you. Please keep me with you.' Hot tears fell. She remained there, until she was sure that the barge had floated away, taking her heart with it.

After that, all she could do was wait, the echoes her only company in the gloom.

2008

If I'd been seated in the passageway still, I'd have not seen him until he was right next to me in the darkness. As it was, one shaky hand still on the gallows supports, I watched him come into the yard through the far archway, looking cautiously around him. Then his gaze fixed on me and he came towards me, appearing slightly off-guard because I waited in the middle of the yard for him. Fuck. This was something I really didn't need now. I thought I'd seen the last of him.

'Look, Owen, I have to warn you, I'm really not in the mood,' I cautioned. This was no time for polite greetings.

'Hello to you too, Jen,' he said softly.

'Hello, Owen. Now, goodbye, Owen. If you really still need to talk to me, we can make it another time, and not here.' His eyes were red-rimmed, with deep shadows under them. He looked far less healthy than he had before. His hair was greasy.

'I need to see you, Jen,' he said. 'I've needed to see you so badly.' There was that look again, the one that gave me the creeps. Don't over-react, I said to myself, just because you're panicky at the moment; he's just a misguided soul with a crush.

'Please, I'm at work now. It's not appropriate that you're here. If the boss finds me chatting to you, I'll be in trouble.' I wondered if a more logical tactic would work. 'We can always meet for a drink sometime,' I lied.

'A drink would be nice,' he said, and I thought his face brightened a little. Shit, what had I just promised myself into?

'I'll call you then,' I ventured hopefully.

'Can I have your number?' he asked, predictably.

'No, I'm sorry, you can't,' I said, realising moments later I should have appeased him and given him a false number.

'You look really nice again today, Jen,' he said, eyes all over me once more. I glared back at him for a moment, unbelieving that he could be so inappropriate, and then I noticed the slight sway in his stance.

'Are you drunk?' I demanded, disgusted.

'No,' he replied, glancing at the floor. I knew I was right; he was lying.

'I wasn't going to talk to you anyway, and I'm certainly not going to talk to you when you're fucking drunk. Just go away!' He seemed pathetic, weaker, which made it easier for me to be commanding.

He took a step towards me. 'But I want to stay.'

'Well, you can't,' I said. The phone in my pocket beeped and vibrated. A text message. My thoughts flew in a panic to Aly. Regardless of the drunken idiot a few flagstones away, I got the phone out of my pocket and read the message.

Hi, hope u feelin better. Girl across road didn't see it happen, but noticed a bloke hangin round she thort was strange. Tall, thin, shoulder-length blond hair. Sound like anyone u know? Hav a think. C u at 4.30 XXXXX

I didn't need to have a think as she instructed. I looked at Owen, swaying slightly opposite me. Shoulder-length blond hair. Tall and thin. My heart thudded and then seemed to stop as a cold, creeping comprehension took hold of me. I stared at him, tried to formulate what to do for the best—confront him, or run from him. I thought of the shattered glass of my window, the violence of the shards of terracotta and sadly wilting flowers on Aly's doorstep. I had no idea what he wanted of me, how he knew about Aly, and my bewilderment didn't help my state of mind. His eyes lingered on my face and they were cold. Instinctively, sickeningly, I knew I was in danger.

CHAPTER FOURTEEN

2008

There was no time to run from him. He saw the understanding in my face, the new level of hostility, and suddenly his mask of semi-drunken innocence fell and I saw a ferocity in his eyes I wouldn't have expected him to possess. In a moment he'd grabbed my hands in his, with surprising speed, since he was under the influence, and sent my mobile phone with a clatter onto the flagstones. I cried out as he pushed me back against the red-brick wall and held me pinned by my hands.

'Was it your dyke girlfriend?' he snarled. 'The one you're interested in instead of me?' Flecks of his saliva sprayed my face and I recoiled from him.

'It was just a friend,' I said hearing the tremor in my own voice. 'Please let me go.' I sounded weak and pathetic, but all of my nerve had gone. His hands were strong and his grip was beginning to hurt.

'Don't lie to me, Jen. You think I don't know? You think I haven't seen? You dumped me in that fucking pub, and the next minute you're running around with that bitch.' His lips curled into a disgusted sneer. 'Do you two fuck? Oh, no, you can't can you? She's a fucking girl!'

His words made me furious, but it was impotent rage and I was too scared to voice it. 'It's none of your business what I do and with who,' I protested quietly, hoping that by staying calm I might elicit a similar response in him. 'And how the hell do you know anyway?' Perhaps if I could make him explain he would relax, give me an opportunity to escape.

I saw a sort of pride in his face, a slyness. I looked away from his glazed eyes and tried to turn from the sure smell of alcohol on his breath. He watched me turn my face away from him and scowled. 'Even now you're disgusted with me aren't you? Well, at least I know now, it's because I'm a man and you're a sick dyke. You're all the same, hating men, thinking we're not as good as you. Well, you shouldn't have underestimated me, should you?'

'What do you mean?' I demanded, trying to wrench my wrists free of his grip and failing. I still couldn't pull the threads of this together in my head and that only made it more frightening, since it gave me no real idea how to appease him.

'Interested in someone else, that's what you said,' he spat at me and then smiled in a sickening way, 'and then I saw you. In the pub, her hands on you. Maybe she was your friend, I thought, and I watched you. When that bloke came on to you, I almost came to get rid of him myself, I wanted to protect you, Jen. Then she was there. I saw her kiss you. Filthy whore.'

The picture began to make sense to me now. A whole new wave of fear swept through me as I became aware of how calculating he had been. I began to shake and tears rushed to my eyes. 'You followed me home?' I asked nervously.

'No,' he said with a proud smile, 'I followed her. I wanted to see where she went. Then I realised, it was your flat she'd led me to. I saw you both through the window, through a gap in the curtain. Just to be sure, I waited. She didn't leave until the morning.' He narrowed his eyes and smiled again, his expression sardonic. 'I'm just curious, Jen, what exactly do you do in bed together? Rub your cunts together and wish one of you had a cock so you could do the job properly?'

His sudden vulgarity made me feel physically sick. I just stared dumbly at him, tears trickling down my cheeks. I could feel my pulse through my whole body. I prayed for someone to come to the yard then, anyone. 'You threw the rock?' I croaked.

He just smiled in satisfaction. 'And then, I followed her again. Stupid bitch didn't even notice, even when I waited at the end of her street and watched which house she went into.'

I didn't even need to ask. It had been him that had vandalised her door, broken her flowerpot. I remembered again my horror at the shattered pot and I shuddered. I thought of him following Aly across town and my blood seemed to freeze.

'I was there last night, when you came home with her too, holding her filthy hand. I watched you looking at what I had left for you, and then going into the house. I saw you in her kitchen. Then you went and got all cosy on the sofa, didn't you?'

'You frightened us,' I said weakly, hoping desperately that it might soften him.

'What, with your tough dyke to protect you?' he scoffed. His face changed to one infinitely softer and in that, more terrifying.

'But you see, Jen, I know you. You're not a dyke. You don't even look like one.' Again his gaze travelled over me, my costume. I remembered the way he had said he liked me in it and I felt nauseous. 'You're just confused.'

'No, Owen,' I said, wondering if brave honesty would deter him, 'you're wrong. I am with Aly, and I want to be. I'm certain of it.'

'But do you really know the other options?' he demanded, more aggressive now. Clearly I'd just made him angrier. Panic turned my insides to liquid. He seemed to gather himself and his expression softened. 'You could have had me, Jen,' he said and his sing-song tone held me dreadfully transfixed. Now I was terrified of his intentions. Someone would come. Someone would come. Someone better fucking come. I struggled against his grip again, experimentally, to see if he would release me. His hands simply tightened and he laughed in my face.

'I've finally got you where I want you. I'm just sorry it had to be this way,' he whispered. My mouth was too dry for a response.

He looked at me curiously for a moment, head tilted to one side. I watched his Adam's apple bob up and down. 'You never recognised me, Jen, did you?' he asked.

I shook my head, incapable of anything else.

'Thing is, Jen, I lied. I've visited the museum six times now. Once you weren't here, there was some bloke in your place. So I came back the next day. I only came to see you. I wanted you the first time I saw you, in that costume.' He licked his moist lips now and I shuddered. 'Five times, Jen, you've looked at me, told me you were going to hang me and bury my body under these stones, and you never noticed me. I was going to the library, looking stuff up, so I could impress you, talk to you, next time I took the tour. Imagine my delight when you were in there.' He smiled a lewd smile now. 'I had to make my move. It was like it was planned.'

'But I'm not interested,' I managed to say. His words were washing over me now, I could only think of how frightened I was, dread what might happen next. I had pins and needles in my hands where he gripped them and the damp of the wall was penetrating my clothes.

'Only because of your new girlfriend,' he snarled.

'No. I'm not interested anyway,' I replied. I immediately wished I hadn't, as I saw the rage grow in his eyes.

In a movement too quick for me to react to, his right hand was around my throat, tightly. I gasped for breath, and my free hand flew to try to pull his away. His fingers were like iron. I felt my face growing hot. Then his other hand was on my breasts, rubbing me too hard. I fought him, but his grip only tightened, until I could barely breathe at all.

1808

Her breasts were still heavy and sore with milk. It seeped to make damp patches inside her dress. Mrs Beckinsale's embrace a fleeting moment of human touch, but her mind was already gone from inside these walls, gone on a ship to Australia. 'Thank you,' she managed to say to the woman who had done so much for her, but there were no more words. The acknowledgment in the tired, grey eyes. They were even more tired today, she thought.

He was there, but she would not look at him. He watched, silently, no taunts, and her sense of victory made her hold her head high. Her life was sailing across the seas now, not here, not for him to take from her. Tears glazed her eyes but did not fall.

A last glance at the inside of the women's gaol. Gilly. Everything whispered to her of Gilly, who cradled her child now. Thoughts of nothing else.

Hands tied behind her back, as they led her through the corridors, and then upwards, out of the gaol, towards the daylight. The injustice no longer mattered; her rage had long since passed away. Let them do as they would, they would not take her innocence, her truth from her. It was safe in Gilly's arms and it was named Verity.

The sun was bright and hurt her eyes, despite the chill of winter in the air. She did not look at the coarse loop of rope waiting for her. She glanced up instead at the tower of the old church opposite. She had shunned the preacher, the communion wine, they had brought to her. She did not want to go to heaven. She wanted to linger in the world, to be with her child always.

She had not seen the front of the building since the first day they had brought her here. The street below seemed as though it led to another world. There were people in the street, faceless people, watching. At the inn across the road, she could see a man drinking beer. Two men were going to their deaths alongside her. One was a murderer. The people were for him, he deserved an audience. She did not. There was no life left in this body for them to take.

The fear only came when they placed the hood over her face and the daylight was gone. She closed her eyes then and saw only her child's face, felt only Gilly's warm arms about her body. The rope was around her neck, but she was no longer there to feel it. Gilly was stroking her hair in the dark, and Verity was gurgling in her arms. Final tears rose in her eyes, and her head felt light. Gilly. Verity. Her life, her truth, and she was with them.

The wooden ground fell away beneath her feet. Her stomach lurched. She felt the rope tighten, and then she felt nothing, as unconsciousness overtook her, long before death made her still.

2008

My eyes began to prickle and I started to feel dizzy. His hand was travelling down my body now and, through a haze of fear and desperation, I saw that he was smiling. 'You like me now, don't you?' I heard him croon. I pushed against him again, but I felt weaker now.

His grip on my throat grew even tighter. He's going to kill me, I thought suddenly. My face was hot and my head was pounding. I tried to kick him, but he dodged my kick. His grip loosened just a little as he did so, but he pushed himself against me now, smiling, and I was repulsed to feel his erection press against my thigh. 'Don't fight it, Jen,' he whispered and, in truth, I wondered if I was able to.

Suddenly there was a scuffle, and in an instant he was torn away from me. I fell to the floor at the foot of the wall, slumping hard onto the flagstones, gasping for breath. I coughed and spluttered, and felt as though I still couldn't get enough oxygen.

I looked up and tried to make sense of what had happened. It was like watching a bizarre nightmare, as I saw Jim from reception, Bill the caretaker, and Mark, his turnkey's tunic flying, struggle with Owen, who fought them hard, managing to punch Mark in the face, before they succeeded in pushing him against the wall where the graffiti was carved, and holding him there. I was on my hands and knees, spitting strings of saliva onto the flagstones, still choking. My arms and legs felt weak and I was dizzy. The adrenaline of fear and the rush of relief made me feel high, and tears flowed down my face, I was shivering uncontrollably.

Owen was swearing as Bill and Jim held him fast against the wall. I felt detached from the scene. I stared blindly at the little group, as Mark left them and came across to me, stroking my back. I thought I was going to be sick and turned away from him, heaving, although the acid did not rise into my mouth.

'Jen?' he was saying, and I hardly heard him. I saw my mobile phone on the floor, the screen cracked and the back separated from the body. I stared at it. 'Jen, are you okay?'

I looked at him. Okay? No. I shook my head, but I wasn't really sure what I was. He put his hand on my arm to comfort me. I looked at Owen again in disbelief, the memory of his hand at my throat making it harder to breathe again. There had been such bitterness in his eyes. I looked at him now and wondered where it had come from. He had stopped struggling now, and was quietly pathetic against the wall. I remembered his face close to mine, his spit spattering my face, and I shivered. Mark felt it.

'Jen?' he said. His face was so concerned.

'It's okay,' I croaked at last, to reassure myself as much as him.

That was when I heard the two sets of footsteps running along the corridor above and then down the stairs, the quick way to the exercise yard. I looked across at the entrance to see Karen, the supervisor, appear, her face anxious and then horrified as she took in the scene. Just behind her was Aly.

I cried out with the relief of seeing her. I let Mark help me to struggle to my feet. She ran to me and snatched me away from him, taking me in her arms and holding me, stroking my back. I clung to her and I sobbed. I didn't give a thought to the people watching us. Her hand soothed my head and I felt her heavy breathing, her heart pounding with mine. She was hot with running and I needed the heat to warm my chilled blood. I cried until I had made her shoulder wet with tears and she still held me tight, as I began to shake again.

Eventually, I began to calm down. Her solid strength surrounded me and brought me back to myself. I looked up at her through teary eyes, and suddenly, remembering her message, the broken phone, I was curious.

'How did you know to come?' I asked her.

'I don't know,' she said. 'A feeling. It was when I sent you that message and you didn't reply. You always reply quickly. With you saying that you thought something bad was going to happen earlier, it put me on edge. The thought of you alone in this place frightened me. And then I remembered about the creepy guy, how he'd come down here that time before.'

'It was him,' I said, gesturing towards Owen, remembering that she wouldn't know any of the details yet. 'All of it was him—the rock, your pots, all of it. He saw us. He's been watching me, coming here. I thought he was really going to hurt me.' Even saying the words made me feel sick again.

Her eyes were full of pain and concern, and more than a little anger. Her emotions were audible in her voice. 'And so, I was so worried that I found the phone number of the museum in the book and got them on the phone. Some bloke answered, who thought I was a nutter. I told him to just check the fucking CCTV and he must have done, because next thing I hear this muffled exclamation and the line goes dead. I got a taxi and then I ran.'

'So you saved me?' I said, with a small smile. I didn't want to think about what would have happened if she'd not called and made them look at the CCTV. I also didn't want to think about what would have happened had I still been in my gloomy passageway, where the cameras didn't reach. 'Thanks,' I said, clinging to her again.

'You're welcome,' she said softly, returning my embrace.

❖

The police were called, of course, and the museum closed for the day. They arrested Owen. As he was led away, hands cuffed behind his back, I stared at him, disbelieving, wondering just what he would have been capable of. He cast a lingering look at me. I almost pitied him. He didn't even look at Aly, who still held my hand.

I thanked Jim, Bill, and Mark, who had a black eye developing for his trouble, and told them they were my heroes. I introduced them to Aly, and was surprised when, despite vaguely inquiring looks, they did not seem at all concerned what the nature of my relationship with her was. I was whisked off, in the back of a police car, no less, Aly beside me, to the hospital. Photographs were taken of the bruises at my throat and wrists, for evidence.

I lay on the trolley in Accident and Emergency surrounded by the blue cubicle curtains, and held Aly's hand. The police came for a statement, which I gave them, and they also asked Aly about the vandalism at her house. All of them knew I was with her, the details of our statements made it clear. I didn't even flinch at allowing them the knowledge. It didn't matter. Her eyes were a mixture of concern and pride as she looked at me.

The doctor who examined me gave me the all clear, but suggested I take it easy, and not spend too much time on my own. I glanced at Aly, and told him, 'It's okay, I've got someone to look after me.' He smiled at her. 'Good,' was all he said, before hurrying off to someone far needier than I was.

I had removed my hospital gown, and was nearly dressed, sitting on the edge of the trolley to pull on my shoes, when the curtains parted and my mum's face appeared, gravely concerned.

'Mum!' I exclaimed, glancing at Aly. She took a cautious step back from me.

'Oh, Jenny, thank God, what happened?' she said, looking in alarm at the bruises on my throat and taking hold of one of my hands in hers.

'I was attacked at work. But it's okay, the doctor says there's no harm done. Who called you?' I looked at Aly again. She was hovering awkwardly, as though wondering if she should leave me alone with my mother. I knew I didn't want her to go.

'It was that nice Mark you work with,' Mum told me. I felt guilty I hadn't thought to phone her myself. 'He's such a nice boy.' I laughed slightly because the nice boy was a year older than I was. She looked at me sharply, as if she suspected I might be hysterical. Then she noticed the bruises on my wrists and her eyes turned fearfully to mine. 'But who attacked you?' she demanded.

'It was this guy that I went for a drink with, and who it turned out had a bit of a thing for me,' I said, matter-of-factly. It still made me shudder to remember, and I didn't want her to be scared and, in making me re-live the incident, add to my own tremors.

'And the police have got him?' she asked anxiously.

'Yes. Jim, Bill, and Mark at work got him off me, and now he's been arrested. Apparently there's enough evidence to convict him of something.' I didn't tell her how desperately I hoped that was true and that there would be no chance of him being released anytime soon.

'I always said that place wasn't a healthy one to work in,' she said. I shrugged. When I didn't respond vocally, she looked from me to Aly. I saw her look her up and down and her eyebrows drew together slightly. Aly was wearing her black jeans today, below a plain blue T-shirt. Though, to me, she was always compelling, there was really nothing especially unusual about her appearance. Still, Mum looked suspicious of her. I tried not to resent it.

'Who's this?' Mum said to me, as if Aly couldn't hear her.

'This is Aly.' I glanced at Aly and beckoned her closer. 'Aly, this is my mum.'

'Hi,' Aly said, and I sensed her awkwardness. I hated putting her in a situation where she would feel uncomfortable. I turned my eyes to hers, drew confidence from the expression I saw there. She understood what I was about to do, I knew she did.

'Hello,' Mum replied to her greeting, 'do you work with Jenny?'

Aly hesitated. I knew she didn't want to lie. Neither did I. 'Actually, Mum,' I began, before Aly was forced to answer, and paused. 'Actually, Mum,' I said again, 'I have to tell you something. It might as well be now as any time. In fact, I think now is the right time, you know, it feels more important suddenly.' Mum was looking from me to Aly and back to me, expectant.

'You see, Mum, Aly doesn't work with me. She's not just my friend. She's my girlfriend.' The word felt odd in my mouth. Odd, but good. It struck me that it was the first time either Aly or I had spoken of our relationship in definite terms. When I looked at her and saw her smile, the pleasure in her eyes, I knew she was happy to hear me say it. Now I waited for my mother's reaction.

Mum gazed at me, not comprehending for a moment. We watched her and waited. 'You mean?' she said finally, raising her eyebrows in surprise.

'Yes,' I confirmed. 'I'm gay.'

Mum blinked. And then she blinked again.

❖

My mother was remarkable. Would she have been the same had my life not been endangered that day? I have no idea. As it was, after a long pause, during which she gazed at me, blinking, she turned her eyes to Aly and held out her hand. 'Pleased to meet you then,' she said in an uncertain tone.

'You too,' Aly replied, squeezing her hand, smiling easily.

'We'll have to talk,' she said to me. 'We don't chat often enough.'

'Yeah, we will,' I assured her. 'I promise.'

'How long have you been—or have you known—or...?' she asked, clearly not sure how to frame the question. Part of me was a stranger to her suddenly.

'I can't put a date on it,' I said. 'But I think I've known for a long time. I just didn't confront it until I met Aly.' From nowhere, that confidence Aly had said I would need had crept into me. I saw Mum's mind working, wondering if there had been signs she should have spotted, wondering if there were things she should have handled differently. I wanted to reassure her. 'And I'm happy, Mum,' I told her. 'I mean, I've been happier than I am right now, after what happened today. But even now I'm happy. Aly makes me happy.' Mum came to me and stroked my hair, as if I was still a child.

'That's all I want. It's all I've ever wanted for you, you know,' she told me softly. I don't think I'd ever loved her as much, or appreciated her as a person, not just my mother, as I did then.

Of course, Mum wanted me to go home with her, where she would nurse me, no doubt with plenty of casserole and hot milk. I knew she had questions for me too. However, I insisted that I was going home with Aly.

'I'll take good care of her,' Aly assured her. I felt warm at the prospect of being looked after by her, and my smile must have given my mum confidence, since she looked at me reflectively for a long moment before agreeing.

'I'm sure you will,' she said, smiling and even managing to meet Aly's earnest gaze. We told her the address so that she could visit. I thought to myself that we had better be sure to paint the door before she turned up. There were some things better kept just between Aly and me. I didn't want to linger on anything that reminded me of Owen, let alone inflict it on my mum. With her response to my revelation, I felt my happiness growing stronger. I had discovered how to be true to myself, and now I could finally be honest with her too. The rest of my friends and family would follow. I wanted them to meet Aly, with no need for lies. The anticipation of introducing her to the people in my life gave me a little thrill, as I reached down to finish fastening my shoes.

❖

I found it very easy to relax at Aly's house. She had already swept up the broken pots, and on my first morning there she painted the door. All the signs of what had happened had gone. Owen was kept in custody, and knowing that, I didn't feel at all fearful, even when Aly went out to work. I'd been given the week off and spent rather a lot of time stretched on her sofa, music blaring, enjoying my exploration of her CD collection, or flicking through her photographic journals.

The police visited me after a couple of days, to ask me a few more questions and to tell me more about the results of their investigation. I listened, horrified and astonished, as they told me it turned out Owen was not actually called Owen at all. His name was Thomas Brooks, and he'd been arrested and questioned in Manchester, when a girl had reported him for stalking. There'd been no evidence and he'd been released. They'd wanted to talk to him in connection with some items that had been stolen from another woman's house, and more accusations of indecent behaviour, this time in Leeds. To my astonishment, considering the academic tone of the conversations I'd had with him, Owen—or

Thomas—wasn't a post-grad student at all. He was unemployed. They told me he must have studied, having decided he liked me, in order to convince me he was genuine.

I told them, yes, of course I would testify in court if I had to. I wanted him to be gone from my thoughts. I wanted to enjoy my newfound freedom without the threat of him to hold me back. The feel of his hands around my neck still lingered in my darker moments. I'd broken down in tears in Aly's arms just the day before. I wanted him in prison. If that meant going to court, so be it; I was sure I could face it, with Aly behind me, her arms to hold me and reassure me.

I told Aly about what the police had said later that night as we sat on the sofa, drinking white wine. She looked as surprised as I did, and I saw the shadow in her eyes. 'Shit,' she said as I concluded, taking a gulp of her drink. I knew what she was thinking. The whole thing had been far more sinister than either of us had given it credit for being. She put her glass on the coffee table, reached for me on the sofa, and wrapped her arms around me. I leaned into her warmth.

'Thank God for you,' I said, emotion tightening my throat. It was remembered fear, relief, gratitude that she had cared enough to worry for me, and pleasure that I was here in her arms, all at once. 'If you'd not had that feeling and thought to phone work, I don't know that anyone would have come.'

'Don't even think about it,' she said, hearing the strain in my voice. 'And anyway, you saved yourself really, by sending me that text. It was what you said that worried me.'

I thought about the anxiety that I had felt in the dark entrance to the passageway at work. I remembered the strangling sensation, the tightness in my chest, the awful cries. A panic attack. But if I'd not had it I'd not have sent Aly the message that had made her suspicious. I remembered my desperation to get into the daylight, clinging to the supports of the gallows in the middle of the yard. Without the panic attack, I'd have been still in the gloomy passageway when Owen had come looking for me. He'd have taken me by surprise, in the dark, with no camera to see. I swallowed hard and clung more tightly to Aly.

'Who'd have thought a panic attack could be so well timed?' I said to her, trying to sound flippant and not quite managing it.

'You think that's what it was?' she asked, stroking my back. We'd looked it up on the Internet. My symptoms were those of a panic attack—

difficulty breathing, dizziness, mysterious pains, a sense of going mad or being about to die. Panic attacks were also usually associated with a place. In my case, it seemed to be the gaol.

'Yeah, I mean, what else was it?' I said.

'I don't know. Those layers of history maybe?' I was amazed how serious she sounded and I looked up at her.

'Do you really believe that?' I asked, curious. It had crossed my mind too, but I'd dismissed it.

'Well, no, not really,' she said, looking endearingly embarrassed. 'But it does make you think doesn't it? There was something, well, fateful about it all, wasn't there? And if it wasn't fate, maybe it was some sort of historical energy or something. Perhaps your panicking was caused by someone else's pain, in some other time?'

What she said appealed to the romantic in me. 'But why would it happen to me?' I asked.

'I don't know,' she replied. 'But there must be some really powerful negative energy in that place. Maybe there's some sort of connection over the years. Or maybe the layers of history just get a bit confused sometimes.' She shrugged her shoulders and I suspected she believed more strongly in her words than she was prepared to admit to.

I thought again of Elizabeth Cooper, of the possibility of a connection with a woman who'd lived two centuries ago. There'd never been anyone called Cooper in my family, at any point in the last two hundred years. I knew enough of our genealogy for that. And besides, she'd been sentenced to death when she was still very young. I thought of my pain layered with hers and all the others in between. Maybe the layers *were* confused sometimes. 'Perhaps,' I said contemplatively.

'And perhaps it was just a panic attack,' Aly concluded with a small smile.

1868

A young man, well dressed in a top hat and black cloak, walked around the bend in the road and gazed at the aged façade of the Shire Hall ahead of him. A sprinkling of white snow lay on the cobbles, and the sky was heavy with winter, and the smoke of industry. It felt very cold. He'd never seen snow before and marvelled at how it gave even the tall factories a softer aspect.

He walked up to the bottom step of the flight of five, and then he stopped. He took in the tall sandstone columns, the grand entrance doors, and the smaller darker door to the left, which led underground, to the gaol. He knew beyond the fine, recently renovated courtroom lay neat rows of cells, each containing a miserable prisoner, serving their time and doing their hard labour. It was difficult to imagine, from out here on the street. He did not know how far the gaol reached back, or that it was carved into the very bedrock of the cliff. The town was still new to him.

How had it been sixty years ago, he pondered? It would have been about then. He'd been told this town had changed beyond recognition in that time, transformed by industry and commerce, and felt compelled to come and look, see if the building still stood. It seemed a very solid entity in the narrow street, quietly guarding its inmates, and its past.

The door of the inn behind him opened and a man left, walking away down the street, leaving footprints in the snow.

He did not remember his great-grandmother very well. She was a hazy memory of grey hair and kindly green eyes. He remembered that he had stood by her chair when he was a very young boy and she had stroked his dark blond hair, looked intently into his eyes, and cried. He had been a little frightened of her after that.

However, he did remember his grandmother. It was from her that he had inherited the blond hair and the shape of his hazel eyes, although she had been mostly grey and her eyes surrounded by fine lines by the time he had known her well. Her name was Verity. He had liked the name as soon as he'd understood it, and had soon begun to ask questions about her. His mother had told him the story, when he was old enough to comprehend, that his grandma Verity had been born in England, in a gaol, and been brought across the sea before she was old enough to remember the journey. His great-grandmother had not really been that at all. His real great-grandmother had been hanged as a thief, a crime of which she was most definitely innocent, his mother insisted. She couldn't quite recall the date, but he had worked it out to be somewhere before 1810.

When he'd suggested they ask his grandmother about it, since she would be able to tell them the exact year she was born, his mother had told him it was best not to. Even she wasn't sure exactly how old her mother was. The year her mother was born was, she reminded him, also the year in which her real grandmother had died. Recalling that his grandma Verity did not like to celebrate her birthday, always spending the day alone, in a chair in the shade of the porch, apparently lost in thought, he had said nothing.

He'd stared at his grandmother though, after he'd heard her story. Later, as she had grown frailer and the opportunity to learn more began to slip away, he had finally asked her about it. He saw a cloud of sadness pass through her eyes, but sensed she was glad he had asked, was pleased by his interest. She told him that she was sad because she had never known her real mother, and that her mother, the lady who had brought her up, who he knew as his great-grandmother, had told her what a wonderful, strong woman her real mother had been. She would've liked to have known her very much, and sometimes thought she felt her presence, watching over her, especially on every birthday. Then she had smiled, and told him that she was lucky though, that she couldn't have had a kinder and more loving mother than his great-grandmother Gilly had been.

It had been after his grandmother had died, last year, that he had made the decision to travel to England. It was not merely that he felt a connection to his family's past there, he wanted to see this distant, cold land of opportunity. His mother had wept as he boarded the boat, but she had understood too.

He'd been here three months now, and knew he'd made the right decision. He was prospering.

This was the first time he'd visited the Shire Hall. This morning he'd had an unexpectedly vivid vision, of his real great-grandmother as a young girl, brave in the darkness of the cells, and he'd had to come here.

He looked up at the façade again. He did not want to go inside, though the shadows seemed to draw him. It was still a place of gloom and punishment, only more controlled now, in these more enlightened times. He thought of his own young wife, and the child that grew in her belly. He put his hand into his pocket and fingered the smooth wooden carved kangaroo that he would give to the baby when it was born, to remind it as it grew of its family's Australian past. Would he tell his son or daughter of the deeper shadows in the family's history? He wasn't sure. It had been a long time ago. Yet he looked at the building in front of him, and he felt the connection stir the emotion inside him.

Wrapping the cloak tighter, he nodded his respect to the building, to the echoes of his great-grandmother, and then he made his way back towards the town, leaving his own footprints in the snow.

2008

I returned to my own flat after a week. The letting agency had had the window repaired. Nothing had really changed, except that I caught the slight sparkle of a few shards of glass still caught in the carpet. Being alone there didn't frighten me at all, but after a week with Aly, I did feel very much on my own. I missed her. It was bloody ridiculous. In every relationship I'd ever had I'd always resisted any attempts to encroach on my personal space, my private time, and yet I found myself wanting Aly in every spare moment I had. It was ridiculous, but still, it made me smile.

I had thought that living with her for the week, after a relatively short acquaintance, we'd have begun to irritate each other, but it hadn't happened. She gave me the impression that she was entirely at ease with me in her house and I hoped whole-heartedly that this was true. Now, in the morning light, having only parted from her the evening before, I missed being able to turn to her and smile, just blurt out my random thoughts to her. To kiss her. I picked up my new phone and sent her a message telling her as much: *Hi sexy. I'm missin u already. Want 2 come 2 my place after work 2day? Hugs XXXX*

She replied quickly, as she usually did: *Hi babe. Just wen I was glad 2 get rid of u... ;) Course I want 2 come 2 urs l8r. Hope ur day gud. Meet u outside at 4.30. Hugs back XXXX*

I smiled, both at the joke in the message and the thought of having her in my flat later. I wondered if we'd get much sleep and laughed out loud as I caught sight of my flushed face and shining eyes in the mirror. Not only did I long for her company, but my libido had apparently become insatiable. Who knew?

I was going back to work today. I dressed in my usual black jeans and T-shirt. I brushed my hair and I walked to the bus stop. It was so easy to fall back into routine, to feel as though everything was as it had ever been. I was coming to terms with what it felt like for everything to be the same, and yet fundamentally different. The differences were good differences. For someone who'd considered herself incapable of making changes, I'd come a long way. Now, returning to work, fitting back into my old pattern, was the final test. I'd made it to the bus stop; so far so good. At no point did I think about actually going back into the building, standing alone in the yard. I was ignoring the nagging in the pit of my stomach.

Town was bustling with people. It was a sunny day and the fountains in the Market Square sparkled. I remembered how the crowds of people usually irritated me and was surprised to find that, instead, I felt excited to be part of it all. Part of the real world at last. Fuck, I was in danger of losing my healthy cynicism and actually being happy. What the hell had Aly done to me? I'd have to remember to show her my appreciation later. I grinned stupidly as I turned automatically to climb the hill to the older part of the city.

However, as I walked around the odd curve of the cobbled street and the Shire Hall frontage appeared before me, as it had so many times before, I felt the nausea rising in me. Shit, surely I was stronger than this? I made it to the bottom step, and I looked at the door, my own coded portal back in time. Still I stood motionless on the bottom step. What was wrong with my legs? I looked up at the sandstone columns towering above me and thought of the gloom and shadows which lay behind this frontage. I thought about how far the gaol dropped down the cliff to my yard.

Not my yard.

The notion was overwhelming: it was the gaol's yard. It belonged to the prisoners who had carved their names in the walls, passed through it to the transportation gate, awaited the miserable end of their lives in the cells of the gaol that surrounded it. It was really nothing to do with me, though I'd passed through just as they had. No, not as they had. I'd used the bars that had trapped them as a way of sheltering from the world. But I was free now, in a way so many of those tortured souls never had been. I thought of the high brick walls, the rattling gates, the shadows that grew longer and more sinister as the day progressed, and I felt claustrophobic. It was not a shelter; those bars imprisoned, they did not protect. It was a place of despair. Maybe all of that negative energy really was soaked into the very bricks of the building, the flagstones of the yard. I'd added my story to it now, my fear and my pain. Did I want to revisit it?

I knew the answer at once. As a group of people walked up the steps past me to peer at the ticket prices and opening times, I imagined them looking at the spot of the wall where Owen had pinned me, strangled me. I heard them laughing with that mock-horror I had so often seen, even encouraged, at the suffering of others. I imagined that laughter being directed at me and felt frightened by the level of detachment I'd developed when it came to the pain of living people, albeit separated from me by hundreds of years.

I was quite calm, remarkably unafraid of re-entering the building. Only I had finally connected with the lives that had passed through this place. Maybe in some layer of history they were still here, still in misery. I didn't want to sensationalise that anymore. Nor did I want to lock myself away from the world and hide in history. I didn't need to; I'd found the key to my freedom, and her name was Aly.

Tears rose in my eyes, as I said good-bye to the shadows of the centuries that lingered within. It was an effort to resist them, pulling me back, but I managed it. Then I turned my back on the entrance and walked away down the street, towards the bustling city centre and the world I didn't need to hide from anymore.

❖

As I walked, I sent Aly a message to tell her I wouldn't be at work, but that we could still meet in town, if she wanted to. I phoned Jim at work, to explain that I wouldn't be coming in again. He was only concerned with my welfare. He wasn't surprised at all, not after what I'd been through, as he put it. No, he was pretty sure I wouldn't have to work my notice, they'd understand. I thanked him again for his intervention, assured him that I was fine, and told him I'd see him around. I'd call Mark and Chloe and tell them sometime soon; hopefully we'd stay in touch. I couldn't have cared less about the rest of them. I wondered what Jade of the bleached highlights would think, and I laughed. At least I'd given them something to gossip about in those long, boring hours. And they could think what they wanted; I didn't give a damn. It was liberating to look at life this way, I discovered.

I spent the day immersed in the flurry of town. I wandered through the shops, browsing idly, and I sat in the Market Square eating an ice cream. My mind turned to what I would do next. I still had no idea of course. When did I ever have any fucking idea? But now it wasn't a problem to me. It was more like a challenge, and a welcome, exciting one at that. If my mum could cope with me having a girlfriend, the chances were she could cope with the disappointment of me not being a teacher. I'd find something.

Aly met me at three in the end, near one of the statue lions in the Market Square, one of the busiest meeting places in the city. I'd not planned it, but when I saw her I couldn't help myself: I wrapped my arms around her, tight around her bare shoulders, since she was in her usual black vest, and kissed her, full on the lips. She felt so good to hold, as her mouth responded to mine. I even hoped someone was looking. I wanted the whole world to know she was with me.

'Well, hello,' she said, her pleasure written all over her face.

'Hello,' I said, grinning and keeping hold of her hand.

'So, what happened? Couldn't face it?' she asked gently.

'It wasn't really that,' I said. 'I think I could have faced it. It's just that I really didn't feel like I wanted to go back in there. I'm not sure I can explain it in any way that makes sense. I guess I just don't want to spend all my time in prison with dead bodies for company any more.' I laughed lightly and wondered if she'd understand.

'I think I get it,' she told me. 'It's time to escape from prison and move on.' I smiled at her assessment; for all my deeper musings, she had summed up the essence of my feelings in one sentence.

'I've already moved on,' I confirmed. 'Going back in there would be going backwards. And from now on I'm not doing that.' She'd help me, I knew she would.

'I like you when you're determined,' she said, grinning, 'and you know, if you're starting to miss it at all, I can always help you out.'

'And how will you do that?' I asked, recognising the sparkle in her eye.

'Well, I do own a pair of handcuffs,' she replied nonchalantly.

'So you do,' I said, nodding. 'Well, I'll keep that in mind.' For all the frivolity of my words, that look in her eye was turning me on. Oh she knew it so damn well. I grinned and blushed all at once.

'Seriously though, babe, I think you've done the right thing,' she said, and her support strengthened me further. 'Not that you asked my opinion.'

'I always want to know your opinion,' I assured her, feeling the truth of my words. 'It helps to have your input about things, it really does.'

'I only say what I think,' she replied with a casual shrug, as though it was unimportant.

'That's one of the things that makes you so special,' I told her, looking into her eyes so that she would be sure I meant it. I didn't know for sure what lay behind those insecurities I suspected she harboured, but I was going to do my best to dispel them. I leaned in and kissed her lightly. As I pulled back I noticed a teenager a few feet away staring at us and smiled sweetly at him. Aly laughed.

'Are you drunk or something?' she demanded light-heartedly.

'No, just happy,' I said. I think it was the first time in my life I'd ever have been able to say that to anyone and really mean it.

Aly smiled widely in response. 'So you're unemployed? As well as happy?' she asked. I loved the fact that she took my declaration of happiness at face-value, didn't look for anything behind it. For six years, or longer, I'd assured people I was happy and they'd wanted to probe, or waited for qualifications. I'd never really convinced anyone. Now my happiness was genuine, and Aly saw it. 'No job, no plans?' she enquired further.

'No, guess not,' I said, 'I really have no idea what I'm going to do next.'

'Fate must be working again today,' she said mysteriously.

'What do you mean?' I asked, curious.

'Well, I was going to talk to you about plans and stuff,' she told me, pushing her hands into her pockets awkwardly, her cheeks flushing a little. My response to her more serious, and frankly almost hesitant tone, was to feel excited. If she wanted to talk about plans, it meant she saw a future for us. I'd barely stopped to consider it until that moment, but I was suddenly acutely aware of how much I wanted her in my life for a long time to come. That was a turn up for the books; I'd never felt like that before about anyone.

'Were you?' I asked. 'How do you mean?' I tried to sound casual, all the time wondering what was coming next.

We strolled to a bench and sat down, thighs touching. She rubbed my leg absent-mindedly, her thoughts clearly on her next words, 'You see the thing is, there's this studio with a flat over it for rent, in the paper.'

'So you're moving?' I asked, beginning to hope that I saw the direction this conversation was going, but barely daring to think it.

'It seems too good to miss,' she confirmed, pausing for a moment and looking at me speculatively, as if trying to predict how I would react to what she said next. 'But it gave me an idea too,' she went on. 'I mean, we got on pretty well this last week, and I like having you around all the time, and we could both use having to pay less rent each…'

'Are you saying what I think you are?' I was conscious that she was nervous asking me. It was about the least direct I'd known her to be. I interrupted her to ease her discomfort and because I couldn't contain the enthusiasm of my response much longer.

'Yeah, I am,' she said, sounding more certain as she took in the barely concealed excitement in my words. 'Do you want to share the flat with me?'

I grinned with pleasure. 'Yes, I do,' I said instantly. It didn't even seem to be a decision.

'You're not going to think about it?' she said, smiling her own satisfaction back at me, but the traces of concern still in her eyes.

'No, I don't need to,' I said, covering her hand with my own. I'd just agreed to move in with a woman I'd only known for a couple of weeks and it felt like the most natural thing in the world. This time last month I'd never have suspected it was possible. But the woman in question was Aly, who had captivated and freed me all at once, who I knew I had fallen in love with. Fuck, did I say love? Even as I thought it, I knew it was true.

'It's all been very quick to be moving in together,' she said, and I understood her caution. Just because I'd thrown mine to the wind, it didn't mean it would be so simple for her.

'Does that worry you?' I enquired, hoping that if it did, there would be something I could say to alleviate those concerns. She looked contemplative for a moment.

'No, actually,' she said, and I was pleased she sounded certain. 'I wouldn't have suggested it unless I was sure, but you know, I don't want you to rush into anything that you'll regret. You've had a lot to cope with lately.' A ghost of a memory flickered across her face. I knew without asking that she'd been hurt before, had been in a situation that she was now reminded of. She didn't want to risk pushing me too hard, and I was grateful, but my overwhelming urge was to reassure her. Whatever had happened to her before, I was convinced it had no bearing on what we shared between us. I hoped she felt the same.

'I don't feel like I'm rushing into anything,' I assured her. 'It seems right,' I added, squeezing her hand. She smiled. I was about to say something to express my excitement at the prospect of living with her, when I realised there was still a hesitancy in her expression, as she drew a deep breath.

'And I thought,' she said, her tone still suggesting I might hate whatever idea it was that she'd had, 'well I'm going to need some help with admin and everything, if the studio takes off. And an assistant, when it comes to that. I was going to ask anyway, but now you haven't got a job to go to…'

'You want to be my boss?' I asked, laughing. I already knew I loved the idea of working with her, helping her reach her goals, artistic as well as commercial. I was instantaneously excited at the prospect.

'Yeah, though there'll obviously have to be a tough application and interview process,' she retorted, amusement in her tone, before her expression became serious once more. 'But for real, what do you say?'

'I say yes. You didn't think I'd say no, did you? Yes, absolutely. It's fucking fantastic!' I wasn't usually quite so enthusiastic about anything and blushed as I concluded. It was the thought of living with Aly, working with her, but it was also the thrill of knowing I had found what was right for me, at this moment. So it was hardly putting my history degree to good use. I didn't care. I needed a break from history anyway. I couldn't believe how well the pieces of my life were falling into place. That had never happened to me before, I'd just stumbled from one thing to another, feeling lost in the dark. Now things just seemed to come together. It should have been too good to be true. For just a moment I wondered if it was. Then I looked at her again, as we sat on our bench in the sunshine, and cast away the last of my doubts.

'We'll run it as a joint business,' she said, quite seriously, as if she had noticed my moment of concern, 'legally and everything, if you want.' I just grinned back at her stupidly, entirely incapable of words that would convey everything I wanted to. Who'd have thought I'd ever be so happy I was lost for words? Certainly not me. 'But we can talk about that later,' she said, discerning from my smile that I really didn't need to talk business. I trusted her and I just wanted to revel in the excitement for a while. She laughed and then looked at me as though she was making a decision about something. 'Right now, come with me,' she said. 'There's something I want us to do.'

'What?' I demanded.

'Just come with me,' she said with an inscrutable smile, pulling my hand as we rose together from the bench.

❖

'You can say no if you want to,' she said, as we sat on stools next to each other in a small ethnic jewellery shop, where I could see she'd bought her customary bangles and pendants from.

'A bit late now,' I smiled at her. 'I said yes didn't I?'

The man who prepared something at a small table to the side of us was tall and dark skinned. He had a bar through his nose and his ears were more metal than flesh, weighed down and misshapen by the weight. I looked at Aly and giggled, partly with nerves, slightly with the joy of the rebellion. For fuck's sake, it was hardly rebellion. But I felt like a born-again teenager and it seemed that way. Clearly it was infectious, for a moment later she was giggling with me.

'Right, who's first?' he said, coming to stand between us and smiling, with lips pierced in three places, at our laughter.

'Her,' Aly volunteered me. 'Then she can't back out.'

'Oh thanks for that,' I retorted. 'I'm not that scared!'

'I know you too well, babe, you're terrified,' she replied with eyes full of mirth. I grinned, but her words resonated with me. She did know me that well, already. I'd never had that level of understanding and interest in me before.

'You'll just have to hold my hand then,' I told her. The man laughed. Aly took my hand, as he swabbed my ear with cold alcohol, just above the single piercing I'd had for years. I clutched at her as he brought the gun up and squeezed it with a snap to push the stud through my skin.

'Ow!' I said, grinning all the same.

'Don't be a baby,' Aly joked, as the man reloaded his gun, and went to swab her ear. She already had two holes in each ear, so hers would be a little higher than mine. She didn't even flinch as he shot the stud, which made a pair with my own, through her ear.

'Don't forget to bathe them,' he told us, giving us each a leaflet on aftercare of piercings. Aly paid him and we left the shop.

'Does this mean we're committed then?' I asked her outside, putting my hand to my hot, vaguely throbbing ear. I suppose mutual piercings were hardly the most usual sign of commitment between lovers, but I recognised how much I wanted to attach that significance to what we had just done.

'Well, kind of,' she said, and I sensed again that her caution came only from not wanting to risk too much too soon, rather than from any reluctance to be faithful to me. Her eyes gave me a more reassuring answer than her non-committal words. Then she smiled a wicked smile, 'Plus I thought it'd be fun.'

'Fun?' I returned, with mock incredulity.

'Have you never heard how close pleasure and pain are?' She grinned.

'Hmmm.' I raised my eyebrows. She knew she'd left me with very little to say, and now she looked mischievous. Fuck, she was sexy with that look in her eye. I wanted to grab her hand and run to somewhere we could be alone.

'I'll teach you, babe,' she assured me.

'I'm sure you will, honey.' We giggled together. It was so easy to laugh with her. We started to stroll down the street, hands still linked.

'But, if you ask me, it does mean we're joined,' she said more seriously. 'I'm not saying it's going to last forever. It might not. You know I believe in living for now, not the past and not the future.'

'I know. I'm just learning how to do that,' I said, 'but with you I can do it like I never did before.'

'Whatever happens, we'll always have a connection now,' she added. I knew she was referring to our pierced ears, but between us there was a deeper understanding that I had to voice.

'We have a connection anyway,' I said, looking into those deep, dark eyes and feeling how strongly I was drawn to her all over again. 'You're my truth.'

She stopped and kissed me in the middle of the street.

AUTHOR'S NOTE

Elizabeth's gaol and Jen's museum are heavily inspired by a very real place, the Galleries of Justice Museum, located in the old Shire Hall and County Gaol of the city of Nottingham, England, where I worked, mostly as a Victorian wardress, during summer of the year 2000. The tour Jen presents to her visitors is very similar to the one I presented to tour groups of my own during those months.

Most of the historical information contained in *Truths* was gleaned during my time at the museum. I am indebted to both the Galleries of Justice and my colleagues of the time for teaching me not only the facts, but also some of the more gruesome and interesting details. The information Jen relates to her audiences is, to the best of my knowledge, mostly accurate.

I have, of course, used a liberal amount of artistic licence in my portrayal of the building and its inhabitants, and their experiences in both time periods. None of my characters are based on real people, and the structure of the real building is similar, but not identical, to my fictional one. The museum has a library, but the one I describe and the archive Jen accesses are my inventions.

Elizabeth's experience in a gaol of 1808 is as historically accurate as it is possible to be, without interfering with the demands of my plot. Prisons in 1808 were not the disciplined, organised places they became under the Victorians. Though, in 1774, two penal reform acts were passed through Parliament, with the intention of improving conditions with such measures as provision of health care and the segregation of the sexes, prisons were still thoroughly filthy and unpleasant places. There was no regime, no uniform, and no real sanitation. Though debtors were often imprisoned for the duration of a prison sentence, most prisoners, especially in Nottingham County Gaol, were simply being held in the prison until their sentences to be served elsewhere were carried out.

The most significant artistic licence I used in Elizabeth's story is that, chances are, Elizabeth would have met her fellow prisoners before her sentencing, as there was often no separation of the convicted and to-be-tried. It is also likely that preparations for her execution would have taken less than three weeks, though the system was far from systematic. One other point to note is that in 1808 executions in Nottingham were still being carried out on Gallows Hill outside of the town. They were moved to the steps of the County Gaol in the 1820s, though in many places in England this move, from designated sites of execution outside of the towns, to the frontages or flat roofs of the County Gaols, happened earlier.

In 1808, two women were executed in England. One was a murderess. The other, Mary Chandler, was executed in Lancashire for the crime of stealing in a dwelling place, the same crime Elizabeth is convicted of and for which forty-six people were hanged between 1800 and 1827. I am indebted to a grimly fascinating Web site, www.capitalpunishment.org, which made it possible for me to check my facts on executions in England in this period.

Before the unsuccessful (for Britain!) conclusion of the War of Independence in 1776, felons were transported from English gaols to the penal colonies in America. When this was no longer an option, transportation began to Australia in 1787. Figures vary, but somewhere in the region of 190,000 convicts had been transported by the time the practice ceased in 1868.

Though Nottingham is very much a real city, not all of the locations are based on real places. Those that are bear no more than a passing resemblance to the actual businesses and localities. This is a work of fiction, after all.

About the Author

Rebecca S. Buck has lived in Nottingham, England, most of her life. She was accepted by the University of Oxford to read History, but soon found that something inside her rebelled against such a rarified academic environment and left to return to her hometown. She graduated from the University of Nottingham in 2004 with a degree in English Studies. She hopes to return to study at postgraduate level in the near future, with a specific interest in literature and culture. She is fascinated by this relationship, especially in an historical context, and the importance of fiction for representing the human experience. This is partly what inspires her to write. She also finds writing an appropriate outlet for an over-active imagination.

Having spent much of her time since 2005 in Slovenia, Rebecca is now living in England once again, and working fervently on her next book.

Books Available From Bold Strokes Books

The Pleasure Set by Lisa Girolami. Laney DeGraff, a successful president of a family-owned bank on Rodeo Drive, finds her comfortable life taking a turn toward danger when Theresa Aguilar, a sleek, sexy lawyer, invites her to join an exclusive, secret group of powerful, alluring women. (978-1-60282-144-6)

A Perfect Match by Erin Dutton. The exciting world of pro golf forms the backdrop for a fast-paced, sexy romance. (978-1-60282-145-3)

Truths by Rebecca S. Buck. Two women separated by two hundred years are connected by fate and love. (978-1-60282-146-0)

Father Knows Best by Lynda Sandoval. High school juniors and best friends Lila Moreno, Meryl Morganstern, and Caressa Thibodoux plan to make the most of the summer before senior year. What they discover that amazing summer about girl power, growing up, and trusting friends and family more than prepares them to tackle that all-important senior year! (978-1-60282-147-7)

In Pursuit of Justice by Radclyffe. In the dynamic double sequel to *Shield of Justice* and *A Matter of Trust*, Det. Sgt. Rebecca Frye joins forces with enigmatic computer consultant J.T. Sloan to crack an Internet child pornography ring. (978-1-60282-148-4)

The Midnight Hunt by L.L. Raand. Medic Drake McKennan takes a chance and loses, and her life will never be the same—because when she wakes up after surviving a life-threatening illness, she is no longer human. (978-1-60282-140-8)

Long Shot by D. Jackson Leigh. Love isn't safe, which is exactly why equine veterinarian Tory Greyson wants no part of it—until Leah Montgomery and a horse that won't give up convince her otherwise. (978-1-60282-141-5)

In Medias Res by Yolanda Wallace. Sydney has forgotten her entire life, and the one woman who holds the key to her memory, and her heart, doesn't want to be found. (978-1-60282-142-2)

Awakening to Sunlight by Lindsey Stone. Neither Judith or Lizzy is looking for companionship, and certainly not love—but when their lives become entangled, they discover both. (978-1-60282-143-9)

Fever by VK Powell. Hired gun Zakaria Chambers is hired to provide a simple escort service to philanthropist Sara Ambrosini, but nothing is as simple as it seems, especially love. (978-1-60282-135-4)

High Risk by JLee Meyer. Can actress Kate Hoffman really risk all she's worked for to take a chance on love? Or is it already too late? (978-1-60282-136-1)

Missing Lynx by Kim Baldwin and Xenia Alexiou. On the trail of a notorious serial killer, Elite Operative Lynx's growing attraction to a mysterious mercenary could be her path to love—or to death. (978-1-60282-137-8)

Spanking New by Clifford Henderson. A poignant, hilarious, unforgettable look at life, love, gender, and the essence of what makes us who we are. (978-1-60282-138-5)

Magic of the Heart by C.J. Harte. CEO Susan Hettinger and wild, impulsive rock star M.J. Carson couldn't be more different if they tried—but opposites attract in ways neither woman can resist. (978-1-60282-131-6)

Ambereye by Gill McKnight. Jolie Garoul is falling in love with her assistant. The big problem is, Jolie is a werewolf. (978-1-60282-132-3)

Collision Course by C.P. Rowlands. Tragedy leaves Brie O'Malley and Jordan Carter fearful and alone. Can they find the courage to take a second chance on love? (978-1-60282-133-0)

Mephisto Aria by Justine Saracen. Opera singer Katherina Marov's destiny may be to repeat the mistakes of her father when she becomes involved in a dangerous love affair. (978-1-60282-134-7)

Battle Scars by Meghan O'Brien. Returning Iraq war veteran Ray McKenna struggles with the battle scars that can only be healed by love. (978-1-60282-129-3)

Chaps by Jove Belle. Eden Metcalf wants nothing more than to flee from her troubled past and travel the open road—until she runs into rancher Brandi Cornwell. (978-1-60282-127-9)

Lightbearer by John Caruso. Lucifer dares to question the premise of creation itself and reveals that sin may be all that stands between us and living hell. (978-1-60282-130-9)

The Seeker by Ronica Black. FBI profiler Kennedy Scott battles ghosts from her past, deadly obsession, and the evil that haunts her. (978-1-60282-128-6)

Power Play by Julie Cannon. Businesswomen Tate Monroe and Victoria Sosa are at odds in the boardroom, but not in the bedroom. (978-1-60282-125-5)

The Remarkable Journey of Miss Tranby Quirke by Elizabeth Ridley. When love enters Tranby's life in the form of a beautiful nineteen-year-old student, Lysette McDonald, she embarks on the most remarkable journey of all. (978-1-60282-126-2)

Returning Tides by Radclyffe. Insurance investigator Ashley Walker faces more than a dangerous opponent when she returns to the town, and the woman, she left behind. (978-1-60282-123-1)

Veritas by Anne Laughlin. When the hallowed halls of academia become the stage for murder, newly appointed Dean Beth Ellis's search for the truth leads her to unexpected discoveries about her own heart. (978-1-60282-124-8)

The Pleasure Planner by Larkin Rose. Pleasure purveyor Bree Hendricks treats love like a commodity until Logan Delaney makes Bree the client in her own game. (978-1-60282-121-7)

everafter by Nell Stark and Trinity Tam. Valentine Darrow is bitten by a vampire on her way to propose to her lover Alexa Newland, and their lives and love are placed in mortal jeopardy. (978-1-60282-119-4)

Summer Winds by Andrews & Austin. When Maggie Turner hires a ranch hand to help work her thousand acres, she never expects to be attracted to the very young, very female Cash Tate. (978-1-60282-120-0)

Beggar of Love by Lee Lynch. Jefferson is the lover every woman wants to be—or to have. A revealing saga of lesbian sexuality. (978-1-60282-122-4)

The Seduction of Moxie by Colette Moody. When 1930s Broadway actress Violet London meets speakeasy singer Moxie Valette, she is instantly attracted and her Hollywood trip takes an unexpected turn. (978-1-60282-114-9)

Goldenseal by Gill McKnight. When Amy Fortune returns to her childhood home, she discovers something sinister in the air—but is former lover Leone Garoul stalking her or protecting her? (978-1-60282-115-6)

Romantic Interludes 2: Secrets edited by Radclyffe and Stacia Seaman. An anthology of sensual lesbian love stories: passion, surprises, and secret desires. (978-1-60282-116-3)

Femme Noir by Clara Nipper. Nora Delaney meets her match in Max Abbott, a sex-crazed dame who may or may not have the information Nora needs to solve a murder—but can she contain her lust for Max long enough to find out? (978-1-60282-117-0)

The Reluctant Daughter by Lesléa Newman. Heartwarming, heartbreaking, and ultimately triumphant—the story every daughter recognizes of the lifelong struggle for our mothers to really see us. (978-1-60282-118-7)

Erosistible by Gill McKnight. When Win Martin arrives at a luxurious Greek hotel for a much-anticipated week of sun and sex with her new girlfriend, she is stunned to find her ex-girlfriend, Benny, is the proprietor. Aeros Ebook. (978-1-60282-134-7)

Looking Glass Lives by Felice Picano. Cousins Roger and Alistair become lifelong friends and discover their sexuality amidst the backdrop of twentieth-century gay culture. (978-1-60282-089-0)

Breaking the Ice by Kim Baldwin. Nothing is easy about life above the Arctic Circle—except, perhaps, falling in love. At least that's what pilot Bryson Faulkner hopes when she meets Karla Edwards. (978-1-60282-087-6)

It Should Be a Crime by Carsen Taite. Two women fulfill their mutual desire with a night of passion, neither expecting more until law professor Morgan Bradley and student Parker Casey meet again…in the classroom. (978-1-60282-086-9)

Rough Trade edited by Todd Gregory. Top male erotica writers pen their own hot, sexy versions of the term "rough trade," producing some of the hottest, nastiest, and most dangerous fiction ever published. (978-1-60282-092-0)

The High Priest and the Idol by Jane Fletcher. Jemeryl and Tevi's relationship is put to the test when the Guardian sends Jemeryl on a mission that puts her not only in harm's way, but back into the sights of a previous lover. (978-1-60282-085-2)

Point of Ignition by Erin Dutton. Amid a blaze that threatens to consume them both, firefighter Kate Chambers and property owner Alexi Clark redefine love and trust. (978-1-60282-084-5)